the Red
SIREN

ISBN 978-1-62029-726-1

Cover Model Photography: Jim Celuch, Celuch Creative Imaging

Published by Barbour Publishing, Inc., P.O. Box 719, Uhrichsville, Ohio 44683 www.barbourbooks.com

Our mission is to publish and distribute inspirational products offering exceptional value and biblical encouragement to the masses.

 Member of the
Evangelical Christian
Publishers Association

Printed in the United States of America.

the Red SIREN

M. L. TYNDALL

BARBOUR
PUBLISHING

But he that received the seed into stony places,
the same is he that heareth the word and receiveth it with
joy; yet he hath not root in himself, but dureth for a while:
for when tribulation or persecution ariseth
because of the word, by and by he is offended.
MATTHEW 13:20–21

CHAPTER 1

August 17-13, English Channel
off Portsmouth, England

This was Dajon Waite's last chance. If he didn't sail his father's merchant ship and the cargo she held safely into harbor, his future would be tossed to the wind. With his head held high, he marched across the deck of the *Lady Em* and gazed over the choppy seas of the channel, expecting at any minute to see the lights of Portsmouth pierce the gray shroud of dusk. Another hour and his mission would be completed with success. It had taken two years before his father had trusted him to captain the most prized vessel in his merchant fleet, the *Lady Em*—named after Dajon's mother, Emily— especially on a journey that had taken him past hostile France and Spain and then far into the pirate-infested waters off the African coast.

Fisting his hands on his hips, Dajon puffed out his chest and drew a deep breath of salty air and the scent of musky earth—the smell of home. Returning with a shipload of ivory, gold, and pepper from the Gold Coast, Dajon could almost see the beaming approval on his father's sea-weathered face. Finally, Dajon would prove himself an equal to his older brother, Theodore— obedient, perfect Theodore—who never let his father down. Dajon, however, had been labeled naught but capricious and unruly, the son who possessed neither the courage for command nor the brains for business.

Fog rolled in from the sea, obscuring the sunset into a dull blend of muted colors as it stole the remaining light of what had been a glorious day. Bowing his head,

Dajon thanked God for His blessing and protection on the voyage.

"A sail, a sail!" a coarse voice blared from above.

Plucking the spyglass from his belt, Dajon held it to his eye. "Where away, Mules?"

"Directly off our lee, Captain."

Dajon swerved the glass to the port and adjusted it as Cudney, his first mate, halted beside him.

"She seems to be foundering, Captain," Mules shouted.

Through the glass, the dark outline of a ship came into focus, the whites of her sails stark against the encroaching night. Gray smoke spiraled up from her quarterdeck as sailors scrambled across her in a frenzy. The British flag flapped a harried plea from her mainmast.

"Hard to larboard," he yelled aft, lowering the glass. "Head straight for her, Mr. Nelson."

"Straight for her, sir."

"Beggin' your pardon, Captain." Cudney gave him a sideways glance. "But didn't your father give explicit orders never to approach an unknown vessel?"

"My father is not the captain of this ship, and I'll thank you to obey my orders without question." Dajon stiffened his lips, tired of having his decisions challenged. True, he had failed on two of his father's prior ventures— one to the West Indies where a hurricane sank his ship, and the other where he ran aground on the shoals off Portugal. Neither had been his fault. But this time, things would be different. Perhaps his father would even promote Dajon to head overseer of his affairs.

With a nod, Cudney turned. "Mr. Blake, Mr. Gibes, prepare to luff, if you please." His bellowing voice echoed over the decks, sending the men up the shrouds.

"Who is she?" Cudney held out his hand for the glass.

"A merchant ship, perhaps." Dajon handed him the telescope then gripped the railing as the *Lady Em* veered to larboard, sending a spray of seawater over her decks. "But she's British, and she's in trouble."

The ship lumbered over the agitated waves. Dajon

watched Cudney as he steadied the glass on his eye and his boots on the sodden deck. A low whistle spilled from his mouth as he twisted the glass for a better look.

"Pray tell, Mr. Cudney, what has caught your eye— one of those new ship's wheels you've been coveting?"

"Nay, Captain. But something nearly as beautiful—a lady."

Dajon snatched the glass back as the *Lady Em* climbed a rising swell and then tromped down the other side. As the vessel's sails snapped in the rising wind, he braced his boots on the deck and focused the glass on the merchant ship. A woman clung to the foremast, panic distorting her features—indistinct through the distant haze. She raised a delicate hand to her forehead as if she were going to faint. Red curls fluttered in the wind behind her. Heat flooded Dajon despite the chill of the channel. Lowering the glass, he tapped it into the palm of his hand, loathing himself for his shameless reaction. Hadn't his weakness for the female gender already caused enough pain?

Yet clearly the vessel was in trouble.

"We shall come alongside her," Dajon ordered.

Cudney glared at the ship. "Something is not right. I can feel it in my gut."

"Nonsense. Where is your chivalry?" Dajon smiled grimly at his friend, ignoring the hair bristling on the back of his own neck.

Cudney's dark eyes shot to Dajon. "But your father—"

"Enough!" Dajon snapped. "My father did not intend for me to allow a lady to drown. Besides, pirates would not dare sail so close to England—especially to Portsmouth, where so many of His Majesty's warships are anchored." Dajon glanced back at the foundering ship, now only half a knot off their bow. Smoke poured from her waist, curling like a snake into the dark sky. Left to burn, the fire would sink her within an hour. "Surely you do not suspect a woman of piracy?"

Cudney cocked one brow. "Begging your pardon, Captain, but I have seen stranger things on these seas."

Faith Louise Westcott flung her red hair behind her and held a quivering hand to her brow, nausea rising in her throat at her idiotic display. How did women feign such weakness without losing the contents of their stomachs?

"They've taken the bait, mistress." A sinister chuckle filled the breeze.

"Oh, thank heavens." Faith released the mast. Planting a hand on her hip, she gave Lucas a mischievous grin. "Well, what are you waiting for? Ready the men."

"Aye, aye." The bulky first mate winked then scuttled across the deck, his bald head gleaming in the light from the lantern hanging on the mainmast.

After checking the pistol that was stuffed in the sash of her gown and the one strapped to her calf, Faith sauntered to the railing to get a better look at her latest victim, a sleek, two-masted brigantine. The orange, white, and blue of the Dutch flag fluttered from her mizzen. A very nice prize, indeed. One that would bring her even closer to winning the private war she waged—a war for the survival of her and her sisters.

The oncoming ship sat low in the water, its hold no doubt packed with valuable cargo. Faith grinned. With this ship and the one she had plundered earlier, loaded with precious spices and silks, she was well on her way to amassing the fortune that would provide for her independence and that of her sisters—at least the two sisters who were left unfettered by unholy matrimony.

She allowed her thoughts to drift for a moment to Charity, the eldest. Last year their father had forced her into a union with Lord Villement, a vile, perverse man who had oppressed and mistreated her beyond what anyone should endure. Faith feared for her sister's safety and prayed for God to deliver Charity, but to no avail.

Then, of course, there was the incident with Hope, their younger sister.

That was when Faith had stopped praying, had stopped hoping, had stopped believing in a God who claimed to love and care for His children.

She would rather die than see her two younger sisters chained to abusive men, and the only way to avoid that fate was to shield them with their own fortune—a fortune she must provide since British law prohibited women from inheriting their father's wealth. Cringing, she stifled the fury bubbling in her stomach. She mustn't think of it now. She had a ship to plunder, and this was as much for Charity as it was for any of them.

The bowsprit of the brigantine bowed in obedience to her as it plunged over the white-capped swells. Gazing into the hazy mist, Faith longed to get a peek at the ninnies who had been so easily duped by her ruse, but she dared not raise the spyglass to her eye.

Putting on her most flirtatious smile, she waved at her prey, beckoning the fools onward, then she scanned the deck as her crew rushed to their stations. Aboard her ship, she was in control; she was master of her life, her future—here and nowhere else. And oh, how she loved it!

Lucas's large frame appeared beside her. "The rest of the men be waitin' yer command below hatches, mistress." He smacked his oversized lips together in a hungry sound Faith had become accustomed to before a battle. Nodding, she scanned her ship. Wilson manned the helm; Grayson and Lambert hovered over the fire, pretending to put it out; and Kane and Mac clambered up the ratlines in a pretense of fear. She spotted Morgan pacing the special perch Faith had nailed into the mainmast just for him. She whistled, and the red macaw halted, bobbed his head up and down, and squawked, "Man the guns, man the guns!"

Faith smiled. She had purchased the bird from a trader off Morocco and named him after Captain Henry Morgan, the greatest pirate of all time. The feisty parrot had been a fine addition to her crew.

Bates, her master gunner, hobbled to her side, wringing his thick hands together in anticipation. "Can I just fire one shot at 'em, Cap'n? The guns grow cold from lack of use." His expression twisted into a pout that reminded her of Hope, her younger sister. "I won't hurt 'em none; ye have me word."

"I cannot take that chance, Bates. You know the rules," Faith said as the gunner's soot-blackened face fell in disappointment. "No one gets hurt, or we abandon the prize. But I promise we shall test the guns soon enough."

With a grunt, Bates hobbled away and disappeared below.

Returning her gaze to her unsuspecting prey, Faith inhaled a breath of the crisp air. Smoke bit her throat and nose, but she stifled a cough as the thrill of her impending victory charged through her, setting every nerve aflame. The merchant ship was nigh upon them. She could already make out the worried expressions upon the crew's faces as they charged to her rescue.

This is for you, Charity, and for you, Mother.

Heavy fog blanketed the two ships in gray that darkened with each passing minute. Faith tugged her shawl tighter against her body, both to ward off the chill and to hide the pistol in her sash. A vision of her mother's pale face formed in the fog before her, blood marring the sheets on the birthing bed where she lay.

"Take care of your sisters, Faith."

A gust of wind chilled Faith's moist cheeks. A tear splattered onto the deck by her shoes before she brushed the rest from her face. "I will, Mother. I promise."

"Ahoy there!" A booming voice shattered her memories.

She raised her hand in greeting toward the brigantine as it heaved ten yards off their starboard beam. "Ahoy, kind sir. Thank God you have arrived in time," she yelled back, sending the sailors scurrying across the deck. Soon they lowered a cockboat, filled it with men, and shoved off.

A twinge of guilt poked at Faith's resolve. These men had come to her aid with kind intentions. She swallowed hard, trying to drown her nagging conscience. They were naught but rich merchants, she told herself, and she, merely a Robin Hood of the seas, taking from the rich to feed the poor. Well, perhaps not the poor, but certainly the needy. Besides, she had exhausted all legal means of acquiring the money she needed, and present society offered her no other choice.

The boat thumped against her hull, and she nodded at Kane and Mac, who had jumped down from the shrouds and tossed the rope ladder over the side.

"Permission to come aboard?" The man who appeared to be the captain shouted toward Lucas as he swung his legs over the bulwarks, but his eyes were upon Faith.

By all means. Faith shoved a floppy fisherman's hat atop her head, obscuring her features from his view, and smiled sweetly.

～

"Aye, I beg ye, be quick about it afore our ship burns to a cinder," the massive bald man beckoned to Dajon.

Dajon hesitated. He knew he should obey his father's instructions; he knew he shouldn't risk the hoard of goods in his hold; he knew he should pay heed to the foreboding of dread that now sank like an anchor in his stomach, but all he could see was the lady's admiring smile beneath the shadow of her hat, and he led his men over the bulwarks.

After directing them to assist in putting out the fire, he marched toward the dark, bald man and bowed.

"Captain Dajon Waite at your service."

When his gaze drifted to the lady, she slunk into the shadows by the foremast, her features lost in the dim light. Odd. Somehow he had envisioned a much warmer reception. At the very least, some display of feminine appreciation.

"Give 'em no quarter! Give 'em no quarter!" a shrill voice shrieked, drawing Dajon's attention behind him to a large red parrot perched on a peg jutting from the mainmast.

A sharp blade of fear stabbed him.

"Captain," one of his crew called from the quarter-deck. "The ship ain't on fire. It's just a barrel with flaming rubbish inside it!"

The anchor that had sunk in Dajon's stomach dropped into his boots with an ominous clunk.

He spun back around, hoping for an explanation, but all he received was a sinister grin on the bald man's mouth.

Alarm seized Dajon, sucking away his confidence, his reason, his pride. Surely he could not have been this daft. He glanced back at the *Lady Em*, bobbing in the sea beside them—the pride of his father's fleet.

"To battle, men!" the woman roared in a commanding voice belying her gender—a voice that pummeled Dajon's heart to dust.

Dozens of pirates spat from the hatches onto the deck. Brandishing weapons, they rushed toward his startled crew. One by one, his men dropped their buckets to the wooden planks with hollow thuds and slowly raised their hands. Their anxious gazes shot to Dajon, seeking his command. The pirates chortled as Dajon's fear exploded into a searing rage. They were surrounded.

The woman drew a pistol from her sash. Dajon could barely make out the tilted lift of her lips. He wiped the sweat from his brow and prayed to God that he would wake up from this nightmare.

"I thank you, Captain, for your chivalrous rescue." The woman pointed her pistol at him and cocked it with a snap. "But I believe I'll be taking over your ship."

CHAPTER 2

With a light kick to his gelding's sides, Dajon prodded his horse into a trot as he made his way down Bay Street. To his right, over the wall that surrounded Charles Towne, the Cooper River swept past the city in smooth ripples that, joined by the Ashley River to the west, poured freshwater into Charles Towne Bay. A muggy breeze eased over him, stealing away the icy chill that had seeped into his bones from a winter spent patrolling the English Channel. Though he had heard tales of the brutal summer heat in the British province of Carolina, he looked forward to the warm sunshine boasted about by the settlers. He had never been fond of the continual dome of fog and clouds draped over England.

He nodded at the women strolling in front of the town's shops and warehouses, shrugging off their admiring gazes, telling himself the women's interest stemmed purely from the Royal Navy uniform he wore. Had it really been four years since he had rejoined His Majesty's Navy—and five years since that accursed woman pirate had stolen his father's ship and forced Dajon to return home in humiliation? Somehow it seemed only yesterday.

Passing one of the town's many taverns, he grimaced at the swarm of men already visible through the windows and pouring out the door into the street so early in the evening. Bawdy music accompanied by the raised voices of men playing billiards and the laughter of women oozed over Dajon like the slimy bilge from his ship,

13

M. L. TYNDALL

reminding him of a time when he, too, had wallowed in
the filth with the worst of them.

Shaking off the bad memories, he urged his mount
forward past a brick Presbyterian church, framed with
dogwood and oak trees, that rose like a beacon of hope.
Dajon scratched his head at the dichotomy of a place
where debauchery and holiness coexisted without
contention. In fact, more than ten churches graced this
tiny port of nearly four thousand citizens, branding it
the "Holy City," a title that warmed Dajon to his soul.

Thunder rumbled as he turned his mount onto
Hasell Street, where moss-draped trees stood like
sentinels dressed in royal robes on each side of the dirt
path. Dajon examined the houses lining the avenue for
the one that matched the description given him by his
old friend Rear Admiral Westcott. Though quite pleased
to have unexpectedly run into the admiral at the powder
magazine the night before, Dajon couldn't halt the pang
of trepidation he felt for what the admiral wished to
discuss with him.

Rain drizzled from the darkening sky, and Dajon
tugged his dark blue bicorn farther down upon his head
just as the only cherry-red house on the street came into
view. Guiding the horse through the open iron gate and
down the gravel path, he lightly drew back the reins at
the front entrance and slid from the saddle. A brawny
man with wiry, long black hair and skin the color of
copper sped around the corner of the house much faster
than his bulk seemed to allow and took the reins. When
the man's dark eyes met his, a spike of familiarity halted
Dajon.

"I'll take care of yer horse, sir." He snapped his gaze
to the ground and shuffled his feet in the mud before
turning away.

"Hold up there. Have we met before?"

The man let out a nervous chuckle. "No, sir." And
kept his eyes leveled at the dirt. "They's awaitin' ye
inside, sir," he said then led the horse around the corner.

A strong breeze blew in from the bay, sending the

palmettos dancing in the front yard and immersing Dajon in the spicy incense of moist earth as he took the stairs in one leap and ducked under the porch's covering. Doffing his hat, he slapped the rain from it on his knee and rapped the brass door knocker. It was only after the clang tolled through the humid air that he noticed it was shaped like a three-masted frigate. He smiled.

The thick oak door opened to reveal a middle-aged man of small stature and rounded belly.

"Mr. Waite, I presume?" He pursed his thin lips and stepped back, allowing Dajon entrance. "Please follow me. The admiral is expecting you." Closing the door, he adjusted his silk waistcoat and led the way through a spacious entrance hall. A marble staircase with shiny brass posts rose to a second story. Candlelight and feminine giggles floated down from above and danced around Dajon, sparking his interest and bristling his nerves.

"May I?" The steward turned and proffered his hand when he reached an open door to his right. Dajon shrugged off his frock and handed it to him, along with his bicorn, and entered the parlor. The admiral sat by a fireplace, intently perusing a document.

"Mr. Waite, sir," the steward announced, and the admiral stood.

"Commander." Rear Admiral Westcott dropped the papers onto a table. "Good to see you again." He shook Dajon's hand and directed him to a sofa.

"Thank you for your invitation, Admiral." Seating himself, Dajon scanned the room. Mahogany bookcases and cabinets lined the walls, an oak desk and chair perched beside open french doors that led to a wide porch, and imported rugs warmed the hardwood floor.

The admiral resumed his seat by the brick fireplace, where smoldering embers added unnecessary warmth to the stifling summer heat. Or maybe it was only Dajon's jittery nerves that caused the beads of sweat to form on his forehead. Could this be the promotion to post captain he had been waiting for? Certainly during the past two years as commander, he had more than proven himself capable during skirmishes with the Spanish and the French. He had heard that promotions came more quickly in the colonies because of a shortage of good officers. It was one of the reasons he had requested a transfer to Carolina.

Wiping the moisture from the back of his neck, he smiled at the admiral, noticing the man wore his gold-trimmed blue coat even when at home. Although the British Navy required no uniform, Dajon took pride in wearing his as well.

An uncomfortable silence permeated the room. "What brings you to Charles Towne, sir?" Dajon began. "I must admit my shock when I came across you in town."

The admiral stared out the window, suddenly looking older than his fifty years. "I fear I needed a change of scenery. Portsmouth holds far too many memories for me."

Dajon swallowed, chiding himself for bringing up the subject and only now remembering that the admiral's wife had died some years ago. "You have my deepest condolences."

The admiral shifted in his seat. "It was a long time ago," he huffed, the sorrow on his face tightening into firm lines. "But I thought it would be wise for the girls and me to start afresh. And what better place than the American colonies?"

"The girls?"

The admiral sighed. "I have been *blessed* with four daughters. Would you believe it? Three have traveled to Charles Towne with me. The fourth remains in Portsmouth with her husband."

Dajon smiled, finding it difficult indeed to fathom the admiral as a father. He was a gruff old man whose booming voice and piercing gaze frightened the most stalwart of sailors. He could not imagine their effect on a genteel woman.

The admiral stuffed a pipe into his mouth and took a puff, folding his hands over his stomach and examining

Dajon as if he were a cadet taking his first lieutenant's exam. "I'm a direct man, Mr. Waite, so I'll get to the point of your visit." The pipe wobbled in his mouth as he spoke. "In your time serving under my command, I found you to be an honorable, trustworthy man."

"Thank you, sir." Anticipation rang within Dajon. He moved to the edge of his seat.

"I have rarely encountered a man so naturally skilled and suited for command in His Majesty's Navy."

Dajon broadened his shoulders. "Due to your excellent tutelage, sir. I was fortunate to learn from one of the best officers in the navy." In fact, Dajon owed his quick rise to commander to Admiral Westcott's hearty recommendation. He clamped his sweaty hands together, his heart skipping a beat.

"Yes, yes." The admiral waved a hand in the air. He scratched his gray hair and flashed his auburn eyes to Dajon—that imperious gaze that could wither the staunchest of hearts.

"But I fear you did not bring me here to recount my success in the navy," Dajon said.

"No, quite right." The admiral stood and began to pace in front of the fireplace, the tails of his coat flapping on the back of his white breeches.

The muted sound of a bird squawking reached Dajon's ears, and he glanced above him curiously.

"Ah yes, my daughter's infernal parrot." The admiral shook his head, drawing Dajon's attention back to him. "She refused to leave the blasted beast behind. Noisy creature and quite messy, to be sure." He puffed on his pipe. "But back to business. I am afraid I have been called away suddenly."

"Sir?" Dajon feigned ignorance at the admiral's reasons for disclosing his plans. But why else would he mention his sudden departure unless he wanted Dajon to assume command of a higher-rated ship in his absence?

"As you have no doubt heard, the Spanish are causing problems in Italy. They have landed a fleet on Sardinia."

"Yes, I have read the dispatches." Dajon blinked, wishing the man would get to the point.

"I am to report overseas in a month in preparation for the possibility of war."

"Nothing to fear, sir. I am sure it will not come to that."

"Egad, man, I am not afraid! 'Tis my daughters that concern me." The admiral's eyes flared with the same sternness Dajon had grown accustomed to when he had sailed under the admiral's command. "This barbarous town is no place for young ladies. When I heard you were stationed here indefinitely, I knew you were the man for the job."

Dajon slowly rose and lengthened his stance. Indeed, he was the man for the job, but what did that have to do with the admiral's daughters? A slight disturbance ruffled his anticipation, like the beginnings of a quarrel in the dark corner of a tavern, but he shrugged it off. "You can count on me, sir."

"I knew I could." The admiral smiled. " 'Tis a big responsibility to force on you so suddenly."

Responsibility? Not to Dajon. Being post captain gave him more power, and more power meant he could protect more people—could play a bigger part in guarding his country, her colonies, and her citizens—and perhaps make some amends for past wrongs. "I am up to the task, sir."

"Very well, then. I shall make arrangements to have your things moved as soon as possible. That way, my daughters can get used to having you around before I set sail."

Dajon's exuberance sank to the floor. "Your daughters?" his voice squeaked.

"Why yes. There is no better man than you to be their guardian in my absence. With the Spanish and Indian attacks of late, not to mention the savage nature of some of the settlers, they need a naval officer to protect them."

No promotion? Dajon's breath halted in his throat.

He wiped the sweat from his brow. A guardian? Of women? Every encounter he'd ever had with females had ended in disaster.

And drastically changed the course of his life.

For the worse.

'Twas one of the reasons he had joined the navy. No women.

Dajon stared at the admiral and knew he could never trust himself to protect a woman again. "Sir, I fear you have the wrong man. I could not possibly—"

"Of course you will not be staying here in the house." The admiral snorted, ignoring him. "That would not be proper, but I will have Edwin prepare a bed for you in the guesthouse out back. I have no doubt you will find it quite comfortable. No need for you to stay on your ship while you are at anchor."

Dajon felt as though he were tumbling headlong into a dark void. "I appreciate your trust in me, Admiral, but 'tis a most untoward request, sir, and I must refuse it."

"I know. You fear your duties will keep you away overmuch?" The admiral slapped him on the back. "Of course your responsibilities in the Royal Navy come first. I only ask that you check on my girls daily and be aware of their comings and goings."

Dajon took a forceful step toward the admiral, trying to formulate his words. How could he deny this man's request—this man who had done so much for him?

The admiral stomped a boot atop the brick hearth and stared into the dying embers, puffing on his pipe. "I daresay any man who can successfully command my three daughters and run my home like a tight ship during my absence"—he chuckled, a disbelieving kind of laughter that said the feat had yet to be accomplished—"now that man would have more than proven his ability to command." He tapped his pipe into a tray on the mantel. "In fact, I might be inclined to promote such a man to post captain." He slowly turned around and gave Dajon a sly look.

Dajon swallowed. So that was the way of it. Admiral

Westcott continued to hold Dajon's future solely in his hands. Making post captain was no easy feat. A commander or lieutenant had to have political influence (of which Dajon had none), win some daring battle at sea (hard to do when one's country was currently not at war), or wait until someone above him died (a rather morbid way to be promoted). The only other hope was by the recommendation of an admiral. And it was clear now to Dajon that he would not receive such an honor unless he did as the admiral requested.

But how could he?

Either way, doom cast an ominous cloud over his naval career like the endless black fog over London. Nevertheless, if he were to remain a commander forever, the position would be more easily borne without the added tarnish of having caused harm to innocent young ladies. And yet he could not agree, no matter the cost to his career. He opened his mouth to speak when a shuffle sounded at the door.

"Ah, there they are." The admiral smiled.

Dajon swerved about to see three women enter the room: One was a petite girl with hair the color of the sun pinned up in a bounty of curls; another had dark hair pulled tight in a bun, a book cradled in her arms. But it was the third woman who drew Dajon's attention and sent his blood racing. She sashayed into the room, flinging her brazen red curls behind her and wearing a saucy smirk on her plump lips.

Dajon's heart crashed into his ribs.

CHAPTER 3

Faith forced the shock from her face at seeing the man whose ship she had once pirated—the man whose ship she still sailed. Perhaps he did not recognize her. Nearly five years had passed, and it had been foggy and dismal that night. If she were still a praying woman, she would pray for no remembrance of her to form in his mind, for if he disclosed her secret, she would face not only her father's wrath but quite possibly the gallows, as well. Alarm stiffened every nerve as she slunk deeper into the shadows behind the door.

"Ladies, may I present Mr. Dajon Waite, commander of the HMS *Enforcer*." The admiral approached his daughters, gestured toward Faith, and then frowned. "Faith, how oft must I impress upon you to put up your hair as befitting a proper young lady? And quit cowering against the wall and come hither to meet Mr. Waite."

Faith took a tentative step forward, keeping her gaze on the floor.

Her father huffed. "Miss Westcott." Then he gestured toward her sisters. "Miss Hope and Miss Grace."

Faith risked a peek at Mr. Waite as he bowed toward all three of them. Then the man opened his mouth as if attempting to say something. Yet not a word proceeded out of it.

"Does he speak, Father?" Faith asked, eliciting giggles from her sisters.

Mr. Waite turned a wary gaze upon her, his blue eyes like ice. A barb of unfamiliar fear scraped down her back. Perhaps he was trying to find a way to break the news to the admiral that his daughter was a pirate.

She looked away as her stomach coiled in a knot.

The admiral gave Mr. Waite a puzzled look. "He was doing quite nicely before you entered."

Mr. Waite's harsh expression melted, and he puffed a breath as if a giant ball in his throat had instantly dissolved. His face reddened. "My apologies, ladies. 'Tis a great pleasure to meet you."

Hope rushed to him and raised her hand.

"Oh, Hope, must you throw yourself at every man who enters the house?" Grace shook her head and turned to replace her book in one of the bookcases.

Ignoring her sister, Hope gave Mr. Waite an alluring smile and fluttered her lashes as he placed a kiss upon her hand. Her low neckline drew his attention, as it did all men's. Faith winced at her sister's blatant coquetry. Why was she always seeking the wrong sort of attention? Yet the commander surprised Faith when he quickly averted his eyes and turned to address her. No recognition tinged his features, just a curious admiration.

He does not know me.

Relief blanketed her tight nerves.

"Father." Hope's voice sounded strained. "I hope Mr. Waite's presence here does not mean you'll be leaving us again?" She glanced at Mr. Waite. "No disrespect to you, Mr. Waite."

Mr. Waite nodded but shifted uncomfortably.

Jutting out his chin, the admiral stared at the bookcases behind Hope. "I have not received my final orders yet, my dear, but you know my job is upon the sea."

"But we have just moved here, Father." Grace clasped her hands together and took a step toward him. "We hardly know a soul, and the customs are so different than in England."

"'Tis a savage place," Hope added with a snort. "Too frightening for us to be left all alone." She twirled a lock of hair at her neck, her features scrunched with worry. "And you must introduce us into society, or we shall be terribly bored."

Faith studied her father. Muscles of annoyance

twitched in his jaw. Yet behind his staunch expression, she detected a glimmer of excitement in his eyes. And she knew. She knew he planned to sail away soon. She knew because she felt the same thrill every time she was about to head out upon the sea. If she and her father were so much alike, then why did he constantly disappoint her?

He straightened his blue coat and put on the indomitable expression of his position. "There are worse things than boredom, Hope. Besides, you have your sisters to keep you company."

Hope lowered her gaze. "With Mother. . .with Mother. . ." She gulped. "And you always at sea, I feel like I am an orphan."

"Egad, an orphan who lives in luxury! Have you ever heard of such a thing?" The admiral gave an angry laugh, his face reddening; then he glanced at Mr. Waite, but the commander had turned aside, pretending to examine a brass figurine on the table.

Grace placed her arm around Hope's shoulders. " 'Tis all right, Hope. Clearly, Father cannot abandon his duty to Britain. And we must always remember that we have a Father in heaven who loves us very much."

Hope flattened her lips and stared at the floor.

Faith touched her father's arm and met his gaze. "Father, can you not stay a little while longer, just until Hope feels more at ease?" But she already knew his answer. She had long ago learned to live without her father's presence, as her mother had before her.

The admiral frowned. A hard sheen covered his brown eyes. He opened his mouth to speak what Faith knew would be an angry retort when Edwin's dull voice interrupted them from the doorway. "Sir Wilhelm Carteret has arrived, Admiral, and Molly informs me that dinner is served."

"Ah yes. Shall we, then?" The admiral blew out a heavy sigh and gestured toward the foyer.

Mr. Waite turned and hastened toward the door as if he couldn't wait to escape. Deciding to face her enemy head-on, Faith slid her arm through his as he passed. "Mr. Waite, please do forgive us for forcing you to endure our family squabbles."

Although he smiled, the muscles in his arm remained as tight as a full sail under a strong wind.

Hope tossed her nose in the air at Faith before exiting the parlor in a swish of satin—no doubt she'd intended to grab the commander herself. Grace and the admiral followed behind.

"Sir Wilhelm," the admiral bellowed. "How good of you to come."

At the sight of Sir Wilhelm, a chill seeped through Faith. He straightened his white periwig and allowed his eyes to slink over her before they landed on Mr. Waite and narrowed. A smile returned when he faced the admiral and bowed. "My pleasure, as always."

"Sir Wilhelm Carteret," the admiral said. "May I present Mr. Dajon Waite."

"An honor, sir." The commander bowed.

Sir Wilhelm grunted and gave him a cursory glance.

"Sir Wilhelm is an acquaintance of the family and dines with us often," the admiral explained as Edwin led the party down the hall to the dining room.

White linen and china glistened in the candlelight on the oblong table that filled the small room. The admiral took his seat at the head, his back to a window overlooking the gardens; rain puddled across the glass, distorting the trees, bushes, stables, and servants' quarters that filled the back gardens.

Once everyone was seated, kitchen maids placed platters of meat, fresh flounder, rice, corn, and biscuits onto the table, in addition to pitchers of wine and water. The savory aroma of beef and creamy butter spiraled over Faith but soured in her churning stomach. She cast a wary eye upon the two men responsible for her lack of appetite: Sir Wilhelm, who flapped his coattails behind him as he lowered to his chair, and Mr. Waite, who took his seat directly across from her.

"A grand feast." Her father rubbed his hands

together before saying grace over the food.

"Sir Wilhelm." Mr. Waite passed a plate of mutton to the man who sat beside him. "Your name is familiar to me. Where have I heard it?"

Sir Wilhelm took the plate and served himself a huge pile of meat, thrusting his chin out before him. "My grandfather, George Carteret, was one of the original eight proprietors of the realm."

"Indeed?" Mr. Waite tucked a strand of wayward hair behind his ear. "Not the same George Carteret who was treasurer of the navy?"

"The same." Sir Wilhelm sniffed and directed his pointed nose at Faith. His epicurean smile sent a shudder through her, and she looked away and grabbed the bowl of rice in front of her.

"Not only that"—the admiral poured wine into his goblet—"but Wilhelm's grandfather was also a vice admiral and comptroller of the navy. A brilliant, powerful man."

Faith watched Sir Wilhelm's scrawny shoulders rise with each praise. She used to think him a large man, but sitting next to the commander, he shriveled in stature. Her gaze shifted to Mr. Waite. His broad chest pressed against his blue navy coat. One rebellious strand of dark brown hair—the color of the rich soil she'd once seen on the coast of Ireland—sprang from his queue, and when his bright blue eyes met hers, glimmering in the candlelight, an unusual warmth spread throughout her.

"So you can imagine," Sir Wilhelm said, leaning forward and drawing all attention his way, "how thrilled I was to discover that an admiral had been stationed here in Charles Towne. I arranged to make his acquaintance as soon as I could. But I never imagined Admiral Westcott would have such lovely daughters." His brash gaze landed on Faith, and she shifted in her chair, wondering why she had the misfortune of being the center of this man's attentions.

"Then do you share your grandfather's love of the sea?" Mr. Waite asked Sir Wilhelm.

Wilhelm poured wine into his glass, clanking the decanter against his goblet so loudly Faith thought it would break. "No, I am afraid my many obligations keep me ashore."

"Indeed?" Faith gave him a crooked smile. "The rumor about town is that you suffer from seasickness."

Hope giggled.

"Faith!" Her father's gruff voice boomed across the room like a cannon blast. "You know better than to put any credence to the foolhardy prattle of the town's biddies. You will apologize to Sir Wilhelm at once."

Sir Wilhelm sniffed and wiggled his nose. "No need. There are many who are jealous of my power and enjoy nothing more than to spread ugly tales about me." He withdrew a handkerchief from his embroidered satin waistcoat and held it to his nose. "I trust, Miss Westcott, you are too clever to fall for such fabrications."

"Forgive my impertinence." She took a bite of beef and eyed him. The ghostly pallor of his face matched the powder in his wig. A dark mole peeked out from behind a cusp of white hair near his right ear, like a bat from a cave.

"Faith is far too wise for such nonsense," Hope added. "She is by far the most intelligent woman I know."

"That she surpasses your own intelligence is no accomplishment." The admiral chortled, plunging his fork into a mound of corn. "My dear Hope was never proficient in her studies."

Hope lowered her eyes, and Faith longed to kick her father beneath the table. Why did he insist on showering Hope with his constant disapproval? Could he not see how it crushed the poor girl, especially now that their mother was gone?

Grace squeezed Hope's arm and cast a matronly look around the table. "It is the condition of the heart that matters most."

"Well said, Miss Grace." Mr. Waite nodded then raised his gaze to Faith. "Forgive me, but I cannot shake the feeling that we have met somewhere before."

Her heart froze. She gulped and willed the screeching voice within her to calm before she dared utter a word. "I fear you are mistaken, Mr. Waite. Unless, perhaps"—she stabbed a piece of meat with her fork, hoping the trembling of her hands was not evident— "you frequented Portsmouth? We may have passed on the streets." She placed the beef into her mouth, but the savory flavor became bitter before it reached her throat.

"Perhaps. But 'tis the strangest thing. Your grooms- man seemed quite familiar to me, as well." A hint of suspicion tainted his voice.

"Lucas?" Faith coughed. "He has a common face." She bent over, trying to dislodge the food stuck in her throat. The commander was toying with her, after all. *He knows. He has to know.* Dread stung every nerve as she pounded on her chest, finally loosening the clump of meat. It wasn't that she feared the gallows. It wasn't that she feared death.

What she feared most of all was leaving her sisters all alone in the world.

"Are you ill, daughter?" The admiral leaned from his seat beside her and laid a hand on her shoulder.

Sir Wilhelm took a sip of wine and gazed at Faith. Something sinister crept behind his grin. " 'Tis probably the climate. Every new settler suffers local infections as they grow accustomed to this humid environment. They call it the seasoning."

"I am quite well, I assure you." Faith glared at Wilhelm. "We have been here over two months and have yet to fall ill."

"Then you have been fortunate, indeed," Sir Wilhelm commented. "In the past twenty years, Charles Towne has been struck by both smallpox and the Barbados fever. Horrid diseases." He shuddered in disgust. "Hundreds died." He gave them a superior look. "Only those of strong constitution survived."

Faith snarled. Strong, indeed. Or too weak and despicable for the disease to waste its energy upon.

The admiral cleared his throat. "Hardly appropriate

dinner conversation in front of the ladies."

"We have nothing to fear," Grace interjected. "God will protect us."

"If we live, dear sister, God will have naught to do with it," Faith snapped.

"You cannot mean that."

"Come now, ladies." The admiral shook his head and gestured for more wine, his face flushed with embarrassment. "Faith, you must repent for such a statement."

Faith flattened her lips and flung her hair behind her.

Grace smiled at Mr. Waite. "Are you a godly man?"

"For heaven's sake, Grace, is that all that concerns you?" Hope sighed, poking at her food.

Mr. Waite swallowed and smiled, grabbing his cup. "Yes, I am, miss."

"To what church do you belong?"

He took a sip of water and set down his cup. "I aspire to the doctrine that the Bible is the divine Word of God and should guide us in all things."

Sir Wilhelm snorted, sending a spray of wine over his plate. "Surely you are not one of those Dissenters, Waite. The Church of England is the only true church."

The commander's jaw flexed. "Where, pray tell, Sir Wilhelm, does it indicate that in the Word of God? I have yet to read that passage." He gave the man a patronizing grin.

Sir Wilhelm squirmed in his seat and huffed in response.

"Well said, Mr. Waite." Grace fingered the top button of her gown, and Faith wondered if perhaps her piety wasn't simply due to a lack of air from the stranglehold her tight-fitting collars had upon her neck.

"You must forgive Grace," the admiral said. "She is overzealous in her faith, as her mother was." He dropped his fork onto his plate with a clank.

"I do not believe you can be overzealous in your love for God, Admiral." Mr. Waite nodded toward Grace.

Faith let out a painfully ladylike sigh. *Wonderful,*

another Puritan in our midst. "You do not know my sister, Mr. Waite."

Sir Wilhelm cleared his throat. " 'Tis best to leave God out of the affairs of men."

Grace cocked her delicate head. "Which would explain, Sir Wilhelm, why man has made such a mess of this world."

Hope frowned then pushed her plate aside and leaned over the table, drawing Sir Wilhelm's gaze to her chest—though obviously not the gaze she intended to draw, as her attention locked upon the commander. "What brings you to Charles Towne, Mr. Waite?"

"After Blackbeard's horrendous blockade of your city this past May, Parliament thought it wise to send some of His Majesty's ships to patrol the area." The commander nodded toward the admiral.

The admiral scowled. "The pirate attack was quite an event, I have heard. The poor citizens of this town held at ransom by a thieving pirate, demanding, of all things, medical supplies. And him holding Samuel Wragg, a member of the council, hostage and threatening to kill him. Absurd."

"I couldn't agree more, Admiral," Mr. Waite said. "Which is precisely why I have been sent here—to capture every pirate patrolling these waters and ensure they are hung by the neck until dead."

CHAPTER 4

The biscuit in Faith's mouth instantly dried, leaving a hardened clump that scraped across her tongue. Grabbing some water to wash it down, she leaned back in her chair, eyed Mr. Waite, and pressed a hand to her stomach, where the food she had just consumed began to protest.

"How exciting!" Hope beamed, clapping her hands. "A pirate hunter in our very own house."

"I am simply doing my duty, miss." Mr. Waite gave Faith a concerned look. "Are you feeling well, Miss Westcott? You have gone quite pale."

Faith nodded, gathered her resolve, and opened her mouth to say something witty, but her voice mutinied.

"I daresay." Hope placed a hand on her chest, her voice a soft purr. "I feel much safer knowing you are guarding our harbor from those vile creatures."

Sir Wilhelm lifted his glass in salute. "We proprietors do appreciate the presence of the Royal Navy to protect our interests in the province."

"We are pleased to be of service." Mr. Waite's gaze drifted over the ladies and landed on the admiral. "Did you say that you have another daughter back in England?"

Leaning forward, the admiral filled his glass of wine for the third time, nearly tipping it in the process. He slammed the decanter down with a thud. Faith cringed. Her father took to drinking only when something vexed him. And the combination was oft more explosive than powder and matchstick. "Charity, my only married daughter, remained in Portsmouth," he said.

Faith's ire rose along with a sudden pounding in

her head. "Imprisoned in Portsmouth, you meant to say, Father." Instantly she wished she had kept her mouth shut—for once—for Father's face swelled like a globefish.

Mr. Waite raised a curious brow in her direction, shifting his gaze between her and the admiral. Faith sighed. She might as well continue what she had started.

"My sister was forced to marry a beastly man who stole the printing business Father had allowed her to embark upon. And. . ." She glanced at Hope, whose countenance had fallen. "And he was unfaithful." A clump of sorrow rose in Faith's throat. She grabbed Hope's hand beneath the table and squeezed against the clammy chill that clung to her sister's palm.

The admiral dropped his knife onto his plate with a loud clank. "And you know better than to speak of such things at my table, Faith."

Sir Wilhelm pointed his fork at her. "Forgive me for saying so, but your sister's husband could hardly have stolen a business that upon marriage became his by law. Besides, women have no sense for business, nor for the spending of money acquired from such ventures. These things are best left up to men."

"Here, here, good man." The admiral lifted his glass.

"And ofttimes a man is forced to seek"—Sir Wilhelm cleared his throat—"shall we say, diversions elsewhere when his life at home is unpleasant." He shrugged before chomping on a biscuit.

Faith shot to her feet, her chair scraping over the wooden floor behind her. Heat inflamed her face. Her fingers tingled, yearning for a weapon, any weapon. Her eyes landed on a pitcher of water. She grabbed it, squeezing her fist over the cool handle. " 'Tis to be expected, sir, only of scoundrels and savages," she said in as calm a voice as possible as she filled her glass. Then, setting the pitcher down in front of Sir Wilhelm—atop a serving spoon— she quickly withdrew her hand as the wavering container toppled over. A cascade of water spilled onto the table, gushed toward the edge, and flooded Sir Wilhelm's breeches before splattering onto the floor.

Springing to his feet, he stumbled over his chair, sending it crashing behind him. "Of all the. . . !" he screeched, reminding Faith of her parrot, Morgan, whenever something riled him.

"Faith!" Her father stood and directed the serving maids to assist Sir Wilhelm. Their shoes clomped over the wooden floorboards like a herd of cattle as they sped off, returning within seconds with towels. "Where is your head, girl?"

"It was an accident, Father." Faith lifted her hands in a conciliatory gesture then clasped them together before facing Sir Wilhelm. "My sincere apologies, Sir Wilhelm. I was not paying attention."

Sir Wilhelm scowled as he snatched a towel from one of the maids with a snap and dabbed at his sodden breeches. "Perhaps, Admiral, you should hire a governess to teach your daughters proper etiquette. Apparently, without their mother, their social graces have lapsed."

"It was an unintentional mishap, Sir Wilhelm," Grace said, ever the voice of calm propriety.

The admiral frowned. For a second, Faith thought he would defend his daughters, but then he grabbed his drink and plopped back into his chair.

After tossing the wet towel back to the maid, Sir Wilhelm adjusted his wig and took his seat. Mr. Waite held his hand to his mouth, and Faith sensed a smile lingered behind it. When his eyes met hers, a spark of playfulness danced across them.

"Sit down, Faith." Her father pounded his boot on the floor and pointed to her chair. "You have insulted our guest enough. If you cannot behave, I will insist you leave this room at once."

Faith sank into her chair, not wanting to leave her sisters to endure Sir Wilhelm's vile opinions without her protection. She squeezed Hope's arm and felt her quiver as a soft sob escaped the poor girl. A heavy weight of guilt pressed down upon Faith. Why had she resurrected such a horrid memory?

"Quit your sniveling, girl," the admiral barked at Hope. "We have guests."

Faith glared at her father. He knew very well what had upset Hope. Yet repeatedly he chose to hide behind the delusion of propriety. He could face battles upon the sea, witness men's legs being blasted into twigs, make snap decisions that changed the course of history, but he could not face what had happened to his own daughter.

"You must forgive my daughters, Mr. Waite." The admiral scratched his thick gray sideburns as the servants cleared the dishes from the table. "Since their mother died, they have not had proper female instruction."

"As you well know, Father"—Faith could not control the acrid bite in her tone—"I have taken that role upon myself. And I will continue to do so." She turned toward her sisters. "Although I know I can never take Mother's place." She eased a lock of Hope's golden hair from her face and saw her mother staring back at her. Faith's heart warmed. "You look so much like her."

Hope smiled, her eyes shimmering.

"Your mother must have been an incredible woman." Mr. Waite's deep voice smoothed the ripples of distress radiating over the table. His warm gaze landed on Faith and lingered there as if he were soaking in every detail of her. "Possessing both beauty and piety." He smiled then looked down and began fidgeting with his spoon.

Faith took a sip of cool water, hoping to douse the heat rising within her at his perusal.

"She is in heaven now." Grace kissed Hope on the cheek.

"God shouldn't have taken her in the first place." Faith released Hope's hand. "We have more need of her here than He does in heaven."

"What you need, my dear, is a good husband to tame you," the admiral said, gulping down another swig of wine.

"I will never marry." Faith shook her head and gave her father a stern look.

The admiral huffed. "Don't be absurd."

Sir Wilhelm cleared his throat and exchanged a knowing glance with her father—a glance that sent dread crawling over Faith.

"If a woman can provide for herself," she said, "she needn't subject herself to the tyranny of a man who restricts her freedom and forces his every whim—"

"As I have informed you, my dear Faith," her father interrupted, his voice strained to the point of exploding, "should you ever find yourself in possession of so great a fortune, I have promised not to arrange a marriage against your will." The wrinkles at the corners of his eyes seemed to fold together as he stared at her.

"Then I hold you to our bargain." Faith squared her shoulders, daring to hope that she could indeed fulfill her end of it. "If I amass this fortune you speak of, you will force neither me nor my sisters into marriage?"

"Yes, of course." The admiral dabbed his mouth with the edge of the tablecloth. "But time runs out. With your mother gone and me so often at sea, I may have no choice but to ensure your future happiness. The sooner you are all married, the better."

"And pray tell, Miss Westcott, how do you intend to procure such a fortune?" Sir Wilhelm asked with a hint of sarcasm.

"I have started a soapmaking business, which I can assure you will be quite successful." Faith stiffened her jaw and focused on her uneaten plate of food.

"Which I have yet to see any evidence of, I might add," the admiral said with a chortle.

Sir Wilhelm joined in his laughter, and Faith reached for her side where her cutlass normally hung but found only her beaded sash. Not that she would have stabbed the horrid excuse of a man, but it would have been amusing to see his face if she had tried. Instead, she rubbed her fingers over the smooth beads.

Grace leaned toward Faith, her mouth pinched in concern. "Marriage is a blessed union of God and should be honored."

With a sigh, Faith returned a gentle smile to her sister. Sweet Grace. So young and naive, but with such a heart of gold. Faith sometimes wished she had been born with so agreeable a nature. But alas, that was not to be. "It is a union not meant for all."

"Nevertheless," the admiral began, leaning back in his chair and folding his hands over his belly, "I believe I have been more than generous with you girls. In the five years since your mother. . .since your mother has been gone, you could have chosen any one of the fine young men clamoring for your attention in Portsmouth." He raised a cynical brow toward Faith. "All of them in possession of a good fortune, I might add."

"Oh pish, Father. They were naught but pompous bores."

The admiral shifted his inquiring gaze to Hope. "And you, my dear?"

"There were far too many of them. I simply could not choose." She waved her hand through the air.

Pursing his lips, he gazed at his youngest daughter. "What say you, fair Grace?"

Grace played with her fingers in her lap. "Like Faith, I do not wish to marry. The apostle Paul instructs that 'tis best to serve the Lord wholeheartedly without the distractions of a husband."

"Ah yes," the admiral sighed. "Grace's pursuit of holy living has kept many possible suitors far away, I am afraid. There's the rub, if you will." He shifted a stern gaze over his daughters. "I fear my only mistake has been in giving any of you a choice. Despite your fallacious opinions, I made a fine match for your sister Charity, a man of title and wealth. I only delayed in procuring the same for you because of your constant bickering and complaining."

"Father." Faith dropped her fork on her plate with a clang. "Despite his title and wealth, Lord Villement is naught but a—"

"Enough!" His roar echoed across the room, silencing all noise save the patter of rain on the window. Then, composing himself, he smiled at Mr. Waite. "So you see my dilemma?"

Sir Wilhelm's salacious gaze slithered over Faith. "Not so daunting a dilemma, Admiral, that a bit of parental discipline could not solve." Then, plunging the last bite of roast between his slimy lips, he patted his stomach. "Delicious."

The admiral poured himself another glass of wine and slowly sipped it as the maids came with pudding and tea. His eyes began to glass over. Shame instantly dissolved Faith's fury. She had upset and embarrassed her father again—and in front of guests. Perhaps it would be better if she excused herself, along with her sisters.

She pushed back her chair, the scrape of wood only adding to her annoyance. "Mr. Waite, you seem like a fine man—," she began, intending to apologize for her brash behavior.

"I am happy to hear it, Faith," her father interrupted. "Because I am making him guardian over you and your sisters until I return from Spain."

Mr. Waite set his teacup onto the saucer. "With all due respect, Admiral, I must refuse the honor, sir." He sat straight in his chair and met the admiral's gaze head-on.

"Refuse?" The admiral slowly rose, his face reddening, his tone filled with incredulity.

"Our guardian?" Faith could not believe her ears. "We do not need a guardian, Father. We have Lucas and Edwin. They can watch over us."

"I think it is a fine idea," Hope added, fluttering her lashes.

"Why ask a complete stranger?" A sultry grin spread over Sir Wilhelm's mouth as his gaze swept over Faith. "It is obvious he protests. I would be honored to protect the ladies in your absence, Admiral." He pulled a jeweled snuffbox from his pocket and snorted a pinch of dark powder up one nostril.

Faith shuddered.

The admiral loosened his white cravat. "Nay, you

have far too many responsibilities, Sir Wilhelm, plus your other involvement with this family."

"What involvement?" Faith demanded.

Mr. Waite shifted his stance and gave the admiral a level stare. "Admiral, might I suggest you choose from one of the local gentry? I am sure there are many willing and trustworthy young men."

The admiral snorted and shook his head, a frown marring his leathery skin. "Do you take me for a fool, Waite? I have searched far and wide through this forsaken outpost, but there is no one else I trust with the safety of my daughters save you." He scratched his thick sideburns and gave the commander such a look of disappointment that Faith nearly melted by proximity. But Mr. Waite held his ground, his eyes locked upon her father's, his stern expression unflinching.

"But I see you will let me down. Very well." The admiral waved a hand at Mr. Waite as if dismissing him.

Faith had to admit she felt relieved herself. The last thing she needed was a pirate hunter living at the house. But something was afoot between her father and Sir Wilhelm, and she intended to discover what it was.

❧

"Come in, Faith. Come in." Faith's father stood at the fireplace later that same evening, lighting his pipe from a stick he pulled from the coals. Mr. Waite had long since bid them all farewell and returned to his ship, and everyone else in the house had retired to their chambers. Sir Wilhelm rose from his chair and gave her a salacious look that nearly sent her scampering from the room. Instead, she took a few steps inside, keeping her distance from him yet staying close to the door should she need to escape. Her mind swam through a thousand reasons why her father had requested her presence in the drawing room after dinner, but now that she saw Sir Wilhelm, only one possibility—one dreadful possibility—surfaced.

The admiral rubbed his temples then glanced at Sir Wilhelm before taking a puff from his pipe. "I have some wonderful news for you, my dear." But the look on his face was not one of joy or excitement, but rather the look a parent gave a child when she was about to be punished. "Please sit down."

Faith threw back her shoulders. "I'd rather stand."

"I insist!" he bellowed, pointing with his pipe toward the sofa.

Lowering herself to the soft cushions, Faith tried to stop her heart from crashing against her chest. Across from her, Sir Wilhelm laid the back of his fingers to his nose and retook his seat, never letting his eyes leave her.

"Sir Wilhelm has made a most generous offer." Her father laid a hand on the mantel and smiled at Sir Wilhelm.

Faith clenched her fists in her lap and glanced out the door into the dark foyer, feeling like a condemned prisoner about to receive her sentence.

"He has asked for your hand in marriage."

A death sentence. The words sped across the deck of her mind, waiting for the final cannon blast to blow them into the water.

"And I have given him my approval."

Hit and sunk. Faith rose from the sofa slowly, methodically, trying to curb her fury. "I have not given *my* approval, Father," she spat through clenched teeth. "I will not be married off like chattel."

"You will do as I say!" He pounded his fist onto the mantel, sending a porcelain vase crashing to the floor.

Faith jumped and stared at the pieces of jagged painted glass littering the wooden planks like the shattered pieces of her heart.

"I know what is best for you." His voice lowered but still retained its fury.

Clasping her hands together, she faced Sir Wilhelm with as much civility as she could muster. "My apologies, sir, if my father has misled you. I do not wish to insult you, but I have no intention of marrying you or anyone else."

Tugging at his lopsided wig, Sir Wilhelm plucked out his handkerchief and fidgeted with it. "Admiral, I am surprised a man of your standing would allow such insolence in his home."

The admiral puffed out his chest until it seemed to double in girth. "Faith, I will have no more insubordination from you. It is already arranged. You will marry Sir Wilhelm."

Panic clambered up Faith's throat. Desperate for any reprieve, she willed tears to her eyes, hoping to soften his resolve. "Father, please reconsider. What of our bargain? I need more time."

The admiral's face swelled red. "Time for what, girl? All the time in the world will not grant you the fortune you need to remain independent. Besides, you are four and twenty, well past time for a proper union. In a few years, no man will have you. Or perhaps that is what you are hoping for?"

"I want to choose my own husband." Faith gave him her most innocent, pleading look—the one that usually pried through the crusty casing around his heart.

The admiral's harsh demeanor softened just a bit, giving Faith a flicker of hope. He took a puff from his pipe. "So you want to choose your own husband, is it?" He paused, and a hint of compassion flickered in his eyes. It was the look she'd often seen when her mother had been alive. "Fine. We shall compromise. Either you will find a suitable husband by the time I return from Spain, or"—he let out a sarcastic snort—"make a sizable profit from this soapmaking business you claim to be running, or mark my words, you will indeed marry Sir Wilhelm."

CHAPTER 5

Tiny pellets of rain blasted over Faith, stinging her face like a hundred needles. Bracing her boots on the foredeck of the *Red Siren*, she yanked the tricorn from her head and allowed the saturated wind to tear through her tangled curls. She flung her arms out wide and closed her eyes, hoping to forget the events of the evening as a wall of salty air, spiced with the scent of rain and sea, crashed over her. While some people went to drink for comfort, Faith went to sea. The thunder and crash of massive waves, the endless horizon, and the freedom of the wind in her hair never failed to soothe her nerves. But for some reason, tonight she could not shake the sickly face of Sir Wilhelm from her mind or his licentious gaze slithering over her when her father had announced their betrothal. She shuddered.

Footsteps sounded beside her, and she turned to see Lucas. Water dripped from the corner of a hat that hid his eyes in its shadow. He smiled.

"I doubt we'll be findin' any ships worth pillaging on a night like this, mistress."

Faith gazed out over the swirling cauldron, dark, save for occasional strips of white foam illuminated by a half-moon that danced betwixt the clouds. Rain formed droplets on her lashes, and she brushed them dry. Lucas was right.

"Not that I mind none," he continued with a snort. "Ye knows I like the smell o' the sea far better than the smell of them stables."

"I suppose I just needed to think." Faith gripped the wet railing, stunned by the chill that ran up her arms.

"But truth be told, it would have been nice to take a prize tonight."

"We done good so far, mistress. That cargo last month of silks and coffee brought us a fair price."

"But I need more." Faith slapped the railing. "Far more."

"I hear ye, mistress. But never ye mind. There's lots o' treasure to be had in these waters."

Lucas probably thought her greedy, but her father's announcement had only incited Faith's urgency. That her father was willing to marry her off to so foul a man as Sir Wilhelm was bad enough, but Hope would be next on his list, and then sweet Grace. Were all the admiral's daughters doomed to lives of abuse and misery? She would not stand for it. She had made a promise to her mother to take care of her sisters, and she refused to allow them to be sold off like prize horses to the highest bidder. She had yet to meet a man she considered worthy to marry—especially so-called Christian men.

Hypocrites, all of them.

Faith glanced at her first mate. Though enormous in size and much harsher in appearance than her father, Lucas Corwin was nothing like the admiral. He understood things like humility, compassion, and loyalty to family. "Thank you for sailing on such short notice, Lucas, and thank the men for me, will you?"

"Aye, they's happy to come." Lucas slapped the air with his hand. "All 'cept Grayson and Mac. I couldn't rouse them from their drink so quick." He snickered.

The loyalty of her crew astounded her. When they weren't out pirating, they spent their time gambling and drinking in town, waiting for her next call. Despite the humiliation of taking orders from a female captain, most of them had chosen to follow her from England to the colonies.

Lucas shifted his weight and fumbled with the hilt of his cutlass. "They's good men fer the most part. And they follow ye 'cause yer fair and ye don't hurt no one like most pirates. They's not after no killin'—just the treasure."

41

Morgan cawed from his post behind her. "Shiver me timbers. Shiver me timbers."

Lucas tugged his waistcoat tighter around him. "That bird be right 'bout one thing. It be so cold tonight, the timbers are quakin'."

Faith nodded as a blast of wind sent a chill through her sodden shirt. Unusually cold for August, to be sure. Not a good omen of things to come.

Lightning etched the sky in the distance, high-lighting the wild dance of the sea—the lawless, tumultuous sea. How she loved it!

A sail cracked above them, and Lucas turned. "Reef the topsails!" he blared to one of the men before facing Faith again. "I thought we was caught fer sure when that cap'n showed up at yer house." He scratched his chin. "Don't knows why he didn't recollect me."

"You were bald four years ago. Remember, the lice?" Faith plopped her tricorn back on her head. "But fortune smiled upon us, for it seems he didn't recognize me either." She shrugged. "Or perchance he just plays with us. But thanks be to Go—the powers that be, that the man had the courage to turn down my father's request to be guardian over me and my sisters, or I fear we would be seeing much more of him."

Thunder drummed across the sky in an ominous echo of her statement.

"Yer guardian?" Lucas laughed.

"Yes, and not only that. The Royal Navy has sent him here to hunt pirates." She gave Lucas a sly grin.

He slapped his thigh. "Why, I'll be a pickled hen. God has a sense o' humor, after all."

"I doubt *God* has much to do with any of this." Faith grew somber.

The ship bucked, sending a spray of seawater over them. Faith shook the water from her waistcoat and adjusted her baldric. Dressing in men's clothing always made her feel more in control—a feeling she had come to crave more with each passing year.

"As soon as my father sails for Italy, we will take the

Siren out as often as possible," she instructed Lucas, who nodded his head and gave her a mischievous grin.

Her father would be gone for at least six months. With a little luck and a lot of pluck, she and her crew could pirate these waters clean of all their treasures. But what to do with Mr. Waite? The last thing she needed was an HMS warship lurking about. He presented a problem indeed. He no longer appeared to be the half-witted lackey she had met five years before. Controlled and cordial, he carried himself as a man of honor. Strength and intelligence shone in his handsome blue eyes. She saw the way he looked at her. And she could not deny the tingle of warmth she felt in his presence.

Nevertheless, she must avoid him as much as possible. The less he knew about her and her family, the less suspicious he would be of her nighttime activities. Not that he would ever believe that the daughter of an admiral was a pirate. But she must play it safe in any case. She had come too far, accomplished too much to get caught now.

"Hard about, Lucas. Back to port," she ordered, eyeing the massive black clouds on the horizon. "For I fear a storm is on the way."

⟜

Dajon knelt before the wooden altar. A chill from the stone floor seeped through his breeches into his knees. Above him on the brick wall, the cross of Christ, his Lord, hung as a reminder of what the Son of God had sacrificed in his stead. He closed his eyes, shutting out the candlelight that illuminated the narrow brick Congregational church of his friend Rev. Richard Halloway. Dajon needed wisdom. He needed comfort, and he sought it from the One who never failed him.

Some time later, after he had poured out his heart to his Father, the scuffle of footsteps accompanied by baritone humming jarred Dajon from his meditation. He opened his eyes to see Rev. Halloway flipping through the pages of a book in the shadows by the communion table.

Clearing his throat, Dajon rose from the altar.

"Ah, my friend, you startled me," the reverend exclaimed as he came into the candle's glow, a wide grin on his ruddy face. He cast a glance behind him where the faint gleam of a new day brightened a window in the back of the sanctuary. " 'Tis early. What brings you here at this hour?" His bushy brows knit together.

Dajon shifted his weight and clutched the hilt of his sword. "I could not sleep."

"Something amiss?" The reverend led Dajon to a pew. "Sit. Tell me." He closed the book on his lap.

Dajon squinted at the title on the volume, unsure whether he should share his fears with his friend. "Richard Allestree's *Whole Duty of Man*?"

"Aye, have you read it?" The reverend lifted the book.

Dajon shook his head and sat beside him.

"I shall lend it to you when I am finished. It will strengthen your faith. But you did not come to discuss what I am reading."

Dajon squeezed the bridge of his nose. "I did not come to talk at all, only to pray."

The reverend patted him on the back. "Then you have already done what is most important."

Rev. Halloway's green eyes sparkled in the candlelight. The crinkle of his leathery skin and the gray flecks in his curly blond hair were the only things that gave away his age. He exuded a genuine concern that always pulled Dajon's darkest secrets out of hiding.

"Admiral Westcott requested that I act as guardian to his daughters while he is overseas."

The reverend let out a deep laugh. "Yes, the Westcott daughters. Newly arrived from England. I have heard men in town speak of their beauty."

"Then you know my dilemma." Dajon sprang to his feet and paced before the altar.

"You speak of Lady Rawlings?"

"Aye." A heavy weight entombed his heart as memories of a past life resurrected. "My answer was no, of course. But I fear my career will suffer for it. He doesn't understand my refusal. But what choice did I have?" Dajon released a heavy sigh.

" 'Twas a long time ago, Dajon."

"Not long enough."

The reverend slapped his hand on the pew. "When will you forgive yourself for what God has already forgotten?"

"How can I? It was my own foolish passion that caused her death." He gazed at the cross. "And I have vowed to God that I would never repeat that mistake."

"He has heard you. He knows your heart. And He will not give you a temptation you cannot resist."

Dajon sighed and gave the reverend a lopsided grin. "Have you seen Miss Faith Westcott?"

"If you mean the redhead, aye, I have." The reverend nodded. "I have taken notice of her as much as the good Lord allows."

"Even though I've just made her acquaintance, something comes over me when she is near. A flame that burns in my gut and befuddles my brain." Dajon plopped down on the pew again and propped his elbows on his knees. "I have the strange sensation that I have met her before, but I know that's not possible." He shook his head. "Of all the men under his command, why did the admiral have to ask me? I have spent the past four years making all the right choices, doing my duty to God and country."

"Perhaps that is why. That he trusts you with his most precious treasures—his own daughters—says a great deal about your character."

Dajon snorted. "If he only knew."

"You are not the man you once were." The reverend leaned back against the pew, the aged wood creaking beneath his weight.

"Perhaps. But it will be a long time hence before I can make amends for what I have done."

The reverend touched Dajon's arm. "You can never pay the price for what God has already paid, my friend."

"As you keep telling me." Dajon attempted a smile.

"Nevertheless, I find I am not ready for such a temptation."

"If you were not, God would not have sent it your way."

Dajon clenched his hands together. "It matters not. I turned him down and now must suffer the repercussions to my career."

"Surely the admiral will not punish you for refusing such a personal favor?"

"You do not know him. He is not called the 'Iron Wall' for nothing." Dajon snickered. "No one who has ever come against him has walked away unscathed."

The door of the sanctuary swung open and crashed against the wall. A stiff breeze whipped through the narrow room, sending the candle flames flickering.

Dajon turned to see two uniformed men marching toward him. He stood. They saluted him, and the one closest to him held out a piece of paper. "For you, Mr. Waite."

Dajon took the paper and broke the seal. It was from Admiral Westcott. As he read, his blood turned to ice.

Mr. Waite,
My orders have come through, and I am to
set sail immediately. I found your refusal to act
as guardian over my daughters in my absence
somewhat surprising and therefore have no recourse
but to assume it was merely due to modesty on your
part. As I am sure you are aware, I consider this
task to be associated with the security of our grand
and glorious nation, long live King George, in that
it will afford me the ability to focus entirely on my
duties rather than on the safety of my daughters. I
must tell you my resolutions are firm, and therefore
I place my daughters in your trustworthy charge.
And I assure you that you shall find yourself amply
rewarded when I return. Instructions have been left
with Edwin Huxley, my steward.

Everything inside of Dajon screamed a defiant *No!*

Yet there was no one present to whom he could protest—at least no one with the power to alter the path laid before him.

> *I did not wish to wake the girls, so I shall leave you the task of bidding them farewell in my stead. I trust you implicitly, Waite. But mark my words, I will hold you personally responsible for the safety and welfare of my daughters.*

> *Signed this day, the 15th of August in the year of our Lord, seventeen hundred and eighteen,*
> *Rear Admiral Henry Westcott*

CHAPTER 6

Tap, tap, tap.

Faith shoved a pillow over her head and rolled over. "Go away."

Tap, tap, tap.

"Miss Faith. You got to get up now." Molly's voice filtered through the door.

Faith fought against the sleep that pressed her deep into the mattress, but then she decided nothing could be important enough to disturb it and allowed it to consume her again.

The door creaked open, and footsteps clicked across the room, followed by a blast of bright light as her curtains were drawn back. "Sorry to disturb you, but you are needed downstairs."

Morgan cawed from his wooden perch next to Faith's bed.

Straining to sit, Faith huffed and rubbed her eyes. "What time is it?" She held out her hand, and Morgan flew to her. "Where is Loretta?"

"Noon, young missy." Molly clamped her hands on her hips. "Far too late for a proper lady to be sleepin'. And I sent the chambermaid on an errand." Molly eyed Morgan. "And a proper lady don't live with no bird, neither."

"But I just retired to bed—" Faith snapped her mouth shut.

"I know when you got yerself to bed. You and that scrap dog Lucas out roamin' the streets all night doin' God knows what." She clicked her tongue. "Shame, shame, shame on both of you."

"It is not what you think, Molly." Faith swung her legs over the side of her bed while Molly sifted through her armoire. *It's actually much worse.* Faith smiled.

"It's not my business to think. I jest keep prayin' for you, and for Lucas, too." Molly broke into a song that sounded like a cross between an African chant and a Christian hymn.

Blinking her eyes in an effort to keep them open, Faith stared at Molly as she selected a gown and undergarments and approached the bed. Two oval black eyes set in glowing skin the color of cinnamon stared back at her. Standing barely over five feet tall, the slender cook more than made up for her size with her determination.

Faith snickered. "Good heavens, what is the rush?" She set Morgan down on the blue satin coverlet.

"Heaven *will* be good, not that you gonna see much of it." Molly tossed a green silk gown, stiff petticoats, and a bodice onto the bed beside Faith. "And the rush is that handsome captain be down below awaitin' you."

"Mr. Waite? Why ever would he be here?" Faith jumped to the floor and tore off her nightdress, anxious to find out what the man wanted and to be rid of him as soon as possible before he ingratiated himself with her family.

Molly strode to the door, shaking her head. "Well, if I'd known that would get you up, I'd a said so in the first place."

After quickly donning her gown, Faith flew down the stairs, but then she halted at the bottom to thread her fingers through her hair and pat her eyes, hoping the puffiness of sleep had subsided. She held a lock of her hair up to her nose and drew in a deep breath. Lemons. She smiled. At least the lemon oil she had sprinkled through her hair masked the scent of the sea—something she knew the captain would smell in an instant.

Turning, she burst into the parlor, intending to make a grand entrance. But she was too late. Hope had already draped herself over poor Mr. Waite.

Grace sat stiffly on the sofa, while Edwin stood beside the admiral's desk, a sheaf of papers in hand.

Plucking Hope's arm from his, the commander turned toward Faith. His dark eyebrows rose as he straightened his blue coat and took a step toward her. The tip of his service sword clanged against the table, and he glanced down. But when he raised his gaze, his blue eyes met hers with such intensity that Faith's heart took on a rapid beat. She chided herself. She was supposed to be getting rid of him, not allowing his good looks and commanding presence to turn her insides to mush.

"Miss Westcott." He bowed, and a strand of his dark hair brushed against his cheek.

Her breath quickened. "Mr. Waite."

"Forgive me if I disturbed your rest." He grinned.

"Rest? Nay. I was reading." Faith waved a hand through the air and gazed off to her right.

"Our sister always sleeps half the day away," Grace said with disdain.

"Grace." Hope patted her silky golden hair, pinned up in a fashionable coiffure, and stared at her sister. "You should not say such things. What will Mr. Waite think of us?"

Mr. Waite shifted his stance, his black boots thumping on the wooden floor. "I will not keep you and your sisters long. I have come to extend your father's farewell and to go over my obligations with Edwin." He nodded toward the steward.

"Farewell?" Faith huffed. "So my father has fled in the night like a coward."

Darting to her, Hope clutched Faith's arm. "Can you believe Father left us without saying good-bye?" Tears glistened in her sister's eyes, and Faith's heart sank. It seemed her father's true love was and always would be the navy. "I am sure he had good reason." She offered her sister a weak smile.

Two black bags sitting by her father's desk caught Faith's gaze. Surely this pirate hunter was not planning to take up residence in their home? Had he not resolutely turned her father down? "Are we to assume, Mr. Waite, that you find yourself equally lacking in fortitude—so much so that you cannot deny my father's preposterous request?"

Mr. Waite gritted his teeth. "I assure you, Miss Westcott, I find the arrangement as displeasing as you do. But I fear I was given no choice."

"Ah." Faith raised one brow. "So he left without speaking to you as well." She flattened her lips. It certainly sounded like the kind of conniving tactic her father might employ. He had never been able to take no for an answer.

"He was called away suddenly." Mr. Waite's tone held no conviction.

"He could not wait a few hours?" Hope sobbed and crossed her arms over her lavender brocade gown—the one that brought out the gold sparkles in her hair and the deep blue in her eyes. "Sometimes I wonder if he loves us at all or simply wants to marry us off and be rid of the responsibility." She swiped a tear from her cheek. "I wish Mother were still with us." She hung her head, her voice tinged with sorrow. "We may not see Father for a year."

"Six months, in fact, miss," Mr. Waite interjected. "At least that is the time period he indicated to Edwin."

Edwin nodded in agreement from his position beside their father's desk.

Forcing back tears from her own eyes, Faith plucked a handkerchief from her pocket and handed it to Hope. "Father loves us in his own way, Hope. And Grace and I are still here. We will not leave you."

Grace rose to join them. "Faith is right. We will never leave you. And you know Father was never good at saying farewell." She eased a lock of Hope's hair from her face and smiled, her green eyes beaming with warmth and love.

Mr. Waite cleared his throat. "I have no doubt he was quite upset at having to leave so suddenly."

Faith cocked her head. "And all along, I was under the misunderstanding that good Christian men were not supposed to lie."

The captain snapped his blue gaze in her direction. "'Twas merely my opinion, miss, and therefore cannot be judged as either false or true."

"Then should we expect to be assaulted with your good opinions on a regular basis?" Faith retorted. Perhaps if she were rude enough to him, he would leave.

"So as not to offend your *tender* sensibilities, I will attempt to keep my opinions to a minimum." He gave her a mock bow.

Tender. Of all the. . .

"The truth of the matter, Mr. Waite, is that we know our father far better than you do." Faith turned and stomped toward the bookcase, trying to mask her anger. "The Royal Navy is his life. I fear we have always come second."

"As Mother did as well." Hope twisted a lock of her hair around one slender finger until it appeared hopelessly entangled.

Grace stilled Hope's hand and began to untwine her hair. "Human love is fraught with shortcomings. Only God's love satisfies."

Faith snorted and waved off her sister's religious platitude as she turned to face them.

Hope eased the loose strand of hair behind her ear. "I have found no satisfaction in God's love."

Grace clutched her sister's shoulders. "You should not say such a thing! And you should not speak poorly of Father either." Releasing her, Grace took a step back, her conflicted gaze shifting between Faith and Hope. "We must honor him as God's Word says." Yet even as the words left her mouth, they rang hollow through the air.

Faith flung a hand to her hip. "It is hard to honor a man who intends to do the same thing to us as he did to our sister Charity. Can you deny that, Grace?"

Hope began to sob again.

Grace slid onto the sofa and shook her head. "I

cannot deny that what he did was wrong, even cruel. But the Bible says we must honor him anyway." She sighed and clutched her gown, twisting it in her hands as if trying to make sense out of the pious rules she dedicated her life to following.

"And how can I honor a man I hardly know?" Hope swallowed and lowered her gaze. "Even when he is home, he seems to find no pleasure in us—only fault."

"Then why are you so distraught when he leaves?" Faith wrinkled her brow.

Hope glanced at Faith, a wounded look in her blue eyes. "Because I keep hoping that someday he'll grow to approve of me and maybe. . .maybe even love me."

Faith's heart shriveled. "Father will always be Father. But we will always have each other, and we have just as much love to give you as any father or mother."

"Even more," Grace added, and Hope's sobs slowly softened.

Faith's gaze landed on the captain. She had forgotten he was still standing there. His annoyed gaze wavered over them and then shifted to the door as though he wanted to make a dash for it and never return. What a handsome vision he presented, even in his flustered state—tall, broad shouldered, commanding in his blue navy coat. A bit of stubble peppered his strong jaw as if he had been too hurried that morning to shave.

"If you ladies would be so kind as to take a seat," he finally said then turned toward Edwin, who stood staring out the window, no doubt bored by what he often called the Westcott sisters' theatrical display. "Edwin, the papers, if you please." Mr. Waite held out his hand.

Faith eased onto the sofa where Grace had taken a seat. Hope slid next to her and squeezed her hand.

"So am I to assume, Mr. Waite, that you intend to become our guardian—despite your earlier protest?" Faith shot him a challenging look.

His sharp eyes locked upon hers. "It seems for the time being that I have been given no choice in the matter. However, allow me to assure you ladies"—he directed a stern gaze at each of them in turn—"you will no doubt find my methods of command no less strict than you are accustomed to."

Faith found her admiration for the man rising. Regardless of the difficult position imposed upon him by their father, Mr. Waite had no intention of shrugging off the responsibility as some men would have. Yet despite her regard for his integrity, it did naught to aid her plan to be rid of him. In fact, quite the opposite, especially if he intended to rule the house with an iron hand. For with their father gone so often, she and her sisters were not accustomed to discipline. And now was certainly not the time to start.

"Mr. Waite, surely you understand this is not your ship and we are not your crew. Are we to be flogged and made to scrub the deck whenever we misbehave?"

Hope giggled.

"If you do not misbehave, Miss Westcott," Mr. Waite said, perching on the edge of the admiral's desk and taking the papers from Edwin, "you will not have to find that out. Now." He shifted through the documents in his hand. "Your steward and I have gone over the admiral's wishes, and we are in complete agreement on every rule."

Edwin moved beside Mr. Waite, arms crossed over his chest, a superior look on his puffy face. But Faith knew how to handle him. It was this new intruder, this resolute captain, who gave her pause.

"Miss Hope," he began. "I will address you first since your father left specific instructions for you."

"He did?" Hope's eyes lit up. She scooted to the edge of her seat.

"It is your father's express order that you have no dealings with a"—the captain peered at the paper—"Lord Arthur Falkland."

Hope shot to her feet. "Impossible! I will not suffer it. Arthur—Lord Falkland—is my beau. We are courting."

"He is also a scoundrel, dear Hope. Everyone in

town knows it." Grace twisted the button at the top of her throat.

"Nevertheless. . . ," Mr. Waite sighed, rising to his feet. "It is your father's desire that you not see him nor a Miss Anne Cormac." He broadened his stance as Faith imagined him doing when commanding his men aboard his ship. But to his obvious chagrin, it did not have the intended effect on Hope, for she began to sob, fisting her hands at her sides.

"Anne is a friend of mine, and if my father cared enough to stay home, he would know Lord Falkland to be a gentleman." She fell sideways on the sofa, and Faith threw an arm around her and glared at Mr. Waite.

The captain tugged his collar. "You may address this issue with the admiral when he returns. In the meantime, you will abide by his wishes or answer to me." He pressed that rebellious strand of hair behind his ear, and Faith suspected he wished he could restrain the three of them as easily. But she had to admit she rather enjoyed the pink hue rising up his face, the twitch of his lips, and the beads of sweat forming on his forehead. His eyes met hers, and he raised a brow as if he saw through her charade.

He flipped the papers in his hand. "Under no circumstances are any of you to travel this city unescorted. Lucas, Mr. Huxley, or myself, when I am not at sea, must be with you at all times whenever you leave this house."

" 'Tis impossible." Grace shook her head defiantly, drawing the captain's shocked gaze.

Grace sat up straight and folded her hands in her lap. "My charity work takes me all over the city. Surely you know that when the good Lord calls us on a mission, we must go immediately. I cannot always wait for an escort."

"What happened to honoring our father?" Hope snickered.

Grace raised her pert nose in the air. "God's work comes first."

Mr. Waite sent Grace an indulgent, if somewhat

stiff, smile. "I appreciate the divine nature of your work, Miss Grace, and I am sure Edwin or Lucas will happily accompany you whenever possible, but these are the standing orders, and they will be obeyed."

Shifting her gaze away, Grace sank back into the sofa.

"Or what, Mr. Waite—will you lock us in the hold of your ship?" Faith teased.

"If I have to, Miss Westcott." His lips curved in a sardonic grin. "And I would not test me on that if I were you."

～

The thumping of regimental drums began pounding in Dajon's head, cautioning him to conclude his business and be gone—back to the sanity of his ship. He flipped through the papers, determined to spout off the remaining rules without further interruption.

"All monies will be under my control," Dajon continued in a hurried tone. "Aside from necessities, which will be provided, please come to me or Mr. Huxley for anything you need."

"I daresay, Mr. Waite." Faith's lips twisted in a mocking grin. "We are big girls and can handle our own money."

"I care not for what you perceive you can and cannot do, Miss Westcott. It is only what you will do that concerns me." He threw back his shoulders and gave them all his sternest look.

Faith widened her eyes. "Do you never break a rule, Mr. Waite?" The pert look on her face was at once alluring and infuriating, and he nearly choked at the tantalizing hold it had upon him.

"Not if I can help it, Miss Westcott."

Intelligence shone behind her sparkling auburn eyes. Was she testing him? He marched to the fireplace and faced them with his most intimidating stare. Surely if he could command a ship full of men, he could control these three women.

Ignoring him, Hope turned toward her sister. "What about that new gown Father promised to buy me?"

"You have no need of another gown, Hope." Grace shook her head. "You should give the ones you have to the poor."

Hope gave her sister a scowl.

Dajon cleared his throat and raised his voice. "These are the rules. When I am not present, Mr. Huxley is in charge. Is that understood?"

Edwin pointed a jagged finger at the girls. "Mark my words. Your father will hear of every infraction."

Hope tossed her nose in the air. "I will not give my gowns to the poor and go about town wearing rags like you do, Grace." She stomped her foot.

Scooting to the edge of her seat, Faith took her sister's hand in hers. "Come now, Hope; of course you will not be forced to sell your dresses. Ladies, let us not forget we have a guest."

Hope eyed Dajon. "He is not a guest anymore. He is our new father—or might as well be. He is just like him."

Dajon dropped his gaze and rubbed the sweat from his forehead. He felt like a zoologist charged with taming a flock of screeching, fluttering jungle fowl.

A bird squawked somewhere upstairs, confirming his assessment.

When a knock sounded at the front door, he prayed it was the admiral returning home, having discovered his orders were in error.

"Pardon me." Edwin gave Dajon a look of pity and left the room as the girls continued arguing.

"Sir Wilhelm Carteret to see Miss Westcott," Edwin announced when he returned.

The white-wigged, sickly man slithered into the room with one hand on his hip, the other hanging in midair, and leered at Faith like a sly serpent.

A pained expression crossed her features as she rose slowly to her feet. "Sir Wilhelm, this is unexpected."

His eyes narrowed. "I heard your father left suddenly and thought you might need company, but I see

Mr. Waite has beat me to it." He pursed his lips in a semblance of a grin and bowed toward Dajon.

"Sir Wilhelm." Dajon set the papers down on the desk, feeling as if he had been snatched from the lion's den. "You are most fortunate in your timing. My business here is finished."

Hope sprang from the couch and rubbed her temples. "Forgive me, but I feel a headache coming on." She nodded to Dajon and Sir Wilhelm and hurriedly made her way to the door like a rabbit under a hawk's gaze.

"I shall help you to your chamber, sister." Grace followed quickly on her heels, leaving a befuddled Faith in her wake.

Throwing back her shoulders, she faced Sir Wilhelm. "Mr. Waite has offered to take me for a stroll." She turned to face Dajon. "Have you not, Mr. Waite?"

Dajon could not mistake the pleading look in her eyes, nor the disgust he'd seen souring within them the moment Sir Wilhelm had entered the room. Did she hate this man so much that she preferred Dajon's company? He shifted his gaze between her urging glance and the rancor burning in Sir Wilhelm's eyes. By thunder, the last thing he needed was to prance about with this red-haired beauty on his arm. Yet the other two girls seemed to hold her in some esteem. Perhaps he could recruit her assistance in keeping order at home. Before he realized what he was doing, he agreed with a placating nod.

"Perhaps we can visit some other time, Sir Wilhelm?" Faith's sweet smile dripped with venom. "But do inform us ahead of time when we can expect your visit." She turned to Edwin. "Please take Mr. Waite's things to the guesthouse."

With a flutter of lashes and a smile that would melt any man's heart, Faith thrust an arm through Dajon's and pulled him into the entrance hall and out the door, leaving a rather disgruntled Sir Wilhelm behind.

CHAPTER 7

Faith shielded her eyes from the sun as she clung to the wobbling jolly boat. Up ahead, the dark hull of the HMS *Enforcer* swelled like a leviathan rising from the sea. Two bare masts towered over her as they thrust into the blue sky, contradicting her belief that sloops were purely single-masted vessels. Truth be told, this ship appeared more the size of a small frigate than a sloop. As they neared the hull, nine gunports gaped at her like charred eye sockets from its side. That would put the ship's guns numbering at least eighteen—provided there weren't any more on deck—eighteen to the *Red Siren*'s sixteen. Still, not terrible odds if their paths should cross at sea.

Faith's gaze drifted to Mr. Waite, seated stiffly at the head of the boat. He smiled then returned his stern face to his crew as they rowed in unison over the choppy waves of Charles Towne Harbor. How she had managed to convince him to give her a tour of his ship, she could not fathom, but she hadn't been able to resist asking him, even if it meant she would have to spend more time with the man she had vowed to avoid. She could not deny that he had come in handy today as a diversion to Sir Wilhelm's slobbering attentions. And she could not expect to completely elude a man living at her home. Besides, since he clearly did not recognize her—or he would have had her arrested already—perhaps she could use Mr. Waite after all.

Nevertheless, excitement coursed through her at the chance to inspect one of His Majesty's Royal Navy ships. It certainly couldn't hurt to learn as much as she could about the ships that pursued her—something her father had never given her a chance to do. *"A navy ship is no place for a lady,"* she could still hear him say.

"Oars up!" one of the men shouted. The eight-man crew hefted their oars straight above their heads as the boat thudded and splashed against the ship's hull.

Faith glanced up at the planks of damp wood that rose above her like the impenetrable walls of an enemy fortress—impenetrable to obvious foes, not clandestine foes like her. For like a tiny white ant, she intended to bore her way through the ship, seek out its weaknesses, and devour it from within.

"Captain's coming aboard!" someone yelled from above.

After the men secured the jolly boat with ropes, a bosun's chair was lowered over the side.

Faith rolled her eyes. She had hoped to avoid this demeaning way men had devised to hoist women aboard ships—as if they were cargo. She could climb the rope ladder as well as any man.

But she couldn't tell that to the captain.

Mr. Waite rose and extended a hand to Faith. "I'm afraid this is the only way we have to bring you safely aboard, Miss Westcott."

"I am sure I will manage." She smiled as she settled into the swaying chair and grabbed the ropes on each side.

Mr. Waite gave the signal to hoist her aboard, and the baritone command "Heave, heave!" poured over the bulwarks as the ropes snapped tight and her chair rose.

"Side by side, lively now, men," another man yelled from above as the captain sprang up the rope ladder with the ease of a man who spent more time aboard a ship than on land.

As Faith rounded the top railing, dozens of eyes shot her way, but the crowd of sailors quickly resumed their forward stares. A line of men near the railing raised whistles and blew out a sharp trill as drums pounded behind her.

the Red SIREN

Mr. Waite grabbed the rail and jumped on board. "Atteeeention!" Every sailor removed his hat, and the captain responded by touching the tip of his.

"Welcome aboard, Captain." A young, uniformed officer with a thin mustache stepped forward just as Faith's shoes tapped the deck. Two seamen assisted her off the wobbling chair.

"Thank you, Mr. Borland," Mr. Waite replied as the rest of the crew dispersed to their duties.

Faith stood amazed at the formality and organization of the sailors, even at port.

"Miss Faith Westcott." Mr. Waite gestured toward her. "May I present Mr. Reginald Borland, my first lieutenant, as well as a good friend."

"At your service, miss." The young man bowed and allowed his narrow brown eyes to drift over her. Then, slapping his bicorn atop his sandy hair, he straightened his blue navy coat. A line of gold buttons ran down the center of each pristine white lapel, winking at Faith in the sunlight.

"Miss Westcott is my temporary ward," Mr. Waite explained, "and has requested a brief tour of the ship. Since we have no current orders to sail, I thought to oblige her."

"Very well, Captain." Lieutenant Borland offered a sly wink toward his captain before turning to leave.

Ignoring him, the captain extended his elbow toward Faith and led her down a set of stairs into the bowels of the ship. Men hustled to and fro but quickly snapped to attention when their captain passed. Dozens of gazes pierced Faith from all directions—even from deep within the shadows. Mr. Waite placed his warm hand over hers as they continued. The protective sentiment sent a spark through Faith that she immediately dismissed.

She had no need of a man to protect her.

"I am at a loss as to how to address you, sir," she said as they turned and proceeded down the aft companionway. "Are you not simply a lieutenant?"

Mr. Waite stiffened beside her and stretched out his

neck as if pulling a cord tight. "Indeed, I am."

Pleased that she had flustered him, Faith grinned, knowing her expression was concealed by the shadows. "Yet my father calls you a commander, and your men refer to you as 'Captain.'"

"There is no formal rank between lieutenant and captain, miss. But because I am the commander of this ship, my men must call me Captain. You may address me as either Mr. Waite or Captain, if you wish."

Oh, how kind of you. Faith shook her head at the man's impudence as she examined the narrow hallway. Lantern light cast monstrous shadows across the low deckhead. With each flicker of the wick or rock of the ship, they altered shape and crouched, ready to pounce upon them—upon her. Not that she hadn't seen a dark companionway on a ship before, but on this ship full of enemies, the shadows seemed more threatening—as if they knew what mischief she was about.

The captain showed her the master's cabin, clerk's cabin, and two storerooms before he approached a large oak door at the end of the hall.

"Allow me to show you the captain's cabin, Miss Westcott, and then I shall give you a tour around the top deck before I escort you home."

Faith blinked. "What of the rest of your ship, Mr. Waite? Surely I have not seen it all."

"'Tis a big ship, miss," he said, reaching for the door handle. "Many areas are not fit for a lady to enter."

Faith let out a huff before she realized it and covered her mouth, pretending to cough. "I beg you to change your mind, Mr. Waite." She eased beside him, a bit closer than propriety allowed. "What have I to fear with you by my side?" She tried to flutter her lashes, but they felt like maniacal butterflies upon her cheeks.

"Have you something in your eyes, Miss Westcott?" The captain leaned toward her, a curious look wrinkling his forehead.

Faith lowered her shoulders and scowled. "Nay, but I beg you. I had my heart set upon seeing the entire ship, and now I find you were naught but teasing me."

She scrunched her lips into a pout as she had seen Hope do so often, but instead of swooning at her feet, instead of apologizing for being so obstinate, instead of offering her everything she wanted, the captain simply laughed and turned away. "Nay, my apologies, miss, but I fear your sensibilities are far too fragile."

My sensibilities? Good heavens. Faith's head began to pound. "My curiosity demands it, sir!" She hadn't meant to shout, but she had to do something to get this buffoon to show her his ship.

Releasing the door latch, Mr. Waite studied her curiously, his eyes narrowing as if he were plotting some battle strategy and she were but a chart laid out before him. "Very well, we would not want you to think me a tease, Miss Westcott, now, would we?" And though his tone was all politeness, the look he gave her was one of a cat about to devour a mouse.

The stench of mold, sweat, and urine assaulted her as he led her down a ladder, past the wardroom then down another ladder into the bowels of the ship. Flinging a hand to her nose, she coughed and took a step back.

Not that she wasn't accustomed to such smells aboard a ship, but this ship housed a lot more men than her small brigantine. And her crew didn't live aboard her ship for more than a day, whereas the men on an HMS warship were oft at sea for months. The captain lifted his lantern to reveal stacks of crates and barrels crowding them on all sides. The patter of tiny feet joined the creak of the wood.

"The hold, miss." He shifted his playful gaze her way. "And as we discussed, 'tis where I throw wards who misbehave." His lips curved slightly, and Faith longed to slap them back into a straight line.

"Watch your step, miss," Mr. Waite warned as a furry beast skittered across Faith's shoe.

She hated rats. Abhorred them, actually, and longed to kick the smelly rodent into the corner, but for Mr. Waite's sake, she let out a tiny yelp and flung her hand to her chest.

When she glanced up at the captain, a smirk sat upon his handsome lips.

He was doing this on purpose. He wanted her to faint dead away from the smells and the rats so he could prove he had been correct in his assessment of the softer gender. *The insolent, unchivalrous knave.*

"Had enough, Miss Westcott?" He gave her a smug look.

A storm began to brew within Faith.

"Why no, Mr. Waite. I have only just begun."

But she soon found she had misjudged her resilience, for the captain seemed intent on showing her the most atrocious parts of the ship: empty stalls that not long ago had housed animals from the crossing from England and still retained a stench that would knock a hardened farmer on his back; the bloodstained operating table and floors of the sick bay that seemed to hold the eerie screams of the dying; and the galley, complete with a bubbling pot of slimy gray stew that reeked worse than the animal stalls. Faith caught a glimpse of weevils digging tunnels through the biscuits laid out for the day, and she held a hand over her mouth and gulped down a clump of bile, ignoring Mr. Waite's smirk. Perhaps she wasn't the tough pirate she claimed to be. For in all her plundering, she had not seen much blood, nor had she been forced to house animals or even hire a cook for her crew. Since she couldn't be away from home for longer than a night, she chose her victims well. Never British vessels. Always small merchantmen, undermanned and undergunned. And not one of them had given her much resistance.

Mr. Waite held out his arm. "Perhaps you need some fresh air?"

As much as Faith would love to go above, she had yet to see the gun deck. But how to express an interest in such weapons without drawing suspicion? She nodded, knowing the cannons were housed on the level above them. "Perhaps we could begin our ascent."

As they made their way to the stairs, they passed a

large room that spanned into darkness in both directions. Hammocks swung from the rafters like a school of fish swimming above tables that crowded a floor filthy with scraps of food and spilled grog. Snores and curses could be heard filtering through the room and bouncing off the moist hull.

"The *Enforcer* houses one hundred and twenty men," Mr. Waite announced proudly as he led her up the ladder.

And Faith believed at that moment she could smell every single one of their unwashed bodies. At least her crew kept themselves somewhat clean—albeit per her orders.

Clutching her skirts, Faith made her way up the creaking narrow stairs and glanced around the ship in awe. Though similar to her sleek brigantine in some ways, this sailing vessel was larger by comparison, and despite the squalor, everything in it, including crew and captain, operated together like a precise machine. But then again, Faith was no Royal Navy captain, nor did she ever intend to run her ship as if she were. Besides, the *Red Siren* could outrun this clumsy old bucket any day. She had nothing to fear.

Beads of perspiration slid beneath her bodice as they approached the gun deck, and she wondered how the crewmen endured this stifling heat below deck day after day. Turning, the captain gestured with his lantern toward another set of stairs. "Just one more flight, miss, and you shall find relief."

Faith offered him a sweet smile. "May I see the cannons first?"

"We call them guns when they are on a ship." He examined her, searching her eyes through the shadows. "I must admit, you are a far more resilient woman than I first surmised, Miss Westcott. Most ladies would have no interest in such deadly weapons."

She wanted to tell him she was not like most women. She wanted to tell him she had an obsession with cannons, with the round iron shot, the ear-deafening blast, the invigorating sting of gunpowder in the air. "I have an interest in many things, Mr. Waite."

"So be it." He nodded for her to precede him.

Faith scanned the gun deck, lined on both sides with nine massive cannons resting in their trucks, their muzzles pointed toward closed ports—twelve-pounders, by the looks of them. Stale smoke lingered in the air. She slid her hand over the cold iron as if it were a dear friend and glanced over her shoulder at the captain. "I never pictured them so large. They must be quite deadly."

"Yes, they can be." Mr. Waite scratched his chin and cocked his head curiously. "As you can see, we have eighteen here and two more on deck."

Twenty guns altogether. Faith made a mental note. "It warms a lady's heart to know she has a brave, strong captain like you protecting her home from pirates." The silly words sounded even more ludicrous lingering in the air between them, and Faith further embarrassed herself with yet another attempt to flutter her lashes.

Mr. Waite stared at her, confusion twisting his features.

She cleared her throat. "Have you killed many of the villains?"

"None as of yet. But rather than kill them, it is my hope to bring them to justice."

"Perhaps they would prefer to die at sea rather than hang by a noose." The words spat out of her mouth with scorn before she could stop them, but the captain didn't flinch. Only the slight narrowing of his handsome blue eyes revealed any reaction at all.

"Am I to presume you hold some fondness for these thieves?" He crossed his arms over his chest.

"Good heavens! Why, of course not." Faith sashayed to his side. She must be more careful. This man was not one to be easily duped. Faith brushed her hand over his arm and felt his body tense. "It must be dreadfully loud in here when you are at battle."

The heat between them rose like steam on a sultry day. The captain's gaze dropped to her lips and remained there for what seemed minutes before he cleared his throat and took a step back. "Yes, I fear you would find it intolerable."

Faith gave him a coy grin. *Intolerable? I can load and shoot one of these guns faster than most of your men can.*

The slight upturn of Mr. Waite's lips reached his imperious eyes in a glimmer. "You do not agree. I can see it in your eyes." His gaze flickered over Faith. Her body warmed under his intense perusal. She plucked out her fan and looked away.

Dash it all, the man sees right through me. "I do not often agree with the opinions of others, Mr. Waite. I prefer to hear the blast myself before I make such a determination."

"Indeed? Well, perhaps I shall fire one for you someday."

Or *at* her, most likely. She smiled.

He offered her his arm. "Shall we? I need to retrieve some papers from my cabin before I escort you home."

The captain's cabin reflected its master in every detail, from the methodical arrangement of the furniture to the disciplined stacks of papers atop his oak desk. Rows of alphabetically ordered books lined the shelves built into the paneled walls. Faith ran a hand along the bindings and glanced at the titles: *Campaigns during the War of Spanish Succession 1704-1711, Handbook for Seaman Gunners, Misconduct and the Line of Duty, Naval Ordinances, Regulations of the British Royal Navy. . .* Below them, all manner of religious books lay reverently side by side: the Holy Bible, its leather edges worn; John Hervey's *Meditations and Contemplations*; Milton's *Paradise Lost*. Faith scowled. Mr. Waite appeared to be as dedicated to his God as he was to his navy.

To the left of the shelves, an open wardrobe revealed pressed and pristine uniforms hanging in a row next to a dark blue frock with gold embroidered trim around the collar. Two pairs of polished boots stood at attention beneath them.

The captain sifted through papers on his desk before

glancing at her. "Forgive me, Miss Westcott, I shall be with you in a moment. Please have a seat."

She ambled over to the other side of the cabin where several plaques, framed documents, and ribbons dotted the wall: a medal for "conspicuous gallantry and intrepidity at the risk of life and beyond the call of duty"; a meritorious commendation medal; combat action ribbons; a plaque signifying Captain Dajon Waite as a naval expert in the use of pistols, swords, and cannons. Faith stole a glance at him. Surely this was a man to reckon with upon the seas.

Not at all like the young sailor she'd encountered on the English Channel five years past. As soon as her men had surrounded him, he'd given up without a fight. Then she'd ordered Lucas to round up his crew and set them adrift in one of their own jolly boats while her crew transferred all their belongings and weapons to his bigger and better-equipped ship.

Mr. Waite's gaze met hers, and he gestured toward a chair. "So what is your opinion of my ship, Miss Westcott?"

"Your ship, Mr. Waite?" Faith flashed a grin. "I thought it belonged to England." She eased into the wooden seat. "Truth be told, I imagine her far too bulky to catch pirates."

"Indeed." He let out a deep chuckle that caused a warm flutter in Faith's belly. "Fine lined and well armed—a beauty upon the water. I assure you, she will encounter no difficulty in her task."

"You speak of her as you would a lover."

A red hue crept up the captain's face, and he returned to his papers.

"I suppose time will tell." Faith enjoyed her ability to embarrass him so easily. "But I thank you for the tour." As she gazed at the strong, commanding man before her, she almost welcomed the challenge of meeting him upon the sea—almost—for what did her experience compare with his? Ah, but what a grand opportunity to test her skill and her crew's against the finest of His Majesty's

Navy. One more glance at the taunting display of medals adorning the wall and she shook her head, wondering at her sanity.

A rap on the door brought her to her senses, and the captain's deep "Enter!" filled the room.

The first lieutenant, Borland, marched inside. He glanced at Faith then faced Mr. Waite. "Pardon me, Captain, but I have a dispatch for you."

The captain extended his hand and snatched the paper, broke the wax seal, and scanned the contents before meeting his first lieutenant's hard gaze.

"May I inquire—" Borland cut off his words and cast a look of concern toward Faith.

Following his first lieutenant's gaze, the captain shrugged, dismissing Faith's presence as having no bearing in the secrecy of the matter.

"A Dutch merchant ship," Mr. Waite announced, "laden with pearls, arriving tomorrow afternoon. We are to rendezvous with her off Hilton Head Island just after noon and provide safe escort from there to our harbor."

Faith's heart thumped wildly as she glanced between the two men.

"'Tis good news, Captain," Borland said. "At least we shall finally set sail again."

Good news, indeed. Faith's gaze shot out the door. She must get home quickly and make plans.

The captain nodded. "Inform the men, if you please."

Borland started to leave then swung back around. "The pirate ship we have been seeking was spotted last night by a local fisherman."

Faith gulped.

"Very good." Mr. Waite nodded. "Then she has not abandoned these waters." He folded the paper neatly and tucked it in his pocket.

"Pray tell, what ship is that?" Faith hoped the tremor in her hands did not reach her voice.

Mr. Borland took her in with a look far too admiring for Faith's comfort. "A troublesome knave who has been plundering these waters for the past few months." He chuckled. "Some say 'tis a woman pirate."

"A woman pirate? Absurd." Faith rose to her feet. "These merchants who spotted her—him—no doubt had consumed too much rum. How can a woman be a pirate?"

The captain circled his desk and leaned back on the edge. "I assure you, they can." His brow darkened. "And it is my first priority to catch this blackguard, man or woman—this one they call the Red Siren."

CHAPTER 8

Dajon eyed the red-haired beauty walking beside him, her delicate fingers tucked into the crook of his elbow as he led her up to the main deck. A solemn mood had settled upon her after the discussion of pirates and treasure ships. No doubt the thought of battles and death upset her—or did it? Dajon perceived a strength beneath the swish of lace and the flutter of dark lashes she so frequently offered him. He could not shake the feeling she was hiding something.

Shame struck him. Although she had urged him to show her the entire ship, he should not have shown her the most repugnant sections aboard. He supposed he had been trying to humble her, but in reality his own pride had reared its ugly head, for he rather enjoyed watching her brazen demeanor slowly dwindle. Silently he repented, for she had obviously suffered under the sights and smells below, but surprisingly, no more than any man unaccustomed to them. In fact, she had moved through the ship with ease, not once losing her footing or cowering in the dark shadows. And her interest in the guns. By thunder, what a fascinating woman.

"Mr. James, prepare the jolly boat," he ordered one of the men standing by the capstan, sending the sailor into action as he shouted orders to the men around him.

As they waited, Faith gripped the railing and closed her eyes. Dajon watched the evening breeze slide its cool fingers through the loose curls adorning her neck, playing with each silky strand, and he found his own fingers aching to do the same. An overwhelming urge to kiss her forced him to tear his gaze away. What was he thinking? His orders were to protect this woman—protect her from letches like himself—a task made all the more difficult when she insisted upon flirting with him all day. Or had she? Perhaps it was simply his own wishful desires.

Oh Lord, give me strength, strength to resist such a tempting morsel laid before me, strength to stay upon the course I have vowed to pursue.

He dared another glance her way. The setting sun transformed her skin into shimmering gold, and Dajon swallowed. Surely this exquisite creature would not be interested in him. More likely, she sought the most convenient alternative to that lecherous Sir Wilhelm Carteret. Dajon flexed his jaw. He would not be so easily taken in by her feminine wiles. Forcing his gaze from her, he watched the sun fling lustrous streams of crimson, orange, and gold into the darkening sky as it sank behind a flowing sea of trees.

Faith smiled and flashed her auburn eyes his way. "Beautiful, is it not? God's creation—untamed and untainted by man."

"Am I mistaken then?" Dajon recalled the animosity toward God she had so blatantly expressed the night before. "You do believe in an almighty Creator?"

"I believe in Him, Captain. I simply do not believe He gives much thought to us, at least not as the Bible implies He does." Faith tossed her chin in the air.

Her declaration stirred both sadness and curiosity within him. "I am sorry."

"Do not be." She raised one brow. "I am not. 'Tis freeing, actually."

"Might I ask what made you give up on God so easily?" He leaned on the railing beside her.

"Easily?" She waved her hand in the air. "You would not understand. You have no doubt led a charmed life."

"Nay, I would not say so." Dajon glanced over the railing and saw the sailors climbing aboard the rocking jolly boat and loosening the ropes. Hardly easy. His life had been riddled with strife and heartache.

Mr. James approached and tapped the brim of his bicorn. "Ready, Captain."

"Very well." Over Mr. James's shoulder, Dajon saw Borland staring at them in a most peculiar way. The first lieutenant dropped his gaze and disappeared below hatches before Dajon could acknowledge him.

"Shall we?" He extended his arm toward Miss Westcott but found she had retreated toward the foremast, allowing two sailors carrying a barrel to pass by. A gust of wind struck the ship, flapping the slack sails and tousling the red curls of her loose bun. She offered Dajon a sultry smile that sent a spark through him. And something else—a memory triggered deep within him. He paused, trying to grab hold of it, but whatever it was evaded him. Perhaps it was her exquisite crimson hair—a rarity among women. He'd seen only a few ladies who had been graced with such an audacious color.

By the time they had rowed ashore and entered Charles Towne through one of the three gates breaching the massive rampart that circled the city, darkness had begun to descend. "My apologies, Miss Westcott, for keeping you out so late."

"I do thank you for showing me your boat, Mr. Waite," Faith replied as she took the lead, weaving around piles of horse manure that littered the dirt of Bay Street.

"Ship, if you please." Dajon rushed to catch up with her and offered her his arm.

Faith smiled but did not take it. "Of course. But there is no need to see me home. You must have preparations to attend to on board. I am quite safe within these walls."

"Aye, I do have a bit of work to do on my ship, but afterward, I'll be staying in the guesthouse per your father's request." Dajon glanced at the stone enclosure that blocked their view of the bay. "To find such a fortified city in the colonies, complete with moat and drawbridge, is quite astonishing." He fingered the hilt of his sword as they passed one of the port's taverns. "But with Spain's recent attacks and the Tuscarora

Indian war, 'tis no wonder the settlers thought it worth the added protection. Not to alarm you, Miss Westcott." He grabbed her arm, forcing her to slow her pace. "But the wall is not impenetrable, and there are dangers lurking within the city as well."

"I realize, Mr. Waite, that you and my father have an arrangement, but any fool can see that it was forced upon you against your will. My father has a way of doing that to people." Faith halted and placed one hand on her gently rounded hip. "Believe me, there is no need for your constant watch. I have been caring for myself and my sisters since my mother died, and I will continue to do so."

His blood began to heat under her ungrateful and dismissive attitude. "You seemed to have need of me when Sir Wilhelm came calling." He gave her a sideways glance. "And when you begged so ardently to see my ship."

She stared at him with the look a spider might bestow upon a fly caught in her web. Finally, she let out a sigh. "My apologies. You have been most gracious." She offered him a smile that seemed to strain the muscles of her face.

However befuddled by the woman's teetering moods, Dajon felt he could not leave her without an escort. "It is unsafe for a woman to traipse through town alone." He cast a wary gaze around them. "Especially this one. And regarding your sisters—surely you do not expect to protect them against everything, Miss Westcott. There are some things best left in the hands of men, due simply to their physical strength and ability."

Her creamy face reddened, darkening the cluster of freckles on her nose. "No doubt another one of your grand opinions? Well, I, for one, have found that conjecture to be naught but a lie perpetrated by men to keep women in submission." Turning, she stomped forward as if she were trying to lose him and turned onto Queen Street. Music from a harpsichord chimed from a tavern to their left.

"Indeed?" Keeping pace with her, Dajon shook his

head, baffled by her insolence, her independence, but most of all, her foolishness. No wonder the admiral worried for his daughters. This one in particular seemed to go out of her way to find danger. He chuckled.

Faith huffed and flashed a dark gaze his way. "I amuse you, Mr. Waite?"

"Amuse and confuse, miss, for not an hour ago, you played the temptress below hatches on board my ship, and now you play the shrew."

"Of all the. . .I did no such thing." Clutching her skirts, she picked up her pace and stumbled over a ladder. The boy perched on top ceased nailing a sign over a doorpost and clung to the wooden tips of the ladder for dear life.

Dajon settled the tottering steps and gave the wide-eyed boy an apologetic shrug before turning to find the wayward redhead. A mob of workers had spilled onto the street from a two-story brick warehouse and joined a surging crowd of sailors and merchants who were headed toward the nearest tavern. Horses clopped by in every direction, weaving around the throng and spewing clumps of mud into the air from their hooves.

Faith was nowhere in sight.

Dread gripped Dajon. His first day as guardian and he had lost one of the admiral's daughters—at night, in one of the worst sections of town. The crowd became a muted blur in the encroaching shadows as Dajon searched for a flash of red hair. Barreling through the throng, he bumped into a well-dressed man in a fine ruffled cambric shirt, swinging a cane. A curled gray periwig perched atop his head.

"I beg your pardon," Dajon said.

The man clicked his tongue in disgust as Dajon dashed across the street before an oncoming coach. The horse reared, neighing in protest. Dajon jumped aside before the beast's hooves could pummel him. They landed with two thuds in a puddle, spraying mud through the air.

"Watch out, you bumpkin!" the driver yelled.

Dajon glanced down at the thick mud sliding down

his white breeches then scanned the street once more. No sign of Miss Westcott.

His chest tightened.

Feminine laughter bounced into the night—familiar laughter. He rushed forward, parting the crowd. A tall man with a portly woman on his arm ambled unaware in front of him. The woman blubbered in laughter at something the man had said, and Dajon darted to the left to bypass them.

Up ahead, light from a crowded saloon spilled onto the street. Three men surrounded Faith.

Sweat broke out on Dajon's forehead. His mouth dried. He bolted forward when another couple stepped in front of him, blocking his way.

Over their shoulders, Dajon saw Faith say something to a burly man then nod in Dajon's direction. Two other men stood on each side of her, smirks on their grimy faces. Passersby quickly looked the other way and crossed the street. Why didn't anyone come to her rescue? Angling toward the right, Dajon sped past the couple and shoved his way through a mob of sailors, ignoring the curses they flung at his back.

Faith grinned before turning and strutting away.

Dashing past an oncoming carriage, Dajon rushed to catch up to her, but the three men who'd been harassing her formed a barricade of human flesh in his path.

The burly man lowered his thick brows and scowled. "The lady don't be wantin' ye followin' her, sailor."

One of the other men took a brazen step toward Dajon. "You navy boys think to be gettin' all the women." Though gangly, the man's frame rose far above Dajon's as he peered down his hawklike nose. Greasy strands of hair stuck to his forehead like tentacles. The stench of sweat and stale fish burned Dajon's nose.

The third man spit onto the ground, cast a glance at the retreating Faith, and returned a surly grin to Dajon.

A bawdy tune blasted over them from the tavern as some of its patrons crept out to watch the altercation. A few men stopped in the street and whispered among themselves. Dajon wondered whether he could count on their assistance or if they were merely assembling for the show.

"Three against one." The first man chortled. "Fair odds, says I."

"Let me pass at once," Dajon ordered the men. In the distance, Faith suddenly halted and swung about, but he could not see her expression in the shadows. Blasted woman. Had she instructed these men to delay him? Surely not. She could not be associated with these ruffians.

The burly man laughed. "Why don't ye go back to yer boat and leave the lady alone."

Dajon drew his sword and leveled the tip beneath the man's hairy chin. "Why don't you step aside and allow me to pass."

The man did not flinch. Not a flicker of fear crossed his steady gaze.

From the corner of his eye, Dajon saw Faith retracing her steps until she stood behind the men, hands on her hips. He wanted to warn her to stay back, but the men appeared to have no interest in her now.

Her eyes shifted to Dajon's. No fear, only annoyance burned within them. "I will have you know, gentlemen," she began in an insolent tone, "that this is the captain of the HMS *Enforcer*, and he is an expert in swordsmanship."

Dajon grimaced and lowered his blade. *What is she saying?* He did not relish a fight. These scoundrels would only take her words as a challenge, especially in front of the crowd forming around them. His palms grew sweaty as he tightened his grip on his sword.

The burly man let out a coarse laugh and slapped his thigh. The other man narrowed his flaming eyes upon Dajon and wiped the spit seeping from the side of his mouth. He eased one hand to his chest. "How are ye with pistols?"

≈

Faith shifted her gaze between her crew and the captain. She'd meant only for them to delay Mr. Waite, not kill him. After she had instructed them to gather the rest of the men at the ship in the morning, her foremost thought was to hurry home, inform Lucas, and get some much-needed sleep, not stroll through town on the arm of the man who would put a noose around her neck if he knew who she was. Besides, the man gave her an unsettled feeling in her stomach, and she didn't like it—not one bit. The less time spent in his company, the better. But she should have realized her men could not resist taunting a commander in His Majesty's Navy.

The captain's eyes drifted to hers again, and in a flash, Bishop plucked a gun from inside his vest and pointed it at Mr. Waite before he could react. But the captain only glared at him—a confident, icy glare that sent a shiver down Faith's back. Her fear for Mr. Waite's safety suddenly shifted to a fear for her crew's.

In one swift motion, Mr. Waite yanked his pistol from its brace and pounded the handle on Bishop's gun, knocking it the ground, then he whipped his pistol around by the trigger and pointed it straight at the man's heart.

"I can handle a pistol as well," he said with an insolent smirk, cocking the weapon.

A cheer rose from the crowd as the three men stood with their jaws agape.

Mr. Waite wiped the sweat from his brow. "Now, if you please, I will be on my way."

Unwilling admiration surged within Faith as she watched the captain dispatch her hardened crew so quickly and with such skill. Without so much as a glance her way, he sheathed his sword, brushed by her men, who backed away from him, and took her arm. He tugged her through the crowd, his pistol still firmly gripped in his hand. When they were well away from the center of town, he housed it again then whirled her around to face him, seizing her shoulders.

"Of all the preposterous, dangerous things to do— wandering around the port at night without an escort." His gaze skimmed over her. "Are you hurt? No, of course you're not hurt." He snorted and released her. "Did you know those men?"

"Nay." She gazed up at him, barely able to discern his features in the darkness. A cloud moved aside, allowing moonlight to flood over him. Somehow the mixture of silvery light and sinister shadows made him appear far more dangerous than he did in full sunlight. Or maybe it was because she'd just witnessed him best three of her most skilled crewmen. And his height did naught but aid the impression. Rarely had Faith, who herself was taller than most women, met a man who towered above her.

"They seemed to know you." Suspicion sharpened his tone.

"I only paid them a shilling to delay you."

"To delay me?" Mr. Waite said. "They could have killed me."

"You handled them quite well, Captain. And besides, I returned as soon as I saw the situation escalate."

"To do what? Protect me?" He snickered and spiked a hand through his dark hair. "All you did was incite them further by telling them who I was."

"Nevertheless, I'm flattered that you were willing to engage them in order to escort me home."

Mr. Waite released a long sigh. "I do not wish to see you harmed. Regardless of your insistence that you can take care of yourself, Miss Westcott, I fear you do not understand the wicked intentions of most men."

Concern burned in his eyes—for her or merely for maintaining his position with her father? He took her hand in his, and the warmth and strength from his touch sent streams of assurance through her. She did not care for the unfamiliar sensation.

A salty breeze blew in from the bay and played with the wayward strand of hair dangling over his cheek. The muted sounds of music and laughter from town swirled around them then combined with the orchestra of leaves fluttering from beech trees that lined the avenue.

A horse and carriage clattered by, startling Faith

back to her senses.

"We should be going."

When they reached the Westcott home, the captain took Faith's elbow and led her up the stairs to the porch. "Quite an interesting evening, Miss Westcott."

She swung about. "I'm glad I amused you, Mr. Waite." She lowered her gaze to his muddied breeches and giggled. "But I see you have soiled your pristine uniform."

"A battle wound worth the pain for your sake." Amusement heightened his voice.

Faith eyed him curiously, finding surprising enjoyment in their repartee.

"I must return to the ship for a few hours," he said. "Afterward, I shall be in the guesthouse should you have need of me."

"And pray tell, why would I have need of you?"

Cocking a brow, he gave her a condescending look. "Simply promise me, Miss Westcott, that you will stay put and not go strolling through the streets at night again."

"You can hardly blame me for what happened," she snapped. "Good heavens, 'twas you who forced me onward with your insulting comments. I simply wished to return home in peace."

"What insulting. . ." He sighed and scratched his jaw. "In any case, you should not be so surprised if you draw the wrong sort of attention. Only unscrupulous women wander the streets at night."

"Why, Mr. Waite." She pressed a hand to her bosom. "I am quite overcome with your concern." She fluttered her lashes again but this time with every intent to appear as silly as she felt.

He broke into a grin as he lengthened his stance. "I daresay, Miss Westcott, you have me quite befuddled. I do not know whether you are trying to allure me with your charms or stab me with your words."

Faith cocked her head and considered which strategy she indeed preferred. "Perhaps both."

A wicked playfulness danced across his eyes. "Until tomorrow." He bowed, slapped his bicorn atop his head, and walked away.

Faith entered the house and slammed the oak door then leaned against it with a sigh. What was she doing? Her plan had been to get home as soon as possible, not engage in witty banter with a man who obviously found her company disagreeable. Not that she wasn't accustomed to that. Her tall stature, intelligent wit, and independent mannerisms never failed to keep suitors at bay. But what did she care?

Confusion trampled over the new feelings rising within her. At least her day had not been a total loss, for she had learned the whereabouts of a treasure ship, and that alone was well worth enduring the captain's company.

"And where have you been?" Edwin crashed into the room, wringing his hands.

"Why, you know very well, Edwin, I was with Mr. Waite." Faith sashayed into the room.

"He should inform me when he will have you home past dark," Edwin huffed.

"I shall be sure to tell him the next time I see him."

"Very well." The lines etched in his ruddy face deepened. "I should inform you that Miss Hope went missing most of the day as well."

Alarm knotted Faith's stomach, but she couldn't show Edwin her concern. No doubt the jittery steward would go running to Mr. Waite with the news. "I am sure she was here. Perhaps she was just avoiding you, Edwin. You worry too much." But Faith well knew her sister's propensity for wayward adventures—one that had become a perpetual thorn in Faith's side. While Faith risked her life to ensure a future for Hope, her sister was intent on destroying it. "Is she here now?" Faith's breath halted as she awaited his reply.

"Yes, miss."

"Then all is well."

Edwin released a big sigh that shook his sagging

jowls. "I knew there would be problems." He turned on his heels and headed toward the back of the house. His whiny voice faded down the hallway. "I told the admiral. I warned him."

At the sound of footsteps, Faith looked up to see Lucas creeping into the entrance hall. "I wanted to make sure ye survived the day with the cap'n."

"That I did, Lucas." Winking, she grabbed the banister and whispered, "We set sail at dawn."

"Do ye know of a ship to plunder?"

Faith grinned. "That I do. A fair prize indeed."

With a mischievous twinkle in his eye, Lucas scrambled away.

Faith lifted her weary limbs slowly up the stairs. She must check on her sisters. She hoped they were tucked in for the night. She could grab only a few hours of sleep before she had to rise and make haste to prepare the *Red Siren* to sail.

For she must reach that treasure ship before Captain Waite.

CHAPTER 9

Darkness smothered Faith as she tiptoed down the stairs. Morgan's jagged talons clamped over her right shoulder, but he remained unusually silent. Clutching her simple linen dress with one hand to keep it from swishing, Faith crept downward, gliding her other hand over the delicately carved oak banister. Yet for all her efforts to move quietly, each step echoed a tune uniquely its own, creating an entire ensemble of creaks and groans by the time she made it down to the entrance hall. Breathless, she halted, listening for any stirrings above where Edwin and her sisters slept.

Guarding the far wall, the grandfather clock drummed a rhythmic *ticktock* that echoed the beating of her heart, yet she could barely make out its stately shape in the darkness. At just past three in the morning, she hoped no one would be awake and she could easily slip away unnoticed. For if she did not set sail by dawn, not only would she not be able to reach the treasure ship before Mr. Waite, but she would risk encountering him along the way. She headed toward the front door, not wanting to risk her normal exit from the back gardens, which could be viewed from the guesthouse where she hoped the captain was still deep in slumber.

As she thought of him, a smile tilted her lips. Today she would best the infamous commander by stealing the treasure he had sworn to protect right from under his handsome nose.

Faint voices reached her ears. Halting, Faith huffed and placed Morgan on the banister, cautioning him to remain. "I shall return shortly." She brushed her fingers over his soft feathers, and he leaned his head against her hand in reply. Then, making her way down the dark hallway, she slunk toward the back of the house, past the warming room, and out the back door, following the sounds drifting from the kitchen.

The muggy night air enveloped her like a swamp. Stars twinkled between the branches of a massive live oak that stood guard against the side fence. Up ahead, soft candlelight and hushed voices flowed through the open windows of the cooking room.

Faith knew she should leave and be about her business, but she thought she had recognized Hope's soft voice. And she could not imagine what her sister was doing up at so early an hour. Hastening into the kitchen, she allowed the swinging door to bump her from behind. A wave of warmth caressed her from the fireplace, where coals smoldered below a three-legged iron kettle. Hope sat at the table nursing a steaming cup of tea. Molly leaned against a baking shelf littered with wooden bowls and rolling pins, a scowl on her face and her hands on her hips.

Fear squeezed Faith's heart. "Good heavens, what is amiss?"

Hope's look of surprise at seeing her sister faded to one of alarm as her gaze shifted to Molly.

The cook shook her head. "Bad enough you kept me up half the night worryin' about you. Now you woke up your sister."

Faith took a step toward Hope, whose gaze immediately dropped to her tea.

Molly huffed. "I tell you what's amiss, Miss Faith. Your sister arrived home only an hour ago."

"I beg your pardon? At two in the morning?" Shock halted Faith as her gaze flitted between Molly and Hope. She had known her sister to venture out without permission before but never so late. "I checked on you. You were asleep when I retired for the night."

Hope's silence sent pinpricks of fear over Faith's scalp. She rushed to her sister's side. "Has someone hurt you, dear?" Horrid memories resurged as Faith knelt and examined her sister from head to toe. Hope wore her best dress—a low-necked French gown of royal blue silk, woven with gold thread—but nary a mark could be seen upon it—or on Hope for that matter. Faith pressed a hand over her heart to still its rapid beat.

"Never you mind, Miss Faith." Molly hiked her skirts up and tucked them into her waistband to avoid setting them aflame then grabbed a cloth and lifted the kettle from the fire. "She be all right, at least in body. In the head, I isn't too sure." She placed the pot on the serving table.

"Where have you been?" Faith demanded as anger replaced her fear. Her throat went dry. "Or should I be asking with whom?"

Wiping a curl of golden hair from her forehead, Hope shrugged. "I assure you, dear sister, I was with Arthur and perfectly safe."

"Arthur? You speak of Lord Falkland?" Rising, Faith blew out a sigh and began to pace. "You call him by his familiar name after only a few months' acquaintance?"

"I feel as though I have known him all my life." Hope smiled, her eyes dancing.

Molly snorted.

Hope's brows drew together. "He loves me."

"Has he declared his love?" Faith threw one hand to her hip. "Has he approached Father for your hand as a true gentleman should, rather than risk your reputation by flaunting you about town at all hours of the night?"

"Not in so many words." Hope raised her chin. "And he was not flaunting me about."

Molly clicked her tongue. "Alls I know is, it's most unproper for a young lady to behave so. If your pappy knew—"

"Father is not here." Hope's icy gaze shot to Molly. "He is never here." She pressed a hand to her stomach. "If you must know, we were at the Sign of Bacchus."

"A tavern?" Faith could not believe her ears. She rubbed her eyes. She did not have time for Hope's petty defiance.

" 'Tis not a tavern," Hope shot back. "Arthur refers to it as a club. They hold concerts, lectures, and balls for the most influential of high society. Everyone who is anyone spends her evenings at the Sign."

Faith had heard of the place. It was said to contain the finest collection of mahogany furniture in town. Original oil paintings of Henrietta Johnson, a local artist, lined the stairwell leading to the nineteen boarding rooms above. Of all the public drinking houses, it was by far the most polished in town.

"Perhaps so, but 'tis still a tavern and no place for a lady," Faith snapped, angrier with herself than with Hope. She must keep a closer watch upon her sister. "I suppose Anne Cormac was there as well?"

"Anne is a dear friend of mine. We share the same passions."

"What passions might those be? Defying your fathers? Associating with gamblers and rogues through all hours of the night like common trollops?"

Hope swallowed hard.

"And what do we know of Lord Falkland?" Faith tried to lower her rising voice. "Nothing, save his reputation as a philanderer and a swindler."

Hope sprang to her feet, her eyes welling with tears. "He is neither of those things. You do not know him. He is a gentleman. Full of passion and life." She swiped at a tear trickling down her cheek. "He tells me I am special."

Faith regarded her sister. *Of course he does, dear one. 'Tis what swindlers do.* Her heart wilted. Sweet Hope. Always the dreamer, always the romantic. Was it her past that forced her into such dangerous liaisons? Fear bristled over Faith. She might be able to protect her sister from these scoundrels, but how was she to protect Hope from herself?

Molly cleared her throat. "Would you like some tea, Miss Faith? Since you up and all."

"No thank you, Molly." Faith sighed. "I'm sorry you have missed your sleep. You should have awakened me when you discovered Miss Hope gone."

"I couldn'a slept anyways." Molly shrugged. "No sense in worryin' the both of us. I was about to alert Mr. Waite—it being his job and all—when Miss Hope come home."

The side door creaked open, and Lucas's tall frame filled the tiny entrance. His questioning dark eyes met Faith's then drifted to Molly and down to her bare ankles. He shifted his gaze. "Morning, Miss Molly, Miss Hope."

Flustered, Molly yanked her skirts from her waistband and allowed them to drop over her legs. Faith had never seen a Negro blush, but she was sure she detected a red hue upon Molly's otherwise flawless cinnamon-colored skin.

"Why, we might as well throw a party seein' as so many of us can't sleep tonight." Molly turned and began stacking a set of wooden bowls on the baking table.

"You're lookin' fine this mornin', Miss Molly." Lucas gazed at Molly's back as he twisted his hat in his massive hands.

Molly veered around and gave Lucas a snort. "Why, I'll thank you not to be lookin', Mr. Corwin." Her voice was caustic, but a hint of a smile danced on her mouth.

The grin slipped from Lucas's face as he ran a hand through the coils of his shoulder-length black hair.

Hope raised a brow. "You and Lucas are venturing out again?" Her words sent a jolt of surprise through Faith. "Yes, I have eyes," she continued. "I have seen you two run off in the middle of the night many a time. What I fail to understand is why 'tis so appalling when I do the same."

Faith balled her hands into fists. "First of all, Lucas is my escort. Secondly. . .'tis none of your concern. I am the eldest, and you will listen to me."

Pain etched across Hope's gaze, igniting into anger. "If I must do as you say, dear sister, then I must also do as you do. Therefore, I shall go out at night whenever I please."

Faith ground her teeth together. How could she

make her sister understand that what she did, she did for Hope? "There is a big difference between what I am doing and what you are doing." Faith averted her eyes as guilt showered over her. With their mother gone, her sisters looked to her to model how a proper, moral lady behaved. She had not realized until now just how closely they watched her.

And how deeply she was failing them.

"I am securing your future," she said simply.

"By running off in the thick of night to make soap, no doubt?" Hope smirked. "You must think me as dull witted as Father does."

"On the contrary, I find you to be quite smart. Perhaps a bit foolish at times." Faith exchanged a knowing glance with Lucas. "All I ask is that you trust me."

"And we best be gettin' to it, mistress." Lucas nodded, his eyes alight with urgency. "Time's a wastin'."

Wringing her hands, Faith glanced out the window, where the square shape of the stables across the yard emerged from the darkness. She had spent far too much time arguing with her sister.

Hope shot her tear-filled gaze to Molly. "Why do you not scold my sister as you do me, Molly?" Wrapping her arms about herself, she hung her head. "Why is everyone in this family against me?"

"Not my place to scold either of you. . .not my place." Molly tossed a rag onto the table and patted the knot of ebony hair at the nape of her neck. "I'm just worryin' for your safety, is all. But there's not much I can do if the both of you keep runnin' off at night." She shook her head.

"I haven't the time to discuss this now." Faith approached the door and turned to face Hope. "We shall talk more when I return."

"Forgive me, sister, if I do not believe you, for you rarely have time to visit with me anymore." The lines on Hope's face deepened, her eyes pleading pools that tugged upon Faith's heart.

"I must go." Faith forced out the words she knew

would hurt her sister, but she had no choice. If she delayed even another minute, they would be too late.

Hope's eyes sharpened. "Perhaps I should discuss this with Mr. Waite? I am sure he has time to converse with me."

Lucas cleared his throat and gestured toward the door.

Faith tightened her lips to keep the anger she felt from firing out from them. "I wish you would not do that." But the pain on her sister's face melted her anger away. She held out a hand toward Hope. "Someday you shall see that all I want is what is best for you."

"You do not know what is best for me." Hope sniffed then took a step toward the door. "If you will excuse me, I am rather tired."

Faith laid a gentle hand on Hope's arm as she passed. "Promise me you will stay home until I return."

Hope nodded, her blue eyes rising to meet Faith's. Despite the tears, they held a sweet innocence tainted by a deep sorrow.

Faith placed a kiss upon Hope's cheek. "Sleep well."

Lucas held open the door as Hope edged by him and disappeared toward the house.

After she left, Molly pointed an accusing finger toward Faith. "You spoil that child."

"She has suffered more than either you or I could imagine." Faith swallowed the burning agony that had risen in her throat and turned to leave.

"She looks up to you, Miss Faith." Molly's sharp tone yanked Faith around again. "If you want to do right by her, be a good example."

"I *am* doing right by her. You will see, Molly." Faith glanced over her shoulder at Lucas, who was still holding the door ajar. They were late. "We must be—"

"I don't want to know where you two are off to." Molly shook her head. "Your family treats me well, pays me fair when most of my people ain't nothin' but slaves in this province. I thank you for that. And for the first time in my life, I feels like I'm a part of a family. So it's not my place to be tattling on you or Miss Hope. I don't want to risk being let go by the admiral. So alls I can do is pray for the good Lord to watch over you."

"I'll take proper care of her, Miss Molly. Don't ye be worryin' none," Lucas said.

"Don't be worryin', you say?" Molly smirked and planted her hands on her waist. "Why, you's just as bad an influence on Miss Faith as she is on Miss Hope. And a grown man, too. Shame on you."

"Let's away, Lucas." Faith nudged him, but his gaze was fixed on Molly, a devilish grin alighting his face.

"Now what's got you grinnin' like the cat that ate the mouse?" Molly asked.

"Only that ye noticed I'm a grown man."

"Any fool can see that." Molly flung a hand in the air with a huff. "Now be gone with you."

Lucas slapped his oversize hat on his head, tipped it at Molly, and disappeared out the door.

"If Edwin or the captain inquires as to our whereabouts when they arise," Faith said, "please tell them we have gone into town for supplies."

"Now you know I can't be lyin' for you. What would the good Lord think of that?" Molly grabbed a rag and tossed it over her shoulder with a disapproving glance.

Faith sighed. "Very well, then. Tell them whatever you wish." She turned and followed Lucas into the darkness.

Before Faith made it back into the house, a sweet hymn swirled over her from the kitchen. Each word of praise to a God Faith no longer spoke to jabbed at her heart.

Out the front door, Lucas disappeared into the shadows and soon returned leading two horses.

Faith whistled, and Morgan flew to her outstretched hand. She set the bird on the horse's back, then clutching her skirts, she mounted her steed, Seaspray, with ease and placed the parrot on the saddle horn. He screeched and flapped his wings, causing the horse to jerk. Grabbing the reins, she steadied the anxious beast until Lucas settled upon his.

The excitement of the coming adventure began to cloud out the disturbing altercation with her sister—for now. But Faith knew she had to address Hope's wayward ways soon, before the girl got herself into trouble.

"Let's be about that treasure, shall we?" She winked at Lucas and kicked her horse, and the two of them sped out the gate and down the lane.

They had not a moment to lose. Faith could not afford to trade broadsides with a British warship, especially one commanded by a highly decorated officer. Such a confrontation not only would result in her ship being sunk to the bottom of the sea but would no doubt leave both her and her crew dead.

CHAPTER 10

Planting her boots on the beakhead of the *Red Siren*, Faith crossed her arms over her chest and braced herself against the oncoming white-tipped swell. The turbulent seas reflected the raging of her heart as the ship bolted then careened over a huge wave. She shook her head, trying to dislodge the memories of the morning. She must concentrate on the task at hand.

After a twenty-minute gallop, she and Lucas had arrived at the bayou, where the *Red Siren* hid in an estuary, anchored safely amid fern and foliage. Her crew had already prepared the vessel with anticipation and welcomed her with greed-infested grins. In less than an hour, Faith had changed into breeches and waistcoat, navigated the ship through the narrow channel, and sent it spewing from the tiny inlet like venom from a snake upon the mighty sea.

A sinister grin played upon her lips. Mr. Waite expected to rendezvous with the treasure ship off Hilton Head in the afternoon, but Faith would meet up with the vessel long before then. By her calculations, the merchant ship would pass Tybee Island—nigh fifteen miles south of St. Helena—near midday, and the *Red Siren* would be there to give her a proper pirate greeting.

A gray haze broke the grip of darkness on the horizon and drove the black shroud back into the sky. Soon splashes of coral, saffron, and crimson dazzled the morning like jewels strewed above the indigo sea.

Closing her eyes, Faith relished the whip of the wind in her hair and the sting of the sea in her nostrils, but thoughts of her sisters intruded upon her peace. Terror drew her muscles taut. After all of Faith's hard work, after all the risks she had taken to protect her sisters from marriages to unsavory men, Hope threw herself at the most unsavory of them all. Word about town was that Lord Falkland acquired and consumed women as frivolously as he did his wealth and in equally as shady a manner. And Lady Cormac—an ill-tempered woman of extreme impertinence—was rumored to be no lady at all but the illegitimate daughter of a local lawyer. What could Hope possibly find so alluring in such disagreeable company?

An arc of bright gold peeked over the horizon, sending a blanket of warmth and light over Faith, lifting her spirits. Depending on her success today, she might finally acquire enough fortune to meet, nay, exceed her father's condition for her and her sisters' independence. Not to mention free her from marrying Sir Wilhelm. How she would answer the admiral when he inquired as to the source of her sudden wealth, she had no idea, but her father never reneged on a promise. At last Faith would be able to stay home and keep a better watch on Hope—and on Grace as well, for truth be told, Faith's youngest sister put herself in no less danger than Hope when she ventured to the shady outskirts of town on her missions to feed the poor and the Indians. Only by the grace of God—no, purely by luck alone—she had not been kidnapped or murdered. Why, oh, why couldn't her sisters stay home and behave like proper young ladies?

The sails above Faith snapped as a gust struck them. She tugged her black velvet waistcoat tighter about her neck against the chill breeze.

Lucas appeared beside her. "All sails be unfurled, and we've caught a weather breeze, mistress. I reckon we'll be at Tybee afore noon."

"Thank you, Lucas."

The ship bucked again, sending a spray of bubbling foam over the bow. Salt stung Faith's eyes, and she examined her first mate.

She wouldn't be a pirate captain if not for him. When she'd rescued him from the streets of Portsmouth, starving and beaten, and convinced her father to hire him as their groomsman, she had no idea he had sailed on a pirate ship for four years under the dread pirate captain Samuel Burgess. When Captain Burgess was brought to Britain and convicted of piracy, Lucas and several of the crew managed to escape, but they faced a fate nearly as horrifying as the noose as they fought for scraps of food on the streets of London.

Lucas taught Faith everything she knew about sailing, navigation, firing a pistol, firing a cannon, even wielding a sword. Together they had stolen their first boat, a small fishing vessel anchored in the harbor at Portsmouth. With that, they began their pirating career and, with each successive conquest, acquired faster ships, until Faith had finally settled on this sleek brigantine—compliments of Mr. Waite.

When Lucas had refused to assume command of the crew, Faith slid into the role of captain with the ease of one putting on a glove. She seemed to have a natural ability to command, make quick decisions, and inspire the men.

Lucas squinted toward the sunrise, a dreamy grin softening his features. But Faith surmised piracy was not on his mind at the moment.

"Am I mistaken, Lucas, or do you fancy Miss Molly?"

The sun gleamed off his perfect white teeth. "Ye noticed?" He shook his head. "She be. . .she be. . .a rare blossom of a woman, to be sure." He shrugged. "But she shuns me, as ye saw."

"Nay, I am not so sure." Faith offered him a coy smile.

"Don't be teasin' me, mistress."

"Despite present appearances, I *am* a woman. And I sense that Miss Molly is not as repulsed by you as she pretends. Trust me."

Lucas scratched his head, his fingers tangling in the black hair that hung in thick wires to his shoulders.

"Odds fish that I do find some comfort in that."

"Is she aware of your heritage?"

"That I be a half-breed? Nay."

"She may not know you have some Negro in you. The color of your skin could pass for a summer day's tan."

"D'ye think it would make a difference?"

"Perhaps. You should tell her about your past."

He scowled. "How my parents were murdered, how I's once a slave, how I run away and became a pirate?"

Faith snickered. "Well, perhaps you should omit that last part."

"Aye, to be sure. She be a godly woman, which is why she don't want to be hearin' about me past neither."

"It might soften her opinion of you." Faith blinked when she realized that she of all people was playing the matchmaker. Yet an undeniable spark crackled across the room when Lucas and Molly were together.

"What would a proper Christian woman like her want with a half-breed, half-witted, thievin' barracuda like me?" Lucas rubbed the back of his thick neck.

"Aye, but there is so much more to you than that, and you know it." Faith flashed him a knowing glance. "Besides, I have never seen you run from anything, Lucas. 'Tis why I'm glad you're my first mate. Fearless, adventurous. You risk your life every day on this ship, but you fear a woman who stands barely five feet tall?"

"Aye, that be about the way of it." He crossed his beefy arms over his chest, and they both laughed out loud.

"Sail ho!" Mac's deep voice bellowed from the crosstrees.

Yanking her spyglass from her belt, Faith raised it and scanned the horizon. Off their starboard beam, the coastline of the New World sped by in sun-kissed shimmers of emerald and honey. Up ahead, nothing but dark blue streaked with foam-crested waves extended to the horizon. "Where lies she?"

"Four points off our larboard bow!"

Shifting the glass to the left, Faith squinted and

spotted the tips of two pyramids, dark against the rising sun. But as the ship grew larger, from her size and colors, she appeared to be naught but a French fishing vessel—too small to carry any fortune of note.

"Let her pass, men. She is not the one we want." She turned to Lucas. "Keep our British colors aloft and alert me when another ship approaches."

"Aye, aye, mistress."

Faith marched to the foredeck ladder then swerved about. "Have Kane check all the pistols and muskets and ensure they are working properly. And tell Bates to ready the guns."

Lucas nodded with a smile.

Three hours later, after catching parcels of sleep in between several ship sightings, Faith emerged from the companionway in a bouffant red-satin skirt, a gold-lace stomacher trimmed with pearls, and a cream-colored bodice that blossomed into double-ruffled sleeves. In one hand she carried a folding fan, in the other a flintlock pistol. A red silk scarf adorned her neck. They had arrived at Tybee Island, and she must dress appropriately for such important guests.

All gazes shot to her, and Morgan squawked a whistle.

With a roll of her eyes, Faith braced one hand on her hip and cleared her throat to allow her most imperious tone. It always seemed harder to command the ship arrayed like a child's doll.

"Prepare to go about!" she barked across the deck, sending the crew up into the shrouds. Plucking the spyglass from her belt, she scanned the coastline, nigh three miles off their starboard side. She must turn the ship around and maintain a leisurely course in the same direction their prey would be sailing, thus allowing their enemies to come alongside with ease when they took the bait.

She heard the familiar hollow thud of Lucas's boots approach.

"Hard to larboard, Lucas, but keep a slow pace." She lowered her glass and squinted at him in the sunlight. A strand of hair slapped her face, and she waved it aside.

With a nod, he swung about and began braying orders. "Ease down the helm! Let go the foresheets and headsheets!"

"Bring down the foresheets, bring down the fore-sheets," Morgan hooted as he paced upon his tiny perch.

The purling of the sea along the hull softened to a trickle as the ship slowed.

Lucas wiped the sweat from his neck. "Helm, bring her about. Raise tacks and sheets." Men scrambled like monkeys across the ratlines, shrouds, and yards that towered precariously overhead.

Faith gripped the railing as the ship veered to port, spitting a fountain of white foam off her stern. After further orders, the yards on the main and crossjack swung around together and braced up sharp on the new tack. Wind eased into the rising canvas, sending the ship skimming through the turquoise water.

Kane joined her at the main deck railing and spit off to the side. The rugged boy's dark gaze took in the expanse of sea before them. "When d'ye expect this ship o' yers, Capitaine?" He folded arms nearly as thick as his thighs across his chest.

"Anytime now. Not to worry, Kane." Faith had never regretted offering a position on her ship to the half-French, half-British seaman she'd found tied to a chain, scrubbing the deck of a French merchant vessel. Later she'd learned he'd been abandoned by his young mother on the streets of Bristol and, at the age of thirteen, press-ganged into the Royal Navy. Now barely eighteen, though his face remained boyish, he had grown into a very imposing seaman.

He flashed a playful grin her way. "I ain't worried none, Capitaine," he said in that peculiar accent of his that still held a trace of French. "Ye have a natural sense about ye when it comes to ships."

"Is the barrel ready to be set afire?" Faith asked.

"Just awaitin' yer order, Capitaine." He pressed both sides of his mustache.

They had not come across any ships of note on the passage south, so she had to assume the treasure ship would soon pass their way. One glance at the sun's position told her it was close to eleven o'clock. She hoped they wouldn't have long to wait.

But wait they did.

Another three hours passed in which no ships were seen save a small fishing vessel that gave them a friendly hail. Standing on the quarterdeck, Faith clutched the railing. The rough wood bit into her skin. Trickles of perspiration slid beneath her heavy gown as the sun, now beginning its descent in the sky, flung its fiery arrows upon them. But she doubted it was the sun that caused her to perspire. Her nerves knotted into balls with each passing second. *Where is that ship?*

"Don't be worryin' none, Cap'n," Wilson said behind her as he steadfastly manned the helm.

She cast him a measured smile over her shoulder. As stout a sailor as ever could be found and none more loyal, Wilson had stood at the ship's wheel for hours without complaint. "Have Strom relieve you, Mr. Wilson."

"Nay, I'd like to stay at me post, if ye don't mind."

Faith nodded with a smile and turned back around.

Lucas's tall figure loomed over one of the men below on the main deck as he assisted him in securing a rope on the belaying pin. The other pirates lingered about like powder kegs ready to explode. Some busied themselves playing dice, others cleaning their weapons. She allowed no drinking on her ship before a raid. Rum dulled the wits and slowed the senses, but the lack of it seemed to keep the men far too jittery.

Faith drew in a deep breath of crisp air, bringing with it the earthy scents of damp wood and tar. Oh, how she loved the smells of a ship! Yet not even sailing upon her precious sea could loosen the dread that now fastened itself around her. Perhaps she was the one who had been duped. She took a quick scan of the horizon and bit her lip. Had the captain known who she was all along? Had he set a trap for her? Her legs numbed.

"Nobody's fool, nobody's fool," Morgan cawed from his perch on the mainmast just below Faith, his words echoing her own impression of Mr. Waite. She frowned at her feathery friend. "Whose side are you on, anyway?"

With a flap of his red and blue wings, he cocked his head upward and stared at her with one eye.

"A sail, a sail!" Mac shouted.

Shielding her eyes from the sun, she surveyed the horizon.

The dark silhouette of a ship bore down upon them.

CHAPTER 11

Pressing the spyglass to her eye, Faith focused on the brimming sails. A three-masted, square-rigged merchant ship rose and plunged over the agitated sea. Dutch and British colors flapped in the breeze over her foremast and mizzenmast. From her lines and size, she appeared to be a *fluyt*, a Dutch-designed ship built to hold a large cargo and a small crew.

But not built to house many guns. Faith grinned.

She focused on the larboard bow. The words *Vliegende Draeck* stood out in blue upon the tan hull. "The *Flying Dragon*," Faith whispered, snapping the spyglass shut.

"Light the fire!" she bellowed then scanned the crew. "Get below hatches and wait for my command."

Clutching her skirts, Faith leaped down the quarter-deck ladder and rushed to the railing, waving her cream-colored fan over her head.

Black smoke curled up from the barrel as several pirates dropped buckets into the sea and then hoisted them up, pretending to battle the flames.

Gripping the railing, Faith leaned over the side and knotted her face into a look of utter despair while shrieking pleas for help toward the merchantman. She made out the silhouette of the captain on the vessel's foredeck and the glint of sunlight off his spyglass as he studied her.

Veering slightly to larboard, the *Flying Dragon* turned and began its approach bow on.

Lucas smacked his lips. "Looks like ye've caught a big fish on yer hook this time, mistress."

"Aye, 'twas easier than I thought," Faith remarked

out of the side of her mouth while maintaining her display of distress.

Ivory foam spewed upon the bow of the Dutch ship as she sped toward her trap. Then, suddenly, the creamy spray slunk back into the sea. The merchant vessel slowed. Down went her topgallants and mainsails until she took up a gliding position just outside the reach of the *Red Siren's* guns.

Faith dropped her fan to her side with a huff. "Of all the nerve. Why does he not rescue me?"

Lucas chuckled and adjusted the captain's hat Faith insisted he wear during raids. "Mebbe he don't favor women."

"Perhaps *you* should drape yourself over the rail, then?" Faith scanned her crew. "Begin to lower the boats, men. And act more frantic. Quicken the fire! We need more smoke. And hurry it up there. Grayson, Strom," she barked at two pirates passing by with buckets in hand. They stopped and gave her sheepish grins. "You need to appear terrified, not like you are carrying water to a Sunday picnic."

"Sorry, Cap'n." Grayson's one remaining tooth perched like a yellowed pyramid among a desert of decaying gums. The portly seaman—with the shortest arms Faith had ever seen, reaching only to his waist— always made her smile. Strom, a gangly, shy youth with hair braided down his back, lowered his eyes under Faith's perusal and trotted after Grayson to fetch more water.

Faith turned to Lucas. "Perhaps 'tis you," she said, looking him up and down. "You do present a formidable figure." She handed him the spyglass. "Gaze at them and give them a friendly wave."

Raising the glass, Lucas perused the vessel. "She sits low in the water."

"That would be the treasure. 'Laden with pearls,' I believe, was the phrase the good Mr. Waite used. Pray tell, what is their captain doing?"

"He be talkin' with three of his crew, mistress—like

he's decidin' what to do." Lucas lowered the glass and gave a friendly wave to the merchant ship. "I be thinkin' ye might 'ave met your match. This captain be smart. He takes no chances with so much treasure aboard."

"Of all the impertinence." Faith tossed her hands to her hips. "What sort of gentleman allows a lady to burn to death?" Shaking her head, she strutted toward middeck. "I suppose we shall have to go after him." The idea was not without its appeal, for she dearly loved the thrill of the chase. Besides, it could take several hours to plunder the ship once they caught her, depending on the amount of treasure in her hold. "Look, mistress, he sends a boat."

Faith spun on her heels and snatched the spyglass from Lucas. Ten men lowered themselves into one of the ship's longboats and shoved off.

"Good heavens, now what to do? When they discover our ruse. . ."

"Can I blow 'em out o' the water, Cap'n?" Bates, her master gunner, had popped up from the hatch and stood before them, a gleam in his twitching eyes.

"Fire the guns, fire the guns," Morgan screeched.

"Nay." Faith slapped the spyglass into the palm of her hand. "We shall take them hostage." She winked at Lucas, who gave her a sly look in return.

"By thunder, I think that'll work, mistress."

"Never fear, Mr. Bates." Faith gave the gun master a reassuring nod. "If all goes well, you will put your precious guns to the test soon enough."

"Aye." Bates's gloomy expression brightened, and he turned and wobbled away on the block of wood that served as his right foot—a souvenir of the Queen Anne's War.

Within minutes the longboat slogged against the hull of the *Red Siren*, and Lucas beckoned the men upward. One by one they leaped over the railing, their cautious eyes roving over the ship. Some had swords sheathed at their sides, others with pistols stuffed in baldrics, but they did not draw them, perhaps lured into a deception of safety by the sight of so few sailors on board and Faith's sweet, innocent smile.

Silence seeped through the ship, interrupted only by the lap of the waves against the hull.

A man of no more than two and twenty, with a comely face and a pointed beard, bowed with a sweep of his plumed hat before Lucas. "My captain sends his regards and bids us assist you in putting out your fire, Captain."

Faith sauntered forward and placed her boot on a stool, drawing the attention of the men—partly, she assumed, because they had never seen a lady wearing boots and partly because she bared the curve of her shapely calf.

"I accept your assistance as well as your captain's regards." Faith grinned as she reached under her skirts and plucked a pistol from a strap around her thigh. "But I must insist you remain on board as our guests." She leveled the gun at the young merchantman as the rest of her crew drew and cocked their weapons.

A horde of pirates spilled from the hatches, curses firing from their mouths. They formed a barricade around the sailors before they could draw their weapons.

"Clap 'em in irons. Clap 'em in irons," Morgan admonished with a flap of his wings.

"Welcome aboard the pirate ship the *Red Siren*, gentlemen." Faith leveled a sardonic gaze upon them. Oh, how she loved saying those words and, even more so, watching the expressions of those who heard it from *her* mouth.

Shock, anger, and fear combined into a whirl of emotions that swept over the men's faces. Their shoulders slumped as they raised their hands into the air.

Faith ordered them bound with rope and wire and taken below, then she turned toward the Dutch ship. As expected, the capture of his crew had not gone unnoticed by the captain. Men darted across the deck in a mad frenzy as sails were raised to meet the wind.

"Hard to starboard, Mr. Wilson. All hands, up tops

and gallants. After her!" she shouted.

The crew flew up into the ratlines as the ship veered to starboard. In moments, the white canvas caught the wind in a jarring snap that sent the *Red Siren* plummeting over the churning waves.

Faith marched to the foredeck as the ship pitched over a roller, spraying her with salty mist. "Raise our colors, if you please, Lucas." She tossed the command over her shoulder, knowing her first mate would not be far behind her.

Lucas repeated the order to one of the pirates nearby, sending him to the ropes. Soon, down came the white, red, and blue British Union Jack and up went the scarlet emblem of the *Red Siren*—a dark silhouette of a woman with a sword in one hand and pistol in the other set against a red background.

Gripping the railing, Faith surveyed her fleeing prey. Although the *Flying Dragon* had all her canvas spread to the breeze, she lumbered through the water like an overstuffed whale. Faith smiled, doubting such a heavily laden ship would live up to her name today.

Blocks creaked and spars rattled above her as they slung aweather and all sails glutted themselves with wind. Sunlight sparkled in clusters of diamonds off the azure sea, reminding Faith of the treasure she would soon possess—and the security it would provide her sisters. Excitement quickened her heart, along with an occasional twinge of fear. She expected no resistance, but there was always the chance someone would get injured. And although her crew had known the risks when they signed on with her, she doubted she could bear it if one of them took a fall.

Faith glanced at Lucas, who stood beside her—ever the rock of calm assurance. He winked then smacked his lips together in anticipation of the battle.

The *Red Siren* rose and swooped over the sea as they bore down upon the doomed Dutchman. Within minutes, they came alongside, matching her thrust for thrust through the choppy waters and positioning the Red SIREN

themselves within gun range.

"Lucas, have Bates fire a warning shot over their bow, if you please."

"Aye, aye, mistress." Lucas jumped down the fore-deck ladder and disappeared below.

Soon the familiar command to fire echoed through the ship, and the vessel exploded in a thunderous boom that sent a violent shudder through her hull. Gray smoke enveloped them and stung Faith's nose. Coughing, she swatted it aside, anxiously peering toward the *Flying Dragon* to see the effect of their threat.

The merchant vessel did not lower her sails.

"Signal them to put their helm over," she roared over her shoulder to Lambert.

Lucas and Grayson joined her on the foredeck while Lambert scrambled aloft to lower and raise the fore topsail, but before he could signal the *Flying Dragon*, her answer came in the form of a volley from the demichasers at her stern. A hail of small deadly shot pummeled the deck, sending the pirates ducking for cover.

"By thunder." Grayson, who did not so much as flinch at the volley, scratched his coarse beard. "That cap'n sure's got some pluck."

"He's naught but a fool," Faith spat. She spun around to face her first mate. "Lucas, bring the prisoners up on deck and place them in plain sight."

He nodded.

"Then bring us in closer and ready the chain shot. If he wishes to make things difficult, I shall be happy to comply."

"Aye, aye, mistress." Lucas stormed away and fired orders across the ship.

Grayson shifted his bloodshot, droopy eyes her way.

Taking his thick, rough hand in hers, Faith squeezed it. "Next time we are fired upon, please protect yourself, Grayson. I would like you to sail with me for a while longer."

With a flash of his single tooth, Grayson's weathered face blossomed into a bright shade of red. "At me age,

105

Cap'n, I'd rather be takin' me chances standing upright than break a bone droppin' to the deck." Chuckling, he ambled away.

Facing forward, Faith braced herself as the *Red Siren* pitched over a wave and angled to starboard. Salt water sprayed a cool mist over her, shielding her from the continual onslaught of the sun.

They must hurry. Mr. Waite would no doubt come in search of the treasure ship when she failed to make an appearance at their rendezvous off Hilton Head. Faith drew a shaky breath. She had no intention of facing one of His Majesty's warships, nor the battle-honored man who commanded her. After checking the pistol stuffed in her waistband, she clutched her skirts, barreled down the foredeck ladder to the main deck, and glanced at her enemy, nigh fifty yards abaft the *Red Siren*'s beam. Men huddled around a swivel gun mounted on her railing, readying it to fire. If Bates did not hurry, they might have to endure another barrage of round shot.

Lucas popped his head above hatches. "Waitin' on your command to fire, mistress."

"Whenever you have the shot."

No sooner had Lucas disappeared below than another thunderous blast rocked the *Red Siren*. Faith grabbed the capstan, closing her eyes against the acrid smoke. Even before it cleared, the distant crack of splitting timbers and the boom of falling wood confirmed their success. Dashing to the railing, Faith gazed toward the *Flying Dragon*, her shape taking form in the dissipating mist. Her foremast was shattered, and fragments of her yards and a tangle of cordage hung to the decks below.

Crowding around the railing, the pirates waited to see their enemy's response. Finally, the merchant vessel dipped her colors in surrender.

Huzzahs and shouts of glee rose from the pirates, and soon the *Red Siren* crashed alongside the Dutch merchant ship to grapple and board her. Faith moved the prisoners, hands still bound behind their backs, within view of their captain.

Then, standing with one boot upon the bulwarks, she cocked and pointed her pistol at the head of one of the prisoners—the young man with the plumed hat who had first spoken to Lucas. Sweat broke out above his upper lip where a slight quiver had suddenly taken residence. She longed to assure him she meant him no harm. But instead she yelled across the expanse to the merchantmen. "I will speak to the captain."

After muffled protests, a stout man with a barrel chest and a mop of brown hair detached himself from the group of sailors and marched forward. With legs spread apart, he crossed his arms over his chest and cast an anxious glance toward the young man at the barrel end of Faith's gun.

"I'm Captain Grainger." His polite nod belied the fury reddening his face.

"A pleasure, sir," Faith said. "Quarter will be granted and your men unharmed, Captain, provided you lay down all your arms and open your hatches. These are my conditions. I suggest you accept them."

"Give 'em no quarter," Morgan squawked from his post, drawing the captain's gaze.

With clenched jaw, Captain Grainger turned and surveyed his men before his dark eyes narrowed back upon her. "Very well. You have left me no choice."

"Excellent." Faith lowered her pistol and nodded to Lucas.

"Prepare to board!" Lucas bellowed as the men armed themselves and crowded at the railing.

The tiny crew of the *Flying Dragon* formed a trembling line of acquiescence as they threw their weapons in a pile.

After ordering two of her men to guard the prisoners, Faith clutched her skirts with one hand, her pistol in the other and led her boarding crew over the bulwarks and into the waist of the ship. She regretted not changing into her breeches, but there had not been enough time.

With a snap of her fingers, her crew jumped to the task of plundering—an undertaking at which they had become quite proficient. Within an hour, they had hauled up a mountain of chests, crates, and velvet boxes brimming with gold ingots, pearls, spices, and sugar.

Faith paced before the crew of the *Flying Dragon*, feeling their gazes scour over her and pierce her like grapeshot whenever she turned her back to them. But she was used to it. They no doubt suffered not only the shock of encountering a female pirate but also the humiliation of being captured by one.

A wave of guilt tumbled over her, but she shook it off as she always did. No one would suffer injury or loss by her actions save the pockets of rich merchantmen. And neither society nor God had provided any other way to save her and her sisters.

Lucas began directing the men to transfer the treasure aboard the *Red Siren*, and one by one, under straining backs and forceful grunts, chests and crates were hoisted over the bulwarks and stowed below in the hold.

Shielding her eyes, Faith glanced upward. As if mocking her, the sun took on a hurried pace in its descent. Sweat streaked down her neckline, and she tugged at her gown, longing for her billowing white shirt that allowed a breath of air against her skin. Removing her scarf, she dabbed at the perspiration and then tucked the crimson fabric into her belt. To plunder the entire ship would take far too long. Surely by now Mr. Waite would be engaged in a furious search for the missing treasure ship. She gritted her teeth and continued pacing, trying to calm her anxieties. But no sooner had the thought crossed her mind than a shout blared from the crosstrees of the *Red Siren*.

"Cap'n, a sail!"

CHAPTER 12

Swinging about, Faith marched to the railing and raised her spyglass. Surging pyramids of white canvas taunted her from the masts of a British sloop of war. The Union Jack stretched proudly atop the foremast, stiff in the afternoon wind. Close-hauled to the northerly breeze and listing to starboard under the weight of it, the ship bore down upon them at full speed.

"Blast!" Faith clenched her fists and stormed across the deck, scanning the pirates who had halted in their tracks.

"Who is she, mistress?" Lucas's normally rigid features crumpled into a frown.

Faith eyed the crates of treasure crowding the deck, ignoring the merchant sailors muttering as they cast hopeful glances over their shoulders toward the British warship.

Her crew had taken barely half the treasure. But there was no time. She glanced back toward the oncoming ship.

"'Tis the HMS *Enforcer*," Faith hissed through clenched teeth. "Back to the ship, men!"

"But what 'bout the treasure, Cap'n?" Wilson complained.

"Aye, we can't be leavin' all this loot!" Lambert added sharply, the other pirates grunting in agreement.

Throwing her hands to her hips, Faith strutted toward her men. "Can you spend it whilst you dangle at the end of a noose, Mr. Lambert?"

Lambert's expression soured. The pirates' gazes shot toward the HMS *Enforcer* as its threatening silhouette loomed larger on the horizon.

"Ye 'eard the cap'n," Lucas shouted. "Unhook these grapnels and be gone wit' ye now. Back to the ship!"

Morgan's loud squawk shrieked over the decks of the *Red Siren*. "Run fer yer lives! Run fer yer lives!" His urgent plea hastened the men as they clambered over the bulwarks, casting yearning glances toward the abandoned treasure.

"Lucas, free the prisoners. Quickly, and then prepare to unfurl all sail." Faith heard the squeak of panic in her voice as she stormed across the deck and assisted Bates, Kane, and Strom with the grapnels. She had no plans to find herself at the end of a noose either, nor to lose everything she had worked so hard to acquire. She glanced at Bates, who battled to pry loose a hook embedded in the splintered deck. "Best get over to the ship and ready the guns."

He rubbed his chin and gave her an understanding look and an "Aye" before he tottered toward the *Red Siren*.

Taking over for Bates, Faith struggled with the iron claw as the snap of sails buffeted her ears. When the last grapnel was freed, Kane and Strom tossed them over to the *Red Siren* and flew over the railings after them. The ships groaned as they began to pull apart. The freed prisoners stood beside Captain Grainger, glaring at Faith.

"Come aboard, mistress!" Lucas yelled at her from the railing, extending his hand to assist her across the wobbling bulwarks.

Faith shot one more glance at the oncoming British warship. Her stomach tightened. The sunlight glinted off the tawny lines of the vessel's sleek body, sharpening each detail. The gaping mouths of nine charred muzzles punched through her starboard hull in a threatening display of cannon power.

Dashing toward Lucas, Faith suddenly halted, spun around, and returned to the captain of the merchant ship. Plucking the scarf from her belt, she handed it to him—a scarlet banner fluttering in the breeze. He fixed her with a cold eye but did not take it. The jeering gleam in his eyes taunted her.

"Forgive me for cutting our visit so short, Captain," Faith said, hiding her rising fear behind an angelic smile. "But if you will do me one last favor and give this to the dear captain of the HMS *Enforcer*, with my compliments?"

With brows pinched, he hesitated, and from the look in his eye, Faith thought he intended to seize her. If it weren't for the *click* of several muskets cocking behind her, he might have done just that.

With a grunt, he grabbed her scarf instead.

"Come on, Cap'n. . .hurry!" Grayson yelled.

The ships began to separate as the wind caught the sails in a series of jaunty snaps.

Lifting her skirts, she darted to the railing then froze. The chasm between the ships yawned a gaping blue mouth that was now too far to traverse. Several pirates stared at her from the other side, fear sparking in their gazes. Two of them still held their muskets firm upon the merchantmen.

Suddenly the air reverberated with the thunder of a twelve-pounder.

Faith turned to see a jet of white smoke drifting above one of the *Enforcer*'s guns. The shot splashed into the sea just ten yards before their bow. Her breath caught in her throat.

Standing atop the crosstrees, Lucas tossed her a rope. She reached for it, but it fell just short of her grasp. Cursing, he hauled it back in.

Below her, the indigo water growled like the carnivorous mouth of a raging monster.

The *Red Siren* drifted farther away.

Faith gulped and thought about praying, but she knew God would pay her no mind, especially in these circumstances. She flexed her hands, trying to stop the tingling fear that numbed her fingers.

Lucas swung the rope again. This time she caught it. Clutching it, she took a running start and threw herself over the side. The rope snapped as her weight pulled it taut. The coarse fibers tore the skin on her palms as she flew through the air and swung her legs high.

Her boots thudded on the main deck of the *Red Siren*, accompanied by the cheers of her crew.

〜

Dajon stood at the quarterdeck railing, his first and second lieutenants flanking him, mimicking his stiff posture. He clenched his jaw and tried to still the fury boiling in his stomach and keep his steady gaze upon the Dutch merchant vessel—the ship he'd been assigned to protect, the ship that was now rubbing hulls with that thieving imp of a pirate.

"She's fleeing, Captain." One of the officers halted at attention on the deck below, where sailors hustled to their stations.

"Fire a warning shot across her bow."

"Yes, Captain." The man touched his hat and shouted an order down the companionway.

A moment later, a gun belched its iron shot in an ear-hammering blast, sending a tremble through the ship. A gust of smoke-laden wind blew over Dajon, stealing his breath.

"'Tis like they knew exactly where she would be," Borland remarked.

"Indeed." Dajon pounded his fists upon the railing. What were the odds that this pirate would be in exactly the right place at the right time? Though many pirates cruised the known shipping lanes, they usually came upon their prey purely by accident and would go days, sometimes months without a conquest. Either this blackguard was extremely lucky, or he had been privy to some ill-gotten information. Dajon hated to consider that he had a traitor on board his ship.

He leveled his telescope upon the pirate ship. The captain had not heeded his warning, but Dajon had not expected him to. He had yet to see a pirate surrender. Most preferred a glorious death in battle to the humiliation of swinging from a noose. He scanned the *Vliegende Draeck*. Her foremast lay in a crumpled heap upon her deck, but it appeared she had suffered no additional damage. Even so, her speed would be severely crippled, and without his protection, she would be easy sport for the next roving bandit.

"Are you going after her, sir?" Excitement lifted the voice of Jamieson, his second lieutenant.

Dajon grimaced. Oh, how he wanted to. How he wanted to put that rapacious rogue in his place. After all, wasn't that what he had been sent to do on these colonial waters?

But he could not leave the merchant ship.

The pirate ship made a swift turn and promptly went about on a southern tack. Her captain had wisely chosen not to risk passing between Dajon's ship and the coast, where they might be trapped. Instead, she ventured out to sea. With her masts a crown of white canvas, she stuck out a rebellious tongue of white foam at him from her mouth at the stern.

"Captain?" A wild entreaty glittered in Jamieson's eyes.

Dajon snorted and clamped tight fingers over the hilt of his sword. Everything inside him ached to give the command to pursue the villains, but his orders. . .

"Nay, Jamieson. With the wind on her quarter, she will be far too swift for us." Dajon heard the hesitancy in his voice, as if he were trying to convince himself of that, as well.

Borland twisted his greased mustache. "You should give chase, Captain. You may not have another chance."

Dajon leveled his brow as he scowled at the fleeing bandit. "I shall have another chance, Mr. Borland; you can wager on that. But for now, I cannot abandon the Dutch ship. I have orders to protect her."

Borland snorted.

"Begging your pardon, Captain," Jamieson said with a snort, "but it seems you are a bit late for that."

Dajon gritted his teeth. "We can yet redeem some

of our honor, as it appears from the jumble of crates strewed about the deck of the Dutch ship, the pirates did not have time to take all the treasure."

The pirate ship tacked to larboard, catching Dajon's eye, and he raised the scope, focusing on the fleeing vessel. His heart leaped at the familiar lines of her hull, the point of her bowsprit, the way she glided through the water. He shifted the glass to the bow, where the words *Red Siren* flashed before him in bold crimson.

He knew that ship. It was the *Lady Em*—his father's merchant ship—he was sure of it.

Hot blood gushed through his veins.

Upon the foredeck, a woman in a red dress stood facing the wind. She wore a large floppy hat shoved so low on her head that neither her face nor even a strand of her hair could be glimpsed. As if sensing his scrutiny, she turned briefly and gave him a full navy salute before swerving back around. Yet he could not make out her face.

"By thunder!" Dajon whacked the spyglass on the railing. "Of all the gall!"

"What is it, Captain?" Borland asked.

" 'Tis my father's ship!"

Both officers gave him curious looks, and some of the sailors on the deck below halted and stared at him as if surprised by their captain's sudden outburst.

"That pirate sails my father's merchant ship—the same one taken off Portsmouth nigh five years ago." Dajon doffed his bicorn and wiped the sweat from his brow. Since he had not shared the humiliating story with anyone, he wasn't surprised by the incredulous gasps coming from his men.

"The great Captain Waite overtaken by a pirate?" Borland mocked. "I would never have thought it possible."

"Many ships have similar lines, Captain," Jamieson said. "How could you possibly recognize your father's?"

"Because regardless of the blasphemous name painted on her bow and the vermin that infest her, I would know my father's ship anywhere, just as I would know that woman pirate anywhere."

"A woman pirate, you say?" Jamieson gave a humorless laugh. "So the tales are true."

Borland grabbed the spyglass and held it to his eye. "Ah yes, there is a woman aboard her—a trace of a red dress upon the forecastle. Yet perhaps she is the captain's mistress."

"Nay, she is no mere mistress." Dajon pictured her insolent salute, and fury hammered through his head until he felt it would explode—fury at how she had beaten him five years before, fury at the agony he had suffered because of it, and fury that she still scavenged the seas with such arrogance—and in his father's ship! Intolerable. But—he felt a grin tugging at his lips—she had made a fatal error in bringing her band of brigands overseas to terrorize colonial waters.

For Dajon was no longer a man to be trifled with.

"We have no choice but to pursue her, Captain." Jamieson swore. "This insult cannot go unanswered. You must retrieve your father's ship."

Borland grinned. "So we have finally crossed paths with the famous pirate ship the *Red Siren*, and her captain is a woman, after all." A malicious satisfaction beamed from his eyes, giving Dajon pause. "A most exciting day."

Dajon stiffened his jaw. "Exciting" was the last term he would use. Every muscle within him twitched to give chase and bring the vixen to justice. But he must obey naval code. He must not allow emotion to rule over him.

Ever again.

"Bring us alongside the Dutchman, if you please, Mr. Borland."

Jamieson's disgruntled gaze darted first to Borland then to Dajon. "But, Captain, she is within our reach."

"Never fear, Mr. Jamieson. I have no doubt we have not seen the last of the *Red Siren*," Dajon said.

Borland turned and bellowed orders below, sending men up to lower topsails.

By the time the HMS *Enforcer* anchored keel to keel

with the *Flying Dragon*, the *Red Siren* was but a speck on the horizon. As Dajon climbed into the longboat and gave the order to shove off, his neck and back ached from the tense rage that had spiked through him the past hour.

Once aboard the *Flying Dragon*, he adjusted his blue coat, threw back his shoulders, and marched over to take his verbal lashing from the captain.

"We thank you kindly for your swift assistance." The captain of the Dutchman smirked in obvious disgust. "Albeit too little, too late."

"Captain Waite, at your service." Dajon removed his hat. "We were told to meet you off Hilton Head, Captain. . . ?"

"Grainger."

"Captain Grainger." Dajon repeated the name between gritted teeth. "When you were not there, I made all haste to find you."

"Made haste or not, 'tis no matter to me. As you can see, you are too late." He waved a weathered hand over the barrels and crates still crowding the deck. "That pirate ran off with half my goods."

"And would have taken the rest if we had not arrived when we did," Dajon reminded him, hoping to put an end to the impudent man's accusations.

"Aye, I'll grant you that." The captain spit off to the side. "But she took most of me pearls—and the rare conch ones, to boot. They would 'ave brought a grand price."

"Conch pearls?"

"Aye, I had just ten of them. Rare pink beauties found only in queen conch shells."

Dajon turned, bumping into Borland, who stood beside him with a smug look of satisfaction on his face. A small band of ashen-faced sailors huddled around the mainmast beside a pile of frayed rope. "Do you need assistance with the injured?" Dajon asked the captain.

"There ain't no injured."

"None?" The revelation shocked Dajon. Pirates

were a bloody breed, known to relish the violence they inflicted upon their victims.

"The scamps didn't harm a soul. They cared only for the treasure."

"Then you made no resistance?"

Captain Grainger shot his fiery gaze to Dajon. "If you're calling me a coward, then say it outright, and we'll settle it like gentlemen."

"I am calling you no such thing, Captain," Dajon said with as much sincerity as he could muster, although the idea of a duel, if only to release his frustration, was not without appeal.

"She had a bloody pistol pointed at my son." He nodded to the slight youth who stood by the mainmast rubbing his wrists. "What did you expect me to do? Besides, we were outnumbered."

"You did the right thing."

"I live for your approval, Captain." His mocking tone elicited chortles from his crew.

Ignoring him, as well as Borland who stood smirking beside him, Dajon continued, "The pirate captain was a woman, then?"

"Aye."

"Can you tell me what she looked like?"

"A beauty, if ye ask me," one of the sailors standing nearby piped up.

"Aye, she was winsome, to be sure." Grainger nodded. "A spitfire, that one." He shook his head. "A mass of red hair the color of copper, with the eyes of a dragon and the face of an angel."

Suddenly a vision of Faith flashed into Dajon's mind, but he tossed it aside. One troublesome redhead was enough for the moment.

"I suggest you store the rest of your goods below, Captain, and raise what sails you have left. I can assure you a safe voyage to Charles Towne from here."

"I should expect nothing less." Grainger thrust out his bristly chin.

Donning his bicorn, Dajon spun on his heel, anxious

to be gone from the captain's insulting demeanor.

"She asked me to give you this, Captain." Grainger's voice halted him, and he turned to see the man flicking a red scarf through the air.

Grabbing the silky cloth, Dajon rubbed it between two fingers and eyed Grainger. "She said to give it to me specifically?"

"Aye, to the captain of the HMS *Enforcer*—with her compliments, I might add."

Dajon examined it again. The initials *R. S.*, embroidered in gold thread, decorated one corner. *Red Siren*. Resisting the urge to rip it to shreds, he crumpled the cloth in his fist instead. The insolence of this woman! Gripping the hilt of his sword, Dajon stormed across the deck. He would catch her. He would catch her and turn her over to the Vice Admiralty Court. Then she would no longer be a plague upon these waters—or a plague upon his life.

CHAPTER 13

Faith gave Seaspray a gentle nudge as they turned the corner onto Church Street. The huge round columns of the First Baptist Church shone like glassy pillars in the moonlight, making the first chapel built in Charles Towne look more like a Roman coliseum than a house of worship.

"Ye took in a fine haul today, mistress." Lucas gave an exhausted sigh as he eased his horse beside hers.

"Yes, a fine haul, indeed, Lucas." Faith tried to match his exuberance, tried to appreciate the wealth they had acquired, but frustration simmered deep in her belly over the treasure lost. After they had counted the plunder and divided it among the crew, Faith had dismissed the men, and she and Lucas had made several trips deeper into the wilderness with the remainder of the booty loaded on their horses. There they spent two backbreaking hours unloading the jewels, pearls, and spices inside a cave—piled atop the rest of the treasure Faith had amassed over the years.

She patted the small pouch hanging on her belt. She'd kept a few of the best pearls with her. Conch pearls. Very rare and very expensive. They would serve to remind her that she was nearly at her goal. Nearly. If only she could have finished the job today.

"Blast that Mr. Waite!" she hissed, twitching the reins to avoid a passing carriage.

"Aye, 'twas poor timin', indeed." Lucas smiled.

His stallion snorted, and Faith smiled at her first mate's ever-gleeful demeanor. How long had he sailed with her? Six years now?

"I fear I would be lost without you, Lucas. I do believe you are the only man I have ever trusted." Truth be told, he was also the only person who knew the whereabouts of her treasure. At first, she had hated confiding in him—hated trusting any man. But without his help, she would never be able to transport her plunder to safety.

An unusually cool breeze blew in from the bay, chilling the perspiration that had taken residence on Faith's neck. She prodded her horse onward, past a three-story, cream-colored house adorned with wrought iron balconies and a narrow piazza that stretched along the side of the building facing the sea to catch the prevailing breeze. She was still growing accustomed to the strange architecture in Charles Towne—so different from the Georgian-style houses back home with their hipped roofs, stone parapets, and massive porticoes in front.

"Ye saved me life, mistress. If ye hadn't rescued me from the streets and gave me a place to live, I'd be lying in me grave by now."

"Ah, but all that wealth must prove a tempting sight, does it not?" Faith regretted the words as soon as they left her mouth. Lucas had never given her reason to doubt his loyalty. To question it now was insulting at best. "Forgive me, Lucas." She rubbed the back of her neck. "'Tis been a long day." And no doubt, the dangers and trials had weakened her faith—in herself and in him as well.

Lucas kept his gaze straight ahead. "Never ye mind, mistress. Ye knows how I feel. All the wealth in the world holds no lure for me—not if takin' it means hurtin' ye and yer sisters. Yer like kin to me now." He regarded her, flipping back his stiff black hair. "'Sides, what would a half-breed like me do wit' all that treasure?"

Faith swallowed a burning lump of emotion. No man, not her father nor any relation nor suitor, had warmed her soul and earned her regard as much as this half-breed castoff of society. How poorly that spoke of the so-called Christian gentlemen she had known.

Exhaustion tugged at her shoulders. Even the

horses struggled as they made their way through the dusty streets, past shops and houses and the curious eyes of the few citizens still lingering about at night. Faith kept to the shadows, thankful she had left Morgan snug in her cabin on board the *Red Siren*, for no doubt, his chattering presence would only draw more unwanted attention their way.

Another breeze wafted over her, carrying with it the scent of salt, fish, and pine. It danced through the loose strands of her hair, and Faith quickly pinned the wayward curls up behind her, drawing the gaze of two passersby. The gentlemen tipped their hats in her direction, and she lowered her chin, hoping they would not recognize her in the dim lantern light. It was bad enough that one of the Westcott daughters roamed the streets at night; two would cast an indelible tarnish on the family name.

Turning down Broad Street, Faith eased her horse toward Meeting Street, where a drawbridge in the inner wall led to Johnson's covered half-moon, over the moat, and then over another drawbridge to the outside of the city. The early citizens, terrified by the many Indian and Spanish attacks, erected the strong double wall, yet already parts of it were being dismantled as the city outgrew its boundaries. Her house was one of those that sat outside the fortification.

Home. She could almost feel the comfort of her warm, soft bed and hoped Edwin had given up on her arrival and retired early with his ritual sip of brandy. She did not feel up to another one of his rattling lectures. Nor did she wish to confront Mr. Waite. Certainly he would still be occupied in securing the *Flying Dragon* at port. With a head start and a fair wind, she had no doubt beat him home, even with the extra time required to store her day's plunder.

Faith made her way outside the wall and then turned Seaspray down Hasell Street, through the open gate, and up to the front porch of her house. She slid off her mount, her boots crunching on the gravel, and handed Lucas her reins. But lights flickering through the windows crushed any hopes of an inconspicuous entrance.

No sooner had she opened the door than a blinding light struck her in the face.

"Where have you been, Miss Faith?"

Taking a step back, she shielded her eyes and pushed the lantern aside to reveal the quivering jowls and tremulous gaze of Edwin.

"Forgive me, Edwin, I did not intend to be so late. Lucas and I were delayed in town."

"Delayed? By what, I might ask? At nine o'clock at night? This is insufferable. What am I to do? And with Mr. Waite gone, too? I had no one to turn to. . . ."

With a huff, Faith allowed Edwin his tirade, praying that without interruption it would run its course and falter for lack of opposition.

"And Miss Molly telling me nothing, and Miss Grace gone all day as well—"

Faith's breath halted in her throat. "Did you say Grace was gone?"

Edwin wrinkled his nose and fixed her with a dark gaze. "Never fear. She arrived in time for supper."

Faith sighed. No doubt her sister had been on one of her charity runs, but Faith would have to speak to her nonetheless. "And Hope?"

"She is home." Edwin rubbed his forehead and began to sway.

Faith clutched his elbow, fearing he would fall. "Edwin, please take a seat." Leading him to a chair, she forced him into it and snatched the lantern from his hand, placing it on the table.

"You do not know what I have endured today," he whined, clutching his heart. "This disobedience is not to be borne, not to be borne, I tell you."

"Edwin, quit your fussing. I was not without escort." Faith blew out a sigh. "Are we not all home and safe now?"

Edwin nodded, blubbering out a sigh.

"You worry for naught." Faith made her way to the stairs and gazed down the dark hallway, hoping to catch a glimpse of the guesthouse through the back window. Nothing but black. She faced the steward. He wrung his hands together like a wet rag, and Faith felt sorry for the man.

His proud eyes rose to meet hers. "You must promise not to be out so late without informing me."

"Of course. But I am too utterly spent to quarrel with you further," Faith said. "Did Mr. Waite arrive yet?"

Edwin shook his head and snorted. "Most unbefitting a guardian, if you ask me."

"You heard my father. His obligations are first and foremost to the navy."

"Perhaps Sir Wilhelm would be more suited for the job. He called upon you several times today."

A chill stiffened her back. "Indeed? Several times?" Thankful she had missed the slimy proprietor, she worried at his persistence, which, if not rewarded, would surely cast suspicions on her activities.

"Yes, twice. He was most concerned for you." Edwin rose and snatched the lantern. "And most disagreeable when I could not inform him of your whereabouts."

"He is a disagreeable man, regardless." Faith placed a hand on Edwin's arm. "Now off to bed with you. Have your brandy and sleep well. You do look pale."

He snorted.

"Everything will appear more cheery in the morning— you shall see."

With a click of his tongue, Edwin grabbed the banister. Faith silenced her giggle as she watched him ascend the stairs, muttering all the while.

Darkness blanketed the entrance hall. Only the sound of Faith's shallow breathing, the ticking of the grandfather clock, and the rustle of leaves outside the windows stirred the silence. She glanced to her right. An open door led to her father's study, where, if he were home, he would no doubt be sitting, smoking his pipe and reading by the warm fire. Now a dark chill seeped from the room and crept over her, reminding her of his absence. Even though they often quarreled, she missed him. She knew he loved his daughters in his own way, but she had come to accept the fact that he loved the sea more. When her mother was still alive, she had filled their home in England with warmth and love. Without her, emptiness haunted every room. Perhaps that was why Hope and Grace sought comfort elsewhere. Faith sighed. If she could seize just one more prize as wealthy as the *Flying Dragon*, she would be able to change not only their fortunes but the shroud of gloom that hovered over this house as well.

Plucking the pins from her hair, Faith shook her head and exited the back of the house, noting the absence of the usual sliver of light beneath the kitchen door. Molly must have retired early. 'Twas no wonder. The poor woman got up at four o'clock each morning to gather the eggs, haul the water, and rekindle the fire.

The door swung away beneath her hand, and the ensuing puff of air from the kitchen, redolent of fresh bread and beef stew, swirled over Faith, sending her stomach grumbling with longing for the supper she had missed. Moonlight spun a silver web across deep shadows as Faith groped her way to the table in search of a candle.

Her fingers bumped into something hard and warm. Hot breath flowed over her.

Jumping back, she screamed at the dark silhouette looming in the shadows. "One more step and I'll slice you!" She reached for the cutlass that no longer hung at her side and then turned to flee. But strong hands grabbed her arms and swung her around.

"Be still, woman, 'tis me." The deep, masculine voice reverberated in the room.

Fear and rage crashed over Faith. Horrifying memories wrestled against her reason, and she thrashed against his grip. She pounded her fists on his chest, but his solid frame did not budge.

"Calm yourself, Miss Westcott. There's naught to fear." His grasp was firm but gentle as he pulled her toward him. He smelled of leather and salt.

Yet her panic made his words sound like unintelligible mumbles. Drawing a deep breath, Faith rammed her knee into his groin.

Instantly, he released her. "Great guns, woman," he moaned as his dark body folded in half.

"Mr. Waite?" Faith took a step back and caught her breath.

"Aye," he gasped. "What is left of me."

Embarrassment flooded her. Then anger took its place at her exposure of her fear—her weakness—in front of him. "You scared me half to death, Mr. Waite! 'Tis what you get for slinking around in the dark." As her eyes adjusted to the dark, she grabbed the candle, now visible on the table, and lit it from the embers still smoking in the fireplace.

The captain's dark hair hung around his face. His breaths came in deep spurts as he leaned over, hands on his knees.

When she approached with the light, he lifted his gaze, and despite the pain in his eyes, a slight smirk played on his lips. With obvious difficulty, he eased himself upright then pressed the wrinkles from his blue coat. The tip of his service sword clanged against the table. "Perhaps next time, a warning shot would suffice?"

"You'll get no warning from me." Faith sent him a fiery gaze. "Not when you come upon me unawares in the dark." She noticed her red scarf poking from a pocket inside his waistcoat, and she suppressed a grin. Twice she had bested him today, yet somehow the second time did not hold the same thrill as the first. If she had known it was the captain, she certainly would not have attacked him. She had no desire to hurt him, and though he tried to hide it, the grimace on his face betrayed his pain.

"Have a seat, Mr. Waite, and I shall fetch you some tea." She started to turn, but once again, he grabbed her arm.

His heated breath, tinged with liquor, drifted over Faith, sending the candle flickering between them. Dark eyes perused her as if memorizing every inch of her face.

Desire and admiration intermingled in their depths, and an unusual flutter rose within Faith's belly. Wayward strands of his hair grazed the stubble on his cheek. A smudge of dirt stained his tousled collar, and his blue coat hung unbuttoned over his wide chest—so unlike the kempt, orderly captain.

He reached up. Faith flinched but remained anchored in place, not wanting him to see his effect upon her.

"'Tis obvious I frightened you terribly, Miss Westcott. Please accept my apologies." He brushed a finger over her cheek.

A warm flush surged through Faith. She snatched her arm from his grasp and turned away. "Frightened?" She waved a hand through the air. "Nonsense. You merely surprised me." She bit her lip. She must remember that Mr. Waite was not only a man—something she doubted she could ever forget—and therefore not to be trusted, but her enemy as well.

But such an enemy. With her back to him, Faith grinned, hoping to turn the tables and have a bit of fun. "Beg your pardon, Mr. Waite, but do I smell a hint of alcohol about you?"

She heard him expel a deep breath. "'Twas a difficult day." The frustration in his voice stung her conscience.

She swerved around and placed a hand to her chest. "I daresay I am shocked, Mr. Waite. I would never have expected a godly man such as yourself to partake of the devil's brew."

"I have a sip of port on board my ship when the occasion calls for it," he replied with confidence. The tiny upturn of his mouth and the playful look in his eyes let her know he was not a man so easily ruffled by her barbs.

She longed to make some sarcastic comment about the occasion that had caused his annoyance. But the way his intense gaze drifted over her sent her insides quivering in a warm pool, and she just stood there, locked in the hold of his blue eyes.

Forcing herself to look away, she set the candle down,

fetched a handful of tea leaves, and tossed them into a pot on the table. Shame weighed upon her. She was not some weak female who swooned over the attentions of a man—albeit a most handsome, honorable man.

No, no, no. Not just a man but an enemy—an enemy who stood between her and her goal of plundering one more treasure-laden ship, an enemy who stood between her and the safety and happiness of her sisters. Anger flared within her, melting her passion and igniting her determination.

~

Dajon watched Faith retrieve two china cups from the cupboard. Her curls cascaded in a crimson waterfall that poured to her waist. He swallowed a lump of desire. What a paradox this woman was. She reminded him of a wildcat: independent, cautious, yet when her claws were not drawn, soft and vulnerable. She had been truly terrified of him in the dark, though he had tried to console her both with his words and his touch. What had happened to her to cause so frantic a reaction?

What was happening to him?

Years ago, he had sworn that the only woman he would ever need would be the ship he sailed upon, for after what happened with Marianne, how could he trust himself with the safety of another lady? His promise had not been difficult to keep—until now.

As he watched Faith cross the room, a picture of femininity yet carrying herself with the confidence and command of a captain at sea, he longed to know everything about her.

"Pray tell, why were you wandering about in the dark anyway?" She placed the cups on the table.

Dajon drew his sword and laid it across a bench before he eased into a chair. "I seem to have forgotten to eat today. I was searching for a lamp when I heard you come in."

"Why did you not alert me to your presence?" She eyed him guardedly. Then, turning, she grabbed a cloth and folded it around the handle of a kettle that hung over the few coals still simmering in the fireplace.

Dajon's gaze swept over her as she knelt, her curves alluring beneath the simple dress she wore. "I thought you might be a robber." He flinched under the prick of his conscience. Truth be told, the minute she had entered the room, he could not take his eyes off her silky skin, the way the moonlight shimmered over it and reflected a glittering red halo around her hair.

Until she had kneed him in the crotch, of course.

Lifting the kettle, she poured the warm water into the pot on the table. As she did, her leg brushed against his, and she jumped, sending her hair spilling past Dajon's face.

The aroma of salt and smoke filled his nose, and he leaned back in the chair, wondering why she did not perfume herself with lilac or rose oil like other women he had known. Suspicion brought his mind to full alert. He narrowed his gaze upon her.

"What ails you now, Mr. Waite? Did I hurt your leg as well?"

"Your hair smells of the sea." He folded his hands over his stomach.

A hint of alarm flickered across her face. She stirred the pot, lifted it, and tipped it over Dajon's cup. "Lucas and I had business at the port today." Her hand trembled, spilling the liquid onto the table. "Oh, good heavens." Setting the pot down with a clunk, she dabbed the puddles of tea with a cloth.

"Aye, so Molly told me early this morning." Dajon lifted his cup. "Must have been important to force you to rise before the sun." He took a sip of the tea, hoping its warmth and her answer would dissolve the ridiculous notions that now filled his head.

"Most important." Faith shifted away and returned the kettle to the hearth. "I had to purchase supplies for my soap business."

"Quite a few supplies, I would imagine, to have taken the entire day to procure, for it seems we both arrived home at the same time this evening."

"Whatever do you mean? I have been here for hours," she retorted without facing him.

"I beg your pardon, miss. When I saw Lucas bedding down two horses in the stable, I assumed. . ."

Faith spun around and flung one hand to her hip. "You assume too much, Mr. Waite." Her gaze flitted down to his pocket, where he'd stuffed the pirate's scarf. "And did you escort your treasure ship to port safely?"

"Yes. Thank you for your concern. The ship is anchored safely in the harbor as we speak." He set down his cup.

With a smirk, she shifted her gaze away.

"But I see you have taken notice of my souvenir of the day's adventures." Withdrawing the scarf, Dajon rose and extended it to her. Since she had lived in Charles Towne for more than two months, perhaps she could give him a clue as to the identity of the owner.

Her face paled, giving him pause.

She lowered her chin and cleared her throat. When she raised her gaze, a different woman lurked behind those auburn eyes. Gone was the hard sheen, the defiant glare, and in its place, a seductive innocence glimmered.

Snatching the scarf, she fingered the initials and rubbed the silk between her fingers. "A lady admirer. Why, Mr. Waite, I had no idea." She turned her back to him. "And all along I thought"—a tiny sob escaped her—"well, I thought you had some affection for me."

Taken aback by her sudden change, Dajon's voice cracked, and the words he had intended to say faltered on his lips. He rubbed the bridge of his nose, where an ache from an old injury rose to haunt him. Had he been absent so long from courting rituals that he no longer recognized a lady's intentions? By thunder, Faith was unlike any woman he had known, to be sure, but he could not be that daft.

Dajon circled her. Placing a finger beneath her chin, he lifted her gaze to his. "I do not know the lady who owns it. I thought perhaps you might recognize it."

"Me? Why, anyone can tell by the bold color that it

clearly belongs to some trollop. What would I know of it?" She lifted the scarf and dabbed at her moist cheeks.

Suppressing a chuckle, Dajon leaned and peered intently into her eyes.

"What are you doing?" she snapped.

"Trying to see if there are two of you in there." He grinned and then furrowed his brow. "The transformation is so swift and unpredictable, I know not which of you to expect, vixen or enchantress."

Batting her tears away, she glared at him, and behind her eyes burned a fury and determination matching that of any brigand he'd ever seen. Thrusting the cloth in his hand, she turned her back to him, flinging her hair behind her in a fiery cloud.

He lengthened his stance. " 'Twas a gift from a pirate—a *lady* pirate—prowling the Carolina seas." Dajon leaned down and drew a whiff of her hair. Smoke, salt, and a hint of lemon. "Her hair is the same color as yours." Since her back was still turned, he took the liberty of caressing a lock between his fingers, enjoying the silky feel and delighting in the way the curl sprang back when he released it. "Odd that she has only made her presence known these past few months. I daresay she appeared about the same time you arrived here in Charles Towne." Why did he enjoy taunting her so? Perhaps because the ache still burned in his groin where she had kneed him. Perhaps because he enjoyed the banter of her sharp wit and the way the freckles on her nose scrunched together when she grew angry. Because even the thought of an admiral's daughter being a pirate was absolutely ludicrous. An impossibility.

She wheeled around, her thick strands slapping his side. "There are many women with red hair in these colonies, Mr. Waite. It is not a crime. And tales of women pirates have been tantalizing the ears of these adventurous pilgrims for years."

"See, now the vixen has reappeared," he teased, noting the fury burning within her eyes.

"Why are you being so cruel? Is it because I kicked

you?" She huffed. "Edwin told me you were still away, and I thought I was all alone." Her voice softened as she inched closer to him. 'Tis frightening to be a woman without protection."

Visions of Faith handling herself fearlessly with the ruffians on the street shot through Dajon's mind, followed by her declaration that she could take care of herself and her sisters without him. But as he felt the heat from her body close to his and as her lemony scent swirled beneath his nose, Dajon had difficulty forming a rational thought from the memories. "I must say, I do prefer the enchantress."

She lifted her head and shifted her misty eyes to his. Her sweet breath puffed upon his chin like an aphrodisiac as her gaze swept over his lips.

Heat stormed through Dajon, weakening his reason and his defenses. The heady pull of her was too much to resist. He lowered his lips to meet hers.

No.

He halted. She was toying with him. He was sure of it. *Lord, help me. I have not the strength to resist her without You.*

A blast of indignation shot through him. What was he doing? He pulled away and crossed his arms over his chest. "Forgive me."

Faith cocked her head. A spark of victory flashed in her eyes. Dajon took a forceful step toward her again and leaned down, his mouth inches from her ear. "You play a dangerous game, Miss Westcott." Then, righting himself, he scoured her with his gaze. "I suggest you not offer yourself in so tempting a manner. Next time, I may well accept your invitation." He gave her a mischievous grin and bowed.

She narrowed her eyes.

Turning on his heels, Dajon grabbed his sword and stomped from the room. A blast of cool air struck him, reviving his reason. He cursed himself for being so weak. Allowing two ladies to get the best of him. He could not let it happen again.

CHAPTER 14

Faith rose early the next morning, determined to spend time with her sisters. With a yawn, she entered the dining room, lured there by their bickering voices.

"Oh, do come in, dear." Hope gestured for Faith to sit in the chair beside hers as the aroma of tea, strawberry jam, and toast danced around her, nudging her stomach awake.

Grace peeked at her from behind *Meditations and Contemplations* and smiled before resuming her reading. "Rising before noon? Whatever is the occasion?"

"Would you care for some tea, Miss Faith?" Miranda, the serving maid, curtsied in her direction.

"Yes, thank you." Ignoring Grace's remark, Faith took the seat next to Hope as Miranda filled her porcelain cup. Fragrant steam swirled off the hot liquid as rays of the morning sun set the silverware, fruit, and china glittering in vibrant colors against the white cotton tablecloth.

"Pray tell, where were you all day yesterday, Faith?" Hope set down her toast and formed her lips into a tiny pout. "With Grace gone as well, I was left with naught to do but sit and read. I wrote Father a letter." She swallowed and lowered her gaze. "Not that he will respond."

"It pleases me to see that you kept your promise and stayed home." Faith drew a slice of toast from the serving plate.

"I fail to see why I was forced to remain here when both you and Grace were free to roam wherever you wished."

Closing her book, Grace set it beside her plate. "I was delivering food to the settlers on the Ashley River. I asked if you would accompany me, but you refused."

"Why would I want to traipse through fields and forest, ruin my gown with mud and filth, and risk being attacked by savages?" Hope said with a huff.

"Perchance to help those in need?" Grace raised a pious brow. "Maybe if you thought of someone else besides yourself, you would not be in so disagreeable a mood all the time."

"I am not disagreeable." Hope turned up her nose and dropped a lump of sugar into her coffee with a plop. "Lord Falkland says I am the kindest and most charming woman he has ever known."

At the mention of Lord Falkland, fear resurged to gnaw at Faith. She determined to discuss the rogue with Hope later, but for now, she turned to her other sister. "Which reminds me, Grace. You are fully aware of Father's rules about leaving the house unescorted."

"Are you not bound by the same rules?" Grace flashed her green eyes at Faith, accusation burning within them.

"I was with Lucas yesterday."

"Mrs. Gibson accompanied me." Grace took a bite of her toast and set it down as if the matter were closed.

" 'Tis not the same thing, and you know it. Mrs. Gibson, although a sweet, godly woman, cannot protect you in the event of some misfortune."

Grace brushed her feathery raven bangs aside and gave Faith a look of scorn. "You can hardly assume to govern us when you are never home. You're as bad as Father is."

Faith winced beneath the sting of Grace's words. She bit her lip to keep from spewing an angry retort. She was nothing like their father. While he went to sea for glory and adventure, ignoring his family at home, she went to sea to better their futures, doing her best to spend as much time with them as she could.

Hope slouched in her chair. "Where were you? You said we could talk when you returned."

"Forgive me. I was delayed." Faith laid a gentle hand over Hope's. "I promise we will talk today."

"Your promises mean nothing." Hope snatched her hand from beneath Faith's. "Grace is right. You are never here. And with Mother gone and Father always away, I feel as though I am not only an orphan but an only child." Moisture covered her sapphire eyes, and she turned away.

Faith stirred cream into her tea, the silver spoon clanging against the porcelain cup as if tolling her guilt. How could she make her sisters understand that her many absences were for their benefit—that their welfare and future were all that consumed her energies and time? Yet she could not let them in on her secret. Grace would be so appalled that she might even turn Faith over to the authorities—albeit to cleanse her from her iniquity. And Hope would only use Faith's pirating as a free license to pursue her own scandalous activities.

Faith clanked her cup down a little too hard and proceeded to butter her toast as if she were sharpening her cutlass.

She risked her life over and over for her sisters, and this was her reward.

Grace sighed and raised one brow. "If you are expecting Faith to be here for us, Hope, you will only face disappointment. For even when she is here, she sleeps half the day."

Faith forced down her anger and smiled. "Why don't we spend the whole day together, just the three of us? How does that sound?" Perhaps she could appease both her own guilt and her sisters' need for her company all at once.

Hope broke into a beaming smile. "That would be lovely."

Happy to have mollified her sister, Faith glanced out the window. The golden flowers of the Carolina jasmine waved in the morning breeze as they clung to a trestle. The pink and violet blossoms of dogwoods and magnolias that had sparkled across the city like jewels early that spring had faded in the latter months of the summer, replaced by coral honeysuckle and sea myrtle, delighting Faith in the variety of unusual flowers that graced this untamed wilderness. She had come to love the beauty of this land and could see her and her sisters settled happily here once their fortune was secured.

Only one person stood in her way.

And as if she could conjure him up by her thoughts, Mr. Waite strode by the window in his blue uniform.

Hope's gaze followed him across the paned glass. "He is so handsome, is he not?"

"I suppose." Faith tried to still the sudden thump of her heart. She sipped her tea, hoping its warmth would sooth her nerves, but instead the acidic taste bit her tongue. In all the discord, she had forgotten to add sugar.

"I thought your affections were for only Lord Falkland," Grace snickered.

"They are, of course." Hope gave her a coquettish smile. "But there is no harm in admiring, is there?"

Grace chuckled. "You are incorrigible."

Faith felt the captain enter even before his baritone voice filled the room like a symphony. "Good morning, ladies."

Hope giggled, and Grace shot him a playful smile.

Mr. Waite harrumphed. "Did I miss something?"

Faith heard his boots shuffle on the wooden floor as she dropped two lumps of sugar into her tea. His warm breath wafted down her neck.

"Good morning, Miss Westcott." The scent of lye tickled her nose. The man obviously kept himself as clean on the outside as he did on the inside.

A heated flush rose from her belly and set her face aflame at the memory of their encounter last night. "Good morning, Mr. Waite," she said without turning, for she was certain her face must be as bright as the red apple that perched atop the bowl in the middle of the table.

His piercing gaze locked upon her as he rounded the table, flung his coattails out behind him, and took a seat across from her. His hair, pulled and tied behind him in a queue, reminded Faith of the color of the roast coffee filling Hope's cup.

She had hardly been able to sleep the entire night. Every time she had started to drift off to a much-needed slumber, the memory of his lips so close to hers kept jolting her awake. The unfairness of it. What was wrong with her? She had thought to tease him, but instead she was the one whose passions had been stirred.

And why was he staring at her now as if he knew her darkest secrets?

Hope twirled a lock of her golden hair. "I trust you slept well, Mr. Waite?"

"Magnificently, thank you." His blue eyes slid to Faith, a smile flickering within them.

Was he mocking her?

"You look lovely this morning, Miss Hope," the captain said as he waved away Miranda and poured himself some tea. Steam rose from the hot liquid in an exotic dance that mimicked the heat radiating within Faith.

Hope flashed him a girlish smile.

"And you as well, Miss Grace." Mr. Waite poured cream into his cup.

"Why, thank you, Mr. Waite. If you don't mind my saying so, 'tis nice to have a Christian gentleman around the house."

"I am finding your home to my liking as well, Miss Grace." He grabbed a slice of toast, spread some jam upon it, and shoved it into his mouth, tearing off a bite.

"My sister has just promised to spend the entire day with Grace and me." Hope's voice lifted with excitement. "Perhaps you could join us?" She tapped Faith's leg beneath the table.

Faith kicked her sister in return. The last thing she wanted was to spend the day with Mr. Waite.

"Ouch." Hope flinched and leaned down to rub her ankle.

"She has? What a grand idea." The captain smiled as if he hadn't noticed anything unusual and brushed the crumbs from his pristine white lapels. "But are you sure, Miss Westcott, you have nothing more pressing to attend to?"

Faith smiled and tried to hide the agitation brewing in her stomach. "Of course I don't. What could you be referring to?"

"Nothing, I assure you. It seems some urgent matter always steals your time away from home." Mr. Waite finished his toast and rubbed his hands together. His strong jaw flexed with each chew as his playful blue gaze flickered over her.

"How would you know? You have been here no more than a few days."

"And yet you are never here."

Faith tightened the corners of her mouth for a moment to keep from spewing angry words at him. When she recovered sufficiently, she smiled sweetly. "I am here now, Mr. Waite."

"Indeed." He sipped his tea and grinned. "And what pleasure I find in your company."

"Can we go to the park?" Hope asked.

"After we attend church." Grace stirred her tea then set down her spoon with a soft clang. "It is the Lord's Day."

"Oh pshaw. Why must we always go to church?" Hope's shoulders slumped.

Grace frowned at her sister and twirled the button on her collar. "Can you not give God back one hour of your time for all He has done for you?"

"What has He done for me?" Hope crinkled her nose and patted her perfectly styled hair. "I am stuck here in this horrid town. Mother is gone. Father is always away, and I am forbidden to have any fun at all."

"Things are not always as they seem, Miss Hope." Mr. Waite plucked an apple from the bowl. "You have plenty to eat, a comfortable home, beautiful clothes, and your health. These are gifts from God. Many do not have such luxuries." He chomped on the apple.

Grace nodded in approval and cast a matronly look toward Hope.

"Faith does not attend church," Hope quipped and tilted her head.

Faith shuffled in her seat. Her sister's mouth always ran wild like a storm at sea.

Mr. Waite raised a brow.

"She stopped attending shortly after Mother died."

"Indeed?" Sorrow tainted his voice.

"It was Mother's wish that you both attend church regularly." Grace rubbed her thumb over the handle of her teacup. "She begged me to ensure that all of us maintained our faith in God." Her voice cracked. "It was most important to her, but neither of you have listened to me at all."

Hope rolled her eyes. "Perhaps if you did not look down upon us from your high and lofty pedestal, we would."

"I do not—" Grace snapped then pursed her lips. "Oh, never mind." Releasing her teacup, she sat back in her chair.

Mr. Waite cast a disapproving glance over them all.

"I am afraid I do not share your faith in God, Mr. Waite." Faith took a bite of her toast. "And it would seem neither does my sister." The jam, however, soured in her mouth, and she swallowed it with a gulp.

"So you have told me. Yet you have not denied His existence. Perchance church would be a good place to hear from Him again?"

If she wanted to hear from God, Faith longed to respond, but she did not wish to incite another argument with Grace. Instead, she remained silent, thankful when she heard Edwin's uneven gait behind her.

"Sir Wilhelm," the steward announced as he halted beside Faith. The bags beneath Edwin's eyes hung lower and darker this morning, no doubt because of his incessant worrying. But Faith refused to concern herself with the skittish steward. Her sisters provided her with enough stress, and to make matters worse, she must now deal with this pompous bore, Wilhelm.

Closing her eyes, Faith wondered what the infernal man could possibly want.

Mr. Waite dropped his apple to his plate then

stood, scraping his chair over the floor, and bowed. "Sir Wilhelm. A pleasure."

Yet there was no pleasure to be found in the captain's gaze. Faith saw only wariness in his blue eyes as he took in the Carolina proprietor. Well, at least Mr. Waite was a good judge of character.

"Mr. Waite," Sir Wilhelm replied, his look of surprise quickly replaced by one of disappointment that tugged on his pasty white skin. "Here again, I see."

"I am afraid I do reside here for the time being." Mr. Waite gestured for Sir Wilhelm to take a chair.

Ignoring him, Sir Wilhelm briefly nodded toward Hope and Grace before his sunken brown eyes fixed on Faith. "Miss Westcott, you are the picture of beauty this morning."

Faith flashed a curt smile but quickly faced forward and fingered her half-eaten toast. *Oh, please go away.*

"'Tis a glorious day, and I have come to inquire whether you and your sisters would do me the honor of joining me on a carriage ride through the country."

Silence struck the table as if a mighty blast of wind stole all their voices and blew them away.

"A splendid idea, Sir Wilhelm," Mr. Waite said, breaking through the shroud of discomfiture. "I was about to escort Miss Hope and Miss Grace to church. But I believe Miss Westcott is available." He raised his sarcastic brow her way. "Are you not?"

The cad. Faith wanted to strangle him but instead forced her lips into a pert smile. "Why, no, Mr. Waite, you misunderstood me. I have every intention of attending church with my sisters today." She gazed up at Sir Wilhelm. "Please accept my apologies, but as you can see, we have plans."

Mr. Waite widened his eyes. "I have a grand idea. Perhaps Sir Wilhelm would like to join us?"

~

Faith shifted on the hard pew as a bead of perspiration made its way beneath her gown. It took a wayward course down her back, twisting and turning before finally being trapped by a fold of her dress. She wondered if it was due to the summer heat or the fact that she had not stepped foot in a church in over seven years.

Mr. Waite sat smugly beside her. She longed to grind her elbow into his side. How dare he use her hatred for Sir Wilhelm to manipulate her into coming to church! To make matters worse, the buffoon had accepted Mr. Waite's invitation to join them and took up valuable space on her right, space she would have preferred anyone else to have taken, even the miscreants down by the docks. There was something grotesque about the man—the sickly smell of him, the way he looked at her that made her stomach shrivel in nausea. And she was not one easily overcome by queasiness.

Her sisters sat on the other side of him, Hope staring into space as if wishing she were anywhere else but here—Faith could well understand her sentiment—and Grace with gloved hands clasped around the Bible in her lap, waiting in anticipation of worshipping a God who surely would neither hear nor care.

Sir Wilhelm slid closer to her until his arm touched hers. She flinched and shifted away, only to bump into Mr. Waite. Heat from his body shot through her until further drops of perspiration slid down her back to join the wet blotch she was sure was forming on her gown.

The captain flashed her one of his charming smiles but made no effort to move aside.

This was going to be a long service.

A rugged, stocky man with sandy hair that seemed to spike out in all directions approached the lectern. He wore normal street clothes of breeches and waistcoat rather than the long flowing robes of the Anglican priests, and Faith assumed he was a simple attendant until he opened a Bible and began to read aloud. Never in all her years of attending church had she seen any priest like him. A simple, humble man. Even when he glanced across the crowd, naught but love beamed from his gaze, instead of the condemnation and vainglorious snobbery she had often witnessed in the eyes of the priests back home.

Above him a large wooden cross hung upon a brick wall, framed on each side with long narrow windows. The sight of it sent a twinge of shame through Faith, making her feel suddenly tainted inside, unworthy. Swallowing hard, she shut out the passage he read— something from the Gospel of Matthew about seeds— and instead focused on a rather handsome man sitting in the front row who kept glancing over his shoulder at Hope.

The square brick building that encircled the fifty or so parishioners was much smaller than St. Philip's, where her father and her sisters usually attended. The crude furnishings and lack of decorations made it seem more like a rustic barn than a place of worship. The scents swirling around her of aged wood, mold, dirt, and tallow only confirmed her assessment.

Still, Faith could not shake the sweet Spirit permeating the place, evident on the faces of those who listened with rapt attention to the reverend's passionate reading:

"But he that received the seed into stony places, the same is he that heareth the word, and anon with joy receiveth it; yet hath he not root in himself, but dureth for a while: for when tribulation or persecution ariseth because of the word, by and by he is offended."

Offended? Had she become offended at God? Confusion tore through her. Perhaps she had. But who wouldn't be offended when the almighty God, the one Being who had power to do or allow whatever He wished, had sentenced her sister Charity to a lifetime of misery, had allowed Hope to endure an unspeakable horror, and had taken their mother from them at so young an age—the only parent who truly loved them. Yes, Faith was indeed offended.

Determined to block out the convicting words, she gazed over the small building, amazed that a church without the beauty of stained glass, without the ivory pillars and gold-inlaid altar, without the incense and white robes could stir more passion within her than she had felt in years.

And she did not care for it one bit.

On her left, Mr. Waite sifted through the Bible in his lap as if it were a delicate treasure he had just found in the hold of his ship. To her right, Sir Wilhelm began to snore, eliciting giggles from Hope, which were quickly stifled by Grace's stern look of admonition.

The reverend continued: "The Son of man shall send forth his angels, and they shall gather out of his kingdom all things that offend, and them which do iniquity; and shall cast them into a furnace of fire: there shall be wailing and gnashing of teeth. Then shall the righteous shine forth as the sun in the kingdom of their Father. Who hath ears to hear, let him hear."

All things that offend, eh? Perhaps God was as offended with her as she was with Him. The only difference was that He had the power to cast her into a fiery furnace. Would He really do such a thing when all she was trying to do was save her sisters? Withdrawing her handkerchief, Faith dabbed at the perspiration on her neck. Perhaps He would. She really didn't know God anymore.

Maybe she never had.

She thought about saying a prayer to Him here in this holy place that seemed so filled with His presence. She thought about it, but the words wouldn't form in her mind. She gazed up at the wooden cross that symbolized the ultimate sacrifice of a man, claiming to be God, who had come down to earth to save His children from their wickedness.

Her wickedness.

Instead of the guilt, the condemnation Faith expected to feel, a strong sense of love drifted over her like a cloud on a hot summer's day. It settled on her and soothed away the rough edges of her nerves. Closing her eyes, she basked in the peace. A gentle call, open arms, the flap of angel wings cooled her in the stifling church.

She breathed deeply, longing to give in to it, longing to let go of her fears, her frustrations—her fight.

No!

Everything inside her screamed in defiance. She would not serve a God who had allowed such suffering in her life.

CHAPTER 15

Dajon had expected Faith to be uncomfortable at church, especially at a church where the powerful Word of God was read out loud, but certainly not as discomfited as she appeared. The poor woman could barely sit still. Her eyes flitted about the church as if she were seeking any possible means of escape. Sigh after sigh poured from her mouth, and tiny groans escaped from deep within her. At one point, she had closed her eyes and seemed to finally settle down, but then she jerked suddenly as if she had been stabbed. Now her breathing sounded like that of a seagull with its beak full of fish.

Rev. Halloway's sermons could certainly be convicting, but Dajon had not anticipated quite so strong a reaction. A breeze wafted in through the open window, teasing him with the scent of lemons. He drew it in like a sweet elixir, the aroma reminding him of Faith's glowing auburn eyes, her rosy plump lips, and the tiny freckles that adorned her nose. With her arm brushing against his, he found it difficult to focus on what the reverend was saying—or on anything else for that matter. Shifting slightly away from her, he tried to shake off the heated daze. Not since Marianne had a woman affected him so ardently. Opening his Bible, he searched through it for words of strength.

Father, please help me. Do not let me fail You again.

After the service, Faith sprang from her seat and snapped her gaze to the back door as if plotting her path to freedom. But before she could make a dash for it, Dajon grabbed her arm.

"Leaving so soon?" he teased. "Come, I would like

you to meet Rev. Halloway."

A look of dread sparked in her eyes as if he had asked her to meet God Himself. "Truly, there is no need." She tugged from his grasp.

"But I insist. He is my dear friend, and I know you will find him most amiable."

Faith looked at him as if he were an annoying bug she longed to squash.

"I would love to meet him," Grace chirped from their right as people began to flow out the front door.

Hope pointed at Sir Wilhelm, still sitting in the pew, his eyes shut, his chin snuggled amid the folds of his waistcoat. Deep breaths fluttered between his lips. She tugged on her sister's sleeve with a giggle. "Should we wake him?"

"Of all the irreverence." Grace shook her head. "Of course, wake him."

"No. Please do not." Faith reached out a hand toward her sisters and shook her head then eyed Dajon with the same warning.

He scratched his chin. "Well, I suppose we could let him sleep a bit longer—while you meet Rev. Halloway, that is."

"Yes, yes, by all means, introduce us to your friend." Pulling her skirts close, Faith inched past the snoring man.

Dajon stifled a chuckle at the lengths she went to, to avoid her intended.

"Rev. Halloway, may I introduce the Westcott ladies, Miss Faith Westcott, Miss Hope Westcott, and Miss Grace Westcott."

The reverend nodded toward all the ladies, but his gaze remained on Faith. He smiled and then cast a sideways glance at Dajon.

Dajon gritted his teeth, hoping Faith had not noticed their exchange, but the moment her narrowed eyes met his, he knew that she had. She faced the reverend. "And how long have you known Mr. Waite, Reverend?"

"Ah, just this past month." He folded his hands over

his prominent belly. "Did you care for the sermon, Miss Westcott?"

"Forgive me, Reverend." Faith shifted her stance and tucked a lock of hair behind her ear. A tiny purple scar marred the golden skin of her neck. In the shape of a half-moon, it curved upward like a smile just below her left ear. Dajon didn't remember seeing it before. An odd scar for a woman.

"But in all honesty," she continued, "I found my mind distracted with other matters."

Although at first taken aback by her forthrightness, Dajon could not help but appreciate her candor. While most people hid the truth behind the excuse of propriety, this lady spoke her mind without fear of consequence. Quite refreshing, indeed.

Dajon watched Rev. Halloway's reaction curiously but was not surprised when he saw naught but humor and love beaming from his friend's gaze.

Grace clicked her tongue and clutched her Bible to her chest. "You are all rudeness, sister." She turned to the reverend. "It was an eloquently spoken word of truth."

He laughed. "Eloquent? I doubt it. But filled with truth—now that I'll agree with."

The reverend tilted his head toward Sir Wilhelm, still asleep in the pew. "Seems your friend shares your view of my sermons, Miss Westcott."

Her mouth quirked in disgust. "I assure you he shares none of my views." She smiled at the reverend.

Faith liked his friend. Dajon found himself oddly pleased at that discovery.

"And you." Rev. Halloway turned toward Hope. "Are you of the same opinion?"

Hope glanced down, obviously unsure how to respond, and a moment of awkward silence settled upon them, conveniently interrupted by the approach of Mr. Mason.

Tanned from many hours working outdoors, Nathaniel tossed his brown hair out of his face and halted next to the reverend, but his gaze drifted over Hope in obvious admiration.

"Ah, Nathaniel." The reverend gripped the young man around the shoulder and shook him good-naturedly as a father would a son. "Ladies, may I introduce my ward, Mr. Nathaniel Mason."

Hope raised her nose. "We have met."

His gleeful expression sobered. "Yes, down at the docks."

"You are building a boat or some such thing." She shrugged and glanced away.

"A merchant brig, miss," Nathaniel corrected, lengthening his stance.

"Nathaniel is skilled at carpentry and shipbuilding," Rev. Halloway said proudly. "He has great plans to own his own merchant fleet someday."

Hope coughed and fingered the lace trim on her sleeves. "Can we go for a stroll in the park now?"

Annoyance flamed within Dajon at the sight of his friend being slighted in such a manner. Truth be told, by the standards of society, Nathaniel was not a man to be noticed. Born to a street harlot who died soon after, he grew up as an orphan on the streets of Charles Towne until Rev. Halloway took him in and raised him as his own son. But the boy—man now, for he was nigh five and twenty—possessed the kind spirit of a parson. Dajon had tried to enlist him as his ship's carpenter, but Nathaniel had plans of his own.

"In a moment, Hope." Faith adjusted her flowered hat, drawing Dajon's attention to the tiny scar on her neck. Most curious. He longed to know the cause of it.

"Shall we go?" She faced him, saw the direction of his gaze, then quickly bowed her head. Tugging on a lock of hair, she pressed it over the scar.

"Holy Chesterfield, is the service over already?" Sir Wilhelm thundered from behind them, staggering to his feet and wiping the drool from his chin.

⌐

A wall of August heat struck Dajon as he escorted the ladies from the church onto Meeting Street.

Sir Wilhelm wiggled his way beside Faith and offered her his arm as he squinted against the bright sun.

She pretended not to notice and instead placed her fingers inside the crook of Dajon's arm. He patted them and glanced down at her, delighting in the way the sunlight sparkled like embers through the curls spiraling from her bonnet. He knew he had only Sir Wilhelm to thank for her attention, but at the moment, he would accept it any way it came.

Dajon drew in a deep breath, hoping to calm his passions, and instantly regretted it. A foul odor hung over the small town. Since most of the settlers were afraid to venture outside the city walls for fear of Indians, garbage and sewage piled up in the streets, not to mention the reek from the many animals that were slaughtered for meat. It reminded Dajon of the smell deep within his ship.

Snapping open his snuffbox, Sir Wilhelm inhaled a pinch of powder into each nostril as if that would mask the stench. "We should return for my carriage. I will not be seen traipsing around town like commoners."

"But we are commoners, Sir Wilhelm." Grace hurried her pace to step beside him, still clutching her Bible to her chest. "All of God's creatures are equal in His sight."

Ignoring her, Sir Wilhelm withdrew a handkerchief and dabbed at the sweat upon his brow.

"Why don't you go back and retrieve your carriage, Sir Wilhelm?" Faith tossed a glance in his direction. "We will wait for you here."

Dajon chuckled, but when Faith squeezed his arm, he quickly disguised it with a cough.

But Sir Wilhelm did not take the bait. Instead, he eased the cravat from his neck and whimpered something about the infernal heat.

Hope blew out a sigh that stirred the golden curls dangling on her forehead. "Can we not go to the park now?"

"That is where we are going, my dear," Faith responded.

As they proceeded past the massive white steeple of St. Philip's, Dajon looked up to see Borland barreling toward him.

The young lieutenant halted and came to attention. "Captain." His gaze scoured over the ladies. "I *thought* I would find you at church."

Dajon flinched. Was that disdain tainting his voice?

"You are needed on the ship at once."

Dajon's first thoughts were of the Red Siren, or perhaps another pirate, Stede Bonnet, one of Blackbeard's associates—a villain Dajon was determined to catch and one he'd heard frequented these waters. "Bonnet?"

"Nay, Captain. Word is he is still holed up in a cove somewhere north of here." Mr. Borland threw back his shoulders and puffed out his chest, no doubt for the ladies' benefit. "And Vane has not been sighted either."

"Oh, pirates, how exciting." Hope flung a hand to her bosom. Borland flashed a smile her way.

Dajon glanced around at his entourage. "Mr. Reginald Borland, may I present Sir Wilhelm Carteret. Mr. Borland is the first lieutenant aboard my ship." He followed with all the introductions, noting the way Borland's gaze lingered far too long upon each lady.

Hope stepped forward and extended her hand, offering the young lieutenant a flirtatious grin.

Sir Wilhelm dabbed the back of his neck and adjusted his white periwig. "Mr. Waite's first lieutenant, eh, Mr. Borland? How do you find the position?"

A church bell tolled in the distance.

Borland shifted his boots on the gravel. "It is good to be led by so great a commander." He flashed a grin.

"But would you not rather be a captain yourself?" Sir Wilhelm asked.

"Someday I shall, I hope." Borland still did not meet Dajon's gaze.

"Mr. Borland is a great seaman." Dajon slapped him on the back. "He has already passed the lieutenant's exam. It is only a matter of time before he is promoted, I am sure."

A carriage approached on their left, spewing up dirt and manure, and Dajon gestured for the ladies to move to the side of the road. The men followed as the *clip-clop* of the horses faded.

"Indeed? You have served in His Majesty's Navy for some time, Mr. Borland?" Sir Wilhelm continued to press poor Borland with his questions, giving Dajon pause. The man was up to something. But what?

"Since I was thirteen, sir. The captain and I joined together." Borland glanced at Dajon, and within his warm smile lay the friend Dajon had come to love as a brother. Fond memories sped through him of those early years when they had both run away to join the navy.

"And you, Mr. Waite?" Sir Wilhelm shifted his beady gaze to Dajon.

"I have served eleven years altogether. I took a leave from service after six years to join my father's merchant business but then returned to the navy five years ago."

"Did you not find the merchant business to your liking, Mr. Waite?" Sir Wilhelm asked.

Dajon gazed at the dirt-encrusted cobblestones and swallowed down a lump of bad memories. "I did not, sir."

"Hmm. A master and commander already, Mr. Waite. Quite impressive, is it not, Mr. Borland?"

Dajon studied his friend, expecting to see his approval, his agreement, anything but the stone-faced expression he wore. He shifted his stance before giving Sir Wilhelm a forced smile. "Quite."

Then, raising his chin, he nodded toward Dajon. "We must go, Captain. An important post from the Admiralty has just arrived."

"Of course." Dajon turned toward the women. "I fear I must leave you ladies in Sir Wilhelm's capable hands." His attempt to conceal a smile faltered, invoking an angry glance from Faith.

"I am sure we can find our way home, Sir Wilhelm." She turned to the man and waved him on in dismissal. "You must have far more pressing matters to attend to."

"Nonsense. I will not stand for it. It would be my utmost delight to escort you home." He proffered his elbow.

"But I thought we were going to the park," Hope

whined, stamping her foot.

"If you will excuse me for a moment." Faith tugged on Dajon's arm, leading him to the side. "You will not leave me alone with this man." She ground out the words as if they sliced her lips.

"Why, Miss Westcott, I had no idea you cared so much for my company." He gave her a mischievous grin, noting the scowl she returned. "But. . ." He cocked his head. "I suggest you get used to Sir Wilhelm, for I fear the fortune you expect to make from your soap business will not be sufficient to care for you and your sisters. I have yet to see you make a single bar."

He winked at her and walked away.

As he made his way down the street with Borland marching at his side, his thoughts shot to the red-haired beauty he had left fuming behind him. Alarm made his skin bristle as another red-haired woman filled his mind. This one no beauty but a vixen, a murderer, a thief—the Red Siren. He must capture this woman pirate, whoever she was, and bring her to justice. But how?

A trap.

Yes, of course. He would spread information throughout town about the location of a treasure ship—a ship whose hull overflowed with jewels, a ship the Red Siren would not be able to resist. Then he would lie in wait and see if she took the bait.

CHAPTER 16

Closing the front door on Sir Wilhelm's appalled, bloated face, Faith blew out a sigh and leaned back against the oak slab.

"I'll be in my chamber," Grace shouted as she bounded up the stairs.

Sweeping the bonnet from her head, Hope giggled. "You shouldn't treat your betrothed with such disregard." A playful gleam danced across her eyes.

"He is not my betrothed, and I simply refuse to spend the day with that imbecile. 'Twas bad enough we were forced to endure his escort home—thanks to Mr. Waite." Insufferable man.

"But a headache? Could you not think of something more believable?"

Faith huffed and rubbed her temples, where a dull burning had formed. "Truth be told, the man does give me a headache." She laughed, and Hope joined her.

"Now we have the rest of the day to spend together." Hope's eyes lit up. "What shall we do?"

Yanking the pins from her hair, Faith ran her fingers through her curls, freeing them from their tight bindings and giving herself a minute to think. After Mr. Waite's skeptical taunt, she knew she had no choice but to devote her afternoon to creating at least the illusion of running a successful soap business. The man was pure exasperation! His suspicions were ruining her plans. But what to do with her sister? "I have just the thing." She forced a smile. "Why don't you help me make soap?"

"Make soap with you?" Hope snapped. "Why would I want to do that? 'Tis smelly and dirty."

"Come now, I assure you it will be enjoyable." Faith slid her arm inside Hope's and smiled. "And you can tell me all about what is going on in your life."

"No." Hope jerked from her grasp and backed away. "You promised to take me for a stroll in the park. You promised we would spend the entire day together, not slave away in some hot, sweaty kitchen."

"I can hardly take you to the park without proper escort. You have Mr. Waite to thank for that." Faith snorted. "And I fully intend to spend the day with you. That is why I am asking for your assistance."

"I should have known." Hope tugged on a lock of her hair and shook her head. "I should have known you would not follow through with your promise. Once again I find you are not to be trusted." She clung to the carved banister in the entrance hall, her chest heaving beneath her violet muslin gown.

Anger stormed through Faith. *Spoiled girl.* "Not to be trusted? How dare you? Why, I am doing this all for you. You and Grace."

"For me, you say?" Hope's laugh took on a caustic tone. She waved a hand back toward the kitchen. "This is not for me nor for Grace. You are doing this for yourself, and you know it. At least be honest about that." She sniffed and raised the back of her hand to her nose.

The words stung Faith in a place so deep within her heart that they left her speechless. She didn't know whether to scream or to cry. Finally, she inched toward Hope, giving her a soft, playful look. "We will have fun, I promise."

Hope's sapphire eyes glossed over with tears. "You are doing this for yourself, and you know it," she repeated, her accusing words echoing in Faith's ears like one of Morgan's shrill parodies.

Faith longed to tell Hope that she would love nothing more than to spend a day in town strolling through the park, enjoying her sister's company as if they were a pair of giddy schoolgirls. She wanted to tell her that her ruse of soap making was merely a cover for the real fortune Faith was acquiring on Hope's behalf.

But she didn't. All she said instead was, " 'Tis your choice. I must make soap. If you choose to join me, I would be most pleased. If not, you can hardly blame me for not spending time with you."

Daggers of fury shot from Hope's eyes as she spun on her heel and ran upstairs. The slamming of her chamber door boomed across the house like an ominous gong. Why did it seem that the harder Faith tried to help her sisters, the greater a mess she made of everything?

❧

Sir Wilhelm Carteret crept into the corruption of his mother's sickroom. Though Miss Westcott had played the timid devotee today, he sensed a true regard, perhaps even affection, growing within her toward him. A pure lady, one inexperienced in the world, would certainly be somewhat frightened at the prospect of marriage—and in particular, the marriage bed. He grinned. That would explain her hesitant and even diffident behavior toward him, to be sure. He squeezed his nose against the miasma of stale breath, sweat, and disease that had taken residence within and now assailed him. A sickly moan reached his ears, and he swerved on his heels, suddenly re-thinking his visit. But he must procure his mother's approval of the match before he pursued Miss Westcott further. And he knew that wouldn't be an easy task.

"Willy, is that you?" The cracked voice split the thick air in the room.

"Yes, Mother, 'tis I." Sir Wilhelm tensed and trudged toward the oak bed at the center of the dismal chamber.

"What are you doing sneaking around in the dark? Light a lamp and come forward." She hacked a moist cough before continuing. "So much like your father. He always was a rat who preferred the darkness."

Retrieving a lamp from the walnut desk, Sir Wilhelm thrust a stick of pinewood into the glowing embers in the fireplace and lit the wick. The fire, which his mother insisted be kept burning day and night despite the weather outside, kept the master chamber both stifling and filled with smoke. Sir Wilhelm strained for a breath of fresh air as he approached the bed, the lantern casting an eerie glow over the walnut desk and chairs that guarded the base of the window and a vanity squeezed into the right corner. Wilhelm rounded a velvet divan and tripped over a pewter basin that protruded from beneath the bed. It was well past emptying, and vile contents of the chamber pot sloshed over his left ankle. Beside it, a bitter vapor wafted from a glazed apothecary bowl full of the physician's latest mixture of herbs intended to cure his mother. A thin sheet of sunlight sliced through an opening in the heavy curtains and landed on the spilled contents of the chamber pot.

Setting the lantern on the bed stand, he sniffed and peered down at the swollen, pasty pallor of his mother's face. She had once been quite comely, but age and sickness, in addition to her constant disagreeable spirit, had sapped her beauty long ago. Dark, hollow eyes shot to his, ever spewing their venom wherever they landed.

On second thought, perhaps she had never been beautiful.

"What have you been about, Willy? I trust you have been down to the House of Assembly as I instructed. You need to ensure the proprietor's voice among these barbaric settlers." She struggled to sit, flinging out a shaky hand for his assistance. "There are rumblings of dissent—especially among those who call themselves the Goose Creek men. They want Carolina to become a British colony. Can you imagine? Then where would we be?"

Wilhelm reached behind his mother and assisted her into a sitting position, holding his breath against the stench of death that clung to her these past several years. "We would still have our landholdings, Mother."

Lady Eleanor Carteret, daughter of the Earl of Devenish, married to the son of Sir George Carteret, one of the original proprietors of the realm of Carolina, squared her shoulders and lifted her regal chin in the air as if her bed were the throne of England. But her breath came in short gasps, and she collapsed on the pillow behind her, breaking the facade of superiority that had more times than not sparked fear in all those around her.

"Land without power is meaningless. There is plenty of land in this new world for everyone." She pointed a crooked finger at him. "Power is what will secure our interest and our future."

Wilhelm turned his head and sneezed, his nose burning in the infested room.

She gestured to a mug on the bed stand. "Hand me my elixir, and tell me your news of Parliament."

Wilhelm grabbed the mug, took a whiff, and nearly gagged at the pungent odor, then placed it in his mother's trembling hands. He held his nose. "What is that putrid stench?" He plucked his snuffbox from his pocket.

" 'Tis the medicines Dr. Kingston has prescribed for me. With these and the weekly bleedings, he guarantees my full recovery." She took a sip, sending the loose skin of her face folding in on itself.

"He will guarantee anything as long as you pay him." Wilhelm sniffed a speck of powder then slumped his shoulders, allowing the calm sensation to filter through him.

"Enough of that. Tell me what is happening in the council."

"I did not attend today. I had some business at Admiral Westcott's home."

"Pray tell, what business? Unless you have overcome your seasickness and plan on following in your grandfather's grand footsteps." She scrutinized him. "Not that you could. I fear you are not made of the same stout material."

"Admiral Westcott has been called to Italy, and. . ." Wilhelm ran a hand under his nose.

"Quit sniffing and be out with it!"

He straightened his back. "He has promised me his daughter Faith's hand in marriage when he returns."

"As wife? Finally. I thought you would never draw the eye of a decent lady. Now perchance I will see grandchildren before I die."

Wilhelm fidgeted with a wrinkle in the sheets by his knee.

"Although an admiral's daughter is certainly beneath your station, I suppose a man like you cannot be too particular." His mother pushed a spike of her wiry gray hair behind her.

Wilhelm shifted the muscles in his back beneath his mother's insults. He should be used to them by now, but for some reason, her words always hit their mark. "Regardless of her lineage, I assure you, she is a fine match. Beautiful, intelligent, strong. You would like her."

"Perhaps." Closing her eyes, she leaned back onto the mound of pillows. "But it would have been nice to see you joined with a lady of your own class. Especially after all I have done for you. Ensuring your place in Parliament and among the lord proprietors instead of your Uncle Phillip. Do you realize the risks I took? The powerful people I crossed?" She coughed and held her chest as if she were taking her last breath. "Without me you would be nothing but a sniveling incompetent. You know everything I have done—everything I ever do—is for you." A tear escaped her eye and weaved a crooked trail around line and wrinkle.

"I know, Mother, and I am eternally grateful. I owe you everything." Without her strength, her brains, her devious plots, his uncle Phillip would have taken over as head of the Carteret family.

Yet he tired of the invisible chain that held him locked to her, as if the umbilical cord had never been severed. It sickened him as much as empowered him.

Lady Eleanor huffed. "Nevertheless, I will be pleased to see you married." She looked away. "But you must promise to attend Parliament and follow my instructions to the mark. The future of this family depends on you."

Wilhelm squeezed his mother's hand. "I will, Mother; I promise." Yet no sooner did his hopes rise upon the wind than thoughts of Captain Waite shot them down.

"Now what ails you, Willy?"

"I fear there is another suitor who might divert Miss Westcott's affections from me."

"How could any woman choose another over you?"

Wilhelm had wondered the same thing himself, but after the past few encounters with Captain Waite and Miss Westcott, it seemed obvious the girl was far too innocent to understand the crafty manipulation and venomous charm of the commander.

"I daresay, then." His mother gave a haughty snort. "She is not as wise as you make her out to be. Dismissing your affections. Upon my word, 'tis unheard of. Who is this suitor?"

"A commander in the Royal Navy, a callow, ignoble fellow."

"A lowly commander? What do you expect from an admiral's daughter? She is not worthy of you." She waved her bony hand through the air. "Let her go."

"I cannot, Mother. I must have her. I have never wanted anything so badly."

True to form, his mother took his hand in hers. "There, there, Willy. There, there. You shall have her, then. No woman dares to shun my dear Willy."

"What am I to do, Mother?" Having accomplished his goal, Wilhelm pushed back from her aged, decaying body. "I cannot force her affections."

"Perhaps not, but you can rid yourself of the competition."

Wilhelm was pleased to see that his mother's desires ran along the same twisted lines as his own. "But how?"

"We must eliminate him by cunning. Dig up his skeletons. Everyone has something reprehensible in his past. Find his and expose it for all to see."

She gripped his hand, her fingers like icy claws. "Ruin the man. Destroy his career." Her eyes narrowed into the cold slits of a hawk hunting its prey. "Do whatever you have to in order to get what you want."

CHAPTER 17

Running her sleeve across her moist brow, Faith stirred the thick cauldron of lye and pork fat boiling in a large kettle atop the fire. She'd had no idea making soap could be so difficult and tedious. A sweltering August wind steamed in through the open door and, joining with the heat from the fire, transformed the kitchen into a giant furnace. She felt like a Sunday goose being roasted alive. As she continued to stir the bubbling fat, the muscles in her arms burned with a searing pain that matched the growing agony in her heart over the argument she'd had with Hope earlier that day.

But now as Faith laid down the greasy ladle and patted her neck with the hem of the stained apron hanging at her waist, she found the task anything but enjoyable, and she supposed she couldn't blame Hope for not wanting to partake of this noxious mess.

She lifted a strand of her curly hair to her nose and cringed. The stench of lard saturated her. Grabbing a ribbon from the table, she tied up her thick tresses and took a step outside for some fresh air.

Shielding her eyes from the bright sun sinking behind the oak trees that lined the fence, Faith watched Lucas brush down a horse across the way in the barn. When he glanced her way, she smiled, and he returned the gesture.

Closing her eyes for a moment, she allowed the slight breeze to cool the fiery skin of her neck and face before she returned to the kitchen.

Staring at the gurgling brew, Faith hoped she had put in the right amount of lye, or the soap would not harden correctly. From what she had learned from the ladies in town, soapmaking was an exact science and took years to perfect, and from the looks of things, it would indeed take her that long before she could produce one decent batch of soap. All her prior attempts had ended in a foul-smelling puddle of slop, not fit to wash the cutlery with, let alone a person. Last month she'd been forced to send Lucas on a two-day journey to Beaufort to buy soap from one of the soap makers in town so she could sell it here in Charles Towne as her own. But she could not afford to be without Lucas for that long again, not when she was so close to acquiring the fortune she needed. Oh, why had she not chosen some other craft like perfume making or quilting?

A deep chuckle sounded from the door. "So ye truly is tryin' yer hand at soap, mistress?"

Faith flung a flustered look over her shoulder at Lucas, whose large frame shadowed the doorway. "The ever-suspicious Mr. Waite dropped his glove of challenge upon me today. I had no choice but to accept."

"He did, did he?" Another hearty chuckle bubbled through the room like the aroma of her fatty stew.

"You find that amusing?"

"Aye, to see the"—he glanced both ways behind him—"notorious pirate captain the Red Siren covered wit' grease and smellin' like a rancid pig, all due to a simple comment from Mr. Waite. Aye, I do find it amusin', the power he holds over ye."

Faith spun around. "He holds no power over me." She tossed the ladle onto the table. Brown sticky globs splattered across the surface. Faith wiped the sweat from the back of her neck. "Other than the noose, I suppose." She gave Lucas a sassy look. "And it will be your neck, too, if we are caught. Perchance then you might not find it so amusing?"

The grin on Lucas's mouth did not falter.

Faith blew out a sigh, relieving her tension. "How else do you expect me to prove to the man where my fortune comes from when it suddenly appears?"

He shrugged. "Seems to me such a man would never buy such a ludicrous tale anyway."

Faith sank into a chair with a huff. "I fear you are correct. But I must at least make a pretense of producing some soap, whether he buys the tale or not."

She batted at a pesky fly that must have found her new scent alluring. "But how else to convince him?"

"All he be knowin', mistress, is that the Red Siren be a lady with red hair." He cocked his head. "That don't prove nothin'."

"Good heavens, that is it." Faith shot to her feet. "I know exactly how to divert any suspicions he may have of my even remotely being the Red Siren."

Lucas's brow furrowed.

Outside the window, Molly strode by the kitchen, hoisting a basket of vegetables atop her head. Following Faith's gaze, Lucas watched her over his shoulder until she disappeared into the house.

Faith cocked her head and grinned. "No doubt, she'll be coming here soon to cook supper."

"I knows."

"Why don't you stay and talk to her, Lucas?"

"She don't want to be talkin' none to me, mistress." Disappointment tugged the corners of his mouth downward.

"I would not be so sure." Faith grabbed the ladle and shuffled back to the boiling pot.

"Oh, saints preserve us. Whatever is that smell?" Molly's voice sliced through the steamy room, and Faith turned to see the tiny cook push past Lucas and explode into the room like a firecracker.

Faith shook her head. How could so much energy be contained in such a small package? "I am making soap, if you must know."

"Not in my kitchen, you're not." Molly set her basket down on the table and threw a hand to her nose.

"Where else do you suggest?"

Lucas stood just inside the door, his gaze taking in Molly as if she were the queen of some exotic land.

Following Faith's glance, Molly turned to the large groomsman. "What you grinnin' at, you oversize fool?"

"I's grinnin' at you, Miss Molly." Lucas crossed his arms over his chest.

Molly's tongue went uncharacteristically still as if the heat in the room had melted it. She stared at Lucas dumbfounded, the attraction between them like a grappling hook pulling one ship to another and neither able to prevent it. "Well, stop it before I wipe that smile off yer face," Molly shot back.

"Good day to ye, then, Miss Molly." Lucas nodded and headed out the door.

"Good day, Mr. Corwin."

Faith gave Molly a crafty look.

"Now don't you be grinnin' at me, neither." Molly began unloading her vegetables onto the table. Ripe tomatoes, green beans, okra, carrots, and summer squash.

Faith's mouth watered at the sight. She had not eaten since breakfast that morning. Resuming her stirring, she wondered why the expected froth had not appeared in her mixture. Flies began to swarm around it as if it were naught but bubbling horse manure. It certainly smelled as if it was. "My soap is nearly done boiling, Molly. Then I shall pour it into the frames and be out of your way."

"I dunno who you trying to fool, Miss Faith, but you ain't made a bar of soap in your life."

"Perhaps, but there is a first time for everything." Faith smiled, remembering the complete look of adoration on Lucas's face when he had looked at Molly. Swinging around, Faith laid down her ladle and wiped the sweat from her brow with her apron. A first time for soapmaking and a first time for love. "I do not know if I should speak of this or not."

"Then don't." Molly directed a stern glance her way. "I ain't in for no gossip."

"It isn't gossip." Lucas would certainly be furious, but she hated to see these two precious friends of hers lose out on something wonderful—something meant to be—due to pure stubbornness. She might as well just blurt it out. "Lucas is sweet on you."

Silence, save for the crackle of the fire and the hum of insects, settled over the room.

Molly did not look up, but a slight quiver in her bottom lip gave her away.

"Mr. Corwin? Hogwash. I won't be hearin' talk like that."

"Come now, surely you have noticed the way he looks at you."

"He looks the same way at the horses." Molly laughed.

Faith threw a hand to her hip. "He is handsome, strong, healthy, and a good worker, Miss Molly. He would make a fine husband."

"Husband?" Molly flinched, and the whites of her eyes widened against the encroaching darkness. "By all that is holy, what d'you think yer doing—matchmaking? You who swears never to marry unless you're forced to. I declare, I never thought I'd see the day."

"I just think you two would make a good match, 'tis all."

Molly's expression sobered. She set down the squash and eased into a chair. "I tells you, Miss Faith. I seen a lot of pain in my life. And it all comes from caring 'bout people."

Faith took a chair beside the cook and gave her an understanding nod. After all, hadn't all of Faith's pain come from things that had happened to those she loved? But it suddenly occurred to her that she really knew nothing about this woman whom she had grown to care for these past months.

"Molly, tell me about your past." Though her voice was soft and pleading, Faith worried her words came out more as an order than a request.

Flinching, Molly straightened her back then gazed at the floor.

As a servant would beneath a harsh command.

A servant, not a slave, for the admiral paid her well for her position. But Faith considered Miss Molly more a friend than a servant. Did Molly know that? Or did the shackles of slavery bind her heart from ever giving itself freely to anyone in authority over her? "You may tell me only if you wish." Faith laid her hand over Molly's. "We are friends."

Molly raised her gaze and smiled. "I was torn from my ma and pa when I was jest ten, Miss Faith." Her smile faded. "Sold as a slave to a landowner in Barbados. A kind family. But by the time I was sixteen, the mistress o' the house got it in her head to be jealous o' the way her husband was lookin' at me. So they sold me."

"How awful." Faith swallowed. The idea of slavery repulsed her. She could not imagine anyone finding it acceptable, let alone civilized. Yet how different was slavery from what had happened to her older sister, Charity?

"Sold me to a vicious sugarcane farmer on Jamaica, a spiteful man, miss," Molly continued. "He did things to me I'd rather not say."

Faith grasped both of Molly's hands and squeezed them. "The only way I survived was by makin' friends wit' the other slaves. They became like family to me." Molly raised her moist gaze to Faith. "But then one day, I watched my owner beat my dearest friend to death for stealin' a banana from a tree. So's I ran away. Left the only people I loved, once again." She shuddered beneath a quiet sob. "That's when I met up with the Franklins. They brought me here to the colonies and taught me to cook. But more important, they taught me 'bout the Lord. That's when I gave my life to Jesus. 'Tain't been the same since." Her sudden grin quickly faded. "But o' course, they both got killed in the Indian wars."

Faith closed her eyes against the burning behind them and swallowed. How could this slight woman have endured so much agony in one life? And yet, oddly, she still clung to a faith that spoke of the goodness of God. Perhaps it was all she had left to cling to—this hope of a caring God, a hope that would surely shrivel beneath the next disaster.

"You see, Miss Faith, everyone I've ever loved been taken from me. I can't stand the pain no more. The only One who will never leave me is Jesus, but I ain't attaching meself to no one else—no man 'specially."

Faith could understand Molly's fear of getting close to Lucas, but she knew her first mate. He would never hurt Molly, would never betray her. Faith forced down an unseemly chuckle at how absurd, though true, her approbation was of a man who was a good groomsman but a better pirate.

"Molly, I am so sorry." She gave the cook's hand a squeeze. "I had no idea you had suffered so much."

"Not yer fault, miss." Her dark cheeks flushing, Molly withdrew her hand and stood. She stomped across the room, grabbed a knife from a counter, and began chopping the heads off carrots as if they represented her ex-owners.

Faith laid a gentle hand on her arm, stopping her. "But I beg you, do not deny yourself love and happiness out of a fear born from other people's cruelty."

A skeptical look crossed Molly's face, but she said nothing.

"Should you not be trusting God?" Faith asked with all sincerity then suddenly cringed. Where had that come from? God had certainly not proven Himself trustworthy in her own life and especially not in Molly's.

Molly laughed then, a warm, hearty chuckle that filled the room. "Well, mercy me, do you hear yerself, Miss Faith? 'Tain't no hope for that batch of soap, but there may be hope for you, after all."

Holding a lantern, Faith knelt in the kitchen by her soap crates to investigate the vile brew's progress. It was well past midnight, and she couldn't sleep. Perhaps it was because of the unusually strained atmosphere at supper that night that stretched across the dining room like a rigid spar. With both her sisters angry at her, Faith had done her best to ease tensions with light chatter and whimsical jests, but to no avail.

Perhaps it was her fear of the noose, brought on by the captain's suspicion of her piracy. Or perhaps it was that she was beginning to realize, as she examined the molten slop in the crates, that she had no idea how to make soap.

"Confound it all, what is that smell?" Mr. Waite's deep voice startled Faith. Springing up, she faced him, one hand subconsciously reaching for her cutlass, which, of course, was not there. Instead, she flung the hand to her breast.

"My apologies, Miss Westcott, I saw the light and wondered who might still be awake at this hour." He bowed and sauntered into the room, looking ever so dashing in his blue uniform.

" 'Tis twice now I have caught you wandering about in the kitchen at night."

"I could say the same of you, Miss Westcott." He raised his nose and took a whiff, his forehead wrinkling. "But the last time we met here, the aroma in the room was much more pleasant. Methinks I should be relieved that I missed whatever was served for supper."

" 'Tis not supper you smell, Mr. Waite, but the batch of soap I made today." Pride lifted her voice, false as it was.

"Indeed?" He approached, the hint of a smirk curving his lips.

Stepping aside, she gestured toward the wooden crates filled with her greasy concoction and prayed Mr. Waite knew no more about soap than she did.

He leaned over them but quickly shrank back as if someone had punched him. "I do hope you intend to add scented oil, Miss Westcott, or I fear you've created the cure for overpopulation."

"How dare you?" Faith stormed. "I have already scented them. What you smell is all part of the curing process." She had no idea why they continued to emit such a foul odor.

His boots scuffed over the floor behind her. Warm

breath heated her cheek, and she winced at her own stench. She had soaked in a hot bath for hours—Molly had insisted on providing oceans of hot fresh water in hopes of removing the smell—and scrubbed her skin and hair until they were squeaky, but for some reason, the abhorrent odor still clung to her.

But why did she care what Mr. Waite thought?

"New perfume, Miss Westcott? I believe I may not succumb so easily to your charms tonight." He took another whiff and then withdrew slightly.

Faith spun around. "Believe me, Mr. Waite, when I tell you that I have since regretted that moment of insanity last evening when we nearly. . .we nearly. . ."

He grinned. "Then you have nothing to fear from me."

Faith studied his eyes, those crisp ocean blue eyes that seemed to hold as many secrets as the depths of the sea.

Does he know? Is he toying with me?

He hid his feelings well behind a wall of sarcasm and wit. Her gaze drifted down to the strong lines of his jaw shadowed with a hint of evening stubble. One lock of hair hung over his left ear, and she wondered if under his facade of obedience and dutifulness there didn't exist a streak of rebellion just like this one mutinous strand.

Her heart took on a rapid pace as he returned her stare with equal intensity. Yes, there was more to this man than he revealed. Something untamed, something dangerous lurked behind his eyes—eyes that were now fixated upon her lips. He swallowed—the long, hard swallow of a man dying of thirst.

Truth be told, Faith's throat had gone dry as well. A flush of heat blasted over her, though the coals in the fire were naught but embers now. What was wrong with her?

Nevertheless, she would not back down from this man, whatever game he was playing.

He cocked his head slightly and grinned—not his usual sardonic playful grin, but a warm, tender one. Then, reaching up, he caressed her cheek with his thumb and cupped his hand around her jaw.

Faith closed her eyes beneath the heady sensations that swirled through her.

When she opened them, his lips hovered over hers.

"I thought I had naught to fear from you," she whispered.

"I thought you had forsaken your insanity."

He drew closer, and Faith found herself suddenly wishing he would either arrest her or kiss her. Either way, this madness would end.

"Miss Faith! Miss Faith!" Edwin's shaky voice snapped her back to reality. She jerked away from Mr. Waite.

Edwin barreled into the kitchen, his belly quivering.

"What is it, Edwin? Whatever is the matter?" She darted to him, alarm spiking through her.

" 'Tis Miss Hope," Edwin managed between gasps.

"Hope?" Faith had checked on her not three hours past, and she had been fast asleep. "Is she sick?"

"A man came to the door." Edwin's gaze flitted between Faith and Mr. Waite.

"What man? What of Hope?" Faith grabbed his shoulders and shook him.

"A friend, a footman from the Brewton home." Edwin plopped into a chair.

Mr. Waite came alongside Faith. "What did he say, man? Spit it out."

"Miss Hope is in trouble."

Faith could make no sense of his jabbering. "In her chamber?"

"Nay, miss." Edwin glanced up at her, a look of hopelessness tugging at his eyes. "Downtown at the Pink House Tavern."

CHAPTER 18

Pressing his handkerchief to his nose, Sir Wilhelm strutted into the dark, sooty room of the tavern. A stout man with greasy hair coiling around his shoulders bumped into him, his tankard of ale sloshing over the sides. "Look out where yer goin'," he slurred.

Sir Wilhelm pushed the man aside and wiped his handkerchief over his velvet waistcoat where the lout had touched him. "How dare you, you vile sot. Don't you know who I am?" Sir Wilhelm offered the man a vision of his profile as he adjusted his periwig, but the sailor simply gave a derisive snort and went his way.

Of all the. . . Sir Wilhelm huffed. This was precisely the reason he never graced these filthy havens with his genteel presence. His mother had been right. Commoners never appreciated the immense responsibility of those in authority nor that the freedoms they enjoyed were only by the sacrifice and grace of their lords. How could they, with such miniscule, narrow brains?

Sir Wilhelm sniffed, his nose burning against the rancid alcohol and body odor that seeped through the air like a fetid fog. As he peered across the shadowy room, littered with indescribable rabble, bloodshot eyes gave him cursory glances before returning to their ale. Why, dressed as he was in black velvet breeches fringed in gold, white satin shirt, and fur-trimmed waistcoat, surely even these miscreants recognized nobility. At least the proprietor of this devil's haven should greet him and lead him to the best seat in the house—he glanced over the crumb-encrusted, liquor-saturated, marred tables and scrunched his nose—if there were such a seat.

He tossed his nose in the air. The devil take them all. Could they not tell he had money to spend—more money than the whole lot of them put together? Hesitating, he longed to turn on his leather heels and storm out. That would show them. But he had heard that Mr. Waite's first lieutenant, Mr. Borland, frequented this vulgar alehouse, and he must speak to him. If Sir Wilhelm's intuition was correct—as it usually was—he might find an ally in Borland.

Sir Wilhelm took another step, holding one hand aloft, and scanned the filthy faces. He had hoped to arrive sooner, before the entire building crawled with vermin, but he had crossed paths with Miss Hope and that pretentious peacock Lord Falkland. Why Mr. Waite allowed the young girl to roam the streets at night with such objectionable company, Sir Wilhelm could not understand. From the looks of her, she had already imbibed too much alcohol. He supposed he should have stepped in and escorted her home, but alas, the admiral had not chosen him as guardian. Instead, he had chosen that nincompoop Waite, and the admiral would have to pay the price for his stupidity.

In the far corner, a blur of blue navy coats crossed Sir Wilhelm's vision. Starting toward them, he wove among the tables, careful not to touch anything—or anyone—but angry voices slithered out like snakes nonetheless, sinking their insulting fangs into his conscience.

"Look, gents, if it ain't our proprietor. Have ye come down from yer castle to the mire to visit the peasants?" one man trumpeted.

"Where were ye when we needed ye?" another man taunted. "When the Yamasee attacked and stole all our food?"

"Ain't you supposed to be protectin' us and not stealin' our money and land?" a doxy spat at him, the mounds of her breasts quivering above her tight-fitting bodice.

Ignoring the taunts, Sir Wilhelm kept his eyes straight ahead, his gaze above the squabbling riffraff.

He and the other proprietors had done all they could to protect the settlers against the massive Indian attack. But what were they supposed to do in face of such a savage enemy? Unappreciative louts!

Mr. Borland turned as Sir Wilhelm approached the table. Setting his mug down, the young officer rose and brushed the crumbs from his coat. "Sir Wilhelm, how good to see you." Lines formed between his narrowed eyes. No doubt he was surprised to see Sir Wilhelm in such a debased place.

Sir Wilhelm nodded in greeting as relief lifted his shoulders. Finally, someone who offered him the respect he deserved.

"Sir Wilhelm Carteret." Mr. Borland gestured toward his friends, who had also stood. "May I present Mr. Copeland and Mr. Willis."

"Sir Wilhelm is a descendant of one of the original proprietors of Carolina," Borland added.

The men bowed. "A pleasure, sir," Mr. Copeland said.

Sir Wilhelm nodded in agreement then faced Mr. Borland. "May I speak with you alone? 'Tis a matter of grave importance."

"Of course." He turned toward his friends, raised his brows, and jerked his head to the right.

Frowning, they grabbed their mugs, nodded toward Sir Wilhelm, and shuffled away.

"Won't you have a seat, Sir Wilhelm?" Mr. Borland gestured toward a chair beside his and then snapped his fingers at a barmaid across the room. "A drink, perhaps?"

"Thank you." Sir Wilhelm flapped his handkerchief across the chair, scattering the noxious crumbs. But upon further inspection of the seat, laden with globs of unidentifiable origin, he spread out the cloth and sat upon it. "It is I who shall buy you a drink, Mr. Borland, if you'll allow me." He eyed the near-empty mug of ale in front of the man. "Perhaps some rum?"

Borland's grin told him the lieutenant enjoyed his liquor. Perfect. A couple of glasses of rum, and Sir

Wilhelm would have the man agreeing to anything.

The barmaid arrived with one hand on her bounteous hip and a look of boredom that her painted lips failed to disguise. Sir Wilhelm plucked a shilling from his pouch and dropped it into her sweaty hand. "Bottle of rum, if you please, and keep the change." The shiny gold lit a greedy fire in her blue eyes. Like flies to the light, these rustics could be controlled with a simple coin. Sir Wilhelm shook his head as she scampered away.

"Begging your pardon, sir, but what brings you here?" Mr. Borland sat back in his chair and folded his hands over his stomach, drumming one set of fingers over the other.

Sir Wilhelm noted the glaze covering Mr. Borland's eyes and gave him his most congenial smile. "I believe we have a common interest."

Borland cocked his head and narrowed his gaze. "I cannot imagine what that could be."

The barmaid returned with an open bottle of rum and two glasses, and Sir Wilhelm quickly poured some into Borland's glass and slid it over to him.

"It concerns your commander, Mr. Waite." Sir Wilhelm wrinkled his nose against a new foul odor wafting his way as he tipped the bottle to his own glass.

"Ah. . .yes. The great Mr. Waite." Borland gave a sardonic chortle and reached for his rum. "What do you wish to do, give him another medal, have a parade in his honor, or perhaps appoint him to Parliament?" He took a swig.

Sir Wilhelm grinned. Just as he had suspected. "Have another drink." He poured another shot into Borland's cup.

Borland grabbed it, tossed it to the back of his throat, then set the glass down. "I don't mean any disrespect, sir, 'tis just that Dajon—I mean Mr. Waite and I do not always agree on things." He twisted his thick sandy mustache between two fingers and stared at his empty glass.

The sounds of the tavern surged around Sir Wilhelm like a hundred ignorant voices pounding in his head. He rubbed his temples. How did people relax in such a place? Even before the thought left him, the crash of a table, the blast of insults, and the smack of fist to face sounded from the front door as a fight broke out. Borland peered through the haze toward the commotion.

"Mr. Waite has cheated you out of promotions that should have been yours, has he not?" Sir Wilhelm drew Borland's attention back to him.

Borland snapped his gaze back, grabbed the bottle, and poured himself some rum. He shrugged.

"No need to reply. I have keen eyes for this sort of thing." Sir Wilhelm plucked out his snuffbox. "And I can also tell a man of worth when I see one. A man with the wits and courage to command." Taking a pinch of the black powder, he sniffed some up each nostril then snorted against the burn. "And a man who is none of those things."

Borland's dark gaze wandered over Sir Wilhelm like a bird in flight trying to find a place to land. His lips wrinkled in a half smile.

Sir Wilhelm sighed. "You, sir, are the one who should be in command of the HMS *Enforcer*, not that ninny Waite." Withdrawing another handkerchief from his waistcoat, he wiped the rim of his glass—only God knew if they ever washed these things—and took a sip. The liquor sped a burning trail down his throat, instantly warming his belly. "Let me guess. He is the type of man who sidles up to the Admiralty like a trollop to a plush merchant—just as he did with Admiral Westcott."

Borland swayed and raised his glass. "But what is it to you, if I may ask?" His wavering cup finally found his mouth, and he took a sip.

A string of foul curses muddied the air behind Sir Wilhelm, and he cringed. The sooner he could leave this place, the better. " 'Tis only that I am a man of justice, as well as a proprietor who wishes our city to be protected by the best man possible. Truth be told, I would sleep far better knowing you were in charge."

Borland leaned his elbows on the table. "Well, what's to be done about it?" he slurred, shrugging again.

"Come now, Borland. You must think like a leader, like a commander." Sir Wilhelm slapped him on the back, nearly toppling him. "Pray tell, how do you confront an obstacle, Mr. Borland?"

"I remove it."

"Precisely!"

Mr. Borland labored to his feet, wobbled, then clung to the edge of the table and thrust his face at Sir Wilhelm. "What are you suggesting, sir? I will do no harm to Dajon. I have called him friend for far too long."

"Harm? Nay, of course not." Sir Wilhelm scrunched his face into what he hoped was a look of complete abhorrence. "Sit down, Borland, if you please." He stood and eased the man down into his chair then wiped his hands with his handkerchief.

Sir Wilhelm reluctantly took his seat again. "All I am suggesting is that we *persuade* Mr. Waite to break some naval code or rule—something that will do him no more harm than to get him dismissed."

Mr. Borland threw his head back and let out a loud chortle that drew the gaze of the crowd around them. Placing his elbows on the table, he leaned toward Sir Wilhelm. "You do not know Mr. Waite, sir. He would never break a rule."

Disgust soured in Wilhelm's mouth. "Egad, he's not God, Borland. Perhaps that is why you cannot defeat him. You think he is some divine being. But I assure you, he is human like you and me."

Hot air blasted in from the open window. The light from the flame flickered across Borland's inebriated expression, twisting his features into a tortured snarl. Sir Wilhelm snorted. How did these navy officers manage themselves in battle?

"He has weaknesses, has he not?" Sir Wilhelm held two fingers to his nose.

From the other side of the room, the eerie sound of

an aged fiddle screeched a ribald tune that grated over Sir Wilhelm like the talons of a huge bird. *What is his weakness, lad? Tell me before I go mad in this place.*

Swirling his glass, Borland stared inquisitively into the rum as if it contained the answer to the question.

"Aye." He finally nodded and lifted his gaze, a hazy gleam in his eye. "He has a weakness for the ladies, I am told. Some tragedy from his past involving a woman."

A slow grin spread over Sir Wilhelm's lips. Since Mr. Waite had only recently arrived from England and no one knew of him here in the colonies, Sir Wilhelm had dispatched one of his men overseas to gather what information he could on the good Mr. Waite's past. From the sounds of it, he would not be disappointed with the results. Power surged through him, strengthening him. Things were going better than expected. He leaned toward Mr. Borland. "Pray tell, what is the consequence for an officer in His Majesty's Navy for, say. . .ravishing a woman?"

Borland shrugged. "Depends on the woman, I suppose. If she were a lady, possibly death. If she were a trollop, most likely no charges would be leveled. But if she were a decent woman, an officer could be cashiered."

"Cashiered?"

"Dismissed in disgrace."

"Perfect." Sir Wilhelm adjusted his periwig and leaned back in his chair. Borland belched and shook his head. "Again, sir, you deceive yourself. Mr. Waite would never commit such an act." He slumped in his chair.

Sir Wilhelm gritted his teeth. How long must he spoon-feed this buffoon? "Do you want command of the ship, or do you not, Mr. Borland?"

"Even with him gone, there is no assurance I will be made commander." Borland drummed his fingers over the ale-sodden table.

Sir Wilhelm raised one eyebrow, feigning patience. "You forget to whom you speak, my dear sir. My grandfather was the comptroller of the navy. My family still has the ear of the Admiralty."

Mr. Borland raised his shoulders. His glassy eyes locked on Sir Wilhelm's. "But why would you do this for me?"

"As I said, I would sleep much better with you patrolling the coast."

Borland nodded, his expression lifted with hope, but then his smile suddenly sank. "Still, we must get him to do the deed, and I assure you, he will not."

Sir Wilhelm huffed. "I can assure you, it matters not what Mr. Waite does or does not do."

Borland's inquisitive gaze met his. A slick smile alighted upon his lips and spread until it seemed to take over his face.

After glancing around them, Sir Wilhelm laid his handkerchief on the table, placed his arm over it, and leaned toward Borland. "Now this is what we shall do."

CHAPTER 19

"Confound it all." Dajon stormed from the kitchen out into the yard still shrouded in darkness. The scent of rain stung his nose, soon stolen by the smell of horses and sweet hay emanating from the stables. Thunder rumbled, sending energy crackling through the air like a cannon about to fire.

Faith's footsteps pounded after him. "The Pink House? Do you know the place?"

Yes, he knew the place, but he had no intention of informing her that it was the most nefarious tavern in town.

Turning to her, he gripped her shoulders and gave her his most confident look. "Never fear. I'll wake Lucas and take him with me. I assure you, I will bring your sister home safely."

"What sort of place is it?" A mixture of fear and anger raged in her eyes, and he longed to ease her pain, to replace it with the joy and admiration he'd seen in her gaze just minutes ago.

"Please do not worry, Miss Westcott." Releasing her, Dajon headed toward the servants' quarters above the kitchen.

"Mr. Waite, I demand you answer me." She marched after him.

Dajon halted and faced her. "It is no place for a lady. That is all I will tell you." A look of frantic despair marred her comely features, softening Dajon's harsh manner. He eased a lock of hair from her face then shook off her bewitching spell and swerved back around. "Go in the house. I will handle this."

"I will do no such thing!"

"I do not have time for your insolence." He entered the small brick house and took the stairs two at a time, praying she would listen to him but all the while knowing she would not.

Minutes later when he dashed into the stables, a sleepy Lucas on his heels, he found a lantern hanging from a hook on the wall and Faith saddling the second of two horses.

"I thank you for your assistance, Miss Westcott, but now I must insist you go into the house."

"She is my sister, Mr. Waite." She cinched the final strap beneath the horse's belly. "I suggest you stop wasting time arguing with me."

Dajon squeezed the bridge of his nose, where a dull pain began to burn. Impudent woman. He had a difficult enough task ahead of him without adding another female to protect.

"I'd let 'er come if I was you, Mr. Waite," Lucas said, leading another horse from its stall. "She can fend fer 'erself."

"Not where we are going." Images of Marianne lying limp in his arms, blood spilling from her mouth, stormed across his vision. He would not bring another lady into a dangerous situation.

Faith adjusted the bit in the horse's mouth and threw her hand to her hip. "You may be accustomed to having your orders obeyed aboard your ship, Captain, but this is not the HMS *Enforcer*, nor am I one of your crew."

Withdrawing a handkerchief, Dajon dabbed at the sweat on his throat then twisted the cloth into a knot, longing to stuff it into her sassy mouth.

"If you leave without me, I shall follow you anyway. Isn't it better I ride under your protection than all alone?"

Fuming, Dajon turned and assisted Lucas with the final horse, realizing he had lost the battle. "You will do what I say when we get there, or mark my words, I shall tie you to a tree if I must in order to keep you out of trouble. Do you understand?" He snapped his gaze to her.

"Yes, sir." She saluted him stiffly then lifted her skirts and swung onto her horse.

As they galloped through the dark streets, Dajon's fears stung him like the tiny pelts of rain that sliced through the night sky. He wondered in what condition he would find Hope. Foolish girl. Had she gone there alone? If so, it would be unlikely she remained unscathed. In fact, it was more likely that she had been robbed of her purity, along with her money, and then tossed into a ditch.

And what of Faith? He glanced at her as she galloped beside him, as at ease upon a horse as she seemed strolling in the garden. Though fear tightened the corners of her mouth, courage and resolution held them in a thin line. He had never met a woman like her. So different from timid, sweet Marianne.

On the other side of Faith, Lucas kept a steady pace, as if the two had ridden in haste side by side many times before. The sight alarmed Dajon. The more he became acquainted with Faith, the more he could see the markings of a pirate within her: commanding, confident, rebellious, and greedy. Not a greed for gold, but for whatever would purchase freedom for her and her sisters. He nearly laughed at the thought. Impossible.

Great guns, he'd almost kissed her tonight—again. Her allure was intoxicating—too heady for him to resist. And that frightened him the most.

His hair had loosened from his queue, and he shook it free, allowing the rising wind to clear his head. He mustn't think of Faith now nor the Red Siren. He must focus on saving Hope, no matter what danger she had thrown herself into.

He tugged back the reins as they passed through the city gates then turned onto Meeting Street. The fetid odors of the city surrounded him, along with the eerie chime of an off-key violin accompanied by devilish laughter. Lightning carved a craggy spike across the dark sky as if warning him of impending danger.

was afoot this night. Dajon could feel it.

He could feel it in the sharp hairs bristling across his neck, in the chill rippling down his back. He could feel it in his spirit.

His thoughts shifted to the only One who possessed the power to protect them from such unseen forces, and he chided himself. Why hadn't he thought to pray for Hope sooner?

Father, please protect Hope. Please let no harm befall her. Keep the villains from her and watch over her until we arrive.

When he raised his gaze, it was to Faith's curious stare.

"Who were you talking to?"

Thunder growled in the distance, announcing a storm. "I was praying for your sister."

"Humph." She nudged her horse into a trot.

Faith thrust her nose in the air but did not respond. Angry voices blared in the street ahead of her. They had not seen a soul since entering the city, all asleep at this hour save for the men down by the docks, the miscreants of the sea who spent their coins on idle pleasures and boastful brawls. In that way, she certainly differed from her pirate compatriots.

Narrow houses sprang up on both sides of the street. Two- and three-story stone structures originally built to house families but now transformed into filthy bordellos. Scantily clad women of all shapes and sizes spilled from the door and windows of one of them as if the house could not contain them all. Men with mugs of ale in hand hung on the trollops like ill-fitting shawls.

Drunken eyes shot toward the trio in the street, and for the first time that night, Faith found comfort in riding between the captain and Lucas.

A flash of lightning drew her gaze to a pink building up ahead.

The Pink House.

Faith swallowed and tried to quiet the pounding of her heart.

Mr. Waite raised a hand to slow them. The horses' hooves clicked over the narrow cobblestone street like the ticking of a clock counting down their demise.

The captain turned in his saddle. "Miss Westcott, I beg you. Allow Lucas to escort you home. Mullato Alley is no place for a lady at night."

So this was Mullato Alley—the most perilous district in town. She had thus far managed to avoid traveling this way, and now she knew why 'twas spoken of in hushed tones. But no matter her fear, no matter her disgust, she must think only of Hope and of bringing her sister home safely. Faith took a deep breath and threw back her shoulders. "My sister is here somewhere, Mr. Waite. Therefore I will stay. She will no doubt need me when we discover her whereabouts."

The captain grunted but said nothing more.

Terror stiffened each nerve within Faith as they proceeded to the Pink House. Men brawled openly in the street. Angry shouts and curses burst through the night like pistol shots. To her right, a ring of boisterous sailors, shouting and thrusting their fists in the air, had formed around two others engaged in a sword fight. The clank of metal on metal rang across the street in ominous tones. Somewhere a gun fired.

What had lured Hope down to this ungodly place? Hadn't she had enough of lecherous men? Faith shivered beneath a rising swell of fear for her sister's safety. An unusual desire to pray gripped her—an urge to appeal to a force outside herself, for as she looked around at the violent depravity consuming the alley, she could not imagine any of them escaping unharmed.

The captain's gaze locked upon the Pink House. Concern tightened his features, and beads of sweat glistened between his eyebrows. She turned to Lucas. "Give me one of your pistols."

Mr. Waite shot her a curious look.

"I know how to shoot it. Never fear." She knew she

181

given him more fuel to feed his suspicions, but she couldn't concern herself with that at the moment. In light of what she saw before her, she realized it was not just Hope's innocence on the line but her very life.

Gripping the weapon, Faith stuffed it in the belt on her gown, finding a small measure of relief at being armed again. Now if she just had her cutlass.

As the captain led them around the side of the Pink House, where several horses stood tethered to a post, Faith tried to ignore the lewd comments tossed her way, tried to allow them to pass over her like the wind rising upon the oncoming storm, but she could not. Instead of disgusting her, however, they only pricked her ire. How dare these men fling such foul, degrading suggestions toward a lady, or any woman for that matter?

At least the captain and Lucas's presence seemed to keep them at bay. No doubt most were too inebriated to follow through with their obscene threats anyway.

Mr. Waite dismounted and held out his hand to assist her from her horse. "I apologize, Miss Westcott, for the insults you are forced to endure, but I fear if I were to attempt to defend your honor for each one, I would be engaged in battle the entire night."

" 'Tis quite all right, Mr. Waite." Faith took his hand, glad for the warm strength that enveloped hers, and hopped to the ground. "I believe I can suffer through it for my sister's sake."

"You are a brave woman." He gave her an admiring look then plucked his pistol from the inside of his coat, primed it, replaced it, and nodded toward Lucas.

Without asking, he placed Faith's hand firmly on his arm. "Stay close to me," he ordered as the three of them rounded the building and slipped through the front door.

The stink of ale, tobacco, and human sweat assaulted Faith. She held her breath against the onslaught and tried to focus. The tavern was a swaying mass of inebriated humanity stretched in every direction. In the right corner, a plump woman perched at a harpsichord banged out a bawdy tune, while a skinny man attempted a vain accompaniment with his violin. An off-key ballad rose from a mob clustered around them, their mugs of ale raised toward the rafters.

A loud thump startled Faith, drawing her attention to a table at her left where two men arm wrestled. A crowd circled them, placing bets. Angry card games exploded with insults and threats from every corner. Women snuggled upon men's laps and cooed into their ears. A narrow staircase led upstairs, its wood creaking under the continual passage of its patrons to whatever wickedness loomed above.

Mr. Waite tensed beside Faith as he scanned the room. Hope was not here, at least not in this part of the tavern.

Some of the patrons fired seething glances their way as they muttered to their companions.

Faith felt his eyes lock upon her long before she saw him.

A man wearing a plumed captain's hat, leather jerkin, black waistcoat, and cocky grin stared at her from a table in the corner. He sat back in his chair with his arms folded across his thick chest. A motley group—his crew, no doubt—sat with him.

A pirate.

His gaze scoured over her as if she were tonight's supper then shot to Captain Waite and narrowed.

"Have ye come to arrest me then?" His eyes dropped to the three gold buttons lining each of Mr. Waite's cuffs. "Lieutenant, is it? Ha." He snorted, his spit splattering onto the table. "They send a mere lieutenant to arrest the great Captain Vane." The men surrounding him erupted into a round of drunken cackles as every hazy eye in the place shot to the trio.

So this was Charles Vane. Faith had heard of his brutality—how he tortured and murdered the crews of his captured vessels, how he never abided by the pirate code and cheated his own crew out of their share of the plunder, and how he had arrogantly snubbed the offer of pardon given by the governor of the Bahamas by setting a French ship aflame and destroying two Royal Navy ships. As she took in his grotesque physique and the pure evil simmering in his gaze, she felt as if a thousand bugs crawled down her back, the sensation made all the more disgusting by the shame of her association with his kind. Averting her eyes, she scanned the room once again for any sign of Hope.

Mr. Waite returned the man's stare and waited until the chortles silenced.

"Ye come here with a mere woman and a slave?" the pirate continued his verbal joust.

Lucas grunted and gripped the hilt of his sword.

The pirate's eyes shifted to the groomsman's threatening gesture, and a wicked sneer played upon his lips.

Mr. Waite raised his brows. "I'll be happy to arrest you if you wish, Mr. Vane," he said nonchalantly, "but I am afraid I have not heard of you."

Faith elbowed the captain and sent an anxious glance his way. Surely he knew who this vile man was. 'Twas sheer folly to antagonize such a volatile beast.

The pirate's face exploded in a purple rage. "Not heard of me?" He shot up, his chair thumping to the floor. The crowd shrank back. "I've plundered o'er twenty ships in these waters." He flung a glance over his men to receive the expected grunts of approbation, even as he slid his hand within his waistcoat.

The captain remained steady and relaxed beside her as if he were talking to a mere servant. Either he was mad, or he possessed more courage than she had ever seen.

"You must be quite proud of yourself, Mr. Vane, but alas, I care not." Mr. Waite gazed off to the right as if the exchange bored him. "We have come in search of a lady."

"Well, ye ain't gonna find a lady in here," blared a man's voice above the noise of the crowd, eliciting a barrage of chortles.

The pirate fumbled within his coat. Faith knew he

went for his pistol. She knew he would have already drawn it if not for the alcohol tugging on his reflexes. Lucas shifted his stance, his fingers stretching beside his own weapon. Faith clutched the handle of her gun. Her moist palms slipped over the cool metal. Why didn't the captain do something?

The laugher abated, leaving a deadly silence in its wake.

A slow smile crept over the pirate's lips. He plucked his pistol from inside his waistcoat. The cock of a dozen pistols snapped through the room like firecrackers—Faith's and Lucas's and the captain's among them. She hadn't even seen Mr. Waite draw his.

Mr. Vane aimed the dark barrel of his pistol at the captain's heart. His grin faded.

The captain did not move, his own weapon trained upon the pirate.

Eight men surrounding Vane leveled their pistols upon the trio, while only their three returned the threat. A maze of deadly steel crisscrossed before them, ready to fire in a lethal explosion.

Fear as she'd never known before dug its claws into Faith and kept her frozen in place.

There was no way out of this. They were all going to die.

CHAPTER 20

Faith gazed at the dark, gaping holes of at least twenty pistols leveled upon her heart and thought this as good a time as any to make peace with a God she had ignored for years. Mr. Waite grabbed her hand with his free one and tried to pull her behind him.

She did not budge.

Though the chivalrous gesture warmed her, better to die alongside her companions than after they had been pummeled with bullets and dropped to the floor at her feet.

Oh God, if You are there. . .I know I haven't spoken to You very much. . .but please help us—for the captain's sake. He's a good man.

From the corner of her eye, Faith spotted a woman in a formfitting purple gown saunter over to Vane. Her brown hair, tied behind her like a man's, curled down her back. Two brace of pistols were slung across her chest.

"Settle down, Charlie." She sidled beside him and gave him a sultry grin. "I know this woman." She winked at Faith. "They mean you no harm. And besides, since when have you ever allowed a navy pig to stir your ire?" She waved a jeweled hand through the air. "Ignore him. He is nothing."

"Anne." Faith lowered her pistol and stormed toward the woman she now recognized as Hope's friend.

"Miss Westcott," the captain hissed urgently behind her.

Vane's glazed eyes flickered briefly to Anne then to Faith, before fixing again on Mr. Waite. His pistol wobbled. Grabbing his mug, he gulped down another swig of ale, foam beading on his mustache, and then switched the weapon to his other hand.

"Do you know where Hope is?"

A spark of alarm flitted across Anne's confident expression. "She did not return home?"

Faith shook her head.

Facing Vane again, Anne placed a hand on his arm holding the gun. "Put the pistol down, Charlie. Pay them no mind. Do we not have better things to do?" she cooed into his ear.

"Gone wit' ye, woman. Leave me be!" Vane jerked her hand away and gave Mr. Waite a venomous look. "Yer outnumbered, sir. Surrender or die."

"I plan to do neither, Mr. Bane," the captain huffed. "But how about this? I will—"

"I said me name was Vane, not Bane!" the pirate interrupted in a spasm of fury. He sent a scathing glance over the room, silencing the few who had dared to laugh.

"Vane, Bane, whatever." Mr. Waite shrugged. "As I was saying, I will not arrest you on the condition that you tell me where our lady friend is to be found. Agreed?" The muscles in his jaw flexed, but Faith could see no other indication of unease in his staunch demeanor.

"I've got me a better idea," Vane snarled. "I'll kill ye where ye stand and take the fine lady ye brought wit' ye fer meself."

Laughter rumbled through the foul air just as a blast of thunder roared outside.

Raindrops struck the roof, at first sounding like tiny footfalls then growing in intensity until the reverberation of pounding drums filled the whole tavern.

A chill slithered over Faith.

Mr. Waite cast a wary glance at her, motioning her to step away from Anne.

She did.

He nodded toward Lucas.

Faith's heart took on a frenzied beat. What was he planning?

He faced Vane. His stern gaze and rigid stance contained all the energy of a lightning bolt about to strike.

Vane snickered and tightened his finger around the trigger of his pistol.

Instantly the captain booted the table that stood between them. Mugs of ale and bottles of rum shot through the air, crashing into pieces against walls and floor and showering the crowd with shards of glass and drops of liquor.

Vane stumbled back. His pistol fired.

Guns exploded.

Faith ducked.

A man grabbed her arm and dragged her from her feet. Twisting, she kneed him in the groin then regained her balance and waved her gun across a circle of men descending upon her.

Lucas tugged her beside him. He shot one man in the leg, dropped his gun, and drew his cutlass.

The man screamed and clutched the wound.

Sword tips bristled at them from every direction.

"Halt or I'll kill him!" Mr. Waite's voice thundered through the room.

Silence, save for the pounding of the rain, descended upon them.

Mr. Waite marched toward Vane, his pistol leveled at the pirate's shocked face. Vane raised his own weapon and gave a sideways grin at the smoke curling upward from the barrel. He tossed it aside with a clank.

"Tell your men to lower their weapons," Mr. Waite commanded. "Or I swear by the love of all that is holy, I will blast what's left of your brains all over the wall."

The pirate's upper lip twitched. A look of insolent defiance burned in his gaze. Faith knew that look. He wasn't going to comply. He would risk his death rather than suffer shame in front of his men.

Without warning, Anne rushed to his side, raised a pistol, and whacked the handle down on Vane's head.

His eyes rolled upward before he crumpled to the ground in a heap.

Murmurs rumbled through the crowd of onlookers, their mouths agape, but Anne turned to face them and threw her hands to her hips. "Go about yer business, ye sotted dogs," she yelled as loudly as any man. "He just needs a wee bit of sleep, 'tis all."

Tension spiked through the room. Faith tried to contain the heavy breath that threatened to burst through her chest. Then, one by one, the men began to laugh. Coarse chortles soon chased out the hostility as the sailors slowly dispersed.

Anne tilted her pretty head toward the captain. "I couldn't let you kill him. I've grown fond of him, you see."

Mr. Waite lowered his gun. "Are you well, Miss Westcott?"

"Yes, I'm fine." She turned toward Anne. "Where is my sister?"

Anne finished giving instructions to Vane's crew to attend to him, then she grabbed Faith's arm. "She was here an hour ago." She gestured for Mr. Waite and Lucas to follow her then led them to the back of the tavern. "I saw her leave through the back door into the garden. I assumed she went home." She glanced over the three of them, concern warming her cold, hard eyes.

"How could you leave her alone?" Faith asked.

"I am not her guardian. She came here of her own accord."

"But you are her friend." Faith jerked from her grasp. "She's not strong like you are."

Anne flinched and narrowed her eyes. "She's more like me than you may think." She allowed her gaze to wander over Faith. She grinned. "And from the looks of you, you are, as well."

Faith ground her teeth. She might be a pirate, but she was nothing like this depraved strumpet.

Was she?

Anne glanced at Mr. Waite and Lucas. "Who are your friends?"

The captain nodded. "Mr. Waite, commander of the HMS *Enforcer*."

Faith gestured toward Lucas. "And this is Lucas, my first—my groomsman," she stammered.

"Your first groomsman, eh?" Anne snickered then pushed aside the massive oak door that led into the back garden. "Like I told you, she went this way about an hour ago."

"Alone?" the captain asked.

"Aye, as far as I could see."

"Did she say where she might be heading?"

"Not to me." Annie cocked her head and grinned, allowing her sultry gaze to drift over Mr. Waite.

The captain brushed past her, grabbing Faith's elbow as he went. "Thank you, Anne. That will be all." He dismissed her as if she were one of his crewmen.

Lucas squeezed by her, as well, eyeing her with caution.

Anne scowled before she released the door and stomped back into the tavern, muttering something about pompous naval officers.

Lightning flashed, illuminating the porch in stark grays and whites before snapping it back into darkness. Two lanterns swaying on poles offered little light over the dismal scene. Rain pounded the slanted covering above them. Droplets squeezed between the wooden slats. One of them slid down Faith's gown, weaving a trail of unease down her back as she scanned the shadows for Hope.

The captain released her elbow and took her hand in his. Lucas came alongside them. Together they took a step forward. Weeds reached up between the cracks of cobblestone and clawed at their feet as they made their way to the edge of the porch and stopped, peering out into the shadows. A brick wall enclosed the small garden, if one could call it that. Thistles and brown shrubs littered the area. A massive tree stood in the center, a cracked stone fountain at its base. Though most of the patrons had gone inside out of the rain, some remained splayed across benches and over the cobblestones in such a drunken stupor that they were oblivious to the raindrops splattering over them.

Faith gulped as a metallic taste rose in her throat. Hope was nowhere in sight.

Thunder shook the sky as they stepped from beneath the overhang. Drops of rain pelted Faith's skin. An eerie ballad snaked through the moist air like a witch's chant. A radiance flickered from beyond the tree.

Mr. Waite squeezed her hand. "Never fear. We shall find her, Miss Westcott." He led her around the trunk and down a path.

Faith's gaze shot to a far corner of the garden where a lantern burned. No, 'twas not a lantern but a fire, a pillar of fire nigh two feet tall. The flames burned bright despite the lashing rain and wind.

Mr. Waite headed for it.

With their backs to the fire, a group of men hunched together against the rain. When they weren't hoisting bottles to their mouths, they belted out a sinister trill that sent chills over Faith.

> *Oh devils, we call ye*
> *Out from yer graves.*
> *Give us yer power;*
> *We are yer slaves.*

Faith snapped her gaze back to the fire. A shadowy figured huddled just beyond it.

Hope.

Faith yanked her hand from Mr. Waite's and dashed toward the corner. Hope curled into a ball against the brick wall, drenched and shivering.

" 'Tis Hope," she yelled over her shoulder, sidestepping the fire and kneeling beside her sister.

"Hope?" She touched her arm, cold as ice. Faith gulped. "What have they done to you?" Hope's eyes fluttered, but she did not open them. A moan escaped her lips. A hundred heinous scenarios crept through Faith's mind. "Not again, Lord. Not again."

"Heaven help us." Mr. Waite stepped around the flame, slid his arms beneath Hope, and hoisted her effortlessly into his arms.

The fire disappeared.

Faith's widened eyes met the captain's. She shifted her gaze to the spot where the fire had been and then to Lucas, who stood frozen in place, the whites of his eyes fixated on the missing flame. No wood, no smoke, nothing to indicate a fire had just burned there. The ground beneath it was not even charred. Faith placed her hand over the spot.

Moist, cold soil met her fingers.

"There she be!" one of the drunken men shouted, arousing the others from their ballad. The mob rose and clambered toward them.

"We've been lookin' fer that lady!" bellowed a slovenly fellow in front, pointing his bottle at Hope.

"Aye, she just disappeared," another commented, and the men grunted in unison.

Faith glanced at Mr. Waite but could not make out his features in the shadows. She wiped drops of rain from her lashes and stood.

Two of the men drew their swords. "We saw her first. She's ours."

Lucas swerved to face them and slowly pulled out his cutlass. The metal against sheath rang an eerie chime across the yard. Yanking her pistol from her belt, Faith aimed it at the mob and counted the dark, swaying heads.

Ten.

Ten to three. And Mr. Waite with his hands encumbered beneath the weight of Hope's unconscious body.

"She does not belong to you," the captain said with all the authority of a king.

"To the devil wit' ye, sir. I'm givin' ye a fair warning. There be powers at work here that ye best be heedin'."

"I agree with you gentlemen," Mr. Waite replied, his tone so calm and steady it astonished Faith. "There are indeed powers at work here. But if I were you, I'd be careful which ones I associated with."

Malefic chortles filled the air as lightning shot a fiery dagger across the sky, flashing a spectral glow over their faces.

Faith swallowed. A chill struck her as if a wall of ice passed through her.

Evil was here.

A malevolent force tugged upon her, weighing her down with dread and hopelessness.

She shook the rain from her face and tried to steady her wobbling gun. What did Mr. Waite hope to gain from this derisive repartee? It would take more than mere words to disarm these men and the wickedness that empowered them.

The captain took a bold step forward, clutching Hope more tightly to his chest. "This woman is not yours. She belongs to God," he roared, "and in the name of Jesus Christ, the Son of the living God, I order you to stand down."

Thunder boomed. The ground shuddered.

The men shrank back as if a broadside had struck them in the gut. Although their eyes narrowed and their jaws tightened, they made no move toward Hope.

Mr. Waite turned and marched across the garden toward the back exit.

Faith glanced over her shoulder as she ran next to him, expecting the villains to give chase. Behind her, Lucas ran backward, his sword brandished toward the band of cursing men.

Mr. Waite kicked open the iron gate. It squealed on its hinges and slammed into the brick wall.

Faith followed him around the side of the tavern where they'd left their horses. One final glance over her shoulder told her the men had not moved an inch.

Grabbing her arm, Lucas pulled her away from the sight.

Mr. Waite halted amid the row of horses and wheeled around.

Faith touched his arm. "What is it?"

"One of our horses is missing."

"Hey, you there." A slurred voice echoed through the alleyway. "Ain't ye the strangers that bested old Charlie?"

Mr. Waited snapped his eyes toward Faith. "We've no time. We shall make do with two. Lucas, mount up, and I'll hand you Miss Hope."

"Aye, aye." Lucas untied the reins, swung onto the horse, then leaned down to receive Hope. She moaned as he grasped her and laid her across the saddle in front of him.

"Hey, I told ye to stop!" A crowd of men formed at the head of the alley. "Are we gonna let this bilge-sucking navy dog come down to our territory an' make a fool o' poor Charlie? Let's teach 'im a lesson."

Groans and "ayes" bounced off the brick walls.

Faith lifted her pistol and stepped out from the horses. "Stay back, or I'll drop you where you stand."

"Ouch now." The man snickered. "Did ye hear that, gents? The lady's gonna shoot us."

He and his companions fell into a fit of laughter.

Lucas backed up his horse and leveled his own pistol upon them.

The captain took a running leap and jumped onto his steed then held down his hand for Faith.

She hesitated, shifting her eyes between him and the crowd. One well-aimed shot by these villains at their fleeing backs and all would be lost. Perhaps she should remain and keep them at bay until Mr. Waite and Lucas could escape with Hope. Perhaps it was the only way to ensure her sister's safety.

"Are you coming? Or do you plan to take on these ruffians by yourself?"

Though she couldn't see his face, she envisioned the sardonic curve of his lips.

"Trust me. I will get you and your sister home safely. Now, please." He stretched out his hand farther even as the horse clawed at the mud, perhaps sensing the impending danger.

Trust. Her chest tightened. Placing her life and the life of her sister in someone else's hands made Faith's stomach constrict so tightly she felt it would explode into a thousand pieces. But she had little choice at the moment. And Mr. Waite had not let her down thus far.

Stuffing the pistol in her belt, she took his hand, and he hoisted her up before him and grabbed the reins.

The men recovered from their gaiety. "Hey, where ye runnin' off to, ye cowards?" One of the men took a step forward and plucked out his sword. "I'm challengin' ye to a duel, ye spineless son of Neptune's whore."

Mr. Waite twitched the horse's reins and faced the man. "Another time, perhaps?" He gave the horse a swift kick in the belly, sending the steed galloping down the alley straight toward the mob.

CHAPTER 21

The drunken men formed an oscillating row. Dajon sped straight for them, intending to run them down if he had to. But at the last minute, they jerked aside, some tumbling to the ground, others scrambling for their fallen pistols. Dajon bolted ahead. He did not look back.

A barrage of cracks and pops split the night air.

A bullet whizzed past his ear.

Dajon jerked the reins to the right and then the left, weaving a chaotic path down the street, dodging the volley of bullets. Lucas galloped beside him doing the same, one arm holding Hope in a fierce grip.

Lightning cracked the sky in a fork of brilliance, casting an eerie gray flash over the buildings that lined the road. Laying propriety aside, Dajon wrapped his arms around Faith's waist and pressed her back against his chest, then they lunged around the corner down Meeting Street. The thud of horse hooves in the mud matched the furious beat of his heart. Thunder bellowed above them as if war in heaven had broken out right over their heads. Faith jumped, and he gripped her tighter as he cast a quick glance over his shoulder. No one followed.

Easing the horse to a trot, he wiped the sweat from his forehead with his sleeve before returning his hand to Faith's waist. Lucas drew up alongside him and cast a glance his way, his expression lost in the shadows.

"Hope." Faith beckoned to her sister, reaching her hand across the distance between them, but no response came from the dark mound bounding at their side.

"She be all right, mistress," Lucas said. "Her breathin' be steady. And I ain't seen no blood."

Faith released a sigh. Her shoulders drooped slightly. Dajon brushed the curls from her cheek and leaned toward her, intending to offer her a word of comfort. Instead, his gaze landed on the black shape of a pistol clasped tightly between her hands.

Reaching around her, he touched her arm. "Give me the pistol, Miss Westcott. 'Tis over now. You are safe." Yet he wondered if she gripped the weapon out of fear—or anger. Truth be told, none of her behavior that evening had portrayed an ounce of fear—and certainly none of the trembling, swooning, or outright panic one would expect of a lady in the face of such danger and debauchery.

She hesitated for a moment then flipped the pistol in the air, catching it by the barrel, and handed it to him over her shoulder, handle first.

Like an expert marksman.

Dajon stuffed it in his belt and swallowed against the horrifying revelation rising in his throat.

He pulled back on the reins, slowing the horse to a walk as they approached the city gates. Visions of Faith storming into the tavern as boldly as she would her own parlor and then standing her ground in a room full of drunken villains, pirates, and ruffians blasted across his mind. Not just standing her ground, but drawing her weapon, demanding her sister's return. Why, she had not even blinked at the lewdness and profanity surrounding her. What sort of lady was she?

A pirate lady.

No. He could not believe it. He would not believe it.

Through the city gates, Dajon turned the horse onto the dirt path to Hasell Street, searching for an explanation for Faith's behavior, any explanation besides the one that kept shoving its way to the forefront of his mind. Perhaps her father had trained her in arms. Perhaps she'd been forced to defend their home in the past. No. He knew Admiral Westcott. He would never allow one of his daughters to behave in such an improper and audacious manner.

She wiggled in the saddle and pulled away from him. "You do not have to hold me so tightly anymore," she shot back over her shoulder.

He leaned toward her ear. "Enjoying yourself too much, perchance?"

"I'm sure many women succumb to your infinite charms, Captain, but I am not among them." Dajon chuckled but kept a firm grip upon her. "I am deeply wounded, Miss Westcott. After all we've been through, 'tis only that I wouldn't want you to fall."

"If you don't control those hands, it won't be me who falls from this horse, Mr. Waite." She shuffled in the saddle again, and the movements of her body against Dajon sent a surge of heat through him. He released her momentarily and cleared his throat. What was he doing? The last thing he needed was to entangle himself with a woman, especially an admiral's daughter—and especially this particular woman who had far too many secrets stowed under hatches.

But Miss Westcott. Never had he encountered such a lady, such a dichotomy of charm and venom all wrapped up in a curvaceous, fiery parcel.

He leaned toward her, longing to savor the moment of her close proximity—one that he doubted would ever come again. But the stench of that awful soap bit his nose, overpowering her normal sweet, lemony aroma. He huffed. Certainly the lady knew no more about soap-making than he did.

She flipped her hair behind her, swatting him in the face with the fetid strands, and glanced toward Lucas and Hope. "I do thank you, Mr. Waite." Her voice had softened, had even taken on a penitent tone. "My sister appears unharmed, at least on the outside. I thought surely all was lost when we entered the tavern and she was nowhere to be seen."

"'Twas my pleasure. I am only glad we arrived in time." Dajon glanced at the groaning petite form in Lucas's arms. "If you and your sisters would simply follow the rules, you could avoid putting yourselves in such danger. That is what rules are for, Miss Westcott—for your own safety and the safety of others."

She gave a most unladylike snort. "I fear your task as our guardian has been much more than you bargained for, Mr. Waite. Perhaps you now wish to reconsider?"

His task? Surprisingly, neither Dajon's obligation to the admiral nor the consequences to his career had even penetrated his decisions tonight. He had acted only out of fear for Hope's safety, and in particular, out of his strong desire to alleviate Faith's distress. When had he begun to care for this family? And more important, when had he begun to put his career, his very life on the line for them?

Surely, Lord, this unselfish act will pay off a portion of my past debt.

He felt a shudder course through Faith. "I fear for what my sister endured before we arrived."

Dajon remained silent. He knew all too well the wickedness that went on in those nefarious dens. As he envisioned the fiendish group of men that had surrounded Hope, he loathed to think what they had done to her, what they had planned on doing. Certainly even more evil had been afoot than ravishing a young woman.

But the Lord had shown up strong! The strange fire, the presence of God that had protected Hope. A surge of faith lifted Dajon's spirits. "Never fear, God was with your sister the whole time, even before we arrived."

A brisk wind swirled, shoving dark clouds aside and allowing the glow of a half-moon to shine upon them.

Faith shook her head.

Lucas cleared his throat. "Beggin' yer pardon, sir, but what exactly did happen back there? I ain't seen nothin' like that before."

"That, Mr. Corwin, was the mighty hand of God."

"But the fire—it jest disappeared."

"Amazing, wasn't it?" Dajon still found it hard to believe himself. Yet how could he deny what he had seen? It reminded him of the pillar of fire God had sent to protect the people of Israel as they traveled across the wilderness. Excitement sped through him.

"And those men couldn'a see Miss Hope till the fire was gone." Lucas's normally hearty voice quivered slightly.

"And the ground was cold and wet beneath the flames after they disappeared," Faith added, awe softening her normal confident tone.

"Aye." He smiled.

Lucas shifted in his saddle, adjusting Hope in his arms. "And those men—they stopped. They didn't chase us after ye commanded them in the name of Jesus to stand down."

"The name of Jesus has been placed 'far above all principality, and power, and might, and dominion, and every name that is named, not only in this world, but also in that which is to come,'" Dajon said, quoting from Ephesians. He felt a tingling sensation throughout his body.

Faith stiffened against his chest.

"God exists," Lucas announced incredulously.

"That He does, Mr. Corwin. That He does."

"I am sure there is another explanation." Faith's sharp tone bit into Dajon's joy. The Lord had rescued one of the Westcott sisters from evil, but the other was still locked in a dungeon of disbelief. *Lord, if this miracle cannot convince her, what will?* Without God, she would forever be wandering through life searching for something that could not be found.

Dajon nudged the horse, prodding him into a trot. Tonight God had used him to do battle against evil to save Hope. And he was more determined than ever not to allow those same wicked forces to keep Faith from the Lord.

⥈

Faith sat on the edge of the bed and rubbed her sister's hand. As soon as they had arrived home, she'd instructed Lucas to carry Hope into Faith's chamber, where she could sit with her until she awoke. Faith considered waking Grace but thought it wiser to allow her sister to rest. No sense in all of them being exhausted on the morrow. So with the chambermaid's help, Faith had undressed Hope, searched for wounds—finding none, not even a drop of blood—and then clad her in a nightgown and wrapped her among the blankets on her bed. Though Hope had fluttered her eyes briefly during the commotion, she had not regained consciousness. And that thought alone terrified Faith more than anything. Something dreadful must have happened to cause her sister to remain ensconced within the dark places of her mind.

Laying her face in her hands, Faith released the tears she'd withheld all evening, allowing them to flow down her cheeks and drip off her chin one by one onto the down quilt. It was all her fault. If she had just spent the day at the park with Hope like she had promised, they would not have fought, and Hope would not have ventured out into the night.

Faith glanced at the blurred shape of her sister lying on the bed. "I'm so sorry, my dear, sweet Hope. Please forgive me." She squeezed Hope's hand then swiped the tears from her own cheeks. No time for crying. From now on, Faith would do better. She would spend more time with her sisters, even if it meant forgoing her sleep.

Releasing her sister's hand, Faith rose and walked toward the window. She clenched her fists then leaned on the ledge, allowing the moonlight to drench her in a wash of silver. If she could plunder one or two more treasure-laden ships, she might have enough to approach her father. Then she would have all the time in the world to spend with her sisters, to protect them, to guide them.

She glanced across the yard where Spanish moss on a red cedar swayed in the breeze. Below, Molly's prize vegetable garden guarded the side wall, framed by purple larkspur, wild geranium, and tall evening primrose, its strong, sweet scent permeating the night air. The storm had passed. Tomorrow would be a beautiful day. Perhaps a new start? She opened her mouth to speak. Then slammed it shut. What was she doing? She had been about to pray—to thank God for saving Hope and to plead with Him for the soundness of her sister's mind and heart. She lowered her gaze to the chipped white paint around the window. Hadn't she prayed at the tavern during a moment of despair, and hadn't God answered her prayers? But why would He, when she had turned her back on Him long ago?

No, 'twas Mr. Waite. 'Twas his prayer God answered. And only his. Yet that would mean God did care for His children—at least some of them.

"Though you have left Me, I have never left you."

Tears surged into her eyes. She shook her head. *No. You've allowed too many tragedies, too much pain. I cannot trust You. I will not.*

"I love you."

A tap sounded on the door, and Faith brushed her tears aside before whispering, "Enter," thinking it must be the chambermaid or perhaps Molly come to scold her for their dangerous escapade.

The door creaked open, and the hollow thud of boots sounded on the wooden floor. She turned, her heart skipping a beat.

The large frame of Mr. Waite filled the doorway. "Forgive me, Miss Westcott, I know this is most improper, but I cannot sleep and thought to check on Miss Hope. May I?"

Swallowing her sorrow and guilt, Faith squared her shoulders. "Of course. Please come in."

He glanced toward the bed and crossed the room. No navy coat hid his broad chest—a chest that stretched his shirt like a full sail under a mighty wind. His breeches were haphazardly stuffed into black boots. His dark hair hung loosely about his collar, and a day's stubble peppered his chin.

Faith's breath halted as he stepped into the moonlight. He nodded toward the bed. "How is she?"

A rush of heat sped through Faith. She took a step back. "I don't know. She has not awakened."

"Were there. . .were there wounds?"

"Nay." She crossed her arms over her stomach, hoping to still the beating of her heart. "Not on the outside, anyway."

He nodded as if he understood. Faith tightened her jaw. As if he could possibly understand the internal wounds of a woman.

"I've sent for the doctor," he said. "There must be a reason she is still benumbed."

"She has been like this before." Faith glanced out the window, feeling her guard weakening before the outpouring of this man's concern.

The captain cocked his head curiously.

"This is not the first time she has been accosted by licentious knaves, Mr. Waite." He blinked then glanced toward the bed. When he returned his gaze to hers, sorrow stained his otherwise clear blue eyes.

Feeling suddenly weak, Faith sank onto the window ledge. Did this man care about Hope, about her? She studied him, searching for a hint of duplicity but finding only sincerity burning in his gaze. Yet nobody cared for anyone unless there was personal gain. He wanted something. But what? She let out a sigh. No matter. He had saved Hope. And for that, he did not deserve to be scorned.

"Forgive me, Mr. Waite. 'Tis just that my sister has suffered much."

"I'm sorry. There is much evil in the world." Without warning, he reached out and took her hand.

His warm fingers enclosed hers protectively. Faith knew she should jerk from his grasp, but the comforting strength of his touch filled a need long unmet. "Evil in the world? Aye. But in your own household?" Faith gritted her teeth against a flood of emotion.

Mr. Waite continued to caress her hand, but he made no reply. He leaned against the wall framing the window, so close to her she could smell the sea upon him. The salty fragrance settled over her nerves, untying the many knots formed during the night's harrowing venture.

Should she tell him? She longed to pour out her heart to this man. Hope moaned from the bed, drawing both their gazes momentarily.

Faith glanced out the window. "My older sister, Charity, is married to a ruthless, cruel man, Lord Herbert Villement. Not only does he mistreat Charity—severely—but he set his wicked eyes upon adding all her sisters to his harem." She shot a fiery gaze his way. "He claims to be a godly Christian man."

Mr. Waite stopped caressing her hand; his fingers stiffened.

Faith swallowed. "'Twas Hope he set his sights upon first. Possibly because I refused to acknowledge his lewd suggestions, and Grace"—she gave a wry laugh—"sweet Grace's piety no doubt disturbed the demons lurking within him. Hope has always been such a flirt, you see." She glanced at Mr. Waite, his dark gaze locked upon her as he listened with interest. "All of it harmless in her innocence and youth. Poor thing. She longed for approval. Still does, I suppose." Faith retrieved her hand and stood, not wanting the comfort to assuage the anger of her memories. She gazed at the shadowy form on the bed. "Papa never appreciated Hope. He finds her ignorant and flighty, and she and Mother were so much alike that they squabbled over everything." Faith let out a pained laugh. "Hope never knew how much Mother truly loved her." Faith's eyes burned, and she pulled her hand from his and stepped into the shadows.

He crossed his arms over his chest, his dark silhouette like a sturdy ship on the horizon.

Faith clasped her hands together. "We tried to avoid our new brother-in-law as much as we could. His salacious dalliance masked behind polite discourse was not lost on us as he must have assumed. But as family, he had access to our home whenever he wished." Her stomach soured as visions of him bursting through their front door shot through her mind, hat and cane in hand, licking his lips in a ravenous grin. "Which was often—usually whenever Father was away and Charity was, of course, home unwell. 'Twas no wonder she had a perpetual headache." Faith snorted and grabbed her throat, trying to dissolve the clump of pain that had taken residence there.

The captain's knuckles whitened as he grabbed the window ledge. Still, he said nothing. He took a step toward her.

Faith held up a hand to stay his advance. She did not want his comfort, his sympathy. She must finish her story. She must let it out, or she feared it would explode within her like the backfiring of a ship's gun.

"One evening, Mother and Grace had gone to the city. Papa was at sea, and most of the servants had been dismissed on holiday, leaving Hope and me alone in the house. I heard her scream."

The same chill that had stabbed through Faith that night stabbed through her now. Wrapping her arms about her chest, she shut her eyes against the image that was forever engraved in her mind.

"By the time I stormed into Hope's chamber, he was donning his pantaloons and spewing foul curses toward her as she lay on the bed." Tears fought their way to the forefront of Faith's eyes, but she willed them back with her fury.

A gentle touch on her arm startled her. She jumped and snapped her eyes open to see the captain's tall figure beside her.

"She was but seventeen," Faith sobbed.

Moonlight glimmered off the hint of moisture covering Mr. Waite's gaze. His nostrils flared, and a tiny purple vein began to throb on his forehead.

Faith stepped away from his grasp. "Then Lord Villement came after me."

CHAPTER 22

Lord Villement came after you?" Dajon's stomach convulsed. He tried to say something, wanted to say something to comfort Faith, but when he opened his mouth, all he found on his tongue was an anchor chain of angry curses.

"Aye." Faith's voice was but a whisper. "He pinned me to the floor by the fireplace, grunting over me like a beast."

"Did he. . .did he. . ." Dajon could not form the words, much less the thought.

She lifted her gaze to his, but the shadows hid her expression. "I grabbed the poker and stabbed him in the leg." She spat the words so quickly and with such finality that it sounded as if there could be no other ending to the dreadful story. But her bunched fists at her sides and the stiffness of her shoulders as she moved to the window told a different tale.

"I threatened to pierce the other leg and would have if he hadn't fled from the house in agony."

Dajon blew out a sigh and raked a hand through his hair. At least Faith had been spared. The moonlight doused her in a halo of silver, highlighting her stiff posture and making all the more noticeable the shudder that now ran through her. He moved closer, longing to take her in his arms, to protect and soothe her. Would she welcome his embrace? Or would she fear him—a man alone in her chamber?

As if in answer, she whirled around and faced the window.

He halted. "I'm sorry."

"It was a long time ago." She snorted and waved a hand through the air. "I have tried to care for both my sisters since, but I fear I have failed miserably. At least Father brought us to the colonies—away from our brother-in-law—but if he forced Charity to marry that cad, will he not do the same to us—marry us off to the first man who comes knocking on his door? Like that vile Sir Wilhelm? I cannot let that happen again." She swayed as if her legs would give way beneath her.

Dajon started toward her again, but she instantly crystallized, her posture rigid. "You take on too much. It is not your job to protect and provide for them."

She shot him a hard glance. "Who, then? You? My father? No. Mother handed me that baton on her deathbed. Not that I wouldn't have gladly taken it anyway."

Anger tightened every muscle in his back. "Surely your brother-in-law was punished?"

Leaning against the wall beside the window, Faith hugged herself but remained silent.

"Did you not report him to your parents?"

She flung her hair over her shoulder, the moonlight setting it aflame in shimmering red. "Yes. Mother was horrified, but what could she do? It was his word against Hope's. Who would believe a seventeen-year-old girl over a lord? Father dove into his usual denial of any problems with his girls and refused to believe the event had ever taken place. Charity believed us, but fear of her husband kept her silent. So naught was ever done." Faith huffed. "Women are of little import. Certainly not enough to make a fuss over."

"Perhaps in some circles, yes. But *I* do not believe so." Anger and sorrow wrestled within Dajon's gut. It was unfathomable that this cretin had gotten away with such a heinous crime. And heartbreaking to witness the effects of it upon both Faith and her sister. And the villain claimed to be a Christian. No wonder her faith had dwindled.

"If I had been there, I assure you the man would

have been punished." He inched closer to her.

"Well, you weren't there, were you?" Faith snapped. "And neither was your God. Apparently He thinks as much of women as society does."

Dajon winced. "I am here now." He touched her arm, and when she didn't move away, he pulled her closer to him.

She stiffened, but then slowly her shoulders sank. She gazed up at him, her glistening auburn eyes only inches from his. "You are here only on my father's orders."

He brushed the back of his fingers lightly across her cheek, enjoying the way she closed her eyes beneath his touch. "Do you really believe that is still my only reason?"

Her lashes fluttered against her cheeks like ripples on a calm sea. She opened her mouth then shut it as he continued to caress her skin. He placed a gentle kiss upon her forehead and allowed his gaze to wander down to her full lips. They quivered slightly.

Was she inviting his kiss?

He licked his own lips, forcing down his passion, forcing down his longing to explore that sassy mouth of hers with his own.

He ground his teeth together, fighting an urge that threatened to crash over him like a powerful wave.

Lord, I need Your strength.

What was he doing?

Faith was vulnerable, upset, and alone with him in her bedchamber. To take advantage of this moment would be incorrigible. Besides, she had suffered enough under the care of men, and Dajon did not trust himself not to add further pain by his own affections, no matter how genuine.

Gathering every ounce of God-given resistance, Dajon released her shoulders. "You are wrong about God, Miss Westcott. He highly esteems women. His love for them is evident throughout the scriptures."

She snapped open her eyes. Was it surprise, disappointment, or perhaps both that flashed from their depths?

Touching a lock of her hair, he fingered the silky strand, unable to resist at least that small token. Their flight through the rainy night seemed to have cleansed it, leaving it fresh and enticing. "You must not blame God for everything bad in this world."

She jerked away and plopped down on the window ledge. "Why not? Is He not sovereign? Can He not snap a finger and do whatever He wishes?"

The overwhelming passion of only a moment ago seeped from Dajon's body as quickly as if a keg plug had been pulled. "Aye, He can. As He did tonight." Dajon raised a brow and crossed his arms over his chest. At all costs, he must rein back the itch to touch her again. "Did He not save your sister?"

Faith snarled. "Perhaps, but why tonight and not five years ago?"

"I do not know. But I do know this"—he leaned toward her—"He has never left you or your sisters."

Faith shook her head stubbornly.

With a sigh, Dajon stepped toward the bed. No wonder she blamed God; no wonder her faith had faltered.

But Hope. His gaze took in her sleeping form on the bed. "I don't understand why your sister continually throws herself in the path of danger. It is as if she is begging for a repeat of her harrowing past. She must listen to her father—to me." He shifted his gaze to Faith, who stood and stared out the window, fingers gripping the sleeves of her gown.

She spun around and threw her hands to her hips. "Adhering to the dictates of men has only caused her pain. She had broken none of your God's rules when she was ravished by our brother-in-law. Naught was broken save her heart and her innocence. And no rule can ever heal the damage done to either of those."

Dajon tucked his hair behind his ear, searching for a way to help her understand that rules were made to protect people—both God's rules and man's—and all too often, broken hearts were the result of broken rules.

"You think me a rule follower, but I have not always been so."

"You? The pious Mr. Waite. Broke a rule or two in your day, have you?" She sashayed over to him, her eyes flashing in the candlelight. "Told a wee lie, perhaps, or neglected to read your Bible ten times a day?" She snickered.

Dajon shuddered. Did he appear so saintly, so sanctimonious? Had he become so good at hiding his true self behind a shield of divine rules that no one thought him human? "Nothing quite so harmless, I assure you. I have a past I am not proud of. I have hurt others. . .caused great harm because of my own foolishness."

"I find that hard to believe." Faith ran her hand over the smooth wood of the bedpost and gazed at her sister.

Dajon wanted to share his sordid past with her, if only to convince her he was as fallen and sinful as anyone else. But he thought better of it. Her hatred of men's treatment of women meant she would not react well to his woeful tale. "I have since found great security in the rules of God and forgiveness in His love."

She darted an icy look his way. "And I have found that regardless of whether you follow God's rules, He does not protect you."

Dajon felt as if a twenty-pounder sat upon his chest. He placed his hand over hers on the bedpost and felt her tremble. "I wish I could take your pain away."

She faced him, her eyes narrowing, but did not remove her hand from beneath his. "Why would you care? What is it that you really want, Mr. Waite?"

A good question. What did he want? How could he tell her when he didn't quite know what he wanted? He allowed his gaze to wander over her face, her skin as lustrous as a pearl, her fiery eyes so full of life, the cluster of freckles on her pert little nose that darkened when her ire was pricked, and those plump lips begging for attention. Taking her hand from the post, he brought it to his lips and placed a kiss upon it, all the while keeping his eyes locked upon hers.

She tilted her lips in a gentle smile—a genuine smile devoid of the tough facade and sarcasm. Dajon's heart swelled under the warmth of it.

And he knew. He knew at that moment that he cared for her. As much as he fought it, as much as he denied it, he was enchanted by this brazen, redheaded, stubborn spitfire of a woman.

"I see you have no answer, Mr. Waite?" she quipped. "Well, what should I expect from a—"

Dajon brushed a thumb over the sleek line of her jaw, silencing her. Relishing in the softness of her skin, he tipped her head toward him and placed his lips upon hers. Why he gave in to the impulse, he couldn't say for sure. Perhaps it was to still her insolent tongue. Perhaps he could no longer resist her, or perhaps it was because she'd asked what he wanted, and truth be told, all he wanted was to kiss her.

She sank into him, receiving his kiss with equal passion. He lost himself in the feel of her, the softness of her lips, the smell of her breath, the warmth of her curves next to him. He felt as though his whole body was aflame and drinking her in was the only way to put out the fire. She reached up and ran her fingers over the stubble on his cheek and moaned.

Releasing her lips, Dajon reluctantly withdrew, kissed her cheek, and folded her in his embrace. He ran his fingers through the curls cascading down her back.

Then, as if another person took over her body, she yanked away from him and gave him a fierce look. "How dare you!"

Dajon flexed his jaw then grinned. "You asked me what I wanted, did you not?"

"Aye, but I did not ask for a demonstration."

"I heard no complaints."

"How could I protest with your mouth smothering mine?"

"Perhaps I mistook the moan you uttered as one of ecstasy instead of dissent? You should be more clear in your intentions." Dajon could not help but laugh.

"Allow me to be absolutely clear now, Mr. Waite." Faith stormed toward the door and flung it open. "Please leave. You have shown me what you want. 'Tis naught but the same thing every man wants."

"Great guns, woman, do you really believe me to be so base?" Dajon approached her. " 'Twas more than passion that ignited that kiss." He halted and sighed. Arms crossed over her waist, she would not look his way. " 'Twas more than passion I felt from you." He eased his fingers over her lips, still moist from his kiss. She did not move. Nay, perhaps he was fooling himself into hoping she returned his ardor. But still she allowed his touch. Her chest rose and fell rapidly; for a moment, he thought she would soften, but she batted his hand away and retreated in such haste that she stumbled over a small table by the door. It wobbled on its thin legs, sending something atop it to the floor with a thud.

Click, click, click. A round object spilled from a small pouch and bounced over the wooden planks.

"What have we here?" Dajon bent and picked up a tiny glimmering bead and held it up to a nearby candle. Alarm pricked his scalp and shot his heart into his throat. He shifted it to his other hand and examined it more closely, not ready to acknowledge what he saw.

It was a pearl. A rare conch pearl.

CHAPTER 23

Dajon stomped through the soggy streets of Charles Towne, ignoring his dark surroundings and the muddy water that splashed over his leather boots and up onto his white breeches. It had been nearly a week since he had seen Faith, nearly a week since he had discovered the conch pearls in her chamber. Unable to face the conclusion the pearls forced upon him, he had avoided her altogether, sneaking home late at night after everyone had retired and rising well before dawn.

Between two fingers of his right hand, he ground the tiny pearl, attempting to crush it and cast the powder into the rising wind—scattering its existence. Perhaps then he could silence its screaming accusation—that Faith, the lady he'd vowed to protect, the lady he had come to love, was also the pirate he must now bring to justice.

But the stubborn jewel would not submit to his pounding fury. It remained strong and round and shiny, like a cannonball shot straight through his heart.

Though she had pretended innocence and swore she had obtained the precious pearls in England, Faith had been unable to hide the guilt shriveling the features of her face. Dajon had charged from her chamber, out of the house, and off into the night to quell the rising storm within him. In his haste, he had forgotten to give her back the pearl. Now, after carrying it around with him for a week, he longed to toss it into Charles Towne Bay where no one would ever find it.

But he could not.

Duty. Duty and honor called to him from every

corner. They had been his only friends these past four years. Faithful friends who had never let him down, friends who had restrained his wild streak—kept him safe in God's will where he could no longer hurt himself or anyone else. They would not forsake him now unless he abandoned them. And he had no intention of doing so. The pearl was evidence. One more bread crumb along the path to capturing the Red Siren.

Yet with each step down that path, Dajon's boots weighed like anchors, tugging at his feet and pulling down his heart along with them.

Why? Why, oh Lord, does it have to be her?

Dajon swallowed hard and clenched his fists as he turned another corner, paying no mind to where he was heading but instead allowing his nose to guide him to port. He had spent most of his evenings sauntering about town, waiting until after midnight to return to the Westcott home. Tonight, however, time had become lost amid the confusion in his mind, and it was far too close to dawn to risk disturbing Faith and her sisters. He would spend what was left of the night on his ship. Perchance there he could make sense of the astonishing evening last week: the miraculous rescue of Hope, Faith's intimate disclosure of their sorrowful past. . .

The passionate kiss they had shared.

And the pearl burning his fingers like a red-hot coal.

The depravity that filled the streets only a few hours ago had dwindled into an eerie silence, broken only by the distant lap of waves against the docks. A blast of hot air struck Dajon, carrying with it the smell of fish and manure and the pungent scent of the rice swamps just outside town. Removing his bicorn, he wiped the sweat from his brow and wondered why he had ever thought trading the cool weather of England for this torrid bog was a grand idea.

A woman's scream split the heavy air, jarring Dajon.

Scanning the surroundings, he realized he had wandered into a pernicious section of town by the docks off Bay Street. Shops and warehouses interspersed with taverns rose like ghost ships on each side of him.

Dajon froze, listening for another scream. Above him, thick clouds churned over a half-moon, flinging bands of light across the scene. He took another step. The click of his boots echoed down the deserted street like the cocking of a pistol. A moan sounded. Dajon jerked to the right. A drunken man sprawled on the porch of a house.

Another scream shot across the street, followed by a whimper.

Plopping the pearl into his pocket, Dajon bolted toward the sound, rounding the corner of a warehouse and dodging down a narrow pathway. Another yell for help sped past his ears. Drawing his sword, he barreled toward the end of the alley. He squinted into the darkness and saw the jumbled shapes of two men hunched over someone on the ground. The lacy edge of a petticoat fluttered between their feet.

"You there! Stand down. Get off her!" Dajon dashed toward the men. They stole a glance at him over their shoulders then scampered away like rats down the alleyway before he could reach them.

For a moment, Dajon thought to pursue them, if only to teach them a lesson, but the tiny moan from their victim brought him to her side.

"Are you all right, miss?" He reached down to assist her off the muddy ground, and she flew at him, her arms encircling his back in such a tight grip, his breath burst from his throat.

"Thank you, sir. Oh, thank you for saving me, kind sir."

"Are you injured?" Dajon laid down his sword and tried to pry the woman off him, but she clung to him like a barnacle on a ship.

"I don't know. I am so overcome with fear." Her high-pitched voice rang insincere in his ears, but he shook it off. Fear did odd things to people.

"Can you stand?" Dajon supported her back. "Let me help you up, and we shall see if you are hurt."

Once on her feet, the woman released him and

entered a swoon. He caught her before she toppled back to the ground. A cloud parted, flooding the alleyway with moonlight, and dark green eyes the color of a tropical sea gazed at him as if he were the only man in the world. The scent of sweet peaches swirled about his nose, chasing away the foul odors of the city. Her breasts rose and fell with each surging breath in the low-cut bodice. Long ebony hair fluttered in the breeze like silk.

Dajon swallowed.

Taking a step back, he cleared his throat and searched for his sword. "You appear to be unharmed, miss."

Retrieving his weapon, he sheathed it and found his eyes drawn to her again. She gave him one of those smiles that women give men across a room to entice them: a mixture of innocence, feminine dependence, and a hint of steamy dalliance.

Heat flared through Dajon even as every muscle tensed within him. He looked away. "You shouldn't be out alone so late at night, miss."

"I know." She sighed. "It was unavoidable, I'm afraid. And I was on my way home when those two beasts. . ." Pausing, she threw her hand to her chest as if to still the beating of her heart then raised it to wipe a tear from her eye.

Dajon touched her arm to offer some comfort. Truly, she seemed quite distraught. "You are safe now."

"Aye, thanks to you." She placed her hands on his blue coat, her fingers exploring his muscular chest. "What would I have done if you hadn't come to my rescue?"

" 'Twas my pleasure, miss." Dajon gripped his sword and stared off into the nebulous shadows of the night, anywhere but into this woman's sensuous green eyes.

"Perhaps I can repay you for your kindness?" She snuggled up beside him and fingered the gold buttons on his coat.

Dajon smelled danger. It wasn't the harrowing kind of life-threatening danger brought on by swords and guns and evil men. It was a delicious kind of danger, the kind of danger a man could lose himself in for days, only to emerge a skeleton of the man he had been, sullied and damaged beyond repair. It was the kind of danger, however, that was almost worth it.

Almost.

Lord, my God and my strength, was all Dajon could think to pray.

He clenched his jaw and allowed his gaze to wander over the woman's voluptuous form. "I thank you for your offer, miss, but I am otherwise engaged."

The woman's eyes grew wide beneath a furrowed brow. She flinched as if he had struck her. "You dare to turn me down?" Her tone carried no anger, no wounded sentiment, just pure incredulity at his rejection. 'Twas obvious she had never received one before.

God, why are You allowing this temptation now? Dajon tightened his grip on the hilt of his sword and rubbed his fingers over the cold silver. Had the week not held enough trials for one man to endure? Now this? His greatest weakness flaunted before him? He nearly laughed as he stared at one of the most alluring females he had ever seen, burrowing next to him and all but handing herself to him as if he were the king of England.

Certainly she was no real lady. Possibly a trollop or perhaps some nobleman's mistress. Who would know if Dajon spent some time with her? What harm would it do? By thunder, he could use some comfort after the shock and dismay of discovering the pearl in Faith's chamber.

Dajon squeezed the bridge of his nose. *No. Lord, I promised to follow You—to abide by Your laws.* A surge of strength leveled his shoulders.

With a cordial grin, he took her hand from his arm and released it. "Truly, you are quite lovely. Irresistible, to be sure. I would, however, prefer the honor of escorting you safely home."

Her green eyes filled to glistening pools. She shook her head. "You are a true gentleman, sir."

Footsteps sounded.

Whisking tears from her cheeks, the woman's breathing took on a rapid pace. The lines on her face tightened.

Dajon snapped his gaze down the dark alleyway as the footsteps drew nearer, but before he could draw his pistol, the lady began pounding his chest and screaming, "Get off me! Help me! Help me!"

Seizing her arms, Dajon shook her. "What are you saying? Have you gone mad? Calm yourself, woman."

She took a step back and clawed at her gown until it tore down the front, revealing her undergarments beneath.

Forgetting about the oncoming footsteps, Dajon stared aghast at her as she pummeled him again with her fists.

"What's this?" A stern voice boomed into the alleyway, and a dark figure rushed toward Dajon and shoved him to the ground. Drawing his sword, the man leveled the tip upon Dajon's chest.

The woman gasped and held her gown together as if a sudden rush of propriety had overcome her.

"Margaret, who is this man? Was he accosting you? I'll run him through right here!"

Dajon struggled to rise, but the man's blade kept him on the ground. He shifted his disbelieving gaze from the woman—Margaret—who continued to feign hysterics, to the man, a large fellow with the gruff face and haggard clothing of a dockworker and the hands of a trained swordsman.

The realization that he had been duped swallowed Dajon like a sudden squall at sea.

What could be the purpose? Surely everyone knew a lieutenant in His Majesty's Navy had no wealth to speak of unless it had been inherited.

He ground his teeth together then eyed the woman with the same look he gave one of his crew when he knew the correct course to take. "Miss, I beg you to tell this man the truth."

A variety of emotions passed over her face like waves on a beach, temporarily disturbing her pristine features: from anger to confusion to remorse to sorrow. Her lips puckered then flattened as her eyes flickered between the men.

Finally, her shoulders lowered, and she released her torn dress. "Nay, brother. He has done me no harm. In fact, quite the opposite." Sorrow alighted upon her features. "He has treated me more like a lady than any man I've ever known."

The anger in the man's dark eyes intensified under a flash of confusion. He gazed back and forth between Miss Margaret and Dajon; then, with a shrug of his shoulders, he sheathed his blade and held out his hand. "My apologies, sir. My sister often finds herself in, shall we say, delicate situations with men." He chuckled.

Grabbing his hand, Dajon stood and brushed off his coat. "I have no doubt."

"I am Henry Wittfield." He gestured toward the woman. "The unfortunate brother of Mrs. Margaret Gladstone."

"Dajon Waite, commander of the HMS *Enforcer*, at your service." Dajon nodded, still stunned by the odd events.

Henry turned to Margaret. "Your husband is worried about you."

She blew out a sigh and grabbed his arm. "As always, brother. Now let's be gone." She tugged on him as if she couldn't get away fast enough.

"Good night to you, sir," Mr. Wittfield said over his shoulder as Margaret hauled him from the alleyway without a single glance back at Dajon.

Retrieving his fallen bicorn, Dajon plopped it atop his head and stared up at the half-moon that had lit the outlandish scene like a stage light pouring down on a ghoulish comedy act. Even as a cloud overtook the glowing orb and shrouded Dajon once again in darkness, even as the cold mud now soaked through his breeches, even as the stink of refuse returned to sting his nose, he was thankful God had given him the strength to resist the sumptuous Mrs. Gladstone.

⤳

Borland tapped lightly on the captain's door. He had heard Dajon return just before dawn, and from the sound of his pounding boots and the slam of his door, he assumed all had gone according to plan. Now, unable to wait another moment, he risked disturbing the captain's sleep with some minor detail of the ship.

He tapped again.

"Enter," the gruff voice laden with sleep bellowed, and Borland pushed aside the oak slab. As he scanned the room, he spotted Dajon sitting on the edge of his rumpled bed, head in his hands.

"What is it, Borland?" Dajon rubbed his eyes.

"Henderson wants to know if he should grease the masts today, Captain."

"You woke me for that?" Dajon gave a disgruntled snort.

"My apologies, Captain. It *is* after eight bells, but I see now you had a rather late night." He delighted to see the dark, swollen splotches beneath Dajon's half-open eyes. "Is everything all right, Captain? Did you encounter some mischief last night?"

"Whatever would make you think that?" Dajon stood, annoyance hardening the lines in his jaw.

"You slept in your uniform. 'Tis unlike you to be so untidy." Borland took a tentative step toward him and pointed at his breeches. "And you're covered in mud." Truth be told, he'd never seen Dajon in such a state of disarray, and that could mean only one thing.

Sir Carteret's plan had worked.

Dajon slogged to his desk. "I had a most eventful evening."

Excellent. Borland could almost hear the constable and his men—or better yet, the marines—marching across the deck to arrest Dajon. He could almost see himself obligingly having to assume command of the ship as they dragged Dajon away.

"Eventful, sir?"

Fisting his hands on his waist, Dajon stared out the window. "Aye. But nothing I couldn't handle, I assure you."

Egad. Nothing he couldn't handle. Mrs. Margaret Gladstone, who was both the wife of a rich tradesman—a silversmith—and a woman in possession of less-than-sterling morals, had been the perfect lure. The only thing that bothered Borland was why the authorities had not been alerted last night as soon as the woman's brother caught Dajon in the reprehensible act.

No bother. It would happen soon enough, and finally the great Dajon Waite's luck would run out like so much seawater through a deck scuttle. Then Borland would assume the command he should have been given long ago. Justice would be served at last.

"Borland. . .Borland?"

Borland snapped his focus back to Dajon, who had turned to face him with a quizzical look. "Yes, Captain."

"I said to tell Henderson to proceed in greasing the masts, if you please." He rubbed the stubble on his jaw. "Now will that be all, or do you have some other pressing emergency?"

"No, Captain. That is all." Borland shifted his boots, unable to force himself to leave without trying once more to discover what had occurred last night. "Are you sure all is well? You seem distraught, Captain. Perhaps I can help."

Dajon eased out of his crumpled coat and tossed it onto a chair with a huff, but when he faced Borland, the harshness in his eyes had softened. "You are indeed a good friend, Borland. I thank you for your concern." He approached and clasped Borland's forearm then released it with a sigh. "But it seems I must bear this particular burden on my own."

A pinprick of guilt prevented the grin that strained to rise upon Borland's lips. He could manage only a nod as he reminded himself that his so-called friend had stolen what was rightfully his. Saluting, he turned and dashed out the door before Dajon's friendly demeanor did any more damage to his resolve for justice.

⤳

Dajon stared at the thick oak door long after the echo of its slam had faded. Mr. Borland was behaving rather oddly. Whatever had gotten into the man? Had he taken up grog so early in the morning? After the events of last night, Dajon wondered if the whole world had gone mad. Rubbing the back of his neck, he walked to the stern window that looked out upon Charles Towne Harbor. Ships of all sizes, ranging from schooners to brigantines to merchant frigates, rocked in the bay, their decks a flurry of activity as men loaded and unloaded merchandise before the heat of the day made the work unbearable. Off in the distance, Shute's Folly Island floated upon the water like an alligator's eye surveying its surroundings. Beyond it, James and Sullivan's Islands formed the entrance to the port of Charles Towne, protecting it from the ravages of the Atlantic.

But also providing an excellent point of entry for pirates—big enough for a large ship to sail through, but small enough to form a blockade and hold the city hostage. Which was precisely what Blackbeard had done not three months earlier.

Dipping his fingers in his waistcoat pocket, he pulled out the shiny round pearl, hoping to pull out a pebble instead, a lump of coal, anything but the conch pearl—hoping he had only dreamed that he'd found it in Faith's chamber. But there it perched betwixt his dirty fingers, winking at him in the sun's rays that beamed in through the paned window. Amazing how one little jewel could turn his life into a pool of bilge.

He tossed it in the air and caught it then dropped it back into his pocket. He had already set in play his plan to trap the notorious Red Siren. And now he must pray—pray with all his heart—that the villain was not Faith Westcott. Gripping the window ledge, he squeezed the rough wood until his knuckles whitened. If he was forced to arrest her, what would happen to her sisters? Her father? Not to mention to Faith herself?

She would be hanged.

All convicted pirates were hanged.

Something solid like a ball of tangled rope stuck in his throat, nearly choking him. How could he go through with it?

He slammed his fists down on the ledge. A splinter jabbed his skin.

Yet how could he not?

Four years ago, he'd vowed to live his life for God and country and nothing else. He would not make another mistake based on foolhardy emotions.

CHAPTER 24

Faith dropped another lump of sugar into her tea and offered the silver bowl, stacked full of sweet clusters, to Hope, sitting beside her on the flowered settee. Her sister shook her head then continued to stare down at the cup of coffee cradled in her hands. It had been a week since the traumatic incident at the Pink House, and although the doctor had pronounced Hope physically well, she had not been her usual exuberant self since. In fact, neither a single complaint nor critical remark had escaped her mouth, not even a plea to go shopping or attend a party. Sad to say, Faith preferred the old petulant Hope to this shell of a woman.

"Grace, have you any plans today?" Faith turned toward her other sister, who sat straight backed in the Queen Anne upholstered armchair, sipping her tea.

"Am I permitted to have plans?" Grace tilted her head, her voice carrying a sarcastic sting.

A light breeze stirred the curtains that flanked the open french doors leading out to the veranda. Faith caught the scent of the sea and took a deep breath, shifting in her seat. Oh, to be out upon those vast, carefree waters instead of sitting in this stuffy room with her equally stuffy sisters. She had thought spending the morning with them in the drawing room would be a good start to a cheerful day together, but she found their humors had not improved overmuch since yesterday.

Faith had remained home the entire week, not daring to take her ship out after Mr. Waite had discovered the pearl in her chamber. Unfortunately, she'd been forced to endure Sir Wilhelm's company on two separate occasions: first when he'd come to inquire after Hope's welfare, and second when he'd intruded on their dinner to invite Faith to a concert at Dillon's Inn. Both times she had ushered him quickly out the door, spouting excuses of ill health and dour humor. But she knew the man would not be put off forever.

However, during her time at home, Faith had been able to keep a stricter eye upon her sisters and spend much-needed time with them, as well as curb their foolish ventures into dangerous territory.

But from the tight expression souring Grace's face, she doubted her sister had been pleased with Faith's constant attentions.

Setting her cup down on the silver service tray with a clink, Grace pressed the folds of her plain muslin skirt. "I had planned to deliver a basket of fresh peaches and bread to the Baker widow. She has four children to feed, you know."

Faith clenched her jaw and felt a knot form in her stomach. "But if I understand correctly, her home is far outside the city walls. Nearly at the Ashley River."

Hope looked up from her coffee. "There have been several Indian attacks there of late." Her monotone voice belied the danger in her statement as she stared into the empty space of the room.

"Indeed, Hope." Faith laid a gentle hand on her arm but kept her firm gaze upon Grace. "And that is precisely why you will not go."

Grace smoothed the side of her raven hair as if a strand had dared to come loose. Which never happened, of course, because she kept them all drawn so tightly in a bun that Faith often wondered if that wasn't the reason her expression seemed so rigid.

Grace's green eyes snapped toward Faith. "It has been most pleasant having you home, Faith, but Father did not leave you as caretaker over us."

Hope glanced out the window as another breeze swirled through the room. "No. He left Mr. Waite."

"Where *is* the glorious Mr. Waite?" Grace smirked.

"Perchance you have scared him off, Faith?"

"I have no idea." Faith fingered the lacy trim on her blue cotton gown as the tea bit her stomach. Pressing a hand over her complaining belly, she glanced at the intricately carved crown molding then at the Dutch floral oil paintings her mother had collected that decorated the violet walls, trying to avoid both of her sisters' imperious gazes.

"I should rather suppose navy business keeps him away." But she knew better. She had learned from Lucas that Mr. Waite had spent every night in the guest-house, always leaving before dawn. Clearly he'd been avoiding her. She pictured the look on his face when she had told him—lied to him—about the pearls, how his brows had pinched together, how his eyes had widened, and how a look of disbelief and sorrow had passed through their blue depths. Most likely he had spent the week gathering the evidence he needed to arrest her. But what proof could he find?

Her ship.

Perhaps he had discovered her ship—or rather *his* ship. Still, he would have no way to link the vessel to her. Lucas had traveled there twice this past week to feed Morgan, and the *Red Siren* had been anchored in the same spot, seemingly undiscovered.

A pang of guilt made her shift in her seat. Guilt for the lies she had told, guilt for the life she had chosen. What was wrong with her?

"Clearly he is quite taken with you, Faith." Grace gave her a smile that revealed a bit of sauciness beneath her prudish exterior.

"Absurd." Setting down her cup, Faith jumped to her feet. "Pure rubbish." She strolled to the window and looked out upon the gardens below where Molly's purple bougainvillea climbed the white fence that guarded the side of the house. "He merely looks out for us as instructed by Father." Then why did she feel a sudden elation at Grace's statement? No matter. Even if Mr. Waite had felt some affection for her, it surely would have suffocated by now beneath his growing suspicions.

"Regardless, I owe him my life," Hope said.

"You owe God your life," Grace retorted. Faith swung around just in time to see Molly enter with a tray of biscuits and another kettle of tea. She nodded toward the cook, who set the tray down on the mahogany table in the center of the room. The buttery smell of the biscuits danced beneath Faith's nose even as her stomach lurched at the thought of eating.

She headed back toward her sisters. "Grace is right. 'Twas a miracle if ever I saw one." And although Faith still had a difficult time believing exactly what she had seen, she could not deny it, either.

Hope set her cup down beside the tray. "It was no such thing. Mr. Waite rescued me."

Molly clasped her hands together. "I beg your pardon, Miss Hope, if you'll forgive me for interrupting, but Mr. Corwin can't speak of nothin' else." Her eyes widened. "How there was a shield of light in front of Miss Hope and how those ruffians couldn't even see her until Mr. Waite arrived. Then how they was held off by some force while you got away. Why, I never seen Mr. Corwin so excited. He's behaving like he's just been made governor of Carolina."

Hope snickered.

"But you, Miss Faith"—Molly shook a long slender finger at her—"you shouldn't have been there at all. A lady in such a place. The shame of it."

"If your God can protect Hope," Faith said, her voice a bit more caustic than she intended, "then He can protect me as well, can He not?"

Molly snorted. "He can do what He wants, I suppose. And you should be thanking Him that He kep' you safe. But the both of you best be staying out of such places, or He may not the next time."

"God always protects me when I journey to do His will." Grace straightened her back and clasped her hands together in her lap. "However, if you're out of His will, no wonder you found yourself in harm's way." The sanctimonious look on her face suddenly collapsed into folds of confusion. "Yet. . ."

Hope scowled at her sister. "Then why, pray tell, did He protect me, Grace?"

"I thought you insisted He did nothing of the kind?" Grace smirked.

Narrowing her eyes, Hope collapsed into the settee with a huff. "I'm still not saying He saved me. I'm simply pointing out that your conjecture is flawed."

Faith eased beside Hope. Her sister had not relayed any of the details of that night to anyone, despite frequent prodding. In fact, this was the first sign of emotion she'd exhibited in a week, and despite the argumentative nature of Hope's words, Faith was happy to see the old Hope come back to life.

Molly grabbed the tray of empty cups. "All I kin say is, it thrills me to know that the Almighty is still active and powerful and kin save us even from our own follies."

"He is the same yesterday, today, and forever." Grace laid a hand on Molly's arm and smiled.

"That He is. I kin see that now. And Mr. Corwin is starting to see things different as well." Molly winked at Faith as if they shared a secret, but Faith wanted no part of this holy alliance. If Lucas decided to follow such an untrustworthy God, then he had best do so on his own time. Turning, Molly began humming one of her conscience-grating hymns as she exited the room.

Faith sighed. She must take the *Red Siren* out. One more good raid, one more shipload of plunder and she would be able to care for her sisters properly, hire protection for Grace—an army if she had to—and Hope would no longer have to vie for the affections of such wretched men as Lord Falkland.

Yet why did she have the nagging feeling that no amount of wealth would be enough to tame her two sisters?

As if in answer to Faith's question, Hope crossed her arms over her chest. "When can I see Arthur. . .Lord Falkland?"

"I beg your pardon." Faith gave her sister a scorching look. "Is he not the one that got you into that mess at the Pink House? He abandoned you. Don't you remember?"

"How do you know that?"

"Your friend Miss Cormac told us."

"You spoke with Anne?" A strange expression of shock fringed with humor danced over Hope's face. "I wouldn't believe her. She rarely tells the truth."

Why Hope would befriend someone who was devoid of honesty was beyond Faith, but that was another issue. "She had no reason to lie. Lord Falkland left you all alone in that heinous tavern to be ravished and God knows what else. You cannot deny he was the one who brought you there."

Hope begrudgingly nodded but would not meet Faith's gaze.

Faith took her hand in hers. "Please, dear. You must see what type of man he is. He doesn't love you."

"He does love me." Hope jerked her hand away. "You don't know him. 'Twas unavoidable. He was called away on a matter of great urgency." Her eyes glistened with tears.

"Could he not escort you home first?"

"He asked Mr. Ackers to do the honor."

"And who, pray tell, is Mr. Ackers?"

"A loyal friend of Arthur's." Hope swallowed and gazed down at the Chinese rug warming the floor at their feet.

"And why did this Mr. Ackers not escort you home?"

"I don't know. He disappeared."

"Disappeared? Of all the. . ." Fury exploded within Faith, sending sharp pains into her belly. She wanted to drag one of her cannons to this Lord Falkland's home and blast it to rubbish. "Seems your Lord Falkland invokes no more loyalty among his friends than a thief in a room full of magistrates."

" 'Twas Mr. Ackers who left me." Hope's lip quivered. Tears slid down her cheeks. "I didn't know what to do."

Faith wanted to tell her she shouldn't have been there

in the first place, but instead, she plucked a handkerchief from her pocket and handed it to Hope. "If it weren't for Mr. Waite—"

"And God," Grace interjected.

"I loathe to think what could have happened to you," Faith continued.

"What difference does it make?" Hope swiped at her tears. "I'm already sullied." Leaning forward, she dropped her head into her hands.

Faith's heart crumbled into ashes. She glanced at Grace, who returned her agonized gaze.

Rising, Grace approached them and sat on the other side of Hope. "You are not sullied in God's eyes."

"God is not here," Hope muttered. "And He does not have to live in a society that allows men to dominate women and then holds the women accountable for the outcome."

Faith waited for Grace's usual retort; instead, tears flooded her sister's eyes, and she put her arm around Hope, saying nothing.

Truth be told, Faith couldn't agree more with her sister's assessment, but what was to be done about it? It was the way of things. Wealth was their only salvation, and until she could garner enough of it, she must stop Hope from destroying what was left of her life. "Nevertheless, I insist you stay away from Lord Falkland."

Hope raised her glassy eyes to Faith. "You cannot order me about. I will see whom I choose to see." No anger tainted her tone, no defiance, no desperation. She had simply uttered the statement as fact.

A chill iced Faith's bones. Rebellious, stubborn girl! How could she make her see the error of her ways before it was too late? "I assure you, Lord Falkland will cause you naught but pain. Why do you insist on destroying yourself?"

"The good Lord may not come to your aid next time, Hope." Grace brushed a honey-colored lock of hair from Hope's face.

"I care not." Shrugging from between her sisters, Hope rose and took a deep breath. "How many suitors do you see lining up at our door? I'm two and twenty already. And I love Arthur...Lord Falkland. He may not be perfect, but he loves me and he has enough wealth to keep me happy."

Faith stood, feeling every muscle tense. Enough of this defiance. If she had to, she'd put her sisters under guard to keep them from harm.

Oh, Mother, I'm trying so hard to protect them, but you didn't exactly give me much to work with. "Hope, you will not—"

Edwin appeared in the doorway, his face even paler than usual. "Mr. Waite to see you, miss." His droopy eyes darted around the room. "He has two gentlemen with him."

"Gentlemen? Officers? Are they in red uniforms?"

"One of them is, miss."

She coughed, gasping for air, and then held a hand over her aching stomach. Had he come to arrest her? She scanned the room looking for a place to hide and then realized how ridiculous that was.

"Edwin, please tell him I'm not feeling well. In fact"—she glanced at her sisters with a pleading look— "tell him we are *all* not feeling well."

"Very well, miss." With a sigh, Edwin left, but no sooner had he disappeared than a scuffle sounded in the hall and Mr. Waite's deep voice bounded through the room.

"Not feeling well? All three of you?" He marched into the room as if it were the deck of his ship. He leveled a hot and loaded gaze straight at Faith.

CHAPTER 25

Dajon patted Faith's gloved hand and gently tucked it in the crook of his elbow. He could still feel the tremble in it even after an hour of strolling downtown. He had certainly expected some reaction from her after the traumatic night they had shared last week, especially after their passionate kiss. But he hadn't expected the complete horror that had shot from her eyes when he had entered the drawing room with Borland and Cudney on his heels. He had only thought to bring the marine at the last minute, as a way to gauge her guilt. And, unfortunately, her reaction had weighed heavily on the scales of iniquity—a pirate's reaction if ever he saw one.

All color had drained from her face. Even the peach of her lips had transformed to gray. Her chest heaved like the swells of a summer squall upon the sea. What other explanation could be offered?

"I thank you, Mr. Waite, for your kind offer." She looked up at him and smiled, her auburn eyes a sparkling mixture of unease and playfulness. "I do admit I feel much better out in the summer air. And my sisters needed an outing more than I, I'm afraid."

"My pleasure, Miss Westcott. I had no idea you have been indisposed."

"Just a bit of fatigue. Nothing to be concerned about." She plucked out her fan and fluttered it through the air.

He glanced at Hope on the arm of Borland as the two of them strolled down the lane. "Your sister seems much improved."

"Yes." Faith lowered her lashes. "She has been melancholy this past week. Only today has she returned somewhat to herself." She sighed and allowed a tiny grin. "Although I'm not altogether sure I am ready for the return of her peevish attitude."

Dajon chuckled, but Faith sobered instantly. "I must beg your forgiveness, Mr. Waite, for my burdening you with our family affairs that night."

"Never fear." Dajon patted her hand again. "You can trust me to keep your confidence."

"I am in your debt, sir." She gave his arm a squeeze that reached up to warm his heart.

Grace, her hand stiffly on Cudney's arm, came alongside him. "We have missed your company, Mr. Waite." She gazed at him with green eyes framed by lashes as thick as a virgin forest. With her petite, curvaceous figure and ebony hair, she possessed an exotic beauty that rarely peeked out from behind her rigid exterior.

"How kind of you to say, Miss Grace. I'm afraid I've been quite busy on board my ship." He eyed his marine, marching beside her. The man's stiff mouth and glazed eyes indicated he wasn't particularly enjoying Grace's company. Perhaps she had been expounding to him the dangers of sin as they strode along.

"Thank you for inviting us to the festival," Grace continued. "My sister was becoming quite the magistrate, forbidding us even to leave the house."

"She was, was she?" Dajon studied Faith, who was fanning the air about her as if swatting away the conversation. "The lady who rides a horse better than most men, enters dangerous taverns in the thick of night, and fires pistols with deadly accuracy? That lady?"

"Yes, exactly." Grace giggled. "She holds us to a far higher standard than herself, it would seem."

"Indeed."

Faith snapped her hard gaze to her sister. "The things I do are for your protection and are quite different from putting oneself in danger's way for naught."

Grace frowned. "I would hardly call feeding the—"

"Nevertheless," Dajon interrupted, hoping to ward off another mind-hammering argument between the sisters. "It is I who should thank you, Miss Grace, for the pleasure of your company." He grinned. With a lift of her nose, she and Mr. Cudney proceeded ahead to join Hope and Mr. Borland.

Dajon had been pleased to discover that the citizens of Charles Towne had planned a small festival celebrating the return of the summer's crops after much of their plantings had been destroyed by the Yamasee Indian raids the previous year. Local artisans agreed to display their wares on the street while musicians entertained passersby. The small event provided the perfect opportunity to invite the Westcott ladies out for a pleasurable day, as well as the perfect distraction for Dajon's real purpose—to bait Faith with the news of the arrival of a merchant ship.

But as he allowed his gaze to sweep over her smooth skin, kissed pink by the sun, her fiery curls dancing in the breeze around the half-moon scar that adorned her graceful neck, even the cluster of freckles atop her nose, he wondered how he could be so deceptive to such an extraordinary woman. He swallowed, gazing at her moist lips, remembering the soft feel of them on his own, her hunger, her passion, her need for him. Shifting his eyes away, he prayed for a cool breeze to blast over him and revive his reason.

But what choice did he have? He had to know the truth, even if it killed him. And somehow today, as Faith walked beside him, clinging to his arm as if she belonged there forever, he knew that it just might.

⌒

Faith adjusted her flowered straw hat, longing to tear it from her head and shake her hair loose in the breeze. Beneath the grueling August sun, her head felt like a poached egg. Or maybe it was the feel of Mr. Waite's strong arm beneath her hand that caused her to overheat.

More than likely, it was the trembling that still coursed through her body. For she had thought for certain when he had marched into their drawing room, marine in tow, that he had procured enough evidence to arrest her.

Turning down Queen Street, she felt a salty breeze waft around her. She took in a deep breath, noting Mr. Waite did the same. He loved the sea as much as she did. At least they had one thing in common. But their similitude stopped there.

The blasted man was taunting her. She knew it.

She shouldn't have accepted his invitation. But as she heard Hope's laughter and saw Grace examining an Indian basket, she knew her sisters had needed a carefree day of amusement.

Perhaps it would be Faith's last one with them.

Perhaps Mr. Waite was simply luring her close enough to the half-moon bastion so when he arrested her he wouldn't have far to throw her in the Watch House prison. Her mouth went dry even as another trickle of perspiration slid down the back of her dress.

When they turned down Bay Street, the cobblestone avenue exploded in a cacophony of sounds and movements. Ladies decked in gay colors, on the arms of men in their finery, flitted across the path to examine shop wares displayed in front of the stores. Music frolicked down the street from a small band positioned under the shade of a hickory tree. Harpsichord, violin, and flute harmonized together in a lively tune.

As they wove their way through the clamoring crowd, they passed exquisitely carved furniture made from oak, mahogany, pine, and cypress, oil paintings from local artists, the latest fashions, shoes, silk fans, musical instruments, and gold and silver jewelry. A variety of languages filled the air, most of which Faith recognized: Dutch, German, French. Charles Towne attracted people from all over the world looking for freedom and a new start in a fresh land, and this day every one of them seemed to be strolling about on Bay Street.

Up ahead, a French trapper and his Indian wife bartered with a shop owner over some pelts flung across his arm. Long matted hair framed his face and swayed across his back as he spoke. Behind him, his wife, wearing dirt-smudged furs, kept her gaze on the ground. Yet not three yards away strolled a man and lady decked in silk and lace—the finest fashions of London society. Faith doubted she would ever grow accustomed to the extreme contradiction of this wild land.

A curricle clomped toward them, and Mr. Waite ushered Faith from its path, placing himself between her and the street. A woman, donned in a silk ruffled gown and white powered wig, gave Mr. Waite an appreciative smile from its seat as they passed.

"Are you enjoying yourself, Miss Westcott?" He leaned down to whisper in her ear. The scent of leather and lye swirled about her nose and quickened her breathing. "You seem a bit tense." His lips curved in that sardonic grin that always sent her heart pounding.

Faith dared to glance into his sharp blue eyes, down to his strong jaw, and over to his dark umber hair pulled behind him. She could understand why he attracted feminine admiration. She averted her gaze before she gave him the satisfaction of seeing her own admiration.

"I fear I am still not quite myself, Mr. Waite, but I am happy to see my sisters enjoying themselves."

Faith closed her eyes, longing to drown out all the sounds around her, save the lap of the bay upon the quays. She took in a deep breath. There it was: the salty smell of the sea hidden among the odor of horse and sweat and city refuse. She could hardly wait to sail upon its mighty waves again where no problems, no guilt, no fears assailed her. Only peace.

That feeling of peace quickly diminished, however, when Faith opened her eyes and saw the Watch House up ahead. She froze, drew a shaky breath, and forced herself onward. The sounds of the city faded into a muddled clamor as she strolled past the ominous building, her hand still clenching Mr. Waite's arm. Unable to avert her gaze, she stared at the circular stone tower that protruded in a semicircle into the bay, a citadel guarding the city's entrance. The brick Watch House loomed just before it. Faith couldn't help but wonder how many poor souls were imprisoned within.

Oh God, please don't let me become one of them.

Good heavens. She was praying again. Yet even as she made the silent plea, she tripped over one of the cobblestones and barreled forward.

Catching her arm, Mr. Waite stayed her fall. "Are you all right, Miss Westcott?"

"Yes, forgive me." His hand touched the small of her back, sending a flame of heat up her spine. She jerked away from him. "I wasn't paying attention."

"You seem a bit unnerved today, miss." The captain shifted his daring blue eyes between her and the Watch House.

"I am concerned for my sisters. Forgive me. I am not very good company."

"That could never be the case." He gave her a sincere smile.

As they continued onward past the Watch House gates, Faith's heart took on a more relaxed beat.

He must not have any evidence against her. He'd probably forgotten all about the pearl, and she had been worried for nothing.

As they passed one of the docks, the wooden frame of a ship projecting from an open warehouse drew Faith's attention. Several men scampered about, and the pounding of hammers and the scrape of saws filled the air.

Faith had never seen a ship being built before, and she stopped, lifting her hand to shield her eyes from the sun. A familiar figure hefting a large piece of wood onto his shoulder emerged from the warehouse, shouting orders to one of the men.

"Is that not the man we met in church?"

Mr. Waite snapped his gaze toward the open warehouse. "Ah yes." He raised a hand to his mouth. "Mr. Mason," he called.

Mr. Mason squinted in their direction then dropped the log from his shoulder and waved. He started to move toward them but froze as if he saw a ghost. Following his gaze, Faith found it had locked upon Hope, who stopped beside her.

Grabbing a cloth from a bench, Mr. Mason mopped the sweat from his face and neck then tossed it aside and approached them.

After nodding his greeting toward Mr. Waite, Faith, and the others, he turned toward Hope. "Good day, Miss Hope." He swiped a hand through his brown hair and drank her in with his gaze. His moist cotton shirt clung to his arms and chest, revealing strong muscles beneath.

Hope huffed. "Whatever are you doing out here in the hot sun like a common laborer?"

His grin fell slack. "I fear I *am* a common laborer." He jerked a thumb over his shoulder. "I am building my third merchant ship." He rubbed his stubbled jaw and crossed his thick arms over his chest.

"Mr. Mason's other two ships are no doubt upon the seas at this moment," Mr. Waite commented. "Someday, Mr. Mason, I fear you will be a wealthy man."

"All I want is to be able to take care of myself, Mr. Waite." Mr. Mason glanced at the captain, then his eyes quickly shifted back to Hope. "And a family someday."

"Still." Hope raised a haughty brow. "Can you not hire someone to do this menial work?"

"I prefer to work alongside my men and make sure the job is done correctly, if that's acceptable to your ladyship." He gave a mock bow.

"Why should I care? I simply do not see the point of getting so filthy and sweaty." A deep shade of red crept up Hope's face.

"Work is good for you, Miss Hope. It gives you something to occupy your time other than pleasing yourself." Amusement flickered in his dark eyes. "You should try it sometime."

Grace giggled, and Faith found herself enjoying the banter between Hope and this common man. She had never seen her sister quite so befuddled, so abashed. Normally Hope would have dismissed the man instantly and walked away, yet there she stood, as mesmerized with him as he seemed to be with her.

"How dare you?" Hope's jaw tightened. She tore her gaze from his, as if waiting for his apology, waiting for him to grovel at her feet as most men did.

"You are the one who stopped to converse with me."

"I did no such thing."

"Yet here you remain." He grinned.

"I shall remedy that immediately, sir." She grabbed onto Mr. Borland's hand. "Come along, Mr. Borland."

With a shrug of his shoulders, the lieutenant followed behind her like a horse-drawn carriage.

Faith and Mr. Waite said their good-byes as Mr. Mason returned to his work, chuckling as he went.

"At last a man who sees beyond our sister's beauty," Grace commented with a chortle.

"Indeed." Faith squeezed Grace's hand. "He is extraordinary at that."

"What an impertinent, rude man." Hope sneered when they caught up to her and Borland.

"I thought him quite charming," Faith teased.

"You would think—"

"Ah, there is Mallory's Tea Shoppe," Mr. Waite interrupted. "I hear they serve an excellent lemonade." He gestured to a small, quaint shop to their right. The wide front porch was furnished with white tables and chairs. "Shall we refresh ourselves, ladies?"

Grace nodded with a smile, and Hope's eyes lit up. "Why, yes. That sounds delightful."

After everyone was seated with lemonade in hand, Mr. Waite rose, scraping his chair over the aged porch floor. "If you will excuse me, ladies. I saw someone inside I need to speak with." He cast a knowing look toward Borland. "I shall only be a minute."

An awkward silence ensued in his absence.

Faith studied Mr. Cudney, whose posture reminded her of a backstay under a stiff wind. What was his purpose among them if not to arrest her? Surely not to socialize. He seemed as out of place as a priest on a pirate ship.

"Mr. Cudney, may I ask how long have you been a marine?"

"A little over two years, miss." His brown eyes met hers with a brief smile then skittered away.

"And do you serve on only His Majesty's ships?"

"Yes."

"The marines fight as infantry aboard the ship," Mr. Borland said. "They carry out guard duties, suppress mutinies, and enforce regulations."

"I see." Faith knew that, of course, but smiled at Borland nonetheless.

"You must be very courageous." Hope rested her head in one hand and cooed in Mr. Cudney's direction. A red hue that matched the color of his uniform marched up the poor man's face.

"Speaking of courage," Mr. Borland began, stroking his mustache and clearing his throat. "We shall need courage like his to protect the *Lady Adeline* sailing in from Martinique day after next."

"Protection from what?" Grace asked, taking a sip of her lemonade.

Faith pressed her cool mug between her hands, the tantalizing scent of lemons swirling about her nose, and willed her expression to remain placid as she listened to Borland's response.

"From pirates, miss, of course, as well as other villains upon the sea."

Grace fingered a button at her high collar. "May God have mercy on their wicked souls."

Frowning at her sister, Faith ignored the unusual guilt needling her heart.

The *Lady Adeline*. A merchant vessel that needed guarding. Precisely the opportunity Faith had been awaiting. But how could she find out more without giving herself away?

"Pray tell, Mr. Borland," Faith said, twirling a lock

of her hair nonchalantly around her finger, "what is so special about this merchant vessel that you believe it to be the target of pirates?" She took a sip of her lemonade, the sour taste curling her tongue.

"Only that she carries a cargo of Spanish gold stolen in a raid. Worth a fortune, I'm told."

Faith coughed and nearly spit the lemonade from her mouth. "So Mr. Waite will be at sea the day after next?"

"Aye, in two days. We are to meet the ship mid-morning off St. Helena Sound but should return to port before sunset." He leaned toward her, a sly look gleaming in his eye. "I suppose 'tis acceptable to relay this information to you and your sisters. Your father is an admiral, after all." He sat back in his chair and straightened his coat. "Is there something you expect you'll need Mr. Waite for day after tomorrow?"

"Nay." Faith waved a hand through the air. "I just wondered in case my sisters and I require an escort into town."

Grace's brow wrinkled. "We can simply ask Lucas or Edwin. You venture into town with Lucas all the time."

"Not that we'll be permitted to go out anyway," Hope added.

The door opened with a creak, and Mr. Waite returned and plopped down beside Faith.

Taking another sip of lemonade, she avoided his gaze. Her heart soared at this fortuitous information. She must return home as soon as possible to make plans for what might be her very last pirate raid.

"Mr. Waite?" A man dressed in a fine ruffled shirt, breeches, and silk hose took the steps up to their table and nodded toward the captain. "Are you Mr. Waite, the commander of the HMS *Enforcer*?" he asked with exuberance as he removed his hat.

"Yes, I am." Dajon stood and took his outstretched arm.

Grinning, the man shook Mr. Waite's hand over and over as if trying to loosen his bones. "I have been searching for you, sir."

"And you are?" Mr. Waite pulled his hand free.

"I am Mr. Hugh Gladstone, a man greatly in your debt." He straightened his velvet crimson jacket.

Mr. Borland's normally tanned face blanched as white as the table. He fidgeted with his mug of lemonade and avoided glancing at the two men as they spoke, and Faith wondered at his sudden agitation.

"Gladstone." Mr. Waite rubbed his jaw. "The name is familiar to me."

"You saved my wife, Mrs. Margaret Gladstone, from great danger last night, did you not?"

"Your wife." Mr. Waite's eyes sparked in recollection, and he shifted his stance. "Yes, of course."

"She informed me how you came upon those ruffians attacking her in the street."

Mr. Waite nodded then led Mr. Gladstone a few yards to their right, uttering, "If you'll excuse me," over his shoulder as he went.

But Faith kept her ear pointed in his direction and her eyes on Borland, who squirmed in his seat as if sitting upon hot coals.

"And you fought them off bravely and saved her reputation and quite possibly her life," Mr. Gladstone was saying.

Mr. Waite cleared his throat. "Any gentleman would have done the same."

"Ah, that is where you are wrong, sir. Many would not have been bothered. Especially with a woman about town so late in the evening." He leaned toward the captain. "They would not have suspected her to be a virtuous lady."

Faith glanced at Mr. Waite. With hands clenched behind his back, he lowered his gaze to the white planks of the porch deck. His brow glistened with perspiration.

Mr. Gladstone's voice lowered to a whisper. "My wife takes laudanum for a painful ailment and ofttimes wanders off at night."

"I am sorry to hear that."

"She has nothing but good things to say about you,

sir. How you behaved the gentleman and risked your own life for hers."

Mr. Borland sipped his lemonade but then began hacking as if it contained sand.

Glancing his way then back at Mr. Gladstone, Mr. Waite responded, "It was nothing, I assure you. Now if you don't object, I must be—" He turned to leave.

"Might I offer you a reward?"

"There is no need." Mr. Waite halted and gave the man a sincere look. "But do take good care of your wife, Mr. Gladstone." His voice held a hint of warning.

"That I will, sir." The man planted his hat atop his head and shook Mr. Waite's hand again before he barreled down the stairs. "You are a hero, sir. A true hero!" he yelled as he dashed off.

By the time Mr. Waite had returned to the table, Mr. Borland was a fuming pot of angst. Was he so competitive with his captain that any noble act on Mr. Waite's part caused such a violent reaction?

Nonetheless, Faith found her own regard for Mr. Waite billowing within her. Truly this man respected women—all women. Even those with less-than-scrupulous behavior. Even those most men would give no notice to unless they sought a night's entertainment.

She faced him, wanting to express her regard, but the ruddy hue creeping up his neck and the way he tightly gripped his mug indicated his discomfort with the topic.

"Lord Falkland!" Hope nearly jumped from her chair, tossing her hand to her mouth. She stood for a moment, staring down the crowded street. Her eyes locked upon something in the distance. "Arthur!" Clutching her skirts, she darted from the table, toppling her chair behind her.

The captain rose and gave Faith a level gaze. "Stay here," he ordered and then stomped after Hope. But she had never been good at obeying commands, especially when it came to her sister's welfare. Dashing past him, Faith ignored his call to her and pressed her hat upon her head as she tried to catch up with Hope. Straining to see past the throng of people and horses, she finally spotted the source of Hope's despair.

Lord Falkland sauntered down the street, decked in a ruffled lace shirt, damask waistcoat, tight-fitting breeches, and a fashionable bicorn, with a beautiful woman on his arm.

"Hope, wait," Faith cried after her sister.

Falkland nudged his hat up and gazed toward the commotion. When he saw Hope, his eyes snapped wide, but they quickly narrowed. With the grace of a serpent, he patted the woman's hand, whispered in her ear, and sent her on her way; then he turned with open arms toward Hope. "Hope, my dear. A pleasure to see you looking so well."

Hope halted before him just as Faith reached her and grabbed her hand, tugging her away from the cur. But Faith quickly realized she didn't have to keep Hope from him. Hope stood stiffly in place, eyes plump with tears, shock freezing her features into tight little lines.

Falkland lowered his arms. "Something bothers you, my dear?"

"Who is she?" Hope's voice carried the tone of a condemned prisoner.

"Who?" Falkland tapped his cane on the street and brushed a speck of dirt from his sleeve.

Faith eyed the man with disdain. Here before her pranced another vain fop who not only cared nothing for her sister but took advantage of Hope's desperate need for love. Not the first time in her life, Faith longed to be a man so she could pound the sneering grin from his face. Her hand curled. She just might attempt it anyway.

"Oh, you mean Mrs. Blackwell." Lord Falkland feigned innocence. "Her husband imposed upon me to escort her to the festival. He is ill with the fever, poor fellow."

"Her husband?" Hope's voice lifted a bit, and she loosened her grip on Faith's hand.

"Yes, dear. You can't be jealous, can you?" He took her other hand in his and raised it to his mouth, placing a kiss upon it.

And in that moment, watching the exchange between Falkland and her sister—the devotion and adoration beaming from Hope's eyes, the flicker of victory and dominance burning in Falkland's gaze—Faith knew.

She knew her sister had given herself to this foul beast, heart and body.

"Why haven't you called on me?" Hope pouted and glanced at him from beneath her lashes.

"I heard you were ill, my dear."

"She was ill because of you," Faith hissed.

Falkland shifted his dark, lifeless eyes to her. "Good day to you, Miss Westcott. You are always a picture of beauty."

"And you, sir, are always a picture of chicanery."

"I beg your pardon?" he huffed and ran a finger over his slick eyebrows.

Mr. Waite joined them, crossing his arms over his chest. "Lord Falkland, I assume?"

"Yes, and you are?"

"Mr. Waite. I am guardian to these ladies."

"Indeed." Falkland glanced at a passing carriage as if bored with the conversation.

Mr. Waite took a forceful step toward him, towering over the man. "And as their guardian, I must insist that you stay away from Miss Hope."

Hope gasped and clung to Lord Falkland's arm. "He will not."

Lord Falkland patted her hand like a condescending parent then plucked it from his arm. "You may insist what you like, sir, but I believe the lady has made her choice."

"The lady"—Mr. Waite stepped in front of Hope, pushing her behind him—"is not safe in your company. Any man who escorts a woman to a place like the Pink House then abandons her is not fit to be entrusted with the care of dogs."

Hope struggled to weave around Mr. Waite, but Faith grabbed her arm and held her in place.

"How dare you!" Lord Falkland tapped his cane into the dirt, sending a puff of dust into the air. "I'll have you know that the lady begged me to go to the Pink House. She rather enjoys that sort of atmosphere—the drinking, the gambling, the, shall we say, interesting clientele. Don't you, dear?" His snakelike eyes peered around Mr. Waite and slithered over Hope.

Hope's forehead wrinkled, and she stared back at him as if he had slapped her. Faith circled an arm around her shoulders and drew her closer. "She does not enjoy associating herself with the same squalor that you do, sir, and she suffered greatly for your negligence."

"I left her in the care of a friend." Lord Falkland raised a hand and examined his nails.

"Your friend abandoned her." The veins in Mr. Waite's neck began to throb, and a strand of his dark hair flicked over his jaw in the stiff breeze. "Do you realize the danger you put her in? Do you realize what almost happened to her?"

"What is she to you?" Falkland's dark gaze shifted between Mr. Waite and Hope. "Ah yes. Now I see. You wish a piece of her for yourself."

Mr. Waite raised his fist and slugged Lord Falkland across the jaw. His lordship floundered like a fish on a dry deck. His cane flew through the air, and he landed with a thud upon the stone street.

Gasps and "Oh mys" shot in their direction, and a crowd gathered to watch.

Faith couldn't help the grin when Mr. Waite caught the silver-hilted cane as it careened to the ground and pointed it at Falkland.

"You are never to see Miss Hope Westcott again. Do I make myself clear?" He flung the fancy stick at Falkland, whose face was already swelling into a sweaty red mass.

"No!" Hope jerked from her sister's grasp and dropped beside Lord Falkland, kissing his jaw where he'd been hit.

Brushing her aside as if she were a mere annoyance,

he stood, wiped off his breeches, and straightened his shirt. "How dare you strike me!" Falkland rubbed his jaw and then lifted it in the air. "Do you realize who I am, sir?"

"No, but I recognize *what* you are," Waite said.

A mixture of pride and relief lifted Faith's spirits.

"Rest assured, Mr. Waite," Falkland twisted from Hope's clawing hands, "you may soon find yourself called out."

"I await the pleasure." Mr. Waite bowed.

Faith laid an arm around Hope's shoulders and tried to pry her away from Lord Falkland's side, but she stomped her foot as if planting it firmly in the ground. She turned her glassy eyes to Mr. Waite. "You cannot keep us apart."

"Never fear, my dear," Falkland announced to Hope, but his piercing gaze remained on the captain. "I *will* see you again. You can be sure of that."

"Do not try me, your lordship." Mr. Waite gripped the hilt of his service sword.

"And I will see you in irons if you dare to strike me again."

With a mocking nod toward Lord Falkland, Mr. Waite took hold of Hope's arm, pulling her from the vile man.

After sending Mr. Borland and Mr. Cudney back to the ship, which was but a few minutes' journey from where they were, Mr. Waite escorted Faith and Grace as they dragged a sobbing Hope back to the house. When Mr. Waite had returned to his ship, and as soon as Faith had seen Hope tucked safely in bed within her chamber, she sought out Lucas and found him in the stables.

He glanced up at her, his initial grin fading beneath what must have been a look of urgency on her face.

"What's wrong, mistress? Ye look like yer loaded and primed and ready to fire."

"Just some trouble in town with Hope, but Mr. Waite handled it." She leaned against a wooden post and smiled. "In fact, I spent the entire day with the commander." She raised her brows. "Which made it the perfect day for the Red Siren to have attacked some poor merchantmen at sea. Grayson and Strom?"

He nodded.

"Tell them to proceed first thing in the morning."

CHAPTER 26

Gripping the taffrail, Dajon gazed over Charles Towne Bay, watching the cream-capped swells coming in from the sea like white ruffles on an indigo shirt. Twenty ships anchored in the harbor; one other Royal Navy ship, the HMS *Perseverance*, a forty-four-gun ship, had recently arrived from Portsmouth, and the rest of them were merchant and trading ships. He knew because earlier today he'd examined each one in great detail through his spyglass.

Anything to take his mind off Miss Faith Westcott.

Yet he still could not shake the strange events of yesterday from his mind. Faith's unusual nervousness, the constant bickering of her sisters, the odd but entertaining exchange between Mr. Mason and Hope, and then the coup de grâce—the infuriating encounter with Lord Falkland. Dajon had to admit that spending the day with the Westcott ladies had been anything but dull. Chuckling, he shook his head, but his grin quickly faded along with the late afternoon sun. The trap had been set.

His insides felt like a lead weight that threatened to drag him to the bottom of the sea. If his suspicions were true, tomorrow he would capture Faith, the notorious Red Siren, and be forced to turn her over to the Charles Towne authorities.

To be hanged.

And no matter how hard he tried to forbid the maddening woman entrance to his thoughts, she barged in anyway, over and over again, proclaiming her many worthwhile qualities—all of which he adored: her independence, her pluck, the fire in her auburn eyes, the

249

depth of love she had for her sisters, her courage, those red curls, and her determination that spoke of deep passions within. He had never known a woman like her and probably never would again. The only thing missing was her love and devotion to God, something he hoped to remedy by a closer association with her—that was, if she wasn't the Red Siren.

But he knew he must prepare himself for the worst possible outcome. He had to be strong. He had to do the right thing.

He gulped as a slow burn seared behind his eyes.

He had to do his duty.

Below him, on the main deck, his crew scampered to and fro, following his orders to ready the ship. Curses and laughter tumbled through the air, as well as the pounding of a hammer in the distance and the scampering of bare feet upon the yardarms above him.

Clenching the railing, he felt the bite of a splinter on his palm, but it did not compare to the sharp pain in his heart.

Oh Lord, I have followed You these four years. I have obeyed all Your commands and never faltered. Please do not test me in this. Please do not let Miss Westcott and the Red Siren be one and the same.

"Captain." Mr. Jamieson's high-pitched voice intruded from behind.

Dajon tightened his grip but did not turn around. "Yes."

"Two merchant sailors to see you, sir. They have some information."

"Of what nature?"

"About the Red Siren."

Releasing the railing, Dajon swung about to see two gruff-looking men standing behind Mr. Jamieson, hats in hand. "What about the Red Siren?" Dajon asked.

The elder of the men stepped forward, his spindly gray hair forming a ring around his sunbaked face. "Captain Milner at yer service, sir." He gestured to his companion. "And this here's Landers."

Dajon nodded and examined the men as Jamieson took his leave. Where Captain Milner was broad and stocky, Landers was slight and short. They smelled of fish, sweat, and salt, and their stained, faded silk waistcoats indicated a failed attempt at noble attire. Seamen, to be sure. Milner looked down and turned his hat around and around as if pondering what to say next. Was that a slight tremble in his hands?

"Yes, yes. Spit it out, man." Dajon's voice shot out louder than he'd intended. "What have you to tell me?"

Captain Milner's gaze snapped to his. "We hear yer hunting pirates. In particular, a lady pirate that goes by the name the Red Siren."

"That is correct." Dajon fisted his hands on his waist.

"Well, we came across her yesterday, we did. Or rather, she came across us." He chuckled at his own joke, and Landers snickered behind him.

"The Red Siren attacked you?" Dajon raised his eyebrows, not daring to hope what he'd just heard was true.

"Aye, sir, that she did." Milner gazed off to the right. "Fired upon me ship then grappled and boarded us."

Dajon's breath formed a ball in his chest. "Yesterday, you say?"

"Took most o' our cargo, too. Spices, coffee, chocolate, and sugar."

"Cursed pirate." Landers spat to the side.

"What time yesterday?"

"'Twas near midday, methinks." Milner glanced over his shoulder at his companion.

"Aye, midday." Landers nodded, but he wouldn't meet Dajon's gaze. "I remember 'cause the sun was right o'er me head."

Dajon rubbed his jaw and eyed the men. Strange fellows, these two, but then again, if they had truly been attacked and boarded by a pirate crew, that would be enough to unnerve anyone.

"Can you describe her?"

"Who?" Landers asked.

"The Red Siren, you dim-witted sluggard!" Captain

Milner shouted over his shoulder then grinned sheepishly at Dajon.

Milner tapped his finger against his chin. "Aye, she was short." He gazed to the right again as if trying to remember. "Fat. Aye, quite plump she was. She had red hair, but it seemed more brown than red when she came up close." He grinned and nodded.

"Aye, she had an ugly scar that ran 'cross her forehead." Landers slid a finger above his brow.

"It weren't her forehead." Milner turned and slapped him with his hat.

"Yes, it was," Landers hissed through gritted teeth, glancing at Dajon.

But Dajon cared nothing about the scar. He had heard enough to convince him.

Faith was not the Red Siren!

Not only had she been with him yesterday during the pirate attack, but she looked nothing like the person these men described.

Dajon felt as if he'd just been released from a long imprisonment in a dark dungeon.

God had answered his prayer.

Thank You, Lord.

Dismissing the merchants, he leaped down the quarterdeck ladder then down the companionway to his quarters. After washing his face and donning fresh attire, he took a cockboat to shore and started for the Westcott home. As the sun set beyond the tangled forest that bordered the town, Dajon felt as though daylight was just rising within him.

He must see Faith. He must apologize to her for his ludicrous suspicions. And he must tell her. . .must express to her something he thought he'd never say, let alone feel for another woman in his life. He must tell her that he loved her.

～

Faith eased her fingers over the horse's soft neck and leaned her forehead against his face. Snorting, the horse pricked his ears toward her.

"Oh, Seaspray, would that I were a simple horse like you, without a care in the world." She sighed and reached up to rub the other side of the horse's neck. Seaspray—named for the steed's cream-colored coat—had taken Faith back and forth to her ship on many an occasion and was one of the few privy to her dual identity. Somehow it made her feel as though they were best friends.

Seaspray licked his lips as if agreeing with Faith's thoughts and then jerked his head back to gaze at her. The gentle glow from a single lantern hanging on a hook filtered over them, and Faith thought she saw a flicker of understanding in the horse's eyes.

Unable to sleep, she had crept down to the stables, where she often came to find comfort among the horses. 'Twas where she had come to know Lucas back in Portsmouth. There the stables had become an escape, a place of refuge from the troubles that plagued her home, and she had passed many pleasant hours helping to care for the horses—that was before she found a much better sanctuary upon the sea.

Grabbing a bristle brush, she began stroking Seaspray's thick mane, her mind drifting to the merchant ship she planned to plunder tomorrow. Forcing down a nagging twinge of guilt, she allowed a flash of exhilaration to charge through her. The chase, the danger, the mighty sea. She loved it all and couldn't wait to be on her ship again. Perhaps that was why sleep had eluded her. Or maybe 'twas a certain captain who kept her thoughts and heart ajitter.

A shuffle sounded behind her in the dirt. She instinctively reached for her sword, but her hand floundered over the soft folds of her nightdress. Gripping the brush with both hands, she spun around, aiming it at the intruder.

Mr. Waite, one boot crossed over the other, leaned against the stable doorframe, a sarcastic grin on his handsome lips. "What are you planning to do with that? Scrub me to death?"

"If I have to." She grinned in return but then, realizing her state of undress, dropped the brush and pulled her robe tighter around her.

Mr. Waite's gaze soaked her in as if she were a dying man's last drink. But the look within his blue eyes carried no malice, no lust, nothing to give her pause. Quite the opposite, in fact. It was a look that sent her belly quivering and her pulse racing. His loose umber hair grazed the collar of a fine cambric shirt that was open at the neck. Black velvet breeches rode low upon his hips. It was the first time she had seen him without his uniform, and she swallowed and lowered her lashes, gazing at the dirt floor, lest he see the attraction in her face. "May I help you with something, Mr. Waite?"

"Forgive me for startling you." His boots rustled in the straw as he moved closer. "I looked for you earlier, but Molly said you had retired."

"Yes, still a bit of fatigue, I'm afraid." Faith slid one foot nonchalantly through the dirt, not caring if her silk slipper got soiled. Truthfully, she had heard him come home but found she could not face him—not knowing what she must do on the morrow. Deceive him. Defy him.

Defeat him.

Why did the idea of outwitting the Royal Navy suddenly cause such discord within her when it never had before? Daring a glance at him, she knew the answer. It wasn't the Royal Navy she was battling this time. It was this honorable, courageous, kind man before her. And the thought made her stomach curl in on itself. She averted her gaze, knowing that if she stared too long into those blue eyes filled with affection, she might not be able to go through with her plan.

But she had to. For her sisters. Especially for Hope. Now more than ever, they were in far more desperate need of the independence that wealth would bring them.

"Then you must be feeling refreshed after your rest?"

"Nay, I couldn't sleep." She nudged a tuft of hay with her toe.

"I fear you have infected me with that disease." His deep chuckle bounced off the wooden walls and landed on her like a warm blanket. Why was he being so cordial? Had Grayson and Strom spoken with him? Had he given up his suspicions of her?

He leaned against the nearest stall. The tantalizing scent of leather and the sea swirled around her and sent delightful needles down her spine. She took a step away from him.

"I must admit to something, Miss Westcott. And I hope you shall find it as amusing as I and will not become cross with me."

Leaning over, she picked up the brush and set it on a stool. Good heavens, what did he intend to tell her? That he knew who she really was? Surely that would not be in any way amusing. "There is no need, Mr. Waite. I assure you." She flicked her hand through the air.

"Oh, but I daresay there is." He touched her arm. "I owe you a sincere apology." Sorrow shone from his eyes.

"There could be nothing you have done that requires it." Faith gripped the edges of her robe and expelled a nervous breath. *Except perhaps the way you make my heart burst and my belly flutter whenever you are near. Except perhaps that I am a pirate and you are a pirate hunter sworn to bring me to justice.*

Clasping his hands behind his back, he turned and took a few steps away from her, his movements lacking the usual confidence she'd come to expect. " 'Tis the funniest thing, actually. For quite some time now. . .well, actually for just a few weeks, I. . ." He turned to face her and rubbed the back of his neck then gave her a sheepish look. "I. . ."

"You what, Mr. Waite?"

"I thought you might be the Red Siren." He blurted the words that crackled with both embarrassment and relief.

The needles of pleasure she'd experienced only a moment ago transformed into jabs of panic. Did he know? Was he testing her?

He began to laugh, and she joined him, holding her stomach and bending over in feigned hilarity. "Me? A pirate?" she chortled.

Seaspray tossed his head over the stall and snorted, nodding as if confirming Mr. Waite's suspicion.

Throwing a hand to her throat to hide the furious throb in her veins, Faith nudged the horse back into his pen. "You teased me about it once, but I thought it mere sport."

"I am ashamed at having ever entertained such a ridiculous notion." Mr. Waite raked a hand through his hair then approached, taking her hand in his. "I came to beg your forgiveness."

"Why, there's naught to forgive, Mr. Waite." Faith tugged her hand away and gripped the railing. "You've made me laugh, and that is enough."

"I do feel quite dreadful about it, really."

"You shouldn't." Faith snapped her gaze to his, unable to halt the booming tone of her voice.

Mr. Waite flinched, and she hoped she had not given herself away. But how could she accept his apology when he had done nothing wrong, and she, everything?

❧

Dajon studied her, trying to make sense of her odd reaction. Unpredictable. It was one of the things he loved about her but also a constant source of frustration. Where he assumed she would have been horrified, even furious at his assumption, she waved it aside as if it were naught but a jest. Her response, in fact, aligned more with guilt than with innocence.

But no.

Not only did he have the testimony of the two merchants, but he'd sent some of his crew into town to verify their story. And, indeed, tales of the *Red Siren* attacking a small merchant ship just off Charles Towne were circulating around the city's taverns.

Flinging her red curls over her shoulder, she brushed her hands over the horse's face, her gaze turned from his.

When he'd first seen Faith standing there so serenely, whispering to the steed, her white robe shimmering in a halo of light and her hair a cascade of glittering red, he could have remained where he was and watched her all night. And when she'd turned to face him, threatening him with the brush, he'd longed to take her in his arms. And now that the wall of suspicion had been toppled between them, he must tell her how he felt.

"There is something else."

She raised her eyes to his.

"It may seem untoward, even improper, after confessing my rather ludicrous and disparaging suspicions, but I..."

Should he tell her? Hadn't he sworn off women after what had happened with Marianne? Hadn't he vowed to God never to put himself in a position to bring harm to another by his own foolish passions?

Why did You bring this precious lady to me, Lord? Why have You allowed me to feel such overwhelming affection for her?

"Yes, Mr. Waite?" The freckles on Faith's nose clumped together under a pert wrinkle.

Dajon brushed the back of his hand over her cheek, relishing the silky feel of her skin and the way she instantly closed her eyes. Perhaps he had learned. Perhaps by God's grace, Dajon had changed. Perhaps God had deemed him ready again.

"Surely you have no doubt as to my intentions, Miss Westcott."

Her lips parted, and she released a tiny sigh as he continued caressing her cheek.

"If your father were here, I would speak to him, but alas..."

Her eyes popped open as if she'd just been awakened from a dream. "What would you need to discuss with my father that you cannot discuss with me?"

"Surely you know." Placing a finger beneath her chin, Dajon raised her gaze to his. Her auburn eyes shone with a moist luster that bristled with desire, admiration, and something else. Was it fear? Frustration? He knew she feared depending on any man, but surely she could see that he was different.

"It would be my honor if you'd allow me to—"

"Please say no more." She tore her gaze away and clasped her robe.

"Court you, Miss Westcott." He stepped closer until there was but a breath between them. "I confess, though I have discovered you are no pirate, you have quite plundered my heart as if you were."

"Please." She jerked away. "You do not know what you are saying."

"On the contrary, it is the only thing I seem sure about of late." Dajon wiped the moisture from his brow, confused once again by her reaction.

A battle seemed to rage within Faith's eyes. One second they sparkled with affection and admiration; the next they stabbed him with defiance and determination. Her jaw tightened, and she swallowed. Dajon had realized that her distrust of men might give her pause when he declared his affections, but he hadn't expected such resistance.

"It can never be," she said sharply and turned to leave.

He grabbed her arm, unwilling to see her go, unwilling to give in to the agony clawing at his heart.

"Release me." She struggled against his grip.

"Tell me you feel nothing for me, and I will."

She bent her knee as if to kick him, but this time he saw it coming and pressed himself firmly against her.

Dajon grasped her face in his hands and pressed his lips against hers. He hadn't planned to kiss her. He had simply wanted to calm her down, simply wanted her to stay, but when she instantly melted into him, he claimed her mouth as his own and kissed her with all the passion that had been building up in him since the day he met her.

When he released her, they stood in silence, their heavy breaths mingling in the air between them.

"I have my answer then," Dajon said, placing a kiss on her forehead.

With a horrified gasp, Faith ripped herself from his arms and fled into the night.

CHAPTER 27

Perched high upon the foreyard, Faith clung to the mast with one hand and a halyard with the other. She thrust her face into the wind, allowing it to blast away her doubts, her fears, and, in particular, her thoughts of Mr. Waite. Curling her bare toes around the yardarm, she spotted Lucas nigh eighty feet below, giving orders to the crew, looking more like a speck of dirt tossed by the wind than a commanding first mate. She loved it up here among the topsails. If she closed her eyes, she could imagine herself a bird, soaring over the vast ocean, unfettered, unhindered—free at last.

"You are most fortunate, Morgan," she said to the red and green macaw balancing on the backstay beside her.

"Gentlemen of fortune, we are, we are," he squawked, making her smile.

Off the larboard side, the rising arc of a brilliant sun poked over the dark line of the horizon. Exhaling a puff of gold, maroon, and copper upon the dark waters, it set the waves aglow with the breath of dawn. She smiled at the matchless beauty of creation. Nothing but wind and sparkling waves as far as her eye could see.

She was home.

Then why did she feel so unsettled?

It was that blasted Mr. Waite. He confused her. He frustrated her.

He delighted her.

She brushed her fingers over her lips. Why had she given in to his kiss? Yet stopping it would have been akin to stopping a cannon from firing after the powder had already been lit. Even now with the chill morning wind swirling about her, her body warmed at the thought. But her passion quickly drowned beneath a wave of guilt. There he had stood declaring her innocent of piracy and announcing his affections for her, and all the while she was about to plunder a ship she had learned about only through him.

But this would be her last time. And though a sudden mourning came over her at the death of her adventurous life upon the sea, she knew the risks were far too high to continue. But then, maybe then she could entertain thoughts of a possible courtship with Captain Waite. Possible, yes. The thought surprised her. Though she had sworn never to depend upon a man, never to marry, this man, this Captain Dajon Waite, might just be a man worth altering her plans for.

Climbing down the ratlines with ease, Faith dropped to the wooden planks below and then marched across the main deck of the *Red Siren*, allowing her bare toes to caress the moist wood as she went. She adjusted her baldric about her chest and leaped up the quarterdeck ladder—something she could never do without the freedom breeches afforded her. Planting her feet firmly on the hard deck, she gave a quick nod to Wilson at the helm before facing the ship's bow as it rose and plunged through the choppy sea.

Morgan soon followed, alighting upon his usual perch on the mainmast.

Taking the ladder in one leap, Lucas positioned himself beside her and scratched his thick dark hair. "And where are we to be expecting to find this treasure ship, Cap'n?"

Faith tugged on the black bandanna she'd tied atop her head and tried to ignore the lack of fervor normally present in Lucas's voice. "Since Mr. Borland let it slip that they were only to protect her from St. Helena Sound onward, I expect the *Lady Adeline* to arrive off Port Royal sometime this morning." She cast him a sly grin. "We should pass her any minute."

"And what's to ensure that Captain Waite won't be passin' our way as well?"

Faith glanced at her first mate, but he kept his gaze upon the sea. "He would have no reason to come this far south."

Lucas huffed and gripped the railing.

"What is it, Lucas?"

"Seems to me yer takin' a big risk." He scratched his head. "Mr. Waite is no fool."

"Aye, I'll grant you that. But he has no further reason to suspect me. Any information Borland disclosed would be considered safe within my feeble feminine mind." She chuckled, but Lucas did not join her. In fact, he rubbed his leathery skin and shook his head.

"Our plan worked, Lucas. You should be pleased."

" 'Tis not that."

"What, then? Where is your usual zeal, your excitement? We are about to give chase and plunder some unsuspecting merchant." Faith gripped the hilt of her cutlass.

"Seems to have lost its allure as of late, Cap'n." Lucas's jaw flinched, and he gazed down at the crew ambling over the deck. "Seems almost wrong to be stealin' so."

" 'We plunder and pillage and pilfer and prey.' " Morgan repeated a pirate's ballad from his perch, only increasing Faith's rising shame.

She felt as if the ship had been struck by a twenty-pounder and was taking on water. Lucas had always been so strong, her stalwart first mate, her faithful partner. Side by side, they had plundered the seas, amassed a fortune, defeated foes. "Please do not tell me you have suddenly grown a conscience." She could not keep the irritation from her voice nor the increasing weight of loss from her soul.

His glance carried both pain and excitement. "It jest be that I ne'er thought there be a God before. An' now I think He exists. . .an' He might even care about me."

"Well, you'd best put that thought out of your mind." Faith crossed her arms over her chest. "You will only be disappointed." Yet hadn't she entertained similar thoughts recently?

Lucas said nothing, only watched the foam spray over the bow of the ship as the orb of the sun rose above the horizon.

"You've allowed that strange event, miracle, whatever it was at the Pink House to befuddle your mind," Faith hissed.

Lucas gave her one of his playful grins. "Nay, I've been speakin' to Miss Molly and to Mr. Waite."

"Oh, now I understand." Faith blew out a sigh. "The God-fearing duo has turned my first mate into a jellyfish." Frankly, she was surprised her sister Grace hadn't joined in the mind-altering conversion.

"Yellow-bellied jellyfish, yellow-bellied jellyfish," Morgan chirped.

Shaking the wind from the coils of his hair, Lucas only smiled.

Faith studied the curve of his lips, and a sudden hope lifted the heaviness from her. "Ah, you almost had me fooled." She pointed a finger his way. "You're just doing this to win Molly's affections, aren't you?"

Lucas shook his head. "Nay. You know me, Miss Faith—I mean, Cap'n. Becoming one of those religious sorts be the last thing I'd be doin', especially for a woman. No matter how remarkable she be."

The first mate glanced at the sails flapping in the breeze before them. "Mac, brace in the foreyard," he yelled across to the man climbing up the foremast rigging.

"What of your past?" Faith asked, blinking back her shock. "What of your slavery, the murder of your parents? Are those the actions of a loving God?"

"Aye, I'll admit I used to think that way." He nodded then leaned on the rail and met her gaze. "But I can't deny what I've seen, what I've felt."

"Felt?"

"Aye, Cap'n. I've been talkin' to God." Lucas's eyes sparkled. "An' methinks He's talkin' back."

"Good heavens." Faith shifted her gaze to the tumultuous waves. Anywhere but into those joy-filled eyes. "What have they done to you?"

"Whate'er it is, I like it, mistress." Lucas lengthened his stance and crossed his arms over his thick chest. "Methinks I like it a lot."

Morgan paced across his perch, bobbing his head up and down. "Mush fer brains. Mush fer brains."

"There you have it. Even Morgan can see the truth." She nodded toward the bird with a smile, but Lucas only shook his head and gazed out upon the sea.

Faith huffed. Of all the people in the world to have fallen for such a hoax, Lucas would have been her last guess. He'd suffered far more pain and loss in his life than she could ever imagine. How could he so easily surrender to a God who had allowed all that to happen?

Temporary madness. With time, hopefully, it would pass.

"Well, you have my word, Lucas: if you help me take in a good haul today, I shall never impose upon your newfound holiness for such a vile act as pirating again."

"I will hold ye to that, Cap'n." He grinned. "For it will surely please me more than anything to see you out o' this life as well."

"A sail, Cap'n!" Kane yelled from the crosstrees.

A slow grin crept across Faith's lips even as exhilaration raced through her veins. "Let's be about it then, Lucas. Once more for old times' sake."

<hr/>

Slamming his logbook shut, Dajon rose from his desk, flung on his frock, and headed up on deck. This was the day he would catch the notorious Red Siren. After discovering—much to his utter glee—that Faith was not one and the same, he had propagated the news of the *Lady Adeline* all over Charles Towne, ensuring all the sailors who traveled these waters knew of the incoming merchant ship and her valuable cargo. Surely word would reach the pirate.

Climbing up the companionway ladder, he emerged onto the deck to a blast of wind and spray that only increased his exuberance. Perhaps now he could keep his mind off the alluring and frustrating Faith. A sharp twinge from an old injury pinched his nose, and he squeezed it, hoping to force down the pain and the memories along with it. Marching across the deck, he gazed upon the morning mist dissipating over the water. If only the fog of confusion hovering in his mind would dissipate so easily.

Faith returned his affections. He knew it. Her body, her voice, her eyes, and especially her lips—a sudden warmth spread through him as he remembered her sweet taste—everything displayed her passionate ardor, everything save her words and the way she had dashed from his embrace. But why?

While only partially aware of his crew's salutes and "good days" as they passed, Dajon watched the golden sun arise from its bed of blue to start anew its journey across the sky.

Fear. That was what he'd seen in those auburn eyes. But of what?

Of men. From her past, no doubt—from the horrible things that had happened to her sisters. And all from the same loathsome ruffian.

Dajon clenched his jaw. The man should be flogged and then keelhauled for what he'd done to these ladies, to this family.

The ship bucked over a rising swell, and Dajon braced his boots on the slippery deck. The jolt seemed to loosen a hidden truth within him. Had Dajon revealed his ardor for her too soon? Had he been too harsh, too passionate with his kiss? Perhaps that was why she had fled. Gripping the main deck railing, he squeezed it and vowed to be more careful, gentler, more patient. He must prove his trustworthiness to her, no matter how long it took. For Miss Faith Westcott was a lady well worth the wait.

Leaping up to the quarterdeck, he took his position beside Borland.

"Sailing trim, Captain, southeast by south," the first

lieutenant stated without glancing his way.

"Very good, Mr. Borland. Any moment, then." Dajon clasped his hands behind his back. They had already passed St. Helena Sound. The pirate ship could turn up anywhere now.

The warmth of the sun caressed his left cheek while the wind slapped the other, reminding him of Faith's ever-changing moods. By the powers, was she never far from his thoughts?

He glanced at his first lieutenant, standing beside him as stiff as a marine, eyes locked on the point of the ship's bow, his jaw rigid and his fists bunched. Dajon had never seen him quite so tense before.

"Did you sleep well, Mr. Borland?"

"Aye, sir." His tone pricked Dajon like icicles.

Perhaps he was frightened about the upcoming battle. But no. They'd been in many skirmishes before, and Borland had always been the epitome of bravery. "Are you unwell, then?"

"No, Captain."

"Very well." Dajon conceded to the man's foul mood, supposing he didn't want to discuss whatever vexed him. "When we have the ships in our sights, lower the topgallants, if you please. We must give this pirate time to shed her snake's skin and reveal her true colors."

"Will she not be able to tell the *Lady Adeline* is a decoy?" Mr. Borland said, although the effort seemed to exhaust him. "I have heard she's a clever pirate."

"Never fear, Borland. I have ensured that the *Lady Adeline* appears in every way a true merchant ship. I even had her loaded with ballast so she sits low in the water."

Mr. Jamieson joined them, his face alight with anticipation.

"Once she raises her colors and fires a shot, then we have her," Dajon continued.

"Very exciting." Jamieson rubbed his hands together and then adjusted his bicorn. He faced Dajon with a look of concern. "Will it not be difficult to arrest a lady?"

Dajon's mind filled with visions of the arrogant, brash woman who had stolen his father's ship from him five years ago, leaving him to return home in disgrace. "This is no woman. 'Tis naught but a callous thief housed in a female body, as devoid of conscience and decency as any other pirate." He gripped the cold silver of his sword. "No, I have no qualms about escorting this lady to the noose."

A dark cloud appeared on the horizon, threatening to cast a shroud of gloom on the promise of a bright day.

"Besides, gentlemen, if all goes well today, we will catch a pirate." He lifted his voice, trying to cheer up his friends. "And not just any pirate. One who has been pilfering these waters for months. Certainly that will shed a favorable light on us back at the Admiralty."

"On you, Captain." Borland finally met his gaze, though the glint in his eyes was anything but friendly. It reminded Dajon of a flaming linstock. "It will shed a light upon only you."

"Nonsense, Borland." Dajon gave a half chuckle, unsettled by the hostility in his friend's gaze. "You know I shall report all of our efforts in the success."

Borland's face twisted as if he were stifling a sharp retort, but he returned his gaze to the sea and said no more.

"Sail ho!" The cry came from above them.

"Where away, Mr. Gibson?" Borland yelled.

"Off the larboard bow, sir. Three points."

"Hold up there!" Gibson bellowed again. "Two sails now, sir."

Dajon plucked out his spyglass and pressed it to his eye. Two ships, indeed. Too far to know who they were for sure, but one swiftly bore down upon the other.

It had to be the *Red Siren*.

"Ease the helm, Mr. Borland. Away aloft and trim the sails. Let's take her in slow." Dajon slapped his glass into the palm of his hand and grinned as Borland repeated his orders to the crew.

"The last thing we want to do is scare her off."

～

"Shouldn't ye be changin' yer clothes, Cap'n?" Lucas asked as he strapped on his cutlass.

"Nay, I tire of hiding behind ruffles and lace." Faith poured priming powder from her horn into the small pan in her pistol, careful not to spill any. "Today I will plunder this ship dressed like a pirate—a true pirate."

Lucas grinned. "'Tis fittin' fer yer last time."

Then, as if noting the gleam in her eye, he added with a raised brow, "It *will* be yer last time, Cap'n?"

"Don't you be pointing that pharisaical eye toward me, Lucas." Faith cocked her head and gave him a sideways glance. "You forget I know you too well."

A blast of wind stole his warm laughter as the *Red Siren* split the waves with each thrust of her bow.

Bracing her boots, Faith leveled the glass on her eye. "Besides, see how low she sits in the water? Heavy cargo." She lowered the glass and winked at Lucas. "Methinks there be gold in that ship." But when her first mate's stern eye did not falter, she conceded, "Yes, Lucas, this will be my last time, I assure you."

Scanning the horizon, she saw no other sails besides the merchant ship, the words *Lady Adeline* painted in black upon her bow, French colors flapping upon her mainmast. Only two swivel guns guarded her deck. No gunports appeared on the hull. Defenseless and as out of place upon these violent seas as a lady in a brothel.

And with all her gold for the taking.

At the thought of stealing this unsuspecting merchant's gold, a weight of shame tugged upon Faith. She winced and furrowed her brow. Was this newfound godliness of Lucas's contagious? Good heavens, she hoped not.

The *Red Siren* surged and plunged over a wave, spraying glittering white foam over the bow. Shaking it off along with her guilt, Faith studied her prey. "Odd. Surely she spots us. Why doesn't she run?"

"Their cap'n seems to be loadin' his swivels." Lucas smacked his lips. "Methinks he is unsure whether we are friend or foe."

"We have not hailed them as either," Faith yelled over the crashing waves. She wrinkled her brow. "But his swivels? Against our sixteen guns? Either he is a fool, or he is completely mad."

Flinging her hands to her waist, Faith marched across the quarterdeck to the railing and gazed down upon her crew readying for battle. The ship creaked and moaned as it forced aside each opposing wave, fighting its way to its victim. White canvas cracked above her like a whip, prodding the ship forward.

"Should I raise our colors, Capitaine?" Kane yelled from the main deck.

Shielding her eyes from the sun, Faith gazed up at the Union Jack bristling in the breeze. "Not yet, Mr. Kane. They appear to be unaware of the danger."

Yet Faith was the one who felt a sudden unease prickle her skin. They would be on the ship in minutes. With so much gold aboard, why did she not at least make a run for it? Swinging about, spyglass to her eye, she scanned the horizon once again. Nothing but azure sea streaked in sparkling white.

"Orders, Cap'n?" cried Bates. The master gunner's twitching eyes met hers from below.

"Lucas," she yelled over her shoulder. "Shorten sail. Down tops and gallants."

Lucas repeated the orders, sending men into the main shrouds and scrambling aloft.

"All hands about ship!" Faith boomed from the quarterdeck railing. "Prepare to board. Mr. Wilson," she bellowed to the man at the helm, "lay me athwart her larboard side."

"Aye, aye, Cap'n." The barrel-chested pirate turned the wheel.

Faith glanced back at Bates. "When we come alongside her, fire a warning shot across her stern, if you please, Mr. Bates."

"Aye." The man gave her a toothless grin and waddled off.

"Let's make our intentions known, gentlemen." Faith drew her cutlass and held it over her head. "For the gold!"

"Aye, fer the gold!" the men echoed and then hurled hearty boasts and curses toward the merchant ship now only fifty yards away.

Jumping down the ladder, Lucas halted at the main deck railing and stared at their prey. Faith joined him and followed his gaze to the sailors buzzing about their swivels as if trying to figure out how to fire them. Her first mate scratched his thick hair.

Minutes later a thunderous blast shook the ship and sent a ripple through the water. Acrid smoke curled from the *Red Siren*'s gunport, and a splash sounded where the shot plunged harmlessly into the sea beyond the *Lady Adeline*.

The crew of the merchant vessel skittered across the deck in a frenzy but soon lowered their colors in a signal of surrender.

"Something's amiss, Cap'n." Lucas frowned. "'Twas far too easy fer a ship carryin' a fortune."

Faith knew he was right. She knew she should hoist sail and flee while she had the chance. But she couldn't. Too much rode upon this last venture. Besides, when would she have another opportunity at such wealth?

Just one more haul. Just one more.

Against every instinct within her, she turned to Lucas. "Then let's take her quickly and be gone," she snapped.

As the band of blue narrowed between the ships and Faith's crew readied the grappling irons, the merchant captain stood amidships and gazed her way. He cupped his hands. "Ahoy, from whence came ye, and what do ye want?"

Bracing her fists at her waist, Faith yelled in reply, "Good quarter will be granted to you, sir, if you lay down your arms, open the hatches, and haul down your sails."

A grin took root and began to spread upon the captain's lips. And before it reached the corners of his mouth, sheer terror struck Faith.

"Cap'n, off our stern!" Lambert's normally steady voice quaked from the crosstrees.

Her heart turned to ice, and she knew before she even turned. She knew what she would see.

The HMS *Enforcer* plunged toward them, white foam exploding off its bow.

～

"We've got her now!" Dajon snapped his spyglass shut, excitement bristling his skin. "Took the bait like the greedy shark she is."

He turned to Borland, who stood beside him at the quarterdeck railing. "Unfurl the topsails and gallants."

Mr. Borland repeated his command, sending the crew aloft. Soon the *Enforcer*'s sails caught the wind in a sharp snap, sending the ship skimming over the rolling swells at top speed.

Fierce wind clawed at his bicorn, and Dajon shoved it down on his head and clung to the railing. Frothy dark water swept over the deck and rolled out the scuppers. The sharp scent of salt and fish tore at his nose as they raced to get windward of the pirate.

"She's raising her sails, Captain," Jamieson said, lowering his glass.

"She'll not catch the wind in time." Dajon crossed his arms over his chest. "Ready the chain shot, if you please, Mr. Jamieson."

"Yes, sir." Mr. Jamieson stormed off and dropped below deck to inform the gun crew.

"Beat to quarters. Clear the deck for battle," Dajon instructed Borland, who bellowed his commands to the crew.

The shrill sound of a whistle screeched through the air, and the crew scrambled over the deck, clearing away barrels and crates, stowing equipment below hatches, and arming themselves with musket and sword.

Spyglass to his eye, Dajon scanned the *Red Siren*—his father's ship. A fire brewed in his belly at the sight of it. At last he would have it back.

Though the pirate crew furiously tugged at the furled sails aloft, they would not loosen the canvas in time. He would be on her in minutes. His gaze shifted to the Union Jack. She had not raised her pirate colors. But no matter—she had clearly come alongside the merchant vessel to plunder it.

And this would be her last time.

They were nearly within firing distance, and Dajon gave the order to lower sails.

The *Red Siren*'s gunports flung open in an attempt, he assumed, to scare him off, making him snort. "She's brazen. I'll give her that."

The *Lady Adeline* had already drifted away and was hoisting sail rapidly in order to escape the impending battle.

"Run out the guns, fire a warning shot, and then signal her to surrender," Dajon commanded.

The thud of port hatches striking the hull reverberated through the ship, one after the other, followed by the clanks of gun trucks grating over the deck. The thunderous boom of a cannon shook both ship and sky, and Dajon peered through the smoke toward his enemy. Would she surrender or put up a useless fight that would surely end in bloodshed?

"She lowers her flag, Captain," Mr. Borland announced with a grin.

Huzzahs erupted from his crew.

Dajon nodded in satisfaction.

"Lower the cockboat, Mr. Borland. Let us pay a visit to the infamous *Red Siren*. Shall we?" He slapped his friend on the back and stomped down the quarterdeck ladder.

"Aye, Captain."

As the boat thudded against the wet hull of the *Red Siren* and rope ladders were tossed over the rail, Dajon rose in the wobbly boat and adjusted his navy coat. He squared his shoulders and gazed up at the dark hull of his father's ship. Pride rippled through him. He had caught the *Red Siren.* He had done his duty and protected the colonial waters and the citizens of this land from the ravages of this vexatious pirate.

Thank You, God, for this victory, he silently prayed, hoping that this courageous act would somehow atone for at least one of his past sins.

Leaping over the bulwarks, Dajon landed with a thud onto the deck, followed quickly by Mr. Borland and ten marines. He scanned the ship, seeing nothing but a crew of scurrilous pirates staring at him, scowls dripping from their faces.

"Your arms, gentlemen. Toss them in a pile, if you please." He gestured toward the center of the deck.

Slowly they complied, each one slogging toward middeck, flinging their weapons onto a growing heap of metal and their curses toward him and his men.

"Now where, pray tell, is your captain?" Dajon allowed his eyes to travel over the crew, shooting each man down with his imperious gaze. "Has she scurried below decks like the coward she is?"

A tall, dark man emerged from the shadows beneath the foredeck ladder. "She has no wish to see you, Mr. Waite." The familiar voice struck Dajon before the face registered in his brain. Even then, it took a minute before Dajon found his breath.

"Lucas." Dajon's jaw hung slack, and for a moment, he thought it would loosen and drop to the deck at his feet. "What in God's. . . What are you doing here?"

"Never mind, Lucas." A feminine voice swirled in the air like a siren's call, and a woman, dressed in breeches and a white flowing shirt, crossed with baldric and pistols, stepped out from behind Lucas. The floppy hat perched upon her head hid her face, and Dajon's heart crashed through his ribs at the sight of her.

She sauntered toward him and pulled out her cutlass.

Instantly the muskets of all ten marines leveled upon her. She snickered. "Frightened of a woman? *Tsk-tsk.*" She shook her head. "I would request a new batch of marines if I were you, Captain."

273

A hint of a smile played under the shadow of her hat.

She handed the hilt end of her sword to Dajon. "With my compliments, Captain." The scent of lemons joined the salty breeze and spiked him like a dagger. His pulse throbbed in his neck. He tried to move, but his boots felt as though they were bolted to the deck.

A green and red parrot flew down and landed on the capstan. "Clap 'er in irons. Clap 'er in irons."

The lady lifted her chin and slowly raised her gaze to his. A tiny scar in the shape of a quarter moon taunted him from her neck. Beneath the shadow of her hat, eyes the color of mahogany met his with a look of determination—and sorrow.

CHAPTER 28

Faith paced across the floor of her cabin, her boots pounding over the wooden planks like the ominous beat of drums preceding a hanging. She gazed at the thick oak door imprisoning her and knew a marine stood guard just outside.

What a fool I am.

Raising a hand to her mouth, she gnawed her nails and stomped toward a case of books on the starboard side of the cabin before swerving and retracing her steps. Sunlight streaming in from the stern window wove a forked trail around her desk and chairs, and she hesitated to step into it, fearing the virtuous light would scorch her wicked pirate skin.

Mr. Waite had set a perfect trap, and she'd fallen for it like a hungry fish led into a shark's cave. So greedy, so desperate to reach her goal, she'd ignored the warnings, the churning in her gut, the trepidation that prickled down her spine, even Lucas's uneasiness.

And now look where she was. Trapped. Caught.

Doomed.

All was lost. Everything she'd worked for. Everything she'd hoped for.

She spun on her heel and retraced her steps again, the pounding of her boots over the wooden floor jarring her nerves like a judge's gavel.

She froze. Her crew would be imprisoned. They'd be hung. It was all her fault. She wiped the sweat from her neck. What had she done? Lucas had warned her against going on this final raid—had not wanted to go himself. Now he would die because of her foolishness, and he and Molly would never have a chance to share their love.

Faith clenched her fists and took up her pace again. And her sisters. What would become of them?

She couldn't shake the vision of the captain's face from her mind. He had not known it was her until that moment. She could tell from the horror and pain that shot from his gaze when he saw her, like daggers piercing deep within her heart.

He'd grabbed her cutlass and tossed it into the sea. The sharp steel formed an arc of spinning light glittering in the sun's rays as it flew through the air. Then the churning waves of the sea reached up to grab it and pull it below, swallowing it up in darkness.

The end of her pirate career.

Then without saying a word, Mr. Waite had ordered his marines to take her below. Although she could hear the rustling of movement above her, she had no idea what he was doing.

Or thinking.

Footsteps approached, the door blasted open, and in walked Captain Waite. Faith froze.

"Leave us," he ordered the marine who had stepped in after him. Then turning, he slammed the door shut. A blast of salty sea air wafted over her—her last breath of freedom.

The captain didn't look at her. Didn't speak to her. Instead, he stomped to her desk, sifted through her charts and books scattered atop it, then gazed across the room, his eyes skipping over her as if he feared looking at her might infect him with some disease.

Faith pressed a hand to her chest. She felt as if a grappling hook had clawed her heart in two. He hated her. And how could she blame him?

He swallowed hard. Tossing his bicorn on the desk, he finally lifted his gaze to hers. "So." He waved a hand across the room. "You are indeed a pirate. The Red Siren, in fact." He picked up a stack of maps from the desk and then slapped them back down. "You must be proud of yourself."

"No, I—"

"All this time," he said through gritted teeth. "While you were fluttering those thick lashes at me and playing the coquette."

"I never—"

He held up a hand, his face a boiling cauldron. "Enough of your lies!" he yelled, and Faith flinched. She'd never seen him so angry before.

"Teasing me. . .playing me for a fool." He raked a hand through his hair, loosening a strand from his queue, then stormed toward her—a six-foot-one, two-hundred-pound cannonball fired her way.

Taking a step back, Faith held his gaze. Halting inches from her face, he rubbed a harsh thumb over her lips, forcing her back, then he jerked his hand from her mouth. "Kissing me. Vixen," he spat the word and turned from her.

Faith lowered her gaze, battling the tears burning behind her eyes. A drop of sweat etched a ragged path down her back.

"And those two men up on deck, Milner and Landers. . .or whoever they are." He faced her once more, and his fiery gaze incinerated her. "You had them lie to me, play the part of poor plundered merchants." He gave a derisive snort. "And all the while they were part of your crew. Great guns, woman, have you no shame?"

Faith opened her mouth to reply, to tell him that no, she had no shame—at least not until recently, not until she had fallen in love with him, not until God had miraculously saved her sister, and not until this moment when the realization flooded her that her continual running away from God had brought naught but disaster in her life. But Dajon didn't give her the chance to say any of those things before he began ranting again.

"Stealing? Thieving and God knows what else." He pounded his fist on the desk, sending the maps, lantern, pen, and coil of rope quaking. "How many men have you killed, maimed while you plundered their ships?"

"I have hurt no one."

His gaze locked with hers, pain screaming from his blue eyes. And she knew immediately that she had indeed hurt someone—someone very dear to her.

"What will your father say?" The captain tore off his frock and tossed it into a chair. It slid from the seat and crumpled into a pile on the floor, but he didn't notice. Instead, he gripped the hilt of his sword and resumed the pacing Faith had ceased.

"I—" she began.

"It will ruin him. Do you know that?"

Of course she knew that. Her father's welfare and especially that of her sisters had been all that consumed her thoughts these past five years.

"And your sisters? What is to become of them? You thought to protect them, but all you have done is secured their ruin. No decent man will have them now."

A burning lump of sorrow stuck in Faith's throat. A weight as heavy as a thousand cannonballs fell upon Faith, threatening to crush her. She'd only meant to save them, to give them the freedom to choose a decent husband or none at all, but in the end, she had caused just the opposite.

"Dajon." She took a step toward him and dared to use his Christian name, but the searing gaze he gave her told her to stay where she was.

The ship careened over a wave, its wooden hull creaking in protest.

"I saw no other way. My mother left them in my charge." A black cloud swallowed up the sunlight beaming into the cabin, only adding to the gloom settling over Faith. "I could not allow what happened to Charity happen to them."

"So you took to piracy?" Mr. Waite's brow wrinkled into folds of disgust, then he gave a cynical shrug. "Of course, a most logical choice for a proper British lady."

A spark of anger overtook her remorse. "How else was I to acquire a fortune to secure our future? Pray tell. Enlighten me, Captain." She tossed her hair over her shoulder. "I won't even inherit my father's estate. That will go to that foul beast, Lord Villement."

Dajon blew out a sigh and stomped to the bookcase.

"Are you aware that this is my father's ship? This"—he pounded on the bulkhead—"was *my* cabin." He arched a contemptuous brow.

Faith nodded.

"Then you knew it was me all along?"

Thunder rumbled in the distance.

"From the moment I saw you." Faith untied the bandanna and tugged it from her head. "You are not a man easy to forget."

He snorted. "Do you have any idea what you did to me that day?" His jaw flexed. "Besides stealing my father's ship and all his cargo?"

A dark red hue exploded on his cheeks and spread throughout his face. He folded his arms across his chest, his fists tight wads of fury.

"I was thrown from the family business—disinherited." His voice was as sharp as the point of a sword. "I spent a year. . .I spent a year doing things I'm not proud of—things that ruined many lives."

Faith gulped and wrung her bandanna into a tight cord in her hands. "I'm sorry."

He faced her with a sneer. "Now you're sorry? But not sorry enough to stop pirating these waters when you knew I was responsible for keeping them safe, eh? Not *that* sorry."

"This was to be my last time."

"Ah. . .of course." He grinned. "Well, as it turns out, it will be."

Dajon drew his sword and placed it on the desk then leaned back upon the worn oak. "Once again you are determined to shame me." He crossed one boot over the other.

"This time the shame is mine, Captain."

"Indeed." His gaze met hers, and she sensed a softening within the piercing blue.

"What was I to do? What choice did I have?" she asked.

"Perchance, Miss Westcott, to trust God. Did you consider that?"

"Hardly," Faith scoffed and eyed the lantern swinging from the wooden beams above her as she tried to rouse her usual fury toward the Almighty. But at the moment, the only anger she felt was toward herself. "Trust God? After my mother died trying to give my father the son he wanted? After my sister found herself imprisoned in a hellish marriage? After my other sister was ravished and ruined? No, sir. I decided God was not handling things very well."

"And I see you have done so much better."

She lowered her gaze beneath his sardonic glare. The truth of his words began to chisel a trail through her stony resolve. No, she had done a far worse job. Every step she'd taken away from God, everything she had tried to do in her own power had only made things worse. Her relationship with her sisters had suffered due to her absences. And consequently, without proper feminine guidance, Grace kept placing herself in terrible danger, and Hope continually threw herself at disreputable men. All while Faith spent her nights scouring the seas, trying to amass a fortune that now seemed suddenly. . .

Quite worthless.

She'd hurt her sisters, she'd hurt this honorable man before her, she would ruin her father and their family reputation, and at the end of it all, she would be hanged.

Her legs began to feel as fluid as the sea beneath the ship, and she shuffled to one of her padded chairs and fell into it, dropping her head into her hands.

"Oh, God, forgive me." Why had she not seen it until now?

Until it was too late.

Dread and shame swallowed the last of her pride, the last of her rebellion, but she would not allow her tears to flow. Not for herself. She didn't deserve them.

No sound came from Captain Waite. Perhaps he waited for her to spend her sorrow before he locked her in the hold below and escorted her to the Watch House.

He was a gentleman, after all. But she had to know one more thing. Taking a deep breath, she sat up and found his gaze scouring over her. "Pray tell, Captain, if God is so loving, if He loves us so much, why did He allow all those horrible things to happen to my family?"

Dajon shook his head. The tight lines on his face had smoothed, and the gleam had returned to his eyes. "I do not know. The world is a wicked place. People can be very cruel." A shaft of sunlight broke through the clouds and swirled around him, framing him in sparkling specks of dust.

Faith gripped the arms of the chair, wanting to rise but unsure if her legs would cooperate. She'd heard this explanation before, but still, it brought her no satisfaction. "But He's God. He can stop them. He can protect us."

"Yes, He can." Dajon nodded and rubbed his jaw. "But perhaps He has other plans. Maybe He allows things to happen that will lead us in a different direction, or bring us closer to Him, or strengthen our character. We do not know. That is where trust comes in."

"Trust?" Faith snickered. "When everything is crumbling down around me?"

"Aye. That is what trust is. 'Tis easy to trust when all is well." Dajon shoved the strand of hair behind his ear, gripped the edge of the desk, and leaned toward her, urgency sparking in his gaze. "Trust that His Word is true, Miss Westcott, that He loves you, that He is with you, 'that all things work together for good to them that love God' and then see what He can create out of life's worst calamities."

The truth of his words hit Faith like a refreshing wave, but regret and agony soon followed in its wake. "That's not difficult for someone like you who loves to follow rules."

His deep sarcastic chuckle bounced across the room. "Not difficult you say? I fear you do not know me very well."

"Still, I do not know if I can simply sit by when

tragedy strikes and do nothing when 'tis within my power to change things."

Dajon approached and gripped the arms of her chair, staring down at her. "But don't you see? You have never really had the power to change anything—except to make things worse."

Faith gazed up at him. A loose coil of hair grazed his stubbled chin. The smell of lye and leather teased her with the scent of a man she knew now she could never have. She longed to throw herself into his arms, to seek the strength and protection she knew she'd find there. . . if only for a moment before he led her away. A moment she would cherish forever.

No longer able to bear the look of pity and sorrow in his eyes, she tore her gaze from his. Once admiration had filled them. Affection—perhaps even love.

Oh God, forgive me.

The stomping of footsteps sounded from above. They were coming for her.

She must prepare herself to accept the consequences of her foolish actions—the consequences she deserved.

❧

Dajon jerked from the chair and took a step back, watching as Faith stared at the wooden planks above her head. Rising, she threw back her shoulders and stepped into a beam of sunlight that set her hair aglow and her skin shimmering.

Dajon gulped.

The fear, the rage, the defiance in her eyes had fled, replaced by remorse and defeat.

"Dajon. . .Mr. Waite." She raised her chin. Such bravery in the face of such defeat. He'd known navy captains with less fortitude. "I have wronged you greatly. I have wronged my sisters, my father, everyone I care about. I know it means naught to you, but I *am* truly sorry." Her auburn eyes glistened, but she kept her tears captive. "I realize now that I blamed God for all the wrongs in my life, instead of believing what I knew deep down to be true of Him."

Silently Dajon thanked God for giving him the right words to help her understand, to help her see the truth of what she'd done. Though he hated to see her so distraught, a crest of admiration rose within him at her quick and humble repentance. But what to do with her now? Agony strangled him at the thought of what he knew he must do.

She let out a small sigh then continued: "I cannot change what I've done, but. . ." She swept a hand through the air. "You have your ship back now, and you have caught your pirate. You shall have your revenge for the pain I've caused you."

"Revenge? By the powers, woman, do you think that is what I want?" Dajon gripped her shoulders, fighting the urge to pull her into his arms. Instead, he turned, stomped to the desk, and plucked a feather pen from its holder. Her lemon scent, the heat from her body, and the submissive appeal in her eyes were driving him mad, but he must keep a clear head. He must not allow his sentiment to cloud his judgment.

Oh God, what am I to do?

The sunlight disappeared as quickly as if God had blown out a candle, and rain pummeled the deck above like the sound of a thousand boots—boots that marched across his heart, that marched to arrest Faith. He began plucking tiny barbs from the pen. If he turned her in for piracy, she would be hanged. How could he bear it? Yet she seemed repentant, remorseful. If she vowed never to pirate again, what good would come of her death? But oh, the harm that would come of it. Her father ruined, her sisters' lives destroyed.

He didn't know what to do. *Help me, Lord. Please.*

Rules and law. They had been his friends for many years. God's law and man's rules. He had vowed to follow both. Whenever he strayed from them in the past, he'd hurt others—people he loved—just as Faith had done. Crimes should be punished, or wickedness would become the rule.

But what of grace? The soft voice, barely an utterance, rose above the pounding rain.

"Captain Waite," Faith said from behind him, her voice devoid of life. "Let us get this over with. I cannot bear it another minute."

Neither could he.

Dropping the pen, he spun around and marched toward her with nothing on his mind but to grab her and hide her away where no one would ever find her.

She flinched at his threatening approach but met his gaze.

He halted. Great guns, she truly thought he hated her. He snorted, shaking his head.

"Do what you must do." She held out her hands so he could bind them.

He took her hands in his. "Dear lady. . ." Releasing her, he rubbed his eyes. "I can't believe I'm saying this." He snapped his gaze back to hers. "But I understand your reasons. You're clearly mad, but I understand."

"Then what has you so vexed?"

"The position you have forced upon me."

"The position, Captain, is to your favor, for you will be hailed a hero for catching the infamous Red Siren." The breath of a smile that lifted her lips instantly dissipated.

"I care not about that if it means I must lose you." There, he had said it. He had said what had been rending his heart in two. He had said the very thing that defied everything he believed in.

"I don't understand." She pressed a hand over the baldric crossing her chest.

"Take your ship back to wherever you keep it." Dajon grabbed his sword and sheathed it. "By the way, where *do* you keep it?"

A white sheen covered Faith's rosy face, and she gaped at him as if he were the ghost of Captain Morgan come back to life.

"Never mind." He huffed. "I don't want to know."

"You're not arresting me?" She blinked and seemed

to be having trouble finding air around her. "But your men. They saw me."

"Mr. Borland may have. But you still had your hat on, remember? I doubt anyone else recognized you."

"But if the Admiralty discovers this?"

"I'll be court-martialed and executed."

"Nay, I won't take that chance." Faith flung out her wrists again.

"You will because I will not see you hang." Dajon grabbed one of her hands even as he forced back a smile. Not only was the lady truly repentant, but it would seem she returned his affections as well. "Do you understand me?"

She tugged her hand away. "No, I do not. You will arrest me at once."

"I give the orders on this ship now." He flashed a superior grin. "And I will do no such thing."

"Look what I have done to you. Stolen your ship, disgraced your name, caused you so much pain." Her face was a knot of confusion.

"Can you be so daft?" He eased a finger over her soft cheek. "You can navigate a ship, play the pirate, ride a horse, fire a pistol, and probably wield that cutlass I tossed into the sea, but you cannot recognize love when you see it."

"Love?" She gasped.

"Yes. 'Twill most likely be the death of me, but I love you, Faith. I cannot help myself." He cupped her chin and caressed her cheek with his thumb.

She closed her eyes. Her chest rose and fell rapidly as if she were running from some unknown danger. One tear escaped the fringe of her dark lashes, then she sank into him.

Entwining her within his embrace, Dajon wished he could always keep her safe in his arms, but keeping this woman safe would be like trying to catch the wind in his sails and hold it there forever. Weaving his fingers through her curls, he leaned his head atop hers and released a sigh.

She gazed up at him, her sparkling eyes shifting between his. The freckles on her nose begged for attention, and he placed a gentle kiss upon them. "Might I say, you look quite ravishing in breeches," he whispered.

She moved her lips closer to his. "I'll wager you say that to all the pirates you catch."

Pressing her against him, he captured her mouth with his, feeling her heartache, her will, her pain dissolve into him. Heat seared through him. He yearned for more of this tantalizing woman, more of her heart, more of her soul, more of her body. Releasing her before he gave in to his desire, he caught his breath. Then, noticing the tears streaming down her cheeks, he kissed them away. "Please don't cry."

"Dajon, I can't allow you to do this." She shook her head, swiping at her tears and backing away from him. "I will not risk harming another person I love for my own mistakes."

"There is no risk. No one need know of this. You never raised your flag and didn't board the ship. I'll tell the men we made a mistake. You are merely searching for a lost relative."

"But what of Borland? What of the *Lady Adeline*? Clearly the captain knew what I was about."

"Borland is a friend. He will keep silent. And the *Lady Adeline* is even now on her way to Jamaica."

"It is too risky." She swallowed. Her jaw tightened.

Dajon gripped her shoulders and gently shook her, hoping to shake loose the sudden fog that had befuddled her brain. "Do you wish to die at the end of a noose? Do you wish to see your sisters miserable, your father ruined?"

"Of course not." She pulled away from his grasp. "But neither do I wish to see any harm come to you." Her eyes flooded with tears again.

"This is the only way." Dajon held out his hand. "Faith, please, trust me. I promise all will be well."

Taking his hand, she leaned her head on his chest. "Very well, I concede. But not for me. I deserve no better than the noose for what I've done. But for my sisters and my father."

"Good girl." Dajon brushed his fingers through her hair.

He held her back from him. "But you must promise me."

"Anything."

"Promise me you will never pirate again."

"Oh, Dajon, I assure you, that is an easy promise to keep."

CHAPTER 29

Leaping from the cockboat, Borland stomped down the wooden dock, feeling it quake beneath his angry march. Raising the collar of his frock against the rain that blasted across his path, he headed toward his favorite tavern.

He needed a drink. A good, long, strong drink.

Anything to squelch the incessant howling in his head. Egad, Miss Westcott was the Red Siren. As soon as he'd heard her voice, as soon as he'd watched her flounce across the deck to Captain Waite, as soon as he'd seen that tiny thread of red hair dancing across her neck, he knew. Yet the captain had the audacity to set her free.

Borland should be overcome with joy.

He would not have to do a thing. This woman, this pirate, would be Dajon's undoing. The event could not have gone better if Borland had spent years planning it—and even then, he could never have conceived of such a fortuitous outcome.

Rain stung his cheek. He lowered his chin and folded his arms across his chest before darting across the muddy street. The screech of jarring wheels and the irritated whinny of a horse jolted him from his thoughts.

"Watch where yer goin', ye bird-witted laggard," the driver of the buggy yelled before flicking his reins and continuing onward.

Thunder roared an angry admonition as Borland plodded forward, the mud clawing at his boots like demons dragging him to the underworld.

Pulling from their grasp, Borland trudged up the stairs of the Blind Arms alehouse and shook off the eerie feeling that he had somehow escaped a perilous ending.

A ribald tune floated through the open window upon flickering fingers of candlelight, beckoning him inside. Borland doffed his bicorn and slapped it on his knee, licking his lips as the smell of ale wafted over him.

"Mr. Borland!" shouted a familiar voice from within the pounding rain.

Peering through the darkness, Borland made out a fashionable calash as it lumbered through the mud and stopped before the tavern.

A footman, with coat dripping and hair plastered to his face, jumped down from the driver's bench, placed a box step in the mud, and held an umbrella aloft as Sir Wilhelm Carteret emerged from the enclosed carriage. He stepped uneasily onto the box then dashed beneath the porch as if the rain would somehow melt him.

"Sir Wilhelm." Borland nodded, annoyed at the delay to his evening's drink. "What may I do for you, sir?"

Sir Wilhelm's lips flattened into a haughty line as he clutched Borland's arm and dragged him to the side. "Why have I not heard of Mr. Waite's arrest?" Sniffing, he raised a hand to his nose. "Mrs. Gladstone refuses to see me."

Borland ripped from his grasp. "You haven't heard then?" He snorted. "Mr. Waite didn't take the lovely Mrs. Gladstone up on her offer, as I informed you he would not."

Sir Wilhelm growled. "That matters not. The brother should have caught them in an embrace, and her word would seal the captain's doom."

Borland drew a shaky breath of the rain-spiced air and tried to quell the searing fury in his belly. "Nay, I fear the lady was so smitten with the chivalrous Mr. Waite that she reneged on our agreement and hailed him her rescuing knight." Borland waved a hand through the air in a royal gesture.

"Gads! I cannot believe it." Sir Wilhelm turned and gripped the railing then snapped his hands from the soggy wood. "This is inconceivable." He swung about, his white periwig slightly askew.

"Aye, and her husband trumpets the captain's praises all about town, even offered him a reward." The vision of Mr. Gladstone all but bowing down to worship Dajon etched green trenches of jealousy in Borland's mind.

Captain Waite's never-ending good fortune.

Sir Wilhelm gritted his teeth. "I must get the blasted man out of the way! Surely you know of some other way—anything that will ruin him." He pounded the air with his fist, lace flopping at his wrist.

Yes, Borland did indeed know of a way to ruin Mr. Waite. He longed to tell Sir Carteret. The juicy news perched on the tip of his tongue and heralded its call so loudly Borland was sure Sir Wilhelm would hear it. But he snapped his mouth shut. He could not do it.

Not yet.

Dajon would not only be ruined. He would be executed.

Borland felt like Satan himself holding the cursed apple. But if he offered the vile fruit to Sir Wilhelm, 'twould be the great Captain Waite who would fall—not only fall but die as well—and while Borland longed to take back from Dajon what was rightfully his, he was not ready to cause the death of his longtime friend.

He slid a finger over his moist mustache and gave Sir Wilhelm a look of defeat. "No, I told you. Captain Waite is perfect."

Sir Wilhelm sneered and waved a hand in dismissal. "Not as perfect as you think. There is another way." His thin lips spread in an insidious grin. "I received some very interesting news from London today." He patted his waistcoat pocket and turned to leave.

"News of Dajon?"

"Of his past," he shot over his shoulder.

"Enough to discredit his naval service? Or more?"

Sir Wilhelm swung about. "Nay, but enough to discredit him with Miss Westcott." Carteret flicked his eyebrows then climbed into his carriage.

Borland's shoulders sank. If Sir Wilhelm only

knew the weapon Borland held, he would no doubt pay handsomely for its possession. Then not only would they both be rid of the infuriating Captain Waite, but Borland would be a wealthy man, as well as the commander of the HMS *Enforcer*. How could any man pass up such an opportunity? Besides, it was his duty to report Dajon to the Admiralty. If he didn't and didn't do it quickly, then he, too, would face a court-martial for withholding the information.

But to inform Sir Wilhelm would mean a certain death sentence for Dajon. And Borland needed to exhaust every other means to discredit his commander before he resorted to such dire measures.

The footman snapped the reins, and the calash lumbered down the street. Borland watched until darkness enveloped the retreating coach before he ducked into the tavern.

He needed that drink now more than ever.

A daring ray of sunlight peeked through a crack in the heavy curtains hanging in Faith's chamber. Pushing aside her coverlet, she slid from her bed and darted to the window. She'd hardly slept at all and had lain in bed the last hour waiting for the sun to rise. Grabbing the curtains, she flung them aside, allowing the morning sun to wash over her, cleanse her, warm her. It was a new day.

A new life.

A tingling sensation radiated from her heart, bringing with it such peace and love as she had not known before. It was the presence of God. She knew because she had felt Him all night long as she spoke to Him from her bed.

"Oh Lord, I have been so foolish. But You never left me."

Moisture filled her eyes, and she closed them as she knelt on the wooden floor and bowed before the holiness, the power, and the love of a God who, even though she had given up on Him, had never given up on her. Tears spilled down her cheeks, plopping onto the floorboards below like sparkling diamonds. She released a tiny chuckle. These tears of joy, tears of submission, were far more beautiful than the worldly jewels she had sought to obtain.

Though she still could not understand the reason behind all her family's tragedies, somehow now deep within her, she knew. She knew God was in control, and His love for them, His desire for their best, had prompted all that had occurred.

"I thank You, Lord. I thank You for saving me from the noose, though that is surely what I deserve—and far worse. I thank You for saving Hope and for keeping all of us safe in Your arms."

Rising, she pulled on her robe, opened a drawer of her dressing chest, and began flinging out petticoats, ribbons, frilly caps, and scarves onto the floor. It had to be here.

Then she saw it hidden among the folds of a chemise. Her Bible.

Grabbing it, she hopped onto her bed and opened it, tracing her fingers over the holy pages. How long had it been since she'd read it? Six, seven years? Even then, it had not made much sense to her. Yet oddly, she had kept it safely tucked away all this time. She flipped a few pages, and her eyes landed on a scripture in Psalms: "Though I walk in the midst of trouble, thou wilt revive me: thou shalt stretch forth thine hand against the wrath of mine enemies, and thy right hand shall save me. The Lord will perfect that which concerneth me: thy mercy, O Lord, endureth for ever: forsake not the works of thine own hands."

Yes, God had revived her, had preserved her life. Not only hers but her sisters' lives as well—even in the midst of terrible trouble.

But not your mother's life. The subtle whisper slithered into her mind even as a chill overtook her.

Faith bit her lip. True, her mother had died, but perhaps taking her home was a form of saving her.

Perhaps physical death was not the most important thing God desired to save them from. Besides, her mother was the most pious woman Faith had ever known. Surely she did not lament the glorious place where she now resided.

And God hadn't said her family would encounter no trouble, only that He would save them through it. Glancing down at the verse again, Faith locked her gaze upon the phrase "The Lord will perfect that which concerneth me." God had a purpose for her, a plan, a reason for everything that happened. But she had stopped trusting Him. Stopped believing that He cared. And sailed off on her own course.

She gently closed the book. "Oh Father, help me to trust You no matter what calamities may befall me or my family."

Her thoughts sped to her mother again, and renewed sorrow burned behind her eyes. Yet despite the pain, God had worked everything to the good. He had brought her Dajon.

Dajon. Thoughts of him bubbled within her like new wine. Honorable, God-fearing, kind, strong, brave—a million adjectives swept across her mind, each one proclaiming his virtues. Not only was he all those things, but he respected women as well—a rarity among the cads she and her sisters had encountered of late. And he was honest. He would never deceive her, never hurt her, never hurt anyone. She hadn't known men like him existed. If she had, perhaps she wouldn't have been so opposed to marriage. Surprise sent her head spinning. Surprise that the thought of marriage had even occurred to her, let alone made every inch of her shiver with joy.

Perhaps Dajon was the answer to her problems. A God-sent answer. A union with him would provide the protection and support she needed—they all needed—giving her time to find proper suitors for her sisters. Not to mention that she would no longer be obliged to marry Sir Wilhelm when her father returned.

Yet she knew the price Dajon had paid to release her. The cost of going against everything he believed in:

truth and duty and obedience. Not to mention the risk he took with his own life.

Truly, he must love her.

⟋⟋

"Good morning, Hope, Grace. Isn't it a lovely day?" Faith floated into the dining room, anxious to see her sisters, anxious to express her affection for them, to tell them that things would be different, that now all would be well. She was met by the tantalizing scent of oatmeal, honey, sweet cream, and orange marmalade. Her stomach rumbled.

Hope, modishly dressed in a cotton lavender gown trimmed in silver lace, gave her a curious glance before returning to her coffee.

"Hope, let me see you." Faith clutched her hand and pulled her to standing, then she studied her sister's sweet features, the golden gleam in her hair, her thick dark lashes surrounding sapphire eyes. Had Faith ever really seen her before? Had she ever really looked at her as anything other than a nuisance? "Such a lovely lady you've become." She hugged her, but Hope was so stiff it felt as though Faith hugged one of the masts on her ship.

When she pulled back, Hope's face had contorted into confusion.

Faith gulped. Was it so unusual for her to express affection to her sisters?

"And Grace." Faith skirted the table in a swish of lace, but her sister flinched and backed away, looking at Faith as if she were the devil himself.

Ignoring her, she took Grace's hand in hers and squeezed it. "Such constant faith in God. What an inspiration you are to us all."

Grace exchanged a glance with Hope then frowned at Faith. "Oh my. Tell me you haven't taken up that vile devil's brew—and so early in the morning?" She rose and began sniffing around Faith's mouth.

"Nay, something far better." Faith squelched her

rising frustration and turned to stare out the window.

"Miss, would you care for some tea?" the serving maid chirped behind her.

"Yes, Miranda, thank you." Faith took her seat, and after the maid had poured her tea, she plopped two lumps of sugar into the steaming liquid.

Sipping the sweet, lemony tea, she enjoyed the warm trail it made down her throat and into her belly. "Things will be different around here," she began, raising her voice in excitement. "I shall be home more often. We shall attend to our studies—art, literature, science—take up the pianoforte, perhaps. Make Father proud."

Hope blinked. "Whatever has come over you? Are you ill?" She pressed the back of her hand to Faith's cheek then waved it through the air. "Please do not make any more promises you never intend to keep."

Faith sighed, feeling as if the sugar had turned to lead in her stomach. She placed a gentle hand on Hope's arm. "Forgive me for being such a horrible sister, will you?" She glanced at Grace. "And you as well? Can you both ever forgive me?"

Footsteps sounded behind her. "What's this about being a horrible sister?" Molly set a tray of cakes down on the table.

"Call the doctor, Molly. I fear some savage fever has captured our sister's brain," Hope said in all seriousness.

Molly leaned over to examine Faith. "Something different about you for sure. A glow, a brightness in yer eye." She straightened her stance. "Well, whate'er has gotten into you, I hope it stays."

"God has gotten into me." Faith grinned.

"God, did you say?" Molly clapped her hands. "The Almighty Hisself? Well, praise the Lord. Jest what I've been praying for."

Grace cast a hopeful glance toward Faith. "Truly?"

Faith gave her a reassuring nod.

Hope dropped her cup into her saucer, the clank echoing through the room. A look of horror marred her face. "Now what is to become of me? I am surrounded."

Faith and Molly laughed.

"Sir Wilhelm Carteret to see you, Miss Westcott," Edwin announced from the doorway.

Carteret. He was the last person Faith wanted to see. Now or ever.

"Escort him to the drawing room, Edwin. I shall be there shortly." She stood, straightening her gown. "Not even Sir Wilhelm will dampen my mood today," she promised her sisters. But as she made her way to the drawing room, her father's ultimatum hit her in the chest like a boarding ax. Unless Dajon proposed, she would be forced to marry this buffoon when Father returned. And although she believed Dajon loved her, she had no idea of his true intentions.

Whom are you trusting? echoed an inaudible voice within her.

Herself again. Faith hung her head. Slipping back into her old ways so soon. *Forgive me, Lord.* She said a silent prayer as she entered the drawing room and barely glanced at the odious man.

"Sir Wilhelm."

"Miss Westcott," he said in greeting. Taking her hand, he placed a warm, slobbering kiss on it.

Faith suddenly wished she had donned her gloves. Snatching her hand away, she took a step back and wiggled her nose at the smell of the pungent starch Sir Wilhelm lavished upon his wig.

He seemed to be waiting with anticipation for her to say something—such as how good it was to see him or to what did she owe the honor of his esteemed visit—but she just stood, hands clasped before her and brows raised.

"Well, you're no doubt wondering the reason for my call." He cleared his throat and adjusted the cravat abounding in waves of white silk around his neck. "I feel we should become better acquainted. We are, after all, betrothed." His thin, pale lips spread into a catlike grin.

The tea in Faith's stomach churned into a brew of repulsion, and she pressed a hand to her belly, hoping its contents would stay put. "I fear you cannot claim that victory yet, Sir Wilhelm. Not until my father returns."

"Victory, ah, yes. It would indeed be so for us both."

Faith scratched beneath her collar, feeling a sudden rash creep up her neck. "Do not presume, sir, to assess my feelings in this matter."

"I make the presumption, Miss Westcott, based on any woman's delight at the prospect of so favorable a future—especially a lady with no title or fortune to call her own."

"I may not have title or fortune, but I have a heart and a will to marry whomever I wish."

"Pshaw!" Withdrawing an embroidered handker-chief, he flapped it through the air. "Women do not have the capacity to make their own decisions, which is why these arrangements are best made between men."

Faith bunched her fists, digging her nails into her palms. "Sir Wilhelm, I do not wish to be impertinent, nor do I wish to offend you, but I must inform you that I am opposed to this match and will do everything in my power to prevent it from occurring."

Sir Wilhelm's face blanched an even whiter shade than Faith had thought possible. But then his mouth curved in a sly grin. "Ah, you play the coquette with me. So charming." He took her hand in his, intending to plant one of his slobbering kisses upon it again, but Faith snagged it back.

"I assure you, sir, I am playing no game." She grimaced as anger tightened every muscle within her. This man's bloated opinion of himself had surely swallowed all his reason.

"You will feel differently, dear, when we are married." His slimy gaze perused her from head to toe as if imagining the event.

"We will never be married," she spat through gritted teeth.

"I realize your aversion to the union, Miss Westcott." Sir Wilhelm flung a hand through the air and left it hanging there as if waiting for some token. "A certain

M. L. TYNDALL

timidity is to be expected among genteel ladies. But I assure you, with my fortune and position, you will be most happy."

The mélange of angst and fury in Faith's stomach nearly boiled over. "As I have said, I seek neither your fortune nor your position, sir, and I fear I must by good conscience inform you that I would rather broil over a savage fire than marry you." She hated to be cruel, but in the face of such arrogant presumption, she had no choice.

Sir Wilhelm swept back the long white curls of his periwig and straightened his silk waistcoat as if preparing to speak to an assembly. " 'Tis that Mr. Waite, isn't it?" His congenial tone turned caustic. "You prefer a poor commander with no wealth or title? Foolish woman," he hissed and snapped his gaze from hers before he took up a slow pace across the room.

"He treats women with dignity. Respect." Faith crossed her arms over her chest. "Something you would do well to observe and learn from."

Spinning on his heel, Sir Wilhelm faced her, his snakelike eyes narrowing. "Perhaps this will change your mind." He reached inside his coat and pulled out a stack of papers, unfolding them with a flap of his hands. "I have discovered that your esteemed Mr. Waite is not who he appears to be."

Sir Wilhelm's confident tone sent a twinge of fear through Faith. "What madness is this? Would you stoop so low, sir, as to slander another man's name?"

"Slander, Miss Westcott, or reveal the truth?" The mole by his right ear seemed to throb with each vile word he spoke.

Faith tore her gaze from it and rubbed her arms. Unease prickled over her, the unease of impending attack, an intuition she'd honed during her years at sea.

Sir Wilhelm gave a satisfied smirk. "It pains me to tell you that not five years ago, your priestly Mr. Waite was involved in quite the scandal outside Brent."

"Scandal?" Faith planted a hand to her waist and

blew out a sigh. "Really, Sir Wilhelm. This is beneath even you."

"See for yourself."

Snatching the papers from his hand, Faith began perusing them, only half listening to his vainglorious drivel.

"Seems your pious captain was known to be quite the coxcomb in his time. Apparently had an affair with a Lady Marianne Rawlings—a married woman." Faith felt his piercing eyes lock upon her, but she did not look up.

The words before her blurred into squiggly lines.

"When she was found with child, he killed her to cover up the sordid event."

Killed. With child. The words scrambled in the air around her just like the sentences did on the page now quivering in her hands. Other words joined them in her memory—words spoken by Dajon in confession of a sordid past.

Scanning the legal document, obviously from a barrister, Faith tried to focus. *Mishap. . .Mr. Dajon Waite and Lady Rawlings involved in a carriage accident. . .Slick roads. . .The Lady Rawlings and her unborn child died from injuries.*

Everything inside of her screamed a defiant *No!*

It couldn't be true. Not Dajon.

He wouldn't have an affair with a married woman. He wouldn't dispose of her and their child as if they were inconvenient trifles.

"Treats women with dignity, did you say?" Sir Wilhelm withdrew his snuffbox and snorted a pinch into each nostril. "Now you see, my dear, since you must find a suitable husband before your father returns and Mr. Waite obviously falls short, you will have no choice but to marry me."

CHAPTER 30

Dajon led his horse down Hasell Street toward the Westcott home. Well past midnight, no need to hurry. Everyone would have retired by now. After he'd watched the *Red Siren* sail away, the HMS *Enforcer* had encountered a foundering merchant ship, taking on water through a rotted hole in her side more rapidly than she could pump it out. He and his crew had spent the rest of the day and part of the night assisting them with a temporary patch and then hauling them into port. After he'd spent the night on his ship, he'd awoken to pressing business from the Admiralty that had stolen his entire day and most of his evening.

It had taken every bit of his will to remain at his tasks, to not drop everything and dash off to see Faith—to see how she fared after her harrowing capture and release, how her renewed faith was settling in, and where her true feelings toward him lay.

He thanked God that no one else on the ship, aside from Borland, had actually seen Faith. No one else knew her true identity. Her flag had not been raised. The *Red Siren* painted on the hull had not been visible from the side they boarded, and she had fired only one shot, a warning shot he easily explained away as the means of an inexperienced captain's daughter to get the merchant ship's attention.

The marines had been quite satisfied with his explanation of mistaken identity. The distraught captain's daughter had only been searching for her missing father after the poor man had been abducted and forced into slavery aboard a ship by a vindictive merchant in payment for an exorbitant debt he owed.

No one recognized Lucas. No one knew Faith, save Borland, and Borland was Dajon's lifelong friend, his partner, his confidant. He accepted Dajon's promise that Faith had vowed never to pirate again.

Then why did guilt continually churn in Dajon's gut? *God, forgive me for my lies, but I did not know how else to save her.*

Daring a glance into the black sky, he hoped for some sign of absolution. Nothing but dark clouds broiled over a sliver of a moon. *Lord, no harm was done. In fact, quite the opposite—a known pirate has repented. Then why do I feel like You have abandoned me?*

Regardless, Dajon could not imagine having taken any other course. Because the only other course available was one that led to Faith's neck in a noose.

Agony choked him at the thought, and he took a deep breath of the night air, fragrant with earth and jasmine. A vision of Faith in breeches and waistcoat stormed through his mind.

A pirate.

He smiled. By the powers, what an incredible woman. He yearned to see her, to take her in his arms, to express his sincere devotion to her; it would have to wait until morning, though, for no doubt she had retired hours ago.

Dismounting, Dajon led his horse through the back gate of the Westcott house. He nodded at Lucas and handed him the reins. "Good evening, Lucas, or good morning, rather. My apologies for keeping you up so late." The air hung like a heavy curtain around them. Not a breeze, not a whisper of wind stirred the thick folds of humidity.

Lucas grunted and took the reins. Unusual for the normally cheerful groomsman, but then, Dajon had caught him at piracy. Perhaps he was concerned for his future. "Never fear, Lucas, I have no intention of arresting you for your part in Miss Westcott's piracy. She explained that your participation was only to assist and protect her and that you have no desire to pirate again."

Lucas shifted his stance but said not a word.

Trying to determine his mood, Dajon peered at him, but the groomsman's features were lost in the shadows. Even the outline of his hair blended into the ebony night.

"Never mind," Dajon said. "We shall discuss it later. I'm spent and wish to retire."

Lucas didn't move.

A thick silence waxed between them. Dajon drew in a deep breath of air burdened with the smell of horseflesh and human sweat. An uneasiness, borne from many battles, pricked his fingers, causing them to grip the hilt of his sword and peer into the darkness surrounding them.

"You may lead him to the stables, Lucas. I am home for the night."

Lucas cleared his throat. "Forgive me, Mr. Waite, but I can't be doin' what ye ask of me."

Before shock could settle in, the snap of a twig and the crunch of gravel drew Dajon's gaze toward the house, where a form appeared out of the darkness. A curvaceous form in a light-colored gown that swished when she walked.

Faith.

He took a step toward her in expectation.

"That will be all, Lucas. Leave the horse where it is." Her harsh tone froze Dajon in place. "Mr. Waite will be leaving shortly."

Dajon gave a humorless laugh. "What are you saying? I have only just arrived." Removing his bicorn, he dabbed at the sweat on his forehead. By thunder, 'twas a muggy night. Perhaps the soggy air had somehow seeped into Faith's brain, befuddling it.

Dropping the reins, Lucas hesitated, shifting his weight back and forth, but one look from Faith sent him shuffling away.

"Why are you awake at this hour?" Dajon asked, beginning to believe that he wouldn't like her answer at all. He held out a hand, hoping she'd take it and relieve him of the fear that now prickled his scalp.

But she did not. Instead, she turned, took a few steps, and positioned herself by his horse. Was that a sword strapped to her side? "I must protect my sisters."

"From whom, pray tell?"

"From you."

Dajon took a step back, as if an icy wall of water had crashed over him. Peering into the darkness that seemed to stretch for miles between them, he searched for her eyes but could only make out two simmering black coals.

Fear gave way to anger. He had done naught to deserve this ill treatment. "What has gotten into you? Yesterday—"

"Yesterday, I thought I knew you," she snapped and crossed her arms over her waist, where Dajon thought he saw the dark shape of a pistol shoved into her belt.

Knew me? Dajon swallowed, sending what felt like lead pellets into his stomach. The hoot of an owl echoed across the garden. Dajon had the odd feeling the bird was somehow warning him to flee. "Miss Westcott, if you'll forgive me, I am in no mood for games."

"I'm not the one playing a charade."

Dajon bunched his fists. Nothing was making sense. It was as if he had walked into a playhouse where one of Shakespeare's tragedies was being performed. Only he was onstage. "Whatever are you talking about? And why do you all of a sudden feel you need to protect your sisters from me? I have done you no harm—in fact, quite the opposite."

She snorted. "Unfortunately, Lady Marianne Rawlings cannot claim the same."

All hope, all joy drained out of Dajon, soaking into the ground beneath him. Only an empty shell of shame and horror remained. Now he understood. "Who told you?"

"Sir Wilhelm."

Ah yes. Dajon should have seen it coming, should have told Faith the truth, but he longed to bury his past forever in the hope that he could forget it as well.

"Tell me it's not true." Faith's stalwart voice broke in a slight tremble.

The owl repeated its eerie call from somewhere above them. No more lies. He would tell no more lies tonight. "I cannot deny it."

She flinched and stepped back, bumping into his horse, who protested with a snort. "Though I am truly thankful for all you've done, I must ask you to leave immediately and never come back." Grabbing the reins, she held them out to him.

Sweat slid behind his collar and down his back—putrid beads of shock, of pain, of remorse. But he could not leave. "Your father left me in charge, Miss Westcott. I cannot abandon my post."

"My father did not know what kind of man you are."

"Perhaps, but I thought *you* might have discovered that truth these past weeks."

"As I said, you play a good charade." The venom in her voice stung every nerve within him.

"I still cannot leave you and your sisters unprotected." He may have lost Faith. He may have lost her love, he may never recover from the gaping hole in his heart, but he still had a duty to perform. "So if you'll permit me." He grabbed the horse's reins and felt her flinch when their fingers brushed. Was she frightened of him or simply repulsed? He started for the stables. "I promise I shall make every effort not to offend you with my presence."

"Which you will find quite easy since you no longer reside here." Faith's seething voice scraped over him, but he stepped around her, leading the horse toward the flickering light in the stables.

The swish of a sword being drawn sliced the thick air. Something sharp pricked his back. "Not another step, Captain."

He slowly turned to face her, just as a cloud eased away from the moon, revealing her tear-stained face. The silver glint of the sword formed a bridge between them, and he wished it were that easy to span the painful gap that now threatened to separate them forever.

"Are you going to kill me, Faith?"

"I will do what I must to keep my sisters safe from men like you."

"You know I would never harm you or your—"

"I don't know anything anymore!" she shouted. Her sword wavered.

In her state of mind, he wouldn't put it past her to run him through. He didn't know exactly what Sir Wilhelm had told her, but if it was anything close to the truth, she now believed him capable of forcing himself upon a decent lady—a married lady at that—stealing her away from her husband and home in the middle of the night, only to have her killed along with their child.

As the point of her sword etched a quivering trail across his chest, he reached for his own sword and drew it in one quick swoop. He batted hers from her hand and onto the ground with a clank that sounded muddled in the humid air.

Faith gasped. Backing away from him, she plucked out her pistol, cocked it, and pointed it at his chest. "Please leave," she sobbed.

Until now he'd heard only the anger in her voice, the spite, but now he heard the pain, like a wail of anguish piercing through the air and into his heart. He had hurt her terribly, and the thought gutted him as if she had indeed run him through with her sword. "Very well. I will leave." Turning his horse around, he faced Faith. "If it means anything at all to you, I am truly sorry." He headed for the gate.

She sniffed. "I suppose you'll turn me in for piracy now."

"Why?" He shrugged and halted. "Nothing has changed. You will not go back on your vow to quit?"

"No."

"Then I have no reason to turn you over to the authorities." He could only pray to the Lord that she wouldn't turn away from God, as well. "Besides, I still love you."

Dajon mounted his horse in one leap and grabbed

the reins. He risked one more glance at the woman he'd grown to love and admire. She held the pistol out before her, leveled upon his heart. Did she really believe he would hurt her? The thought sank him to the depths of the sea. "If you need anything, you know where—"

His words faltered on his lips.

The owl gave his eerie hoot for a third time, announcing Dajon's exit back into shame and regret.

Nudging his horse, he rode off into a darkness so thick, so black that he truly believed it would never be light again.

~

"Why we goin' to the ship?" Lucas asked, bringing his horse alongside Faith's.

"I told you. I have to clean it out. Get all of our things removed. Bring Morgan home. 'Tis not my ship anymore." Faith adjusted her straw bonnet against the rising sun. "I must return it to Mr. Waite."

The thought saddened her. The *Red Siren* had been a faithful friend these past five years. Her ticket to the sea, to wealth, to freedom. But that was all gone now. Perhaps Mr. Waite would have allowed her to take the ship out upon the seas now and then, once she proved to him her pirating days were over—and after the name *Red Siren* was scraped from the hull, of course—but that was no longer an option.

She now longed to be rid of anything associated with Mr. Waite. "I still have a hard time believin' he let ye go like that," Lucas said as the trail narrowed and they entered a thick patch of trees.

Beams of glittering morning sun streamed through the forest like ribbons of hope, transforming the leaves of hickories and sweet gums into sparkling emerald and their barks into columns of amber. It appeared more like a magical forest from a fairy tale than a Carolina woodland.

Faith huffed. Just like her short-lived romance with Mr. Waite. Destined to live only in a storybook where endings were always happy. Not in real life where they never were.

As if mimicking her faltering mood, the air thickened around her with the earthy, pungent smell of rotting wood and dank moss. Something stung her neck, and she slapped a mosquito.

Lucas struck his arm where another blood-sucking beast had landed. "An' especially after ye near run 'im through with yer blade last night." He snickered.

Faith made no reply as the events of the night drilled through her mind for the thousandth time. So enraged at Mr. Waite's betrayal and the revelation of his true character—or lack thereof—her only thought had been to put as much distance between the loathsome man and her sisters as she could. She hadn't considered that he held the power to throw her in prison, not until after she'd pointed the pistol at him.

Why had she confronted him? Perhaps deep down, despite the proof stamped upon documents now littering her drawing room floor, she hoped it wasn't true—that Dajon. . .Mr. Waite would deny the allegations, would offer some explanation. But when he hadn't, when he had only confirmed her biggest fears, she flew into a rage. She would rather see him dead than harm her sisters.

"The day is young, Lucas. Mr. Waite could be alerting the authorities about us as we speak." The daunting thought had occurred to her even before she'd opened her eyes that morning. She wanted to believe Mr. Waite would stick to their bargain, she wanted to believe he was a man of his word, but she'd been trusting a man she no longer knew. Dread consumed her. It was as if Faith, her sisters, and her father were lined up before a loaded cannon and Mr. Waite stood nearby, holding the linstock that would set off the blast.

A bird the color of a turquoise sky flitted across their path, chirping a cheerful tune, followed by several of his friends. Faith envied their carefree life.

"Mr. Waite'll not be turnin' ye in." Lucas loosened his neckerchief then used it to dab the back of his thick

307

neck, revealing the pink tip of a scar beneath his shirt. Faith cringed. She had never gotten used to seeing the molten stripes marring her friend's back. Yet even after being nearly whipped to death as a boy, Lucas now allowed God to give him hope for the future.

"The man loves ye; any fool can see that," he said.

"The only fool here is me." Faith dipped her head beneath an overhanging branch. "For I believed Mr. Waite was the God-fearing man he claimed to be. A man like him is incapable of love."

They rode side by side in silence. Only the clump of their horses' hooves over the sandy trail and the orchestra of birds and buzzing insects accompanied them.

The faint snort of a horse sounded, and Faith grabbed her pistol. Lucas did the same. They both scanned the thicket of trees then shot a glance behind them. Nothing. Not many people dared to venture into the backwoods surrounding Charles Towne, especially with all the Indian attacks recently. Most likely a trapper or a lone Indian, neither of which would be a threat to them.

Returning her pistol to her baldric, Faith tugged on the leather straps, hoping for a breeze to ease inside her cotton gown and cool her searing skin.

Lucas shifted in the saddle and stretched his broad back. "I's praying fer you, mistress. An' fer Mr. Waite."

"You need not bother, Lucas," she retorted. "Mr. Waite was a man of prayer, a man of faith, but he turned out to be naught but a scoundrel who preys on the affections of innocent women." Faith's heart shriveled even as she said the words. "Just like all men." Then she bit her lip and glanced at Lucas. "Yourself excluded, of course."

Lucas flashed a set of pearly teeth that matched the whites of his eyes. "Why, thank ye, mistress. But whate'er Mr. Waite done, 'twas a long time ago, eh?"

"Aye."

"Thanks be to God that He not only forgives but forgets the sins o' our pasts."

"Only if we repent of them." Faith slapped another mosquito and wondered for the first time if Mr. Waite had been sorry for his actions.

Not that it would matter to Faith.

Lucas scratched his hair. "Seems to me Mr. Waite ain't nothin' like this man you done heard about."

True. Mr. Waite had proven himself to be naught but an honorable, God-fearing man these past few weeks. A clump of moss hanging from an almond pine grazed over Faith's shoulder as she tried to brush away thoughts of the man's admirable character. He was a swindler. That was all.

"Perhaps. Perhaps not," she said. "But I cannot forget the abuse of an innocent woman. Not after what has happened to Charity and to Hope."

"God changes people. He already be changin' me, mistress."

Faith studied her first mate, groomsman, and longtime friend, unable to deny the new lightness in his bearing and hope in his eyes. "I must forbid you to spend any more time with Molly—or Miss Grace, for that matter." She gave him a playful grin. "I find I prefer the old nefarious Lucas"—she deepened her voice—"first mate on the pirate ship *Red Siren*, than this charitable, high-spirited optimist." They both laughed.

Lucas grew serious. "I just hoping ye don't lay blame fer Mr. Waite's failings on God." Concern warmed his dark eyes.

Did she? No. She knew that would be pure foolishness, for that would thrust her right back where she started, blaming God for everything wrong in the world and in her life. Truth be told, God had never left her or her sisters. He had more than proven that with His miraculous rescue of Hope. Then what Faith had felt in the cabin of her ship when Dajon had confronted her, what she had felt in her chamber—the very presence of God, the love, the hope, the forgiveness that had blanketed her—was more real than anything she had known. In fact, it seemed to be the only reality she could count on anymore.

"No, Lucas. I fear that I, too, have been forever changed."

They rode the rest of the way in silence, battling the insects and the heat, and finally emerged onto the lagoon where the *Red Siren* floated in the midst of a glassy pool fringed in green moss and algae. The bare masts of the ship thrust into the sky, blending with the myriad trees surrounding them. No one would see the ship unless he happened to emerge right at this spot, and even then the anchor chain was bolted by a hefty lock that would forbid it to be raised. So far, the ship had remained safe.

After dismounting, Faith assisted Lucas in uncovering a nearby canoe, and then together they paddled out to the ship and gathered her flag, Morgan, some of her books and charts, a small chest of doubloons and rubies, and the silver swept-hilt rapier she'd captured from a French privateer. By the time they made it back to shore, the heat rose like steam off the tepid swamp.

As she and Lucas silently loaded her things into packs they had slung over their horses, Faith swallowed down the sorrow clogging her throat and avoided gazing at her ship. This might be the last time she would ever see it and definitely the last time she would call it hers, the last time she would march across its decks as they rose and fell over the tumultuous waves, the last time she would be in command. She didn't regret her change of heart. She knew now that what she had done was wrong, but it didn't seem to dull the pain of loss she felt—not only the loss of her ship but the loss of Mr. Waite.

A harsh scuffle sounded behind her, followed by a thud and a gurgle.

"Avast! Head for the shoals! Head for the shoals!" Morgan squawked from his perch on the saddle horn.

Gripping the handle of her pistol, Faith swerved around to see a beefy man, his thick arm clamped around Lucas's neck, pointing a knife at his throat. Her first mate's pistol lay useless on the dirt by his feet, and the fear flickering in his eyes seemed more for her than for himself. The beast of a man behind him slowly widened his mouth into a grimy, yellow-toothed grin.

In an instant, Faith had her pistol cocked and pointed at the intruder, but before she could utter her ultimatum, the sound of footsteps scraped across her ears. She spun her weapon in the other direction. The gun nearly fell from her hand when Sir Wilhelm Carteret emerged into the clearing. His periwig perched atop his egg-shaped head, slanted precariously as if at any minute it would slide off. Powder-muddied sweat oozed from beneath it onto his forehead and down his bloated, reddened cheeks.

"Load the guns! Load the guns!" Morgan screeched, and the flap of his wings filled the air as he, no doubt, headed for the safety of the trees.

Coward.

"Well, well." Sir Wilhelm placed one hand on his hip and the other in midair. "I daresay, what a surprise, my dear." His pretentious gaze combed over the *Red Siren.*

"You followed me," Faith spat as she tried to surmount her shock and plot her next step.

"You can't say I didn't warn you. I told you that you would pay for your refusal and your insolent behavior. Did I not?"

"I will shoot you where you stand." Faith's finger itched over the trigger, longing to put an end to this miserable man's life, while at the same time knowing she could not take another's life, even when her freedom and her very life were at stake.

"Nonsense. You will do no such thing." He smirked and gestured toward Lucas with a nod of his head. "Not unless you wish to see your slave here die." He loosened his cravat from his neck and flapped it through the air, trying to banish the swarm of gnats enamored with his wig.

Faith dared a glance at Lucas. A line of blood marred his bronze neck, but his eyes carried more annoyance than fear.

"He is not my slave. He is my friend."

"No matter." Sir Wilhelm waved a hand of dismissal

toward Lucas. "You will put down your weapon, or I will order my man to slit his throat."

Faith studied Sir Wilhelm's icy gaze and knew he meant it. He would kill Lucas and get away with it. Lucas was a Negro and a pirate, after all. Releasing the cock, Faith tossed the pistol to the ground.

Sir Wilhelm's thin lips broke into a malicious grin. "So—you are indeed the notorious Red Siren? I am all astonishment." He nearly giggled with glee. "This is most fortuitous." His normally dull eyes blazed with a hard, calculated look.

Ignoring the fear and nausea spinning in her stomach, Faith planted her fists on her waist. "What is it you want?"

"Hmm." Approaching her, he took her hand and rubbed his clammy, cold fingers over hers. "You know what I want." He leaned toward her, inundating her with the stench of snuff and starch. "You will marry me."

Yanking her hand from his, Faith retreated. "I will not."

"Then I shall be forced to turn you in for piracy."

CHAPTER 31

Faith plopped down onto the moist floor, laid her head against the rough brick wall, and brought her knees to her chest. In this far corner of her cell, tucked in among the shadows, she could escape the licentious gazes of the other prisoners. Their ogling had begun to grate on her nerves like acid on an open wound. Grasping a handful of straw, she shoved it beneath her bottom, both to soften her seat and to shield her from the damp stones. An archway of bricks formed the ceiling above her, upon which hung a lantern whose flame was often extinguished, enshrouding her in the nightmarish gloom of the Watch House dungeon.

The dismal cage had been her home for a week, and she could no longer smell the human waste, fear, and death that thickened the air around her. That was not a good sign. She wondered if she would also grow accustomed to being imprisoned within these dank walls, but if her fellow inmates—who had obviously been here longer than she—provided any clue by their constant complaining and cursing, she would never get used to losing her freedom.

Her only joy was the remembrance of Sir Wilhelm's face when she'd informed him that she'd rather hang for piracy than become his wife. He had bent over so violently that she thought he was going to choke on his own vile spit. His periwig flew to the ground, leaving naught on his head but a bald, heat-prickled scalp.

After he had composed himself and covered his fury with a veneer of unruffled arrogance, Faith had convinced him that she would go with him peaceably if he would release Lucas unharmed. She had watched his beady gaze flicker between her and Lucas—who was still being restrained by Sir Wilhelm's henchman—and knew he realized what she already had. That Wilhelm was not man enough to contain her without his man's help.

After the henchman had withdrawn the knife from Lucas's throat, Faith had ordered her reluctant first mate back home with the admonition that he send for her father and take care of her sisters until the admiral returned. The assurance of her faithful friend's loyalty had been the only beam of light in the otherwise dark, hopeless void that continued to close in around her with each passing minute.

Thoughts of her sisters and their precarious futures bombarded Faith in her loneliest hours. With her imminent demise and their father returning from overseas, they would no doubt find themselves married off to the first suitors who would accept them before further scandal racked the family. A sob rose to her throat, but she refused to release it. She deserved her fate. Her sisters did not deserve theirs. She longed to see them one last time, if only to apologize for her foolish actions. Why hadn't they come to see her? Perhaps ladies were not permitted in the dungeon of the Watch House. And as she listened to the depraved conversations and fiendish threats of the men around her, Faith could understand why.

But no word, either?

Nothing from Lucas or Edwin—or Dajon. Not that she expected to see the captain after the malicious way she had thrown him from their home.

Much to her deep chagrin, the only visitor she'd had was Sir Wilhelm, who had come to call upon her twice with the same proposition. If she married him, she would be released and exonerated of all charges, and he would take care of her and her sisters for the rest of their lives. All her problems would be solved with one simple yes. Just one yes seeping through her lips but, oh, the bitter taste.

She had begun to pray—to plead with an invisible God, to humble herself before His power and majesty and ask for guidance. It felt odd, even scary at first, asking for help, relying on someone else, trusting someone else, but the more she prayed, the more she relished the companionship of her heavenly Father.

And she had felt God telling her to trust Him— that He had another plan, a better plan, and for once, she resisted taking charge of her own life. Only now as her faith dwindled along with her strength, she wondered if she had made the right choice.

I know You forgive me, Lord. I'm trying to do the right thing now. Is it too late for me? Is it too late for my sisters? Please do not punish them for my sins. Please protect them and provide godly men to be their husbands who will love them and cherish them.

She swiped away a tear before it slid down her cheek. No more crying. Perhaps she had strayed too far into the wickedness of this world, done too many bad things to be redeemed. But surely it was not too late for her sisters.

She heard the jailer before she saw him. The scrape of his bare, impotent foot over the stones had become an omen of bad tidings. Soon he emerged from the shadows carrying a bucket that seethed with the odor of animal fat and rotten eggs. Sweat gleamed atop his head, which was as big as a melon, while greasy strands clinging loosely to its sides swayed with each step. Halting, he gaped at her with the permanent grin of a hungry alligator.

"Here's yer grub, missy. Come an' get it."

"Just push it beneath the bars, if you please, Gordon."

"I'll thank ye to be callin' me *Lord* Gordon, like I told ye to."

A chuckle erupted from the cage beside hers, and Gordon pressed his face up to the rusty iron bars of her cell and whispered, "If ye be nice t' me, thar's privileges I can do fer ye to make yer stay more agreeable." Lust dripped from his bloodshot eyes.

A shudder of disgust gripped Faith just when she thought she had no more left. "I thank you, *Lord* Gordon, but I'd rather be flogged and tossed to the sharks."

Wicked chortles bounced through the air.

His eyes narrowed. "That can be arranged, ye high an' mighty wench," he growled as he dipped the ladle into his bucket of slop. But instead of pouring it onto her plate, he dumped it into her chamber pot, sitting just inside the bars. "Enjoy your meal." He laughed and slogged off, a wake of obscenities spilling from his lips after him.

But Faith had grown cold to those as well.

"Scorned ye again, old Gordie," one of the prisoners chortled.

Faith turned off the sound of the men's vulgar grumblings as Gordon made his rounds. Soon he dragged himself back in front of her cell and, with a reluctant grunt, gave her the news that she had a male visitor.

A visitor? Sir Wilhelm had already seen her earlier in the day. Faith dashed to the bars. *Lucas.* It had to be. Perhaps with word from her sisters. Faith's heart swelled. It would be so good to see a friendly face.

But it wasn't a friendly face that appeared a few minutes later lumbering down the tower steps—at least not friendly any longer. Mr. Dajon Waite, donned in a disheveled uniform, took the last step and headed toward her, his boots clomping over the stones. Gordon withered under the captain's imperious gaze, and he scampered away before Mr. Waite's blue eyes shifted to Faith's.

Backing away from the bars, Faith gripped the folds of her filthy gown as anger, fear, and—to her surprise—joy waged a fierce battle within her at the sight of him. "Come to gloat?"

He snorted. "Hardly." Anguish burned in his gaze. "I would have come sooner, but Sir Wilhelm's scrawny arm is more powerful than it appears."

Faith nodded. Indeed. The gaunt man and his noble connections did wield a mighty sword among Governor Johnson and the assembly. Her wisp of faith dwindled yet again. Who could stand up to such a powerful man?

Dajon approached the bars. Gray shadows clouded

the skin beneath his eyes. His dark hair grazed his collar. He spiked a hand through the unruly strands and then scratched the stubble littering his chin. Faith wasn't sure which of them looked worse.

He swiped a lock of hair behind his ear and met her gaze in a hold so intense that she could feel his passion, his torment—his love—span between them like a sturdy plank, drawing her near.

Suddenly his past made no difference to her. Her heart had lodged in her throat when he'd entered the room and had remained there. She loved him—no matter what he'd done. Her stomach coiled into a knot as she fought the urge to run to him, to touch him, to feel his comforting strong hands on hers, but instead, pride allowed her to say only, "Why have you come?"

He swallowed hard and looked away. "To see how you are doing."

"So you see"—she swept a hand over her cell as if she were showing him her parlor—"I'm quite comfortable."

He frowned, and she chided herself for being so caustic.

"Faith." He took a step toward her. "I have sent a dispatch to Bath up north. Governor Eden harbors sympathies toward pirates wishing to reform. He has granted the King's Pardon to many who have sworn to change their ways."

Hope, an emotion Faith had abandoned during the week, sprang to life. "Why would you help me?"

"You know." The intense look in his blue eyes said more than enough.

He still loved her.

Hoots and coarse jests blasted over them. Dajon gazed down the row of gloomy cells, but the prisoners only increased their vile banter. "I'm sorry you have to hear such lubricity."

Faith raised a shoulder. "I have learned to ignore them."

"It may take a month to arrive, but I have sent my recommendation along with the urgent request."

Dajon spit the words out quickly, as if doing so would help speed the process. "My position in His Majesty's Navy should carry some merit with the governor, who appreciates our presence in the colonial waters."

"But what of Sir Wilhelm?"

"His powerful arm does not stretch as far as Bath, thanks be to God."

Sweat broke out on his forehead, and he wiped it away with his sleeve then shrugged off his waistcoat and draped it over his arm. His damp shirt clung to his muscled chest. Power exuded from him, an angry, pent-up frustration that knifed into the air all around him. His jaw tensed.

Faith gazed at him in awe. She'd done naught but deceive him, lie to him, force him to risk his life and his career, and then nearly shoot him, and here he stood, his eyes filled with love as he tried to save her life.

"There is one problem," he continued, drawing in a deep breath. "Sir Wilhelm is rushing your trial through the courts. He could possibly have you convicted and. . ." Dajon's gaze did not falter, though his voice did.

"Hanged." Faith swallowed.

Dajon clasped a bar with one of his hands. "Before the pardon arrives."

Wicked laughter shot off the brick walls. "Aye, afore too long, we all be dancin' the hempen jig."

Dajon gripped the hilt of his sword and stared into the dungeon as if he intended to slice the prisoner's throat. Slowly he returned his frenzied gaze to hers. "Sir Wilhelm has many powerful allies."

The hope that had risen within Faith dissolved and fell into her stomach like an anchor. "Then rest assured, he will have his way."

❧

"I won't allow him." Dajon leaned toward her, not caring when the iron bars bit into his skin. He would not watch the woman he loved die.

Not again.

The pardon would arrive in time. It had to. But as he gazed at Faith, her red curls flaming around her face, her auburn eyes still simmering boldly beneath a shroud of defeat, he wondered for a brief moment if she would indeed abide by its conditions.

"He found you at the *Red Siren*?" Dajon hated to ask, but he had to know if she had planned on pirating again—if the news of his past had driven her so swiftly back to her old ways.

"Aye, with my colors in hand." Faith gave a sardonic smirk, then her eyes widened. "I wasn't taking the ship out, Dajon, if that's what you're thinking."

The sound of his Christian name on her lips—even with a hint of spite—flowed over him like honey.

"I was only removing my things," she added. "To return the ship to you."

Rubbing the sweat from the back of his neck, Dajon studied her. Her steady stance and the pleading sincerity in her eyes convinced him that, for once, she told him the truth. "I believe you."

"So easily." She shook her head and lowered her lashes. "When I wouldn't even allow you to explain your actions to me."

"I hope you'll allow me to do so now."

"It matters not. All is lost." She turned her back to him and wrapped her arms around herself. A sob rippled down her back.

"Your opinion of me matters a great deal." Dajon rattled the bars, longing to rip them from their moorings and go to her, take her in his arms. But his outburst only brought a cloud of dirt raining down upon him and a cacophony of chortles from the other prisoners.

"After you stole my father's merchant ship. . ." He cleared his throat at the memory, finding it hard to believe he loved the same woman who had ruined him that day. "I was banished from the family business."

Turning around, Faith met his pained gaze with hers, but she said nothing.

"I fell in with some bad sorts—wealthy, titled bad

sorts, that is. I took up gambling, drinking, carousing." Flashes of those sordid memories burned trails of guilt and remorse across his mind. His throat constricted. "Then I met Lady Rawlings. Her husband, Lord Rawlings, was a cruel, abusive man who beat her frequently."

"Much like Charity's husband." Faith's voice came out barely above a whisper.

"Perhaps worse." Anger still flared in his belly at the remembrance of the man's brutality.

"Our acquaintance was quite innocent in the beginning, I assure you. For a time, we seemed to flow in the same circles, same country dances, same balls and playhouses. Her sweet spirit and innocence drew me to her, especially after the sordid company I had grown accustomed to keeping." Dajon hesitated, unsure how much of the affair to disclose to Faith. Would she turn from him in disgust? No matter. 'Twas time to lay out the details before her and let her decide.

"When I discovered her horrendous predicament at home, it only served to draw me closer to her, to comfort her and help her. But what could I do?" He shrugged. "I had no business being with her. She was married, and I had nothing to offer her—but my love."

"Ah, ain't that sweet." The man in a cell kitty-corner from Faith's clung to the bars and thrust his deathly pale face toward them.

Ignoring him, Dajon eyed Faith, trying to assess the effect of his tale, but she stood riveted in place, nothing but concern beaming from her gaze.

"When I discovered she was with child. . .our child"—Dajon lowered his voice to a whisper—"we planned to run away together. But Lord Rawlings learned of our plot and chased us. The roads were slick." Dajon jerked back from the bars, hoping to dislodge the vision of Marianne's lifeless body in his arms. "You know the rest," he choked out.

A familiar pain seared through his nose, and Dajon reached up to rub it. When the carriage had careened off the road, overturned, and plummeted into a ditch, his nose had been smashed. The haunting ache was a constant reminder of his failure to care for the woman he loved. He deserved much worse.

Now Faith knew the truth. Dajon braced himself for her reaction. But much to his surprise, Faith rushed to the bars and reached out a hand toward him. He gripped it like a lifeline and drew close to her. Placing a gentle kiss upon her fingers, he cringed at the red marks marring her delicate skin. The hint of lemon battled against the dungeon's fetid smells and made its way to his nose.

He sighed and raised his gaze to hers, afraid of what he might see, but no condemnation shot from her eyes, only compassion and concern. "I did love her, Faith, or at least I thought I did. But I see now how every step I took was wrong. Everything I did went against God's plan, His law, and because of my disobedience and stupidity, I caused her death—and the death of our child." Renewed agony threatened to strangle him, and he swallowed against the burning in his throat.

"I'm so very sorry, Dajon." Reaching through the bars, Faith pressed her other hand over his heart. The warmth and tenderness of her familiar touch soothed him like a healing balm. Her auburn eyes enveloped him with a kindness he didn't deserve. "I thought you were no better than my sister's husband or Sir Wilhelm—or most of the men I've met—but I see now that you meant only to save this lady, to protect her."

"A lot of good I did her." Dajon snorted. "I suppose I've been trying to make up for it ever since, to pay some sort of penance."

"But don't you see?" Faith's voice lifted. "You can never pay the price. None of us can. I have realized that in the long hours I've spent down in this dungeon."

Dajon brushed a finger over her cheek, still as soft as silk. She closed her eyes beneath his touch. "Very wise for one so newly returned to God."

She opened her eyes and smiled. "He and I have had

much to discuss this past week."

"Aye and He's been speaking with me as well. I now see that adhering to a list of rules just for the sake of following them does not please God. Nor does it atone for any past sins. Jesus has already done that on the cross."

Faith smiled. "And how did you come to this grand conclusion?"

"When I set you free." He uttered a low chuckle. "The guilt of breaking a rule ate at me day and night, but at the same time, I knew deep in my gut that it was the right thing to do. It was then that I realized God does not concern Himself so much with rules as He does with us. Doing what's right will then flow naturally out of our relationship with Him."

Tears filled her eyes, and she leaned her forehead on the iron bars. "I cannot believe I've been such a fool."

"We have both been fools." Dajon brushed a cluster of matted curls from her face. His stomach tightened. "These blasted bars." He jerked them again, longing to hold her, to wipe away her tears, to steal her away from this horrid place.

"Don't bother. I've tried." She forced a smile then lowered her voice to a whisper. "But please, tell me you are safe. No one knows that you let me go?"

"Only Mr. Borland."

"And you trust him?"

"Aye. Although we had a bit of a falling-out last week." The hatred and fury on Borland's face during their argument had shocked Dajon. Borland had wanted to pursue Stede Bonnet, a pirate known to be holed up in Cape Fear, but Dajon had deferred to a local hero, Colonel Rhett, who had volunteered to bring him in. Dajon couldn't very well run off and leave Faith alone in prison, her future so uncertain. Borland had not agreed and had defiantly resisted until Dajon had been forced to pull rank and silence him. It was the first time Dajon had noticed Borland's fervent ambition.

"It was nothing." He shook the memory from his head, preferring to drown it with happier times they had spent together. "We have been friends for years."

Faith's lip quivered. "Dajon, I could not bear it if harm came to you because of me."

"I love hearing you say my name." He swept his thumb over her still-rosy lips.

"I am serious." She frowned.

Gripping her face, he drew her near, brushing his mouth against hers. He felt her tremble.

"Dajon," was all she said.

He consumed her lips with his, ignoring the ribald howls from their audience.

Cold, hard fingers of iron bit into his cheeks, forbidding him to have more of her.

Dajon pulled away. "I love you, Faith," he whispered between thick breaths.

"And I you, Dajon." When her eyes lifted to his, they brimmed with all the admiration and love he'd only seen glimpses of before.

He eased his hands onto her shoulders and nudged her back a step. "How are you truly?" he asked, eyeing her soiled gown, torn and tattered around the hem, the mud stains on her neck and arms, and the abrasions on her hands and her sunken cheeks. How remarkable that he still found her ravishing. "You've not been eating."

She lifted her nose in the air. "That stench you smell?"

"Aye."

"That's supper, I'm afraid."

Dajon raised a brow. "I see. I shall sneak down some decent food."

"Don't bother. I'm sure I shall be relieved of this place soon enough, one way or another." She bit her lip. "Any word of my sisters?"

"You forbade me to see them, remember?" he teased, but when worry creased her face, he grabbed her hand again. "Never fear. I have inquired of Lucas. They are worried sick about you, but all is well."

Her expression tightened, and she shifted her shimmering eyes to his. "Dajon, if I…if the pardon does not…"

She took a deep breath. "Please take care of them." She squeezed his hand. "Promise me you will."

"I am going to get you out of here." Dajon brought both of her hands to his lips and sealed his vow with a tender kiss. "That's the only promise I will make."

Trouble was, he didn't know if it was a promise he could keep.

CHAPTER 32

Borland paced across the elaborate drawing room of the Carteret mansion. His boots clicked over the tile floor to the rhythm of the brass clock that mocked him from atop the fireplace. He had been ushered here nearly a half hour ago by a rather pretentious butler, who had admitted him only as a result of Borland's volatile persistence. Though Borland had sent several posts during the past week to Sir Wilhelm, the pompous halfwit had made no response nor any attempt to contact him. A frustrated anger sizzled within Borland for being ignored by a man who, no doubt, thought he had no further use for him.

Sir Wilhelm would certainly be surprised to find out differently today.

As Borland passed through the streams of sunlight flowing in through two french windows, he eyed the exquisite jewel-encrusted cornices above them, the gilded sconces lining the wall, and the collection of Ming vases displayed on a bureau by the entrance. He clicked his tongue. A waste of wealth on a buffoon like Sir Wilhelm.

Heading for the marble fireplace, Borland's boots thudded over the Chinese carpet at the room's center as he wove around a velvet settee and a pair of elaborately upholstered chairs. Above the mantel, an oil painting of what must have been Sir Wilhelm's grandfather, Sir George Carteret, glared down at Borland with the same supercilious arrogance of his grandson. Yet behind those oppressive dark eyes burned a wisdom and strength conspicuously absent in Sir Wilhelm.

A rabid sweat broke out on Borland's neck. What was he doing? Could he truly betray his lifelong friend?

Friend, indeed. What has he ever done for you? A chill slithered down Borland's spine.

Memories of the argument with Dajon last week replayed in his mind, rekindling his fury. He could still envision Dajon's red, fuming face when he had turned to Borland and yelled, "Enough! I am the captain, and you will obey my orders," forcing Borland to relent, to submit, and finally to admit. . .

That Dajon was his captain, not his friend.

Perhaps they had been friends once, but those days were long gone. And if Borland was to consider Dajon by rank alone, then his captain had made a terrible mistake. Allowing the Red Siren to slip from his grasp was bad enough, but then to refuse to chase after Stede Bonnet when he had been spotted so close to Charles Towne was beyond incorrigible. By refusing to do his duty, Dajon had in effect caused his entire crew to miss out on the glory, the praise that the capture of a pirate would bring them back at the Admiralty. And for what? A trollop—a pirate wench, at that!

Borland blew out a snort. He would show the mighty Dajon Waite who the real captain of the HMS *Enforcer* should be.

Guilt stabbed his gut, twisting and turning its blade until he could almost feel the pain. But what else could he do? He threw back his shoulders. It was his duty to report the captain. And if he was going to command one of His Majesty's ships, he'd have to learn to make tough decisions.

Even if it cost Dajon his life.

But no. He would not let it get that far. And that was why he needed Sir Wilhelm. That and the considerable fortune he knew the man would hand over for the information Borland possessed.

"Sir Wilhelm." The butler's drone buzzed into the room from the arched doorway, announcing the entrance of his master as if he were the king of England himself.

Sir Wilhelm floated into the room on a puff of stale air and gave Borland a cursory glance before plopping down onto the settee as if coming downstairs had completely exhausted him.

"Devil's blood. What is it, Mr. Borland? You know I am a busy man."

Borland gritted his teeth. Pity he needed this vainglorious nitwit to carry out his plans. "I have sent you several urgent posts. Did you not receive them?"

"Of course." Sir Wilhelm adjusted the lace that drooped about his sleeves. "I cannot be bothered with every minor correspondence."

Borland grabbed the back of one of the chairs and nearly punctured the fabric with his violent grip. "I have information which may greatly aid your cause."

Sir Wilhelm's brows flashed upward with interest. "And pray tell, what cause is that?"

"Your quest for the red-haired Westcott lady." Borland crossed his arms over his chest, feeling some of the man's power drift his way. "I hear she is about to be hanged."

"Yes." Sir Wilhelm shifted his gaze, but not before Borland saw the anger and bitterness fuming in his eyes. "What is your news?"

"It concerns Captain Waite."

～

Something scampered over Faith's arm. With a start, she jumped to her feet and swiped at her soiled gown. A cockroach skittered away beneath the straw. Shuddering, she gripped her arms. She knew she should be used to the bugs by now, but for some reason, the huge cockroaches still made her skin crawl. Filthy, tormenting beasts—like demons from hell.

She glanced at the sludge and refuse littering the murky dungeon, felt the heat sear her skin and the reek sting her nose. Hell. Perhaps this was it, after all.

But no. Yesterday a bright light had pierced this sepulcher. Dajon had come to see her. And surely God would not allow an honorable man like him to visit a damned place like hell.

It was near midday. She knew because the heat became unbearable at this hour and the air so thick with fetor that she gasped for every breath. She'd given up on her pacing and had succumbed to a moment's sleep, a near impossibility in her nest of bugs and rats.

A jangle of keys, a crank of a lock, and the scrape of a door opening, followed by the sound of footsteps, perked her ears. Was *Lord* Gordon coming with another proposition? Making her way to the bars, she strained to see the bottom of the stairway, daring to hope she had another visitor, longing to see Dajon again or perhaps Lucas or her sisters.

The thump and scrape of Gordon's limp foot on the wooden stairs grew louder until finally the jailer emerged into the dim lantern light, followed by the shiny buckled shoes, white stockings, and velvet breeches of a stylishly attired man. Bile rose in Faith's throat. Sir Wilhelm again. No doubt seeing if she'd had enough of this place and would agree to his proposal.

When he approached her cell, the eyes that met hers did not contain the usual pleading conceit but instead beamed with a victorious confidence most unnatural for the silly, diffident man.

Faith's throat went dry. "What do you want?" she huffed, backing away from the bars lest he try to touch her. Odd that she now found her cage a refuge instead of a prison.

"Me, want?" He snickered. "Why, I believe 'tis you who will be wanting something from me."

Uneasiness pricked the back of Faith's neck. "Never."

Sir Wilhelm turned to Gordon, who casually leaned against the stone wall across the way. "Leave us."

Scowling, the jailer shuffled back up the stairs, dragging his foot behind him.

Withdrawing a handkerchief, Sir Wilhelm held it to his nose. "Still so brave, so spirited after living in this muck for days." Was that a twinge of admiration in his gaze? He coughed and tugged upon his cravat. "However do you stand this place?"

"Somehow I find it preferable to your company." Faith retreated into the shadows, hoping that if he couldn't see her, he would give up his quest and leave.

Hideous laughter echoed through the dungeon, and Sir Wilhelm turned and stared down the row of cells before shifting his cold brown eyes back to her. "Would you find the death of your precious Mr. Waite preferable to my company?" The corner of his thin lips lifted in an exalted smirk.

Alarm fastened onto Faith like a leech. "What nonsense is this?" She fisted her hands on her waist, bracing herself against this desperate cur's lies.

He leaned toward the bars. "I know that your illustrious captain caught you before I did." His whisper hissed over her like a snake. "And that he let you go."

All remaining strength drained from Faith's legs. They began to wobble. Ambling farther into the shadows, she leaned against the wall for support, not wanting Sir Wilhelm to see her fear. Gathering her wits, she responded in her most unruffled tone, "He did no such thing. And besides, what does it matter to you?"

"Nothing." He adjusted his wig and jumped when a cockroach scurried by his shoes. The folds of his face contorted in disgust as he watched the insect dart away. "It matters naught to me. In fact, Mr. Borland intends to have his captain arrested soon."

The realization struck Faith as violently as if the ceiling of the dungeon had crashed down on her. *Mr. Borland has betrayed his best friend. But why?* "Mr. Borland?"

Sir Wilhelm grinned, obviously detecting the crack of alarm in her voice. "Yes, you remember, my dear, Mr. Waite's first lieutenant—the man standing upon the deck of your ship, the *Red Siren*, when he and Mr. Waite boarded her?"

Faith pressed a hand against the wall. The craggy stone scraped her raw skin. So Borland had told Sir Wilhelm everything. A chill overtook her, even in the

329

tepid heat. It made no sense. "If Mr. Borland intends to arrest Dajon. . .Mr. Waite, then why hasn't he done so already?"

"Mr. Borland and I have an arrangement." Sir Wilhelm blew his nose into his handkerchief then scanned above him with wary eyes, no doubt looking for flying insects. Faith prayed for a sudden swarm to nest in the man's elaborate wig.

Pushing off the wall, she crept toward the row of iron bars, longing for them to disappear so she could use her remaining strength to throttle the beast.

Sir Wilhelm tugged off his cravat and blotted the sweat covering his brow. The white, sickly skin of his neck matched the ghostly pallor of his face. A tuft of grizzly black hair peeked around his lapel as if looking for an escape. "You will marry me in two days," he announced, the tone of his voice leaving no room for argument.

"And if I don't?"

"Then I fear Mr. Borland will arrest Mr. Waite for treason." Sir Wilhelm waved his handkerchief through the air. "And as you know, he'll be court-martialed and executed."

Faith approached him, ignoring the way his gaze slithered over her and the resultant brew of disgust churning in her stomach. Something still didn't make sense. "What is in it for Borland?"

"Let's just say Mr. Borland is a much wealthier man today than he was yesterday." His eyes glinted with cruel delight.

Would Mr. Borland betray his captain for money? Perhaps. The greed for wealth and power often drove a man—or a woman—to malevolence. She cringed at her own guilt.

Oh God, what am I to do?

"You have two days to ponder my proposal. Otherwise, I fear Mr. Waite shall meet an untimely death. And I know you do not want that on your conscience along with everything else." Withdrawing his snuffbox, Sir

Wilhelm snorted a pinch into each nostril then stared at her. A shameless grin angled over his mouth, and he extended his hand through the bars.

Faith retreated beyond his reach—at least for the moment.

He snapped back his hand. "Never fear. I can wait. It shall make our union all the much sweeter."

Faith longed to respond, to tell him that if he ever took her as wife, it would be anything but sweet, but her love for Dajon stilled her tongue.

Twisting on his heel portentously, he sauntered toward the stairs then swerved back around. "Oh, and by the by, I've given strict orders forbidding Mr. Waite to call upon you again. Although I *have* permitted your sisters to visit. Perhaps that will soften your opinion of me and give you more reason to consider their futures rather than just thinking of your own." He snickered and began his ascent. The stairway soon swallowed him up, along with his bestial laughter. Faith wished he would disappear from her life just as easily.

But before she had a chance to fully absorb the implications of Sir Wilhelm's threat, the thumping of footsteps sounded on the stairs, and much to her delight, behind Gordon, Lucas's burly body descended. And following him, Molly, Hope, and Grace emerged in the darkness. Sunlight from above filtered down upon them, highlighting their colorful gowns and glowing cheeks— like a grand parade filled with all the people she loved.

Faith's heart nearly burst through her chest. It was by far the most wonderful sight she'd seen in quite some time.

"Faith!" Hope gathered her skirts and dashed to the cell, thrusting her hands through the iron bars and grabbing her by the shoulders. Tears streamed down her sister's reddened cheeks.

Grace slid beside her and clutched the rods, a frightened look pinching her face.

Lecherous comments assailed them from deep within the dungeon. Hope's eyes widened, and Faith felt her sister's tremble through her hand. A crimson blush stole over Grace's ivory skin.

"Ignore them. They can't harm you." Faith took Hope's and Grace's hands in hers. Grace's eyes locked upon Faith's, but strength beamed from behind her anxious look.

Faith gave an appreciative nod to Lucas and Molly standing behind them.

Darting a frenzied gaze over Faith's cell, Hope raised a hand to her nose. "Oh, Faith. Pirating?"

"'Twas quite lucrative." Faith cocked one penitent brow, hoping to alleviate her sister's distress with a bit of levity.

"I'm sure. But the Red Siren. Mercy me." Grace shook her head, but instead of giving Faith the expected disapproving glare, her eyes filled with tears.

"Lucrative but wrong." Faith let out a jagged sigh. "Very wrong. I didn't mean to hurt you, Grace." She glanced at Hope. "Nor you, sweet Hope."

"I didn't want this for you." Grace swallowed. "I've tried so hard to keep us all from any pain. How often have I told you that bad things happen when you disobey God?" Grace shook the bars as if trying to force home her point. "Look what happened to Mother, to Charity."

"Whatever did they do wrong?" Hope swiped a tear from her cheek and frowned at her sister.

Grace flattened her lips, her green eyes etched with sorrow. "You know Mother was not, shall we say, the most virtuous woman in her youth, and Charity. . .how oft did she have trouble telling the truth?"

"Oh, bah. I care not. I think being a pirate would be exciting." Hope sniffed then snapped her gaze to Faith. "Why didn't you tell me? I could have joined you."

"That is precisely why I didn't tell you," Faith shot back, but her slight smile soon faded beneath a wave of shame—shame for her, shame for her sisters, shame for their family. She released their hands and looked away. "No matter what you think of me, I was doing it for you—for us."

"Yes, Lucas explained." Grace leaned her head on the bars. "I'm so sorry that you believed you had no other recourse. I had no idea the burden you bore for our welfare—what you must have gone through to try to ensure our future. Please forgive me."

"You bear no blame, sweet Grace." Faith brushed a black curl from her sister's face.

A baby rat scampered across the stones by Hope's shoes, and she screamed and jumped back. "Oh my. How do you stand it in here?" She sobbed. "All that time when we thought you had abandoned us, you were risking your life for our welfare."

"Please do not make it a noble venture," Faith huffed.

"But we could have helped you." Hope reached through the bars again and brushed a reassuring hand over Faith's arm. "We could have worked something out together." She smiled at Grace. "We are sisters, after all."

"Yes, we are." Faith took Hope's hand in hers. "What I should have done is trusted God to take care of us."

Grace smiled.

"Can you both ever forgive me?" Faith asked, sorrow clawing at her throat. She wished more than anything she could go back in time and make things right. Do the right thing. Make the right choices. Save her sisters all this pain. But she couldn't. "I've made quite a mess of things."

"Of course we forgive you," Grace said, and Hope nodded.

Foul insinuations followed by fiendish chortles pierced their ears, and Faith bit her lip, angry that her sisters must endure this for her sake. Yet one more harmful consequence of her stupidity.

She gazed at them. Perspiration dotted Grace's upper lip, and Hope, like a precious flower, seemed ready to wilt at any moment.

"You mustn't stay long. 'Tis quite beastly down here, I'm afraid." As much as Faith longed to see her sisters, she could not force them to bear a punishment fit only for her.

"Nonsense." Hope squared her shoulders. "If you can endure it for this long, then we can surely abide it for a few minutes."

Faith blinked at her sister's sudden bravery. Reaching through the bars, she grabbed Grace's hand, too, and brought both sisters close.

Grace's tender gaze swept over Faith. "Your gown is in tatters. And you look so thin. How much longer must you stay here?"

"What will happen to you, Faith?" Hope's voice was strained with fear. "They hang pirates." New tears forged trails down her cheeks. "First Mother, now you. I cannot lose you both." She broke out into sobs, and Grace released Faith's hand and swung her arm over Hope's shoulder.

"We can pray, Hope. We *will* pray."

"Oh, what good will that do?" Hope snapped the words out between wails.

Grace continued to console her, tears filling her eyes.

As she watched her two sisters suffer for her mistakes, Faith wished the ground would suddenly open up and swallow her alive. *Oh, Mother. I'm so sorry. I have failed you. I have failed my precious sisters, and most of all, I have failed God.*

She battled against the tears burning behind her eyes.

They need me, Lord. They cannot endure another loss. It cannot be Your will that I hang. Please, Lord, save me. Not for my sake, but for theirs.

But perhaps God had already given her a way out. If she married Sir Wilhelm. . . Releasing Hope, Faith pressed a hand over her roiling stomach. Truth be told, she deserved to live out her days with the odious man for the pain and suffering she had caused.

Faith shifted her gaze between her sisters. "Listen to me. You aren't going to lose me. Do you hear?" Faith shook off a quiver of repulsion at the thought of becoming Sir Wilhelm's wife. "I shall be out of here in two days."

"Truly?" Hope sniffed.

"Aye. I promise, and we will all be well taken care of."

"I don't understand." Grace furrowed her delicate brow. "How is that possible?"

"Governor Johnson will issue me a pardon," Faith said, trying to use a confident tone. No need in upsetting them further by telling them it was Sir Wilhelm who would procure it.

"Ye ain't gettin' no pardon, missy!" a dark voice bellowed. Lucas started toward the other cells as if he could silence the men, but then he suddenly stopped.

"Ye'll be hangin' wit' the rest of us," the man cackled like an old hen.

"I fear he's right. Governor Johnson hates pirates. And after what Blackbeard and his crew did to this town, he has vowed to hang every single one of them he catches," Grace said.

"Never mind about that." Faith tossed her hair over her shoulder, trying to hide her own apprehension that even someone as powerful as Sir Wilhelm could squeeze a pardon out of Robert Johnson. Hoping for a diversion, she gestured for Lucas and Molly to come closer. Their intertwined hands separated as they took up places on each side of her sisters.

"Aye, Cap'n." Lucas nodded then peered into her cell. Repulsion and agony burned in his gaze. "I should be in there wit' ye."

"Oh, good heavens, Lucas, what good would that do?" Faith sighed then shifted her smiling eyes between him and Molly. "Were you holding Miss Molly's hand?" She knew what she had seen, and the prospect it posed delighted her.

Lucas flashed a gleaming white smile that brightened the dingy dungeon.

"They are courting," Hope interjected, dabbing her cheeks with a handkerchief. "Isn't it marvelous?"

Faith swept her gaze to Molly, who had lowered hers and was shuffling her shoe against the stone floor. "Molly, I do declare, what happened to your fear of caring for anyone—especially a man?"

Molly shrugged one shoulder and smiled. "When I see you turn to trusting God after all you been through, I figured I needed to start trusting Him, too." She cast an adoring look at Lucas, which he quickly returned. "An' I always had a soft spot for reformed pirates."

"Well, at least one good thing has come out of all this mess." Faith forced a smile. "I am most pleased."

Facing Lucas, she grew serious. "How are things at home?"

"I sent a dispatch to the admiral. I don't know when he'll get it, but I's sure he'll be comin' home when he does. Everything else is fine." Lucas cast a sideways glance at Hope that gave Faith pause.

Faith studied her two siblings. "Have they behaved, Lucas?"

Hope's expression sank.

"Miss Hope's done run off wit' that Lord Falkland a couple of times, mistress. I can't seem to keep an eye on her all the time," Lucas replied, folding his hat in his hands.

Faith snapped her gaze to Hope. "Hope, why? Why do you throw yourself at a man who will only use you?"

"He's leaving, Faith." Hope's blue eyes swam.

"What do you mean?"

"He sets sail tomorrow for England."

"The sooner the better." Molly snorted.

"He won't take me with him. I love him, Faith." She dabbed her eyes with her handkerchief. "I thought he'd make me an offer of marriage before he left."

Faith clenched her jaw. "The man is a scoundrel, Hope. He cares for no one but himself."

"You are wrong." She stamped her foot. "He promised to marry me when he returns."

"Oh, he did, did he?" Faith's heart sunk at the naiveté of her sister. The ruffian would most likely never return, and Hope would either wallow in grief for years or find comfort in the arms of the next man who smiled her way. But at least Faith wouldn't have to worry about Lord Falkland anymore.

"Remember, Hope, how God protected you from those scoundrels at the Pink House?"

Hope did not raise her gaze.

"Perhaps He is doing the same thing now," Faith continued, praying the Lord would reveal His love and mercy to Hope as He had done with Faith. "Perhaps He is protecting you by sending Lord Falkland away."

"If He is, then He is cruel," Hope said in a sharp tone that sliced through Faith's heart.

Retrieving her arm from around Hope, Grace tucked a loose tendril of her sister's hair behind her ear. "How can you discuss something so trivial as Lord Falkland when our sister is locked up in a dungeon?"

"She inquired of me," Hope snapped with a pout. "And besides, she said she would be pardoned in a few days."

"That's right," Faith said. *Freed from prison one day, only to be chained to a madman the next.*

Hope coughed and drew her handkerchief to her nose. "The smell in here."

"You should leave. It isn't good for you to be down here." Faith turned to Molly. "Please take my sisters upstairs. I need to speak with Lucas for a moment."

"No, I don't want to leave you," Hope pleaded.

Faith forced herself to smile. "I'll see you in a few days."

"She'll be jest fine, Miss Hope." Molly began to lead Hope away. Grace swallowed hard and flashed a wavering grin toward Faith before turning to join them.

"Grace." Faith tugged on her sister's arm, halting her. "If something goes wrong. . .I mean with the pardon. . ."

Grace's green eyes became glistening pools. "Please don't say it."

"Promise me you'll take care of Hope. She will need your strength."

Grace nodded as a tear escaped her lashes and sped down her cheek. "You will get out of here. I know it."

"Pray, Grace. Please pray."

"I'll be prayin', too, Miss Faith," Molly said over

her shoulder as she led both girls to the bottom of the stairway.

"Lucas, I need you to get a message to Mr. Waite for me."

"Aye."

No matter what Faith's future held, she must warn Dajon. "Please inform him that Mr. Borland is not his friend. He has told Sir Wilhelm that Mr. Waite let us go free."

Lucas's dark brows rose, and alarm burned in his eyes.

"Mr. Waite is in danger," Faith said.

"But Sir Wilhelm, don't he want the cap'n out of his way? Why don't he and Borland just have him arrested?"

"Because I have made a bargain with them to prevent it."

Lucas gave her a puzzled look. "What sort of bargain?"

Faith ground her teeth together, barely able to spit out the words. "I have promised to marry Sir Wilhelm."

CHAPTER 33

Dajon leaped up the foredeck ladder and charged across the wooden deck, making his way to the bow of the ship. Anger tore at him, ripping his self-control to shreds. He had to calm himself before he faced Borland, or who knew what he might do. He thrust his face into a blast of salty air. A metallic scent bit his nose, a sharp smell that made his skin crawl and permeated the air with a feeling of unease.

Friend. Some friend, indeed. He snorted, clutching the railing as the HMS *Enforcer* lunged over a rising swell then slapped the back of the wave, showering him with warm spray. He shook his head, scattering the droplets onto the railing, where they shimmered like diamonds in the moonlight.

Two of his crew lazed nearby, but one steely gaze from him sent them hustling away. He needed to be alone. He had to think. He had to patch the wound from Borland's treachery, and then he had to decide what to do with the rat.

After Lucas had delivered Faith's message, Dajon had tried to visit her, but upon being prevented from doing so, he had weighed anchor and headed directly out to sea. He'd always heard the voice of God more clearly when he coursed through the vast, untamed ocean, and he hoped that would be the case tonight. If not, he feared he'd be forced to follow through with his original impulse of strangling Borland and then tossing his lifeless body to the sharks.

God, help me. Is there any pain worse than the betrayal of a friend? Then he remembered how the Lord had been betrayed by all His dearest friends—those who had sworn their love and loyalty to Him. *How did You bear it, Lord?*

"Forgive." The word floated on the breeze, weaving around the strands of his hair.

Dajon shook his head and doffed his bicorn, tossing it to the deck. *I don't know if I can.*

Booted steps clumped over the deck, but Dajon didn't turn around. He clenched his jaw and prayed it wasn't Borland. He'd been avoiding the man quite successfully and hoped to continue to do so for a while longer.

"Captain." The voice spiked over him—one that used to lift Dajon's spirits but now only clawed at his heart. "What brings us out upon the waters this fine night? News of a pirate nearby?" Borland planted his boots firmly on the deck beside Dajon and crossed his arms over his chest.

A blast of hot wind, laced with salt and fish and betrayal, tore over Dajon, and he lengthened his stance and stared at his first lieutenant. The wind played havoc with the coils of Borland's sandy hair, tugging them from his queue. He wouldn't meet Dajon's gaze. In fact, Dajon couldn't recall the last time he'd seen the playful camaraderie that had often danced across his friend's brown eyes.

Blood surged to Dajon's fists. How dare the man even speak to him after what he'd done? But here he stood, feigning a friendship that had probably never existed and all the while betraying Dajon's confidence. "Why, Borland?"

Borland flinched, and the side of his mouth quirked, but otherwise he remained still. "Why what, Captain?"

Dajon grappled the hilt of his service sword, longing to draw it and end this charade. "No more games."

Borland's jaw tightened. "I see you are not quite yourself tonight, Captain." He turned to leave. "I shall speak to you at another time."

Seizing him, Dajon twisted him around. "You will speak to me now."

Borland's eyes flashed with a fury that startled Dajon. "Very well." He tugged his arm from Dajon's grasp as if he detested even his touch. "What is it you wish to discuss?"

The ship bucked, forcing both him and Borland to grab the rail. Dajon took the time to draw a deep breath to restrain his rising fury. "Why did you betray me?" he growled through gritted teeth. "And to that ninny Sir Wilhelm?"

Borland's eyes darted about wildly before they met his, fear skipping over them, but then a cold sheen swallowed up the fear and his body stiffened. "I was doing my duty."

"Your *duty*? You agreed that if Miss Westcott abandoned her piracy, we would allow her to go free."

"No," Borland snarled. "*You* agreed to that. I merely listened and obeyed." He shifted his gaze back to the sea. "Which is all I ever do."

Shocked by the hostility firing from his friend's eyes, Dajon stared out over the churning black sea that spanned to an even darker horizon. The moon illuminated crystal foam upon the waves and frowned at him as if she disapproved of the goings-on below. He wished she would fling some light upon his current situation, for no matter how far back he searched, Dajon could think of no time he had mistreated Borland or any of the other men on his crew. "You do what I say because I am in command." Dajon spoke with grave deliberation.

"Yet in doing so, you ask me to risk not only my career but my life." Borland dared to laugh. "Our friendship does not extend that far."

Dajon clenched his jaw, wondering if their friendship extended any further than Borland's self-interest. "You know very well that if I were caught, I would never divulge to anyone that you had any knowledge of what I did." Dajon gripped the railing. "Nevertheless, you should have informed me of your true feelings instead of placating me with lies."

Borland crossed his arms over his chest. " 'Twas my

responsibility to turn you in. A captain who does not abide by the articles of war should not be in command of one of His Majesty's ships." He flicked the hair from his face and gazed out upon the sea. "Yes, perhaps this ship needs a new commander."

The hull of the ship creaked and moaned in protest, and it took every ounce of Dajon's control not to slam his fist into Borland's jaw. "Jealousy? That's what this is about?" Dajon roared. "You envy my position—is that it? After all these years?"

Storming to the foremast, Dajon punched it, but all he did was cause searing pain to shoot through his fingers and into his wrist. Shaking his burning hand, he faced Borland, who remained a rigid bulwark.

"Then our friendship has been naught but a pretense." Dajon returned to his side and thrust his face toward him.

"Not always."

"When did you begin to hate me so?" Dajon gripped the roughened wood of the railing.

"When you received command of this ship over me—with fewer years' service and no connections. Egad!" Borland gave Dajon a scorching look. "You even resigned for two years and then came back, like the prodigal son expecting a lavish party upon your return."

"And you the faithful son," Dajon muttered, cursing himself. He'd never considered that his friend might be envious of his promotion, never once thought Borland would be anything but happy for his success. "I have been a fool to trust you."

"You don't understand, Dajon. You never have." Borland shot him a look of disdain and thrust out his chin. "If I do not make a success of myself in the navy, I will be a disgrace to my father, my entire family. It is what they expect of me."

Watching the Union Jack flapping on the bowsprit, Dajon tried to recall his friend's history. Borland came from nobility—a second son, not in line to inherit the family fortune but nobility nonetheless—and from a long line of naval captains. "I did not ask for the honor, Borland."

"No, of course not." Borland's voice burned with sarcasm. "The great Dajon Waite, praised for his heroic encounter with a Spanish flotilla off Càdiz that prevented a resurgence of hostilities. Pure rubbish, I say. I was there right beside you, but did I receive a command?" His fists clenched as if trying to squash the memory.

"So you send me to my death."

"No." He slid his dark eyes over to Dajon. "My intent was to simply have you removed from the navy." His upper lip twitched beneath a slick mustache.

Fury rampaged through Dajon, shattering all control. Gripping Borland's stiff collar, Dajon thrust a fist into his stomach. Borland folded with a groan and stumbled back.

"Treason is an offense punishable by death," Dajon said through clenched teeth, landing another blow on Borland's jaw, snapping his head to the side. Then, clutching his coat, Dajon shoved him toward the bow and hauled his limp body precariously atop the railing.

Borland gripped Dajon's hands, trying to detach them from his neck. His eyes exploded with terror as he glanced below him at the raging water. "Do you think me so vile as to have you killed to further my own career?" he squeaked.

Dajon tightened his grip and jerked Borland's head farther down toward where the bow of the ship crashed through the ebony water in a frothy, raging V. Only the weight of Dajon's body prevented the man from tumbling into the water. Just one inch to the left, just one shove and Dajon would be rid of this menace forever. Without his testimony, Dajon would live, and Faith would not have to marry Sir Wilhelm.

"Forgive as I have forgiven you."

The words splashed over him along with the salty spray of the sea, but Dajon shook them off.

"Sir Wilhelm promised me you will not be executed." Borland clawed at Dajon's fingers, his face as ashen as the moonlight that spilled over it.

The muscles in Dajon's face knotted into tight balls. His fingers began to ache. Fury urged him onward. Fury and the pain of betrayal, of being played for a fool. He could not remember a time he'd ever been this angry, a time when he wanted to kill.

A beaming spire of white light lit up the eastern sky. The sharp sting of electricity hung in the air, sending the hair on the back of Dajon's neck spiking. His breath grew ragged and deep as he remembered the pillar of fire—God's pillar of fire—that had saved Hope. A fire of grace. For Hope had done naught to deserve it. In fact, quite the opposite.

"Please, Dajon," Borland begged, his eyes sharp with panic, his hands clamping over Dajon's wrists as if they were his only lifeline.

Grinding his teeth, Dajon held him farther over the edge, trying to fight the rage that took control of him.

Lightning flashed again, this time closer, and Dajon wondered why there was no thunder, no clouds. A chill crawled over his skin. His hands no longer ached. His muscles bulged with strength. And he knew all he had to do was release the squirming wretch and Borland would tumble into the sea.

God's grace. A free gift of forgiveness for a debt that could never be paid. Like Dajon's debt. Like Borland's. The Almighty had lavished His grace upon Dajon; who was he not to do the same for his enemies?

"You insolent buffoon." Dragging Borland's stiff body back over the rail, Dajon released him.

Stumbling backward, Borland gripped his throat and tripped over a hatch coaming.

Dajon drew his sword and pointed the gleaming tip at Borland. He no longer intended to kill him, but certainly God would allow him this small satisfaction of seeing his friend continue to squirm. "Sir Wilhelm exaggerates his power. I'll grant you, the jingle-brained man has some authority here in Carolina where his grandfather was one of the eight lord proprietors, but his word carries no weight with the Admiralty. He could no more stop an order of execution from a court-martial than he could stop the recent Indian raids or Spanish attacks."

Shock followed by a sudden realization passed over Borland's expression as he wavered over the deck, trying to regain his balance while avoiding Dajon's blade.

Angry waves slapped the hull, reaching white fingers onto the deck as if they were yearning for the prey that had escaped them. Instead, they spit their salty spray over the two men. Dajon gazed into the night sky, clear save for the sparkle of stars and the glimmer of the moon. The lightning had vanished. Had he only imagined it, or was it some wicked force tempting him to commit murder?

Shaking off the frightening thought, Dajon lifted Borland's chin with the tip of his sword. "And look what you have forced upon Miss Westcott. Now she'll have to marry that feeble knave." Dajon grimaced, nauseated at the thought of that man's slimy hands touching Faith.

Borland straightened his coat and threw back his shoulders as if hoping to regain his dignity. Or perhaps he'd seen the bloodlust dissipate from Dajon's eye and no longer feared his fury. " 'Tis a better fate than the noose. Besides, that she would resign herself to marry such a maggot to save you is quite noble."

Dajon raised one brow angrily. "Except you and I both know that I shall be arrested as soon as she is wed."

Borland shrugged. "That was the plan." He eyed Dajon's blade. "But I beg you to believe me—I thought you would lose your commission, not your life."

Dajon studied his first lieutenant, wondering if that were true, if there was a scrap of decency left in the friend he once knew. "It matters not anymore."

"You can run." Borland swallowed and stared at Dajon pleadingly. "Change your name; lose yourself in the colonies or, better yet, the West Indies. A man can make a fortune as a privateer, I'm told."

"Only during wartime or else be hanged as a pirate."

"Never fear. I'm sure we shall declare war on France or Spain soon enough." Borland chuckled.

Dajon blew out a harsh breath. When disaster had struck his career so long ago, he'd run away, away from his family, away from God. "Nay. I'm tired of running." He lowered his blade and waved it toward the ladder. "Get out of my sight."

Borland eased away, keeping his eye on Dajon, before turning and making haste for the ladder. But suddenly he halted and turned around. "What will you do?" No anger, no hatred stained his voice, just curiosity.

"Why, turn myself in, of course." Dajon sheathed his sword, the sharp hiss of metal sealing his decision. "First thing in the morning. Then"—despite his dire future, he allowed himself a speck of joy that reached his mouth in a grin—"I shall send word to Miss Westcott that she no longer need marry Sir Wilhelm."

❧

Borland shook his head, trying to dislodge the water in his ear. Perhaps he had misheard his captain. "Turn yourself in?"

Dajon crossed his arms over his chest but said nothing.

Borland inched his way back toward him, certain that his captain no longer intended to kill him. There had been a moment, a brief moment, when Dajon had held Borland over the railing that he could not claim such confidence.

But now the rage had fled, replaced by a calm, sincere resolve. "But why? Why submit to certain death?"

"What is it to you?" Dajon faced the sea.

"But you can still save yourself."

"I told you, I will not run away."

Borland peered at his friend inquisitively. Perhaps Dajon had not thought things through. "Surely you realize that if you leave, Sir Wilhelm will no longer have a card to play in this mad scheme of his. Miss Westcott will not have to marry him. And you'll be free to live out your life."

"And you'll be free to assume my command at no

expense to your conscience, eh?" Dajon's sharp gaze bit into Borland. "Isn't that it?"

Shifting his eyes away, Borland recoiled in shame. Dajon was right. After all the trouble Borland had caused, he still thought only of himself.

"Nevertheless, you are correct." Dajon released a sigh and gripped the railing. "I have betrayed my country. I allowed a known pirate to go free. And I will not run, nor will I abandon Miss Westcott in her greatest hour of need."

Borland searched his mind for some other plausible explanation, some other reason for which a man would willingly die, certainly not for honor and duty, and certainly not for a foolish woman. "There will be other women, Dajon. You attract them like sailors to grog."

Flinching, Dajon frowned. "None like Miss Westcott, I'm afraid."

Sentimental fop. "This is madness, Dajon. You have been bewitched. Regardless, you still won't have her. You'll be dead, and if she doesn't marry Sir Wilhelm, she will soon join you."

The *Enforcer* dipped over a swell, nodding in agreement. Milky froth leaped onto the deck and swirled about Borland's boots like the confusion in his mind.

"Perhaps." Dajon tore off his waistcoat, draping it over the rail. "Or Sir Wilhelm will relent at the last minute, or the King's pardon I've requested will arrive in time." He shrugged. " 'Tis in God's hands. At least she will not be forced to marry a man she abhors just to save me. Because there will be no saving me. But if she is hanged"—Dajon winced as if the thought pained him—"then you are correct. We will be together in a far better place."

Wiping the sweat from his neck, Borland suppressed a chuckle at his friend's foolhardy faith. "Don't tell me you truly believe that."

"With all my heart," Dajon replied without hesitation, his tone neither defensive nor patronizing. "I took my eyes off eternity for far too long and put them

347

upon rules, regulations, and things of this world. But no more."

"But are you not relying on your rules again by turning yourself in?" Fear squeezed Borland until sweat began to form on his brow. If he couldn't convince Dajon to run, the captain's death would be on his hands forever. He doubted he could live under the weight of that guilt.

Scanning the dark, churning sea, Borland wondered at the existence of so grand a God-King that men would willingly die to follow Him. "So am I to believe that God wants you dead?"

"I don't know. But I do know this." Dajon shot him a confident gaze. "He doesn't want me to run."

"You stand ready to turn yourself in for treason, willing to be executed, and for what? To follow the leading of this unseen God." Borland grunted and shifted his boots over the damp wood. A bell tolled, echoing over the deck, followed by another, announcing the change of watch.

Crazy, sanctimonious fool. Turning, Borland began pacing across the deck, trying to make sense out of something that could not be made sense of. He halted at the edge of the forecastle and studied Dajon. His captain stood tall and strong, gazing out over the ocean as though deep in conversation. A peaceful power exuded from Dajon that drew Borland back. When he reached his side, the captain glanced his way.

Borland lowered his gaze. "How can you bear to be near me?" he asked, rubbing his sore neck, remembering that only a moment ago, Dajon indeed hadn't been able to bear it. "I am the reason you find yourself in this predicament. I am the reason you will die."

A flash of anger sparked in Dajon's eyes but quickly dissipated. "No, Borland. I must admit I was angry at your betrayal, but truth be told, I broke the law and I deserve my punishment. What's done is done. In the end, I'm no better than you."

Borland swallowed a burning lump in his throat. "How can you say that? You're the most decent, honorable man I know." He shook his head and followed Dajon's gaze to the onyx sea. A sudden calm had overtaken it. Only a slight rustle stirred the black liquid. The frown of the moon reflected off the dark waters as a large fish broke through the mirror with a crystalline splash. A dolphin, perhaps. A breeze tickled the angry sweat on his neck and brow, and Borland lowered his shoulders. Peace settled over him, but it was more than peace. It was a knowing.

"I can't do it." His voice rent the stillness of the night. Dajon glanced his way.

"I won't testify against you." Borland locked his gaze upon his captain's. "I've told only Sir Wilhelm. It's his word against mine. I will simply tell the court I have nothing to say in the matter."

Dajon's eyes narrowed as if he pondered whether he could trust him.

Borland ground his teeth together. "I don't blame you for your mistrust. What I have done is far too ghastly to forgive. But I now see that my indomitable pride, my envy, and my selfishness have led me down this vile trail. And I find I detest the direction they have taken me."

"Sir Wilhelm will still bring charges." Dajon tore his gaze away.

"No doubt. But without witnesses, what can he do?"

The captain tightened his lips. "That would depend on whether the Admiralty Court would believe him or not." He flashed a disbelieving smile at Borland. "A moment ago, I wanted to kill you."

"And a moment ago, I had a plot in place to kill you." Borland cocked a conciliatory brow.

"And you say there is no God." Dajon clutched the back of Borland's neck and tossed him back and forth.

"Careful with the neck, Captain."

Dajon released him, and both men grew silent for a moment.

"We should tell Miss Westcott immediately," Borland said. Grabbing Dajon's coat and hat, he handed them to his captain.

"Sir Wilhelm forbids me to see her."

"Then I will go."

Dajon scratched his jaw. "Nay. Find out when the wedding is to take place." A slow smile stretched across his lips. "I have a better idea."

CHAPTER 34

"Great guns, Mr. Jamieson. Where are all the cockboats?" Dajon scanned the empty braces perched atop the deck then glanced over the port side as Borland dashed toward the stern and leaned over the taffrail.

"None here, Captain—sir!" Borland yelled.

"Who took them out?"

"Midshipman Salles took one out, sir," Mr. Jamieson offered.

"Yes, but who else?" Dajon spiked a hand through his hair. "I gave no one else permission to leave the ship." He glanced up at the smoldering sun now halfway across the sky and swiped the sweat from his brow.

He must get to shore. He had only an hour before Faith would marry Sir Wilhelm. Alarm gripped him, squeezing hope drop by drop from his heart. Everything, his entire future and that of Faith's rested solely on his perfect timing.

Fisting his hands on his waist, he scanned Charles Towne port, nearly a mile from the ship. Nothing but indigo waters, stirred only by passing ships and diving pelicans, separated him from reaching his dreams.

Borland approached on his left. "I don't understand it. All the boats have disappeared."

⋙

Faith slid her silk shoes up the stairs of the brick courthouse, the clank of the irons around her ankles ringing a death knell with each step she took. Reaching up, she tried to wipe the perspiration from her neck, but the chains binding her wrists forbade her. On each side, deputies of the assembly gripped her elbows and assisted her onward. If she wasn't so distraught, she would laugh at all the fuss they were making over one small woman.

But she was a pirate, after all.

And after assessing the slight men beside her, she'd decided they were wise to use such precautions. Freed from these chains and with a cutlass in hand, she had no doubt she could dispatch them with ease.

But regardless, she wouldn't dare attempt it. Not with Dajon's life on the line.

Would she never see him again? The pain of that possibility stabbed her deep in the gut. What had he done when Lucas had given him the news of her decision to marry Wilhelm? Perhaps he had gone to Bath himself to speed up Governor Eden's pardon. She had no way of knowing where he was, no way of informing anyone of the abominable event about to take place. After Lucas, Molly, and her sisters had left, Sir Wilhelm had prevented anyone from calling upon her again.

Two giddy girls shuffled along behind her, fussing over the lacy trim around her hem and waist.

"Oh, Miss Westcott, you do look so beautiful," one of them said.

"Beautiful. I so love weddings," the other girl chirped, reminding Faith of Morgan's meaningless squawking.

She longed to spin around and ask them if they did not see the chains that bound her feet and hands but thought better of wasting her energy. They were naught but young girls, with no more brains than begonias, hired by Sir Wilhelm to prepare her for this loathsome farce of a ceremony.

Choking down a rising clump of disgust, Faith took the final step, the silk of her emerald gown swishing over her stockings. Neither her warm sudsy bath, nor the beautiful gown now adorning her, nor the string of pearls at her throat had been able to remove the filth of the dungeon from her skin.

Or the repulsion of marrying Sir Wilhelm from her heart.

One of the deputies shoved aside the massive oak door, and a blast of mold, human sweat, and decay assailed her.

She swallowed, hesitating as her legs seemed to melt. The deputies tugged on her elbows, but snatching them from their grasp, she stepped inside of her own free will. She would not be led like a condemned prisoner to her death. She had made her choice.

Faith took another step inside, and the girls scrambled to get by her and take their places at the front. The door slammed shut, showering Faith with dust from the rafters and locking her in a vault from which there was no escape. As her eyes became accustomed to the dim interior, the form of Sir Wilhelm took shape like a specter at the far end of the room. He stood before a long, upraised judge's table dressed in all the finery of his class. Turning to face her, he licked his gaunt lips as a grin slithered over them. Beside him, a man dressed in a fine cambric shirt and a richly embellished velvet waistcoat and breeches eyed her with suspicion. A priest, wearing the flowing white robes of the Church of England, stood at the front, sifting through the pages of a small book.

Sir Wilhelm beckoned her forward like a snake into his coils, sunlight glinting off his jeweled fingers. The deputies nudged her from behind. Her chains scraped over the wooden floor as she glanced out the window to her left. A wooden platform broiled in the hot sun, two nooses dangling lifelessly in the windless day. No doubt Sir Wilhelm had planned the ceremony within sight of her alternative.

Pompous half-wit. Little did he know she would gladly put the noose around her own neck rather than marry him. 'Twas only thoughts of Dajon that kept her feet moving toward a fate worse than death.

Oh God, help me. I know I deserve this and far worse. But if there's any way in Your mercy to rescue me while sparing Dajon and my sisters, even if by my death, please come to my aid.

Faith inched ahead, praying for a breeze to whip in through the window, but the air remained tepid, static as doldrums at sea. No movement, not a single wisp stirring. Dead, like her heart.

Keeping her face forward, she finally reached the front.

"Miss Westcott, may I introduce Judge Nicolas Trott." Sir Wilhelm gestured toward the finely dressed man beside him.

Trott. Faith had heard of the man. An Anglican priest, descended from a highly influential British family, he was known for his lack of mercy and his particular hatred of pirates.

With an arrogant snort, he perused her.

Sir Wilhelm retrieved a paper from his coat and waved it before her face. "On Judge Trott's recommendation, Governor Johnson has graciously given me your full pardon."

How she longed to snatch the document and stuff it into his pretentious mouth.

The judge snapped a quick glance her way as if staring at her too long would infect him. "I trust you'll not be pirating again, Miss Westcott."

"I trust I'll not be doing anything pleasurable ever again, sir."

A hint of a smile lifted the judge's lips.

Perspiration streamed down Faith's back, drawing the silk close against her skin. Somewhere in the distance, a bell tolled. Sir Wilhelm took his spot beside her, rubbing his arm against hers. Disgust swept over her like raw refuse, and she stepped away.

The young girls giggled with delight from their seats, oblivious to the nightmare playing out before them.

Faith glanced over her shoulder at the thick wooden door holding her captive, the deputies flanking each side. Oh, that Captain Waite would come barging through those doors and whisk her away from this madman, but she knew that would never happen. He probably had no idea this marriage was even taking place, and if he did, to halt it would mean his certain death.

As if reading her mind, Sir Wilhelm leaned toward her with a sneer. The smell of starch and stale breath curled in her nose. "Looking for your Mr. Waite, perchance? Hoping for a heroic rescue, my dear? Even if he knew about the proceedings, I've arranged for him to be detained today. We wouldn't want our blessed nuptials to be interrupted, now, would we? Besides, if he dares show his presumptuous face, I'll have him arrested on the spot." He brushed a speck of dirt from his waistcoat as if it were Dajon himself.

Regardless of the man's omens of doom, a spark of hope lit within Faith. Dajon was still free—and alive! And that speck of knowledge gave her the courage to continue.

She thrust her hands toward him and rattled her shackles. "Do you suppose you could unchain me for the ceremony, Sir Wilhelm, or am I to be kept in irons our entire marriage?

A lecherous fire glinted in his eyes. "If it keeps you forever mine."

"All the chains in the world will never accomplish that, sir."

With a curse, he snapped his fingers and called for one of the deputies.

After her chains were removed, Faith flexed her ankles and rubbed her aching wrists, sure they were red beneath her pristine gloves.

"We are ready, Reverend." Sir Wilhelm faced the priest, who had been observing the odd proceedings with both interest and disapproval. For a moment, Faith hoped he would not agree to perform such an obvious mockery of the sanctity of marriage, but all hope was dashed when he adjusted his red sash and said, "Very well. Let us begin."

~

Dajon pulled himself out of the bay and crawled onto the wharf. He stood and shook the water from his hair.

Wiping the drips streaming down his face, he eyed the dockmen and sailors who stood slack jawed, gaping at him. He had no time to explain to them why he'd just emerged from the harbor like a fish from the water. Instead, he bolted down the dock, weaving around crates and barrels and clusters of men, ignoring the hollers and yelps that followed in his wake—and the curse when he accidentally bumped one man into the water.

"My apologies!" he yelled without looking back.

Barreling past the docks, he charged onto the street and was nearly trampled by a pair of geldings pulling a carriage. He waved off the driver's rather obscene expletive and shielded his eyes from the sun. There in the distance, the bricks of the courthouse shone bright red against the other brown buildings. He dashed down the crowded street, ignoring the sharp rocks scraping over his bare feet, and prayed harder than he ever had.

Just a few more minutes, Lord. Can You hold them up for just a few more minutes?

⌒

" 'Dearly beloved, we are gathered together here in the sight of God, and in the face of this congregation, to join together this man and this woman in holy matrimony, which is an honorable estate, instituted of God in the time of man's innocence, signifying unto us the mystical union betwixt Christ and His church. . . .' "

The priest droned on, reading from *The Book of Common Prayer*, and Faith's legs transformed into squid tentacles beneath her. She stumbled backward, and Sir Wilhelm gripped her around the waist and drew her near, imprisoning her against his languid body, only further increasing her nausea.

" '. . . is not by any to be enterprised, nor taken in hand, unadvisedly, lightly, or wantonly, to satisfy men's carnal lusts and appetites, like brute beasts that have no understanding.' "

Brute beasts? Faith dared a glance at Sir Wilhelm, wondering if he recognized himself in those words. But he stared ahead, a supercilious smirk planted on his mouth.

" 'I require and charge you both, as ye will answer at the dreadful day of judgment when the secrets of all hearts shall be disclosed, that if either of you know any impediment, why ye may not be lawfully joined together in matrimony, ye do now confess it.' "

The priest paused, looked up from his book, and glanced around the room. His gaze took in the deputies guarding the door, the frivolous girls squirming with excitement in their seats, and Judge Trott, who retrieved a pocket watch from his waistcoat and looked at the time with a sigh.

No one uttered a word. No one came to her rescue.

Sir Wilhelm tightened his grip around her waist, and she suddenly felt as though she were chained to an anchor, sinking deeper and deeper into a bottomless sea.

The priest's searching gaze then passed over Sir Wilhelm and landed on Faith. He raised his brows as if encouraging her to respond.

Lowering her gaze, Faith bit her lip then clenched her jaw and held her breath—anything to keep the words blasting forth from her mouth that yes, she knew of an impediment to this marriage. She knew exactly why they should not be lawfully joined together. *Joined.* A shudder ran through her, and she pressed a hand over her rebelling stomach.

But for Dajon's sake, she remained silent.

Casting an anxious glance over his shoulder, Sir Wilhelm waved a hand through the air. "If you please, Reverend. We are in a hurry."

Giving Sir Wilhelm a look of annoyance, the priest cleared his throat and resumed his reading.

"Sir Wilhelm Carteret, wilt thou have this woman to be thy wedded wife, to live together after God's ordinance in the holy estate of matrimony? Wilt thou love her, comfort her, honor and keep her, in sickness and in health, and forsaking all others, keep thee only unto her, so long as ye both shall live?"

Sir Wilhelm opened his mouth and said something, but his answer was drowned beneath the enormous thud of the door crashing open behind them.

Wheeling around, Faith squinted at the tall figure standing in the doorway, her eyes adjusting to the light that blazed behind him. Water dripped from his breeches onto the wooden floor like droplets of hope.

"I hope I'm not too late for the wedding." Sarcasm rang in his deep voice.

Dajon.

Faith's heart leaped and then took on a frenzied beat, stealing her breath away.

Sauntering toward them, Dajon shook water from his cotton shirt. His blue eyes were riveted on her, laughter and love sparkling within them.

Sir Wilhelm thrust his pale face into the reverend's. "I said, *I will.* Now carry on."

Dajon tore Sir Wilhelm's hand from Faith's waist and pushed himself between them. He swiped a hand through his wet hair, its dark ends dripping onto his shirt. The wet fabric clung to his muscled chest still heaving from exertion. He smelled of the sea and of salt and life.

He winked at Faith, and a warm, peaceful sensation flooded through her, quickly extinguished by her fear for his life. "What are you doing here?" she whispered through clenched teeth. "They will arrest you."

Ignoring her, he turned toward the priest. "I protest this union, Reverend."

"Finally." The reverend snapped his book shut and folded his arms over his robes.

"I order you to continue." Sir Wilhelm's rabid gaze shot over them and then locked onto the reverend as if he would devour him whole.

But the priest simply shrugged as if the situation were out of his control.

"Deputies, arrest this man at once!" Sir Wilhelm ordered the men standing guard at the now open door, then he glanced at Judge Trott, who stood to the side watching everything with a stern yet detached gaze.

A sickening wave of dread washed over Faith. She had done everything to prevent this very thing from happening. *Why, God? Please help us.*

"On what charge, may I inquire?" Dajon asked in a tone that bespoke no fear of the answer.

"Treason." Sir Wilhelm threw back his shoulders and faced the judge. "Judge, this man willingly allowed this pirate to go free."

"Indeed?" Judge Trott rubbed his chin, seeming to be more amused than appalled.

"Yes, I have a trustworthy witness from his ship. His own first lieutenant."

Faith studied Dajon, his body a statue. Not a tremble passed through him. No fear shot from his clear eyes. In fact, he stood nonchalantly as if he were awaiting his breakfast. She grabbed his hand and squeezed it, and he raised it to his lips, locking his gaze upon hers—a sultry, playful, dangerous gaze.

"Is this true, sir?" Judge Trott shifted his stance.

"That Sir Wilhelm has a trustworthy witness?" Dajon released her hand and cocked a brow at the judge. "Or that I let this lovely pirate go free?"

Judge Trott grunted. "Never mind. This is a matter for the Admiralty Court. I shall ensure they are assembled as soon as possible."

"Pray don't trouble yourself, Your Excellency." Dajon bowed slightly. "The witness Sir Wilhelm speaks of cannot seem to recall the incident. But it doesn't matter. . . ." He cast a sly glance at Faith. "I resigned my commission yesterday to the commander in chief aboard the HMS *Perseverance.*"

Faith gasped. Dajon's career meant everything to him. She could not believe he would willingly resign.

Dajon shrugged one shoulder. "You may speak to him yourself, if you wish."

Judge Trott plucked his watch out again, eyeing the time. "Very well. Very well." Returning the watch to his pocket, he eyed Sir Wilhelm. "Unless this lady protests,

I believe this wedding is canceled." He tilted his head at Faith and awaited her response.

She could hardly believe her ears. Was this truly happening, or was she dreaming? She dared not move for fear of waking up.

"Indeed, I do not, sir," Faith said.

Sir Wilhelm barreled toward Judge Trott, his eyes alight with fury. "But, sir. I insist you arrest this man."

"Do you have some other charge to make against him?"

Sir Wilhelm's face turned purple as he sputtered curses and shot his fiery gaze over the room.

"Then this matter is closed." The judge released a heavy sigh. "Now if you will excuse me, I have far more pressing business to attend to." He started for the door.

"Then I insist you hang this woman for piracy." Sir Wilhelm's quivering, frantic voice bounced off the brick walls and screeched through the room like a wail from a badly tuned violin. He pointed his bony finger at Faith.

She clung to Dajon's wet arm and swallowed, knowing well this man's vengeance was not beyond watching her die.

Dajon laid his strong, warm hand over hers.

Judge Trott spun on his heel, his face puffed out in exasperation. "Egad, man. She has been pardoned."

Sir Wilhelm plucked the paper from his pocket, holding it up for all to see. Then, gripping it between his fingers, he started to rip it, but Dajon was on him in a second and snatched it from his hand. "Thank you. So kind of you."

Judge Trott turned and marched from the room, his deputies in tow.

Sir Wilhelm faced them, his face contorted into a sickly knot, his eyes afire with hatred. For a brief moment, it seemed as if he contemplated charging Dajon, but he must have seen the futility of such an action, for he remained in place.

"You have not seen the last of me." He spat and wiped the saliva from his chin.

"To my utter despair," Dajon replied.

Sir Wilhelm turned and marched from the room, flinging a chain of foul curses over his shoulder.

Faith fell into Dajon's arms. The moisture from his shirt soaked into her gown like a refreshing ointment. "Is this really happening?" She leaned back and gazed up at him. "I cannot believe you came for me."

He took her face in both hands and shook his head. "How could you ever believe that I would not?" He kissed her forehead, her nose then placed his lips on hers.

Heat inflamed her belly, threatening to overtake her, but feeling the reverend's eye upon them, Faith pushed from Dajon's embrace and threw a hand to her hip.

"What took you so long? I nearly married that buffoon." She glanced at his powerful physique, all the more evident through his wet attire. "And why are you all wet?"

" 'Twas such a hot day I thought I'd swim into port instead of taking a boat." He chuckled, a playful gleam in his eyes. "And I had to wait until I was sure Sir Wilhelm had procured your pardon, which I knew he must do before you wed."

"Will there be no wedding?" the whining voice of one of the girls asked. Embarrassment flushed over Faith. She had forgotten the silly girls were still present.

Dajon cocked a brow and gazed at Faith then at the reverend, who had remained before the judge's bench like a pillar of aplomb, a look of satisfaction on his face.

Faith's breath kindled anew, sending her chest heaving. Once again her legs wobbled beneath her.

Dajon took her hand in his and gazed down at her, his blue eyes so assured, so true, so loving.

"Miss Westcott, will you marry me?"

CHAPTER 35

Leaning on his elbow, Dajon gazed at the beauty sleeping beside him. Sunlight streamed in through the stern window, setting her curls sparkling in an array of red, orange, and gold. Dark fringes of lashes shadowed her golden cheeks, and a tiny cluster of freckles danced upon her nose. Stirring, she moaned and snuggled close to his chest. The scent of lemon and lilies danced around him, reminding him of the glorious night they'd spent in each other's arms. He allowed his gaze to wander down her creamy neck, across her bare shoulders, and down to where the coverlet forbade his eyes to go farther. He couldn't believe she was his wife.

Thank You, God. Thank You for this precious gift.

The ship rocked over a wave, shifting the sun across her eyelids that she slowly fluttered open. When she focused on him, a delicate grin adorned her lips. "Good morning, husband."

"Good morning, wife." He brushed a thumb across her cheek.

Reaching up, she ran her fingers through his hair and then allowed her hand to boldly caress his shoulder, then the muscles in his arm, then over to finger the hair upon his chest.

His body warmed. "I'm real, I assure you." He grabbed her hand and kissed it.

"I would never have believed I could be so happy." She shifted her shimmering auburn eyes to his. "Yesterday I faced either the noose or Sir Wilhelm's bed—both equally repugnant." She smiled, but then a flicker of sorrow pinched her features. "I had lost all hope. And now here I am, not only freed from those hideous fates but the wife of the most wonderful man I've ever known."

The snap of a sail sounded above them, followed by the creak of the hull.

"And I'm at sea." Her eyes widened with glee, and she sat up, holding the coverlet to her chest. "And I'm on my ship"—she gave him a measured smile—"*your* ship, I mean."

Dajon chuckled and toyed with the curls cascading down her back.

Faith traced a trail over his arm with her finger. "What a grand idea to spend our wedding night aboard the *Red Siren*. I'm so glad you brought her to port."

"After I resigned my commission, I must admit I felt naked without a ship to command." Dajon caressed the silky skin of her back, his mind and body shifting to the soft feel of his beautiful wife.

Leaning down on her elbow, Faith frowned, the mirth of only a moment ago drained from her face. "I can't believe you did that for me. You love the navy. Your career—it meant so much to you." She lowered her gaze and began to pick at a loose thread on the coverlet.

Placing a finger beneath her chin, he raised her eyes to his. "Truth be told, as soon as I began to understand the enormity of God's grace, I realized I didn't need the navy to redeem me from my past sins." He shrugged.

"But you love the sea as much as I do."

A lock of her hair fell over her shoulder and grazed the bed. Dajon twirled it between his fingers. "You gave up your seafaring career as well, did you not?"

"Career?" She giggled. "If you can call it that, but aye, I did. For the Lord."

"Then perhaps He has other plans for us upon the sea." He pulled her down beside him, showering her neck with kisses until she pushed him away, laughing.

The tiny purple scar below her left ear caught his eye. He traced the half-moon with his finger. "Where did you get this?"

"In a sword fight." She gave him a sassy look.

"Of course." Dajon laughed. "I know I should be horrified to discover my new wife is a swordsman"—he cleared his throat—"or swordswoman, but somehow I find it quite enticing."

A challenge sparked in her eyes. "Perhaps we can try our hand at swordplay someday."

"Perhaps, but I fear you are not a woman accustomed to defeat."

"Nay and why would that change?" One side of her mouth curved in a grin.

"Speaking of pirating." Dajon thought better to change the subject before she challenged him to a duel. "What of all the treasure you've stolen?" He raised his brows.

Faith held a finger to his lips. "The Lord has already shown me what I am to do."

"Indeed?"

"Since I cannot return the wealth to its proper owners, I shall give it all to charity—to the poor, to those in need."

"What about providing for your sisters and their future?"

"I won't deny I'm a bit uneasy about it." Faith sighed. "But I need to trust God. I know He has a plan for all of us—a good plan—if we will only trust and follow Him."

Dajon smiled, feeling the warmth of her statement spread down to his toes.

"All save this ship, that is." She gave him a sideways smile. "I have returned her to her rightful owner."

"Nay."

"What do you mean? The *Red Siren* is yours."

"I am giving her back to you. . .as a wedding present."

She shook her head. "I don't deserve such a gift. Not after I stole her from you."

"You stole my heart, too." Dajon brushed a thumb over her cheek. "And I'm giving that back to you as well."

Her eyes moistened. "Then I vow to take good care

of both." She pulled him down and met his lips with hers. For a moment, Dajon lost himself in her taste, squeezing her closer, his body heating.

As if completely unaware of her effect upon him, she pushed him back. "What shall we do with the ship? Merchant or"—her voice sparked with excitement—"privateer?"

Dajon chuckled. "Only in wartime, my little pirate, or we shall be right back where we started."

"Oh, very well. But we shall command her together." Faith folded the top of the coverlet and patted it with finality.

"Together?" Dajon cocked a brow. "Nay, my love. I never share my command."

Her lips leveled in a satisfied smirk. "Well, 'tis time you begin, my husband."

"Having such a notorious pirate for a wife should prove quite interesting." He rubbed a thumb over her lips, longing to kiss them again.

She kissed his finger and smiled. "We should return home soon and tell my sisters the good news. They must be worried sick about me."

"Yes, we shall." Dajon crept closer. "But 'tis far too early."

Faith ran her fingers over the stubble on his cheek and frowned.

"Why the sad look?" he asked.

"I am too happy for words. What if I am only dreaming?"

"I assure you, you are not." Dajon brushed her curls from her forehead. "But perhaps I need to prove it to you."

"And how do you intend to do that?" Her tone held a challenge.

He gave her a roguish grin.

She smiled at him in return, her gaze beaming an invitation.

And Dajon lowered his lips upon hers to accept it.

EPILOGUE

Faith pushed open the front door of the Westcott home and nearly ran over Edwin. He stumbled backward, his bloodshot eyes rounding like saucers.

"Miss Westcott. What. . .where. . .how?"

Dajon entered behind her and led the tottering steward to a chair beside the grandfather clock. "There, there, man. Have a rest. I assure you we are not ghosts."

Edwin slid into the seat. "But you were in prison."

"I am aware of that, Edwin. Now, if you please, where are my sisters?" Excitement rippled through her. Faith gripped the banister and peered upstairs. At nearly one o'clock in the afternoon, everyone should be up and about.

"In the drawing room, I believe," Edwin stuttered, withdrawing a handkerchief and dabbing his forehead.

After closing the door, Dajon proffered his arm with a smile. "Shall we?"

Gripping his elbow, Faith allowed him to lead her up the stairs. She still couldn't believe that the extraordinary man beside her was her husband, and she couldn't wait to share the news with her sisters.

"Miss Faith! Miss Faith!" Molly's high-pitched voice pulled them back to the bottom of the stairway. The cook sped down the hallway, her muslin skirts flailing behind her. "I thought I heard yer voice." Her eyes landed on Dajon, and she halted. "Oh, Mr. Waite. Warms my soul to see you." She caught her breath as her gaze shifted suspiciously between them, then she darted to Faith. "How did you get out of prison, Miss Faith?" She reached up as if she wanted to hug her but hesitated.

366

Throwing her arms around her, Faith embraced Molly, and they both broke into a jumbled mix of sobbing laughter.

Pulling away, Faith held her at arm's length. "I have much to tell you."

Grace's soft footsteps upon the stairs drew Faith's attention. Her normally glowing skin seemed pale in the light coming in through the back window. Dark smudges tugged on her glassy green eyes. Clutching a book in hand, she inched her way down to Faith as if she didn't quite believe what she was seeing.

The back door slammed, and a thud of boots sounded before Lucas barreled into the foyer, hat in hand and smelling of hay and horses. His eyes shimmered as a beaming smile took over his mouth.

"Lucas!"

"Miss Faith. How did ye—"

Grace flew down the remaining stairs and into Faith's arms, stopping Lucas's question in midair and nearly knocking Faith over. "Praise be to God. I'm so glad to see you."

"And I you, sweet sister." Faith squeezed her then took a step back. "You're trembling." She took both her hands in hers. "Everything will be okay now. I am free."

"Free," Molly repeated. "Why, heaven be praised!" She clapped her hands together.

"I have such good news to share. Where is Hope?" Faith started for the stairs. "I want her to hear this, too. Is she in her chamber?"

A sullen silence struck the room. No one's eyes met hers.

Dajon took her hand as if he sensed something was amiss. "Where is Miss Hope?" His question flung into the room like a net and hung waiting for an answer to fill it.

Grace stepped forward. "She left a note in her chamber yesterday morning."

"What did it say?" A sweat broke out on the back of Faith's neck.

Grace's bottom lip quivered even as her eyes pooled with tears.

"She has stowed away aboard Lord Falkland's ship heading to England."